"Dear God, Slayde, You've Endured So Much— Far More than I."

Courtney's voice dropped to a whisper. "Yesterday you said you would undo my loss if you could. Well, right now all I wish is that I could undo yours."

The earnest proclamation was the last reaction Slayde had expected, and the most impacting one he'd ever endured. Something profound moved in his chest, soothing his remembered anguish in a rush of warmth. "That's the most selfless offer I've ever received," he heard himself mutter, realizing even as he said it that it was true. "Thank you, sweetheart."

The endearment, uttered in a tender, husky voice, was more intimate than a caress . . . and just as pivotal, given the heightened emotion spawned by the past few minutes.

An invisible barrier was traversed.

Slayde's heart began slamming against his ribs, a compulsion like none he'd ever experienced propelling him forward. Acting on that compulsion—and a pure instinct he'd never known he possessed—he lowered his head and captured her mouth under his.

The world shifted—permanently. . . .

"Kane lulls her readers down romantic hallways, which at first seem familiar, only to take a sudden and refreshing new twist in the journey to the story's end."

—Publishers Weekly

Books by Andrea Kane

My Heart's Desire
Dream Castle
Masque of Betrayal
Echoes in the Mist
Samantha
The Last Duke
Emerald Garden
Wishes in the Wind
Legacy of the Diamond

Published by POCKET BOOKS

ANDREA KANE

Legacy of the Diamond

POCKET BOOKS
New York   London   Toronto   Sydney   Tokyo   Singapore

This book is a work of fiction. Names, characters, places and incidents are products of the author's imagination or are used fictitiously. Any resemblance to actual events or locales or persons, living or dead, is entirely coincidental.

An *Original* Publication of POCKET BOOKS

POCKET BOOKS, a division of Simon & Schuster Inc.
1230 Avenue of the Americas, New York, NY 10020

ISBN: 0-671-53485-8

First Pocket Books printing February 1997

10 9 8 7 6 5 4 3 2 1

POCKET and colophon are registered trademarks of Simon & Schuster Inc.

Cover art by Matthew Rotunda

Printed in the U.S.A.

To Andrea Cirillo, for preserving sanity, restoring faith, sharing laughter, and inspiring a herring worthy of a tiger

Acknowledgments

My thanks go out to:

The Gemological Institute of America, who graciously provided me with both historical and descriptive data on the rare and ever-mysterious black diamond.

To Bob, for sharing his watch expertise, his vast library of relevant historical books, and, most of all, his time.

To Brad and Wendi, my ever-present "rocks" of love and support. When words profound enough to express all that you guys mean to me are invented, I promise to be first in line to claim them. 'Til then, *thanks* and *I love you* will have to do. So, thanks . . . I love you with all my heart.

Legacy of the Diamond

Chapter 1

Devonshire, England
May 1817

It was the third ransom note in as many days, the fifth in a week, but only the second that rang true.

> Pembourne:
> The exchange will be made tonight. Eleven P.M. Ten miles due south of Dartmouth—in the open waters of the English Channel. Take a small, unarmed boat. Come alone, accompanied only by the diamond. Heed these instructions or your sister will die.

Shoving the terse message back into his coat pocket, Slayde Huntley, the ninth Earl of Pembourne, gripped the wheel of his fishing vessel with one hand, simultaneously tilting his timepiece toward the dim light of the lantern. By his calculations, he'd traveled more than nine of those ten miles. He steeled himself for the confrontation ahead, maneuvering the boat deeper into the fog-shrouded waters of the channel, waters far too choppy for a boat this size.

He should have brought the brig. Every instinct in his body cried out that not only was this craft unsuited for rough seas, its very construction left him utterly vulnerable to the enemy. But the kidnapper's message had been precise. And, instincts or not, Slayde dared not disobey for fear of jeopardizing his sister's life.

Aurora.

The thought of her being held by some filthy pirate made Slayde's skin crawl. For the umpteenth time, he berated himself for falling short in his responsibilities, for allowing this unprecedented atrocity to occur. In the decade since he'd become Aurora's guardian, he'd successfully isolated her from the world and, despite his own frequent and prolonged absences, ensured her safety by hiring an army of servants whose fundamental roles were to keep Aurora occupied and Pembourne safeguarded against intruders. Events had proven the latter easier to accomplish than the former. Still—as the accountings he received each time he returned bore out—seldom did Aurora manage to venture beyond her revered lighthouse without being spotted and restored to Pembourne. So how in the hell had this happened?

Vehemently, Slayde shoved aside his frustration and his guilt. In a crisis such as this, there was room for neither. Interrogation and self-censure would come later. Now, they would only serve to dilute his mental reserves, thus lessening his chances of accomplishing what he'd sailed out here to do: deliver the ransom and recover his sister.

Ransom—the detestable black diamond whose legend had dug its talons into his past and refused to let go, whose curse haunted the Huntleys like some lethal specter, a specter whose presence did nothing to dissuade hundreds of privateers from stalking the coveted gem.

Pondering the glittering black stone now wedged inside his Hessian boot, Slayde's knuckles whitened on the wheel. What made him think the claims in this ransom note were not mere fabrications invented strictly to procure the jewel? What if, like most of its predecessors, this message were a hoax? What if this pirate didn't have Aurora at all?

Again, Slayde abandoned his line of thinking, refusing to contemplate the idea of returning home without his sister. There had been three generations of blood spilled already. Aurora would not fall victim to the greed and hatred spawned by that loathsome jewel. He wouldn't allow it. Come hell or high water, he would find her.

The sound of an approaching vessel breaking the waves made Slayde's muscles go taut. Eyes narrowed, he searched the murky waters, seeking the outline of a ship.

At last it came.

Steadying his craft, Slayde waited while the ship drew closer.

As anticipated, it was a brigantine, moderate sized, but well manned and, doubtless, well armed. The whole situation was almost comical, he thought, his mouth twisting bitterly. Here he was, miles from shore, alone and unprotected in a meager fishing craft, being challenged by a hostile vessel ten times his boat's size that was now closing in, primed and ready to blast him out of the water in a heartbeat.

And there wasn't a bloody thing he could do to save himself.

Except surrender the gem and pray Aurora was on that ship, unharmed.

"Pembourne—I see you followed instructions. Hopefully, all of them." The kidnapper's raspy voice cut the fog as his ship drew directly alongside Slayde's. "Did you bring the black diamond?"

Slayde tilted back his head, wishing the mist would lift so he could make out the bastard's features. "I have it."

"Good. If that's true, you'll remain alive. I'll send my first mate down to fetch it."

There was a whooshing noise, followed by the slap of a

rope ladder as its bottom rungs struck the deck of Slayde's boat.

"Where's Aurora?" Slayde demanded, his fingers inching toward his waistcoat pocket—and the pistol he'd concealed there.

"Halt!" the kidnapper's order rang out. "Touch that weapon and you'll die where you stand."

An electrified silence. Slowly, Slayde's hand retraced its path to his side.

The harsh voice commended: "A wise decision, Pembourne. As for your sister, she's being brought topside. Ah, here she is now."

As he spoke, two men dragged a struggling woman onto the main deck. She was of slight build. Her arms were tied behind her, and a strip of cloth covered her eyes.

It *could* be Aurora—but *was* it?

Slayde squinted, intent on discerning the woman's identity. He had little time to do so, for she was shoved unceremoniously into a sack, bound within its confines, and tossed over the shoulder of the first mate.

"Wait," Slayde said as the man began his descent down the ladder's rungs.

The first mate paused.

Addressing the shadowy form on the deck above, Slayde inquired icily, "What proof do I have that the person in that sack is my sister?"

"None," the captain retorted, a taunt in his tone. "It appears you'll have to take me at my word."

Slayde's jaw set. He was on the verge of revoking his earlier claim that he'd brought the diamond with him, ready to swear that it was, in truth, ensconced at Pembourne Manor, when his gaze fell on the squirming sack on the first mate's arm. From the partially open end at the top, several long tresses tumbled free, hair whose color not even the fog could disguise.

A shimmering golden red.

Aurora.

Reassured that his efforts were about to be rewarded,

Slayde nodded his compliance, now eager to complete the transaction and be gone. Aware he was being scrutinized, he allowed none of his impatience to show, instead remaining impassive while the first mate completed his descent and paused three rungs above Slayde's deck.

"The diamond, m'lord," the sailor requested, extending his hand.

Wordlessly, Slayde studied him, noting—with some degree of surprise—the twinge of regret on the first mate's face; it was almost as if the rogue were being forced to act against his will.

"Please, Lord Pembourne," the sailor reiterated, balking beneath Slayde's probing stare, "the stone."

"Very well." Deliberately, Slayde leaned forward, slipping his hand inside his boot. "I'm fetching the diamond, not a weapon," he clarified, taking pity on the cowering fellow. "My Hessian is unarmed." So saying, he extracted the gemstone, holding it out so the first mate could see the truth to his words.

Relief flashed on the weathered features.

"Take it, Lexley," the captain bit out.

With a start, Lexley jerked forward, snatching the diamond from Slayde's palm.

Simultaneously, the woman in the sack began struggling furiously, catching Lexley off guard and toppling from his arms.

With a sickening crack, the sack smashed against the boom of the fishing boat, the impact hurling it outward, where it plummeted down to the railing below.

It hit with a hollow thud.

Slayde lunged forward, grasping nothing but air as the small craft pitched, upsetting his balance and butting the sack yet again, this time overboard.

A glint of silver struck his deck.

Then, an ominous splash as the sack plunged headlong into the rolling waves and vanished.

"Dear God." Lexley made an instinctive move toward the water.

"Get back on board," the captain bellowed. "Now."

The first mate froze. "M'lord—" He turned terrified eyes to Slayde. "You must . . ."

Slayde never heard the rest of the sentence. Having regained his balance, he charged forward, pausing only to gauge the distance to the enveloping swells that divulged the sack's location.

Then he dove.

He sliced the surface in one clean stroke and was swallowed up by darkness.

"Please, God," Lexley prayed, staring at the foam in Slayde's wake, "let him save her. And God—please forgive me."

With that, he scooted up the ladder and onto his ship, dragging the ladder in his wake.

Slayde propelled himself downward, groping blindly in the pitch-black seas. The eclipsing combination of fog and night made it impossible to distinguish anything. He could only pray his calibrations had been right.

Perhaps his prayers were heard.

With a surge of triumph, Slayde felt the coarse edge of the sack brush his fingertips. He latched on to it, hauling the cumbersome bag against him, locking it securely to his body. Kicking furiously, he battled both the weight of his own water-logged clothing and the additional constraint of his unwieldy bundle.

After what seemed like an eternity, he broke the surface. Gasping in air, he heaved the sack over the edge of the deck, then hoisted himself up after it.

The sack thudded softly, then lay motionless.

Kneeling, Slayde was only minimally aware of the rapidly retreating brig, far too worried about Aurora to concern himself with the fate of his gem. His fingers shook as he gripped the loosely tied cord atop the sack, cursing as the wet fibers resisted, ripped at his flesh.

He whipped out his blade, slashing the material from top to bottom, shoving it aside to give him access to the woman within.

She lay face down, her breeches and shirt clinging to her body, masses of wet red-gold hair draped about her.

He rested his palm on her back.

She wasn't breathing.

Shifting until he was crouched at her head, Slayde cut the bonds at her wrists, folded her arms, and pillowed them beneath her cheek. Then he pressed down between her shoulder blades—hard—finishing the motion by lifting her elbows in a desperate attempt to force water from her lungs.

He repeated the action five times before he was rewarded with a harsh bout of coughing.

"Shhh, it's all right." Relieved as hell, Slayde shifted again, trying to soothe the wracking shudders that accompanied her coughs, determinedly helping her body expel all the water she'd swallowed and replace it with air.

At last, she lay still, unconscious but breathing, battered but alive.

Gently, he eased her onto her back, now taking the time to assess her injuries, simultaneously releasing her from the confines of imprisonment. Broken ribs were a certainty, he thought with a grim scowl, given the force with which she struck the boat. A concussion was a distinct probability as well. Not to mention cuts, bruises—and Lord knew what else. His mind racing, Slayde tucked aside her hair and pulled the obscuring cloth from her eyes.

Blinding realization was followed by a savage curse.

The young woman was not Aurora.

Chapter 2

Courtney felt as if she'd been struck by a boulder.

Excruciating blows hammered at her head, throbbed in her skull.

"Papa . . ." The very utterance of her hushed word triggered a violent bout of coughing—and a vague awareness that something terrible had happened, something too devastating to endure.

"Don't try to talk."

Whose voice is that? she wondered between coughs. She was acquainted with every member of her father's crew, and the deep baritone belonged to none of them.

"Papa?" she rasped again.

"Just rest. We'll be on shore in a matter of hours."

Shore? They were miles and days away from delivering their cargo to the Colonies. So why in the name of heaven were they headed for shore?

Valiantly, she brought her choking under control,

fought the pain that separated her from reality. "My head . . . and chest . . . ache so . . ."

"You swallowed a great deal of water. As for your head and chest, you struck them both—violently. That's why I want you to lie still; I believe you have a concussion and several broken ribs. Not to mention some impressive bruises, any of which could be harboring broken bones. Unfortunately, I haven't the necessary supplies to tend to such extensive injuries. But we'll rectify that as soon as we reach land." A pause. "Can you tell me your name?"

"Name . . ." She wished she knew who this man was. Cracking open her eyelids, she could make out only his powerful frame, which seemed to fill the entire length of the vessel on which she lay. Then again, that wasn't so impressive a state of affairs, considering how small a vessel it was. Small and unfamiliar—with an equally unfamiliar, though anything but small, captain. "Who are you?" she managed.

"A victim. Just as you are."

Victim. That one word opened the portals of Courtney's memory, spawned a deluge of unbearable images. Her father . . . being attacked by that filthy pirate, torn from the quarter-deck, bound and gagged . . . wrested from his rightful place at the helm. And Lexley . . . complying at pistolpoint, tying a huge sack of grain to her father's leg, looking anguished as he ordered Greene and Waverly to take Courtney below. Oh, how she'd kicked and fought as they dragged her off. Then . . . her father's scream, followed by that sickening splash.

He was gone.

"No!" With an agonized shout, Courtney sat upright, then fell back with a strangled cry. Blinding pain merged with waves of nausea, and she felt the oncoming sickness an instant before her stomach emptied its meager contents.

Evidently, the signs of nausea were visible, for the man standing at the wheel pivoted and snatched her up, carrying her to the side of the boat and holding her while wracking spasms seized her, her eyes blinded by tears.

"Papa." She fought the dizziness, the memories, the unalterable reality. "He's dead," she choked out as the roaring in her head intensified. "That monster—he killed him."

With that, the world tilted askew and everything went black.

Where the hell was Aurora?

Slayde slammed down the pile of ransom notes, having reread them a dozen times and learned nothing in the process.

Bitterly frustrated, he prowled the length of his study, trying to fit the pieces together. It made no sense. Every one of the notes made reference to the black diamond. Yet, if all the kidnapper wanted was the stone, why hadn't he contacted Slayde and made the exchange, stated his bloody demands? What was he waiting for? Why was he playing with Slayde like a child with a toy?

Unless it wasn't just the gem.

The prospect crept into Slayde's mind like an odious insect.

Could all those notes be fake? Could whoever had Aurora want something more than just the diamond—something more menacing, like vengeance?

There was only one man who hated Slayde's family enough to exact such cruel revenge, a man whose thirst to uncover the black diamond *and* to seek retribution was twisted enough to spawn an action as ugly as this.

Lawrence Bencroft.

Rage surged through Slayde's veins. The elderly duke was drunk more often than he was sober. Still, that wouldn't preclude him from . . .

"Lord Pembourne?"

Slayde snapped about, facing the slight, graying man in the doorway. "Gilbert—how is she?"

The physician removed his spectacles, wiped them with his handkerchief. "Lucky to be alive," he replied.

"Had you reached her any later, she might not have been so fortunate."

Slayde scowled. "Her injuries are that severe?"

"It's not her injuries alone, or even the amount of time she spent under water. Her condition prior to the"—Dr. Gilbert cleared his throat discreetly—"accident was deteriorated, to say the least."

"Stop talking in riddles. Tell me what you found when you examined her."

"A severe concussion, numerous damaged ribs, several deep lacerations, and a wealth of cuts and bruises. She's also terribly weak and severely lacking in both food and, most particularly, in water—ironic as that might seem, given the circumstances. In short, she is one very ill young lady."

"But she'll recover?" Slayde demanded.

"With the proper food, attention, and—most of all— rest, yes, I believe she'll recover." A frown. "Although I'm troubled by the fact that she reverted back to such a deeply unconscious state, despite the fact that I gave her only enough laudanum to dull the pain. It's almost as if she doesn't want to awaken."

"That might very well be the case," Slayde concurred, recalling the girl's agonized state of mind.

"Well, periodically, she must be roused. Just to ensure that she's lucid. I explained this to Matilda, who will awaken her in a few hours—unless, of course, she stirs on her own." The physician shoved his spectacles back into place. "I've done all I can, my lord. The rest is up to nature."

"Please, don't whimper, child. Whatever it is, it's over now."

The crooning female voice seemed to come from far away.

With the greatest of efforts, Courtney's lashes fluttered.

A heavy-set woman with a neat gray bun was perched at her bedside, leaning forward and frowning as she checked something white that lay directly across Court-ney's brow. "Whatever agony you've endured is far more painful than even these wounds," she muttered, evi-dently unaware that her patient was conscious. "Poor child."

"Where am I?" The question emerged in a croak as, once again, Courtney struggled to regain mastery of her body. For the life of her, she couldn't seem to overcome the pain or clear the fog from her mind.

The woman started. "At last. You've awakened." She sprang to her feet. "His lordship will want to know at once."

"His lordship?" Courtney repeated vacantly. But her attendant was already dashing out the door.

Groggily, Courtney lifted the bedcovers, wondering why she still felt as if there were an oppressive weight on her chest. She glanced down and surveyed herself, blink-ing in surprise. She was clad in a nightdress, beneath which she could make out the outline of a thick bandage. More bandages decorated both her arms and legs—*and head,* she added silently, discovering the last as she reached up to touch her pounding skull. *So that's what that nice lady had been tending to,* she deduced. *My head.* The man in the fishing boat had said something about a concussion. She frowned. What else had he said? And how had she sustained all these injuries?

The water.

Abruptly, more flashes of memory ensued. She'd fall-en from Lexley's shoulder. There had been sharp pain, then a deluge of water.

And then that man in the boat. Clearly, he'd rescued her, brought her . . . where?

With great care, she inched her head to one side, enough to get a glimpse of her surroundings without heightening her discomfort. The room was a palace . . . ten times the size of her cabin, with furnishings that could be no less grand than those belonging to the Prince Regent himself. The desk and dressing table were a rich reddish brown wood—mahogany, if the descriptions her books had provided were accurate, the carpet thickly piled, as was indicated by the deep indentations made by the bedposts, and the ceiling high and gilded.

Whoever "his lordship" was, he was indeed a wealthy man.

Not that it mattered.

A surge of emptiness pervaded Courtney's heart. Her father was gone, murdered by a bloodthirsty pirate who had usurped her home, bound and starved her, and used her for bait in his obsessive quest.

Why couldn't she have died, too?

Tears were trickling down her cheeks when the bedchamber door opened.

"Ah. I see Matilda was right. You arc awake."

Courtney recognized the voice at once, her dazed mind making the connection that "his lordship" and her rescuer were one and the same man. Valiantly, she brought herself under control. After all, this man had saved her life and, whether or not that meant anything to her any longer, she owed him her thanks.

Dashing the moisture from her face, she eased her head slowly in his direction.

He was as tall and broad as she'd initially perceived, his hair as black as night; his eyes, by contrast, were an insightful, silvery gray as they bore into hers. His features were hard and decidedly aristocratic, and there were harsh lines etched about his mouth and eyes that made him look both older than he probably was and cynical—as if life had robbed him of youth and laughter.

Somehow she sensed he would understand her suffering.

"Yes. I'm awake," she murmured.

Crossing over, he took in her pallor, the dampness still visible on her lashes, the torment in her eyes. "What pains you so, your injuries or the events that preceded them?"

She swallowed. "I would gratefully endure ten of the former if I could erase the latter."

With a nod, he pulled up a chair and sat. "Do you recall Dr. Gilbert's visit?"

"Who?"

"My personal physician. He tended to your injuries several hours ago. Luckily, no bones appear to be shattered. Your lacerations are varied, the most severe being the gash on your brow. That one is deep and bled profusely throughout our excursion to shore. Since you also have several damaged ribs and quite a concussion, there will be a fair amount of pain—more so in a short while when the laudanum has worn off."

"Laudanum?" Courtney murmured vaguely.

"Dr. Gilbert put a dose in the brandy you drank." A faint smile. "The brandy you apparently don't remember drinking. In any case, it helped you sleep and numbed the effects of your injuries. When it wears off, the pain will intensify. So you'll need continual doses of laudanum over the next several days, and complete bed rest for a week." Her rescuer's smile vanished. "It seems your body is badly depleted of food and water. You'll need to replenish your strength by consuming a great deal of both. In short, you're going to have to stay abed and let others minister to you until you're well enough to take care of yourself."

"I—" Courtney wet her lips, his lordship's words grazing the periphery of her mind. Stay in bed? Let others take care of her? Terrified realization struck. She had no bed, no home, no one to treat her wounds. She also had no money, no worldly possessions, and nowhere to go.

"Did you hear what I said?"

"I—yes, I heard." Shattered or not, Courtney was determined to retain the one thing she still *did* have: her pride, that wondrous pride with which her father had gifted her. "You dived in after me . . . when I . . ."

"Yes."

"I thought so." She spoke slowly, in breathy fragments that caused minimal movement to her chest. "Thank you. For risking your life. For bringing me here. And for

14

fetching . . . your physician . . . to treat my wounds. I realize it must have been . . . a great inconvenience . . . to you and your family. I also realize you saved my life."

One dark brow rose. "That sounds more like regret than appreciation."

"If so . . . the fault is certainly not yours." Courtney rested a moment, her fingers clenching as she fortified herself to go on. "I'm sorry," she managed at last. "But the truth is . . . I have nothing to offer you in return. Nothing at all."

"All your belongings were on that ship?"

Her lips trembled. "My belongings, and a great deal more."

"So I gathered." He cleared his throat. "May I ask your name?"

"Courtney . . . " she whispered, wondering why the pressure in her head and chest seemed to be intensifying. ". . . Johnston."

"Well, Miss Johnston, one of your belongings did, in fact, survive the ordeal. In fact, I only wish your transfer to my vessel had been as smooth." He reached over, lifting a gleaming silver object from the nightstand. "I believe this belongs to you." He pressed it into Courtney's palm.

She stared, her eyes brimming with tears. "Papa's timepiece." Instinctively, she tried to sit up—and whimpered, the resulting pain too acute to withstand.

Instantly, his lordship rose and strode across the room, stepping into the hall. "Matilda," he summoned in a commanding tone, "bring some brandy. Miss Johnston needs another dose of laudanum."

"Yes, m'lord."

Courtney fell back weakly, needing to find the words to thank him, to try to explain how much her father's timepiece meant to her.

"I . . . Papa gave me . . . "

"Later," he replied, returning to her bedside. "After you've rested, and the next ration of laudanum has had a chance to work."

"It hurts," she managed, eyes squeezed tightly shut.

"I know. Just lie still. The medicine is on its way."

Courtney hadn't the strength to respond. It seemed an eternity before Matilda delivered the requisite brandy, supporting Courtney's head so she could sip it.

"Drink the whole thing," her rescuer's voice instructed from a distance. "Every last drop."

She did.

"Poor lamb," Matilda murmured, settling Courtney in and drawing up the bedcovers. "She's as weak as a kitten. Well, never you mind. A little care and attention and she'll be good as new."

"Care . . ." Courtney whispered, her lashes fluttering to her cheeks. "I have . . . no one . . . nothing . . ." Her voice trailed off, and she sank into a drugged sleep.

The timepiece fell from her fingers to sleep beside her.

"My ship, the *Fortune,* is just inside that cove. We'll anchor alongside her."

Sewell Armon propped his booted foot on the deck of the brig and pointed. "There." He scowled as Lexley ignored his orders, instead glancing anxiously out to sea. "You've done that a hundred times," the pirate captain growled. "The bloody girl is dead. Stare all you want, but unless your eyes are good enough to see clear to the bottom of the English Channel, you won't find her."

"Thank you for that assessment," Lexley replied bitterly, the past week having rended his soul, extinguished his hope—and, as a result, sharpened his tongue. "But a conscience is not always amenable to reason. *If* one has a conscience, that is."

"I've had just about enough of your defiance, you rebellious old man," Armon spat, whipping out his sword. "You've been nothing but trouble since your captain and his precious daughter drowned. Well, you'll soon be joining them. Now anchor. You're wasting time—mine." He nudged Lexley purposefully with the tip of his blade. "My crew is waiting."

"And what will happen to *our* crew?" Lexley asked,

wincing. "Do you mean to kill everyone on the *Isobel,* or only me?"

"You'll find that out soon enough. But if it's leniency you seek—for any of your men—I'd suggest you comply with my instructions. Or else . . ."

Armon's attention was diverted by a welcome sight, and a broad smile supplanted his irritation. As the *Isobel* rounded the next jagged inlet of the Channel, the *Fortune* came into view, tucked away and awaiting her captain's return. Armon's smile widened as a whoop of recognition erupted from the deck of his ship and, in response, he whisked the black stone from his pocket and waved it triumphantly in the air.

The whoops transformed to shouts of victory. "'E got it! 'E got the black diamond!"

The instant the two vessels were close enough, Armon swung over to his own deck, flourishing the diamond for all to see.

"What about *them?*" his next-in-command muttered, jerking his thumb in the *Isobel*'s direction.

"Grab the cargo. Sink the ship." His black eyes flickered dangerously. "Take the crew."

"Take 'em? Why not just kill 'em?"

"Because the useful ones, we'll keep. And the others— the ones who've been a constant thorn in my side—" Armon flashed a venomous glance in Lexley's direction. *"Those* I have plans for, plans that'll make them pray to die."

"What kind of plans?"

Armon rubbed his bristled jaw. "Can you still navigate the waters around Raven Island?"

"Ye know I can," the stout pirate answered proudly. "Not in the *Fortune,* of course—I wouldn't risk damaging 'er on the rocks. But in a longboat? I'm the only one who can whip Raven's currents and come out alive."

"Good. In that case, don't sink their ship—yet. Transfer all but the troublemakers onto the *Fortune.* Then, board the *Isobel.* A handful of our crewmen are still

there, awaiting instructions. Have them tie up our unwanted *passengers.* Sail out to Raven." A malevolent
leer. "At which point, toss the bastards into the longboat,
row them out to the island, and leave them there—to
starve and rot."

"I get it." An admiring nod. "In the meantime, ye and
the *Fortune* will be headin' to Dartmouth to make yer
exchange."

"Exactly. Once you've disposed of your cargo, sail to
Dartmouth in their ship. *Then* sink it, reboard the
Fortune, which will be in the cove we agreed on, and
await my arrival." So saying, Armon held up the black
gem, pivoting it slowly in order to admire all its facets.
"I've waited a long time for this day. And no one and
nothing is going to stand in my way."

"Good morning."

That deep baritone penetrated Courtney's haze, and
she blinked, taking in the sunlit room, the disheveled
bed—and the man who stood at its foot.

"How do you feel?" he inquired.

"You changed clothes," she murmured inanely, assessing his fine waistcoat and polished boots, a sharp contrast to the rolled-up sleeves and muddied breeches of
the man who'd rescued her.

Startled, he glanced down at himself. "I customarily
do at the onset of the new day. Is that unusual?"

"No. But before you looked like a fisherman. Now you
look like a . . ." Her brow furrowed. "What is your title
anyway? Duke? Marquis?"

His lips twitched slightly. "Sorry to disappoint you. A
mere earl." A penetrating look. "You haven't answered
my question. How do you feel?"

"Like I've been beaten, inside and out." Speculatively,
she glanced at the tangle of sheets surrounding her.

"You had a restless night," the earl explained. "Each
time the laudanum started to wear off, you became fitful.
I hope you'll have an easier time of it today. In any case,
you must begin replenishing your strength. When Matil-

da advised me you were coming around, I sent my housekeeper, Miss Payne, to fetch some tea. Perhaps later you can manage some toast. It's the only way you're going to improve."

As the earl spoke, bits of memories trickled into Courtney's mind in ugly, measured increments.

Abruptly, she grabbed at the bedcovers, sifting through to find the treasure she'd been holding during her last conscious period.

"Your timepiece is safe," her rescuer assured her. "I placed it in the nightstand drawer. I was afraid you would break it when you began thrashing about."

Courtney stilled, emotion clogging her throat. "Thank you. As for sparing the watch, your efforts were for naught. 'Tis already broken. It broke the day Papa died." Turning her face into the pillow, she confessed in a trembling voice, "I prayed I'd awaken to find this was all a horrible nightmare."

"I understand."

Slowly, she lifted her head from its protective nest, pivoting until her anguished gaze met his. "I'm not sure why," she whispered, "but I believe you do."

A heartbeat of silence.

The earl cleared his throat, clasping his hands behind his back. "Miss Johnston, I realize you've been through an ordeal, one you'd prefer to forget. Nonetheless, I must ask you some questions—if you're physically able to answer them. Are you?"

Before Courtney could reply, a willowy woman of middle years entered the chamber, carrying a tray. "The tea you requested, my lord."

"Thank you." He indicated the nightstand. "Leave it there. Miss Payne, this is Courtney Johnston, the young woman I spoke of. She'll be staying here while she recuperates."

"Miss Johnston." The housekeeper nodded. "I know Matilda has been tending to your needs. You couldn't be in better hands. Still, as I am overseer of the female staff, please let me know if there's anything I can do for you."

"Thank you, Miss Payne. You're very kind," Courtney managed awkwardly.

"Tell Matilda to get some rest," the earl advised. "I'll administer Miss Johnston's next dose of laudanum. Once the medicine takes effect, she'll sleep until midafternoon, so neither you nor Matilda will be needed. However, once Miss Johnston awakens, perhaps the two of you could entice her to eat some toast."

"Of course," the housekeeper agreed immediately. "'Twould be a pleasure, my lord." With a polite smile in Courtney's direction, she took her leave.

The earl gave Courtney another probing look. "Is the pain severe?"

"I can bear it, if that's what you mean. Ask your questions. The laudanum can wait a few minutes."

"Damn, I feel like a cad," he muttered.

"Don't. Obviously your concerns are serious."

"Serious? Yes. Or I wouldn't be pressuring you like this." A pause. "My sister's life is at stake."

"Your sister?" It was the last thing Courtney had expected.

"Yes. The pirate who seized your ship used you as bait. He wanted something from me, something quite valuable. And he's not alone. Hundreds of greedy bastards want the same prize. And one of them—I don't know who—kidnapped Aurora. Hell, he might even kill her, and all to get his hands on that bloody gem."

Gem. Another vivid recollection fell into place. The pirate . . . taunting her with instant death *if* whoever he was awaiting didn't deliver the requisite stone. "Of course," Courtney murmured, "that jewel he kept muttering about."

"He spoke to you?" Her rescuer lunged forward like a panther.

Courtney gazed into the handsome, tormented face. "Only in fragments." At last, she gave voice to the question she'd wanted to ask a dozen times since awakening in the fishing boat, had that question not vanished into nothingness each time she'd tried to speak it. "Who are you?"

For a moment, he seemed not to have heard. Then, he replied, "Slayde Huntley. The Earl of Pembourne."

"Huntley . . ." Reflexively, Courtney came up off the bed, then sank back on the pillows with a moan.

"I see you've heard of me. I needn't ask in what context. Although I am a bit surprised. I hadn't realized my family history was nefarious enough to reach all who travel abroad."

"I'm not traveling. The *Isobel* is my home, and its captain—Arthur Johnston—is my father. *Was,*" she corrected herself, her voice breaking. "Now I've lost them both."

Something flickered in Lord Pembourne's eyes—a glimmer of the past, a flash of remembered anguish. "You have my deepest sympathy. It's obvious your father meant a great deal to you." The offering was straightforward, uttered in a thoroughly composed tone. Perhaps Courtney only imagined the compassion that hovered just beneath the surface, given what she'd just learned—who he was, the stories she recalled of his own tragic past. Perhaps that tragedy was long forgotten, his empathy a mere trick of her mind. But, valid or not, her fleeting perception was enough to dissolve the final thread of her self-control.

Covering her face with her hands, she burst into tears, sobbing as if her heart would break, ignoring the increased pounding in her head and ribs induced by her actions.

She felt the earl hesitate, then walk around and reach for her, drawing her against him until her face was buried in the wool of his coat. Gratefully, she accepted this small measure of comfort. "I'm sorry," she choked out.

"No. *I'm* sorry." Gently, he cradled her head to still any sudden, jarring motions. "If I could undo this loss for you, I would."

"He can't be gone." Her hands balled into fists, digging into Slayde's shirtfront. "He *isn't* gone. I won't believe it."

"I know," Slayde replied, with a conviction only firsthand experience could afford. "And you don't think you can withstand it. But you can. Not now, but later. For now, cry. Cry until the tears are gone."

Courtney did just that, weeping until there was nothing left inside her, nothing but a hopeless, unending void.

At last, she drew back, gratefully taking Slayde's proffered handkerchief. "You've been more than generous, Lord Pembourne. Once again, I thank you." Shakily, she eased herself down to the pillows. "I'll tell you everything I recall. It's the least I can do."

A muscle worked in his jaw. "Are you up to it?"

"Yes."

He pulled over a chair and sat, fingers gripping his knees. "Tell me what happened—the details."

Ghosts haunted her eyes. "That monster and his crewmen—I believe there were about six of them—boarded the *Isobel* . . ."

"When?"

She frowned. "My sense of time is still muddled. How long have I been here?"

"A day and a half, nearly two."

"Then it was five days prior to the night you made your exchange when he seized our ship. He forced Lexley—that's Papa second in command—to thrust Papa overboard. He imprisoned me below. I was permitted no visitors, food, or water. He tied me to a chair and left me in my cabin. Hence, I was privy to very little of what occurred topside, until the night when they dragged me up and shoved me into that sack."

Hope died in Slayde's eyes. "So there's nothing you can relay."

"I didn't say that." The screaming pain in her skull was back, but Courtney refused to succumb to it. "First of all, I can describe the scoundrel from head to toe. He was broad and stocky, with curling black hair, black eyes, and a thickening middle. He wasn't young—about forty, I should say. His nose was scarred. It had definitely been broken—my guess is more than once. He wore a silver ring on the little finger of his left hand. It was engraved with the letter *A.*"

Slayde's brows rose. "You certainly scrutinized him closely."

"Very closely." Courtney's chin jutted forward. "I memorized his features, his walk, his voice. I intend to identify him the precise instant I next see or hear him, at which point I intend to kill him for what he did to Papa."

"I see."

"Yes, I believe you do." Courtney swallowed. "In any case, he made repeated trips to my cabin to ensure I was properly bound, muttering about how I was worth a fortune to him and about how much smarter he was than the two of them—whoever 'they' are."

"I assume he was referring to my great-grandfather and Geoffrey Bencroft, the late Duke of Morland."

"Morland—wasn't he the other nobleman who vied with your great-grandfather for the recovery of the black diamond when it first disappeared?"

"I'm impressed."

"Don't be. I've spent many years at sea listening to Papa's crew spin their yarns. And your family is legendary." Courtney shifted a bit, the resulting slash of pain across her ribs nearly making her cry out. "Where was I? Oh, the pirate kept boasting about the wonderful hoax he'd engineered, a hoax that would win him his treasure."

"Indeed." Slayde's mouth thinned into a grim line. "And that hoax was you."

"I don't understand."

"Aurora—my sister. You bear an uncanny resemblance to her. At least in all the ways that would matter to that greedy snake: your slight build, your diminutive height . . . and the most crucial thing, your hair. Not only its texture, but its extraordinary color. Even I was fooled." Slayde slammed to his feet, began pacing about the room. "Oh, that bastard knew exactly what he was doing when he sent me those ransom notes."

"Ransom notes?" The pounding in Courtney's head escalated. "What ransom notes?"

Slayde gave her a measured look. "You're in excruciating pain."

"What ransom notes?"

"I'll answer this question, and this question only," he said firmly. "The conclusion of our conversation will have to wait until later."

"All right." Courtney couldn't help but agree; the pain was too agonizing.

"From the minute Aurora disappeared, one week ago today, I've been receiving letters promising me her life in exchange for the black diamond. Most of them were clearly hoaxes. But the two I received from the pirate holding you were chillingly genuine—and more than persuasive. They each contained strands of Aurora's—*your*"—Slayde corrected himself—"hair."

"Where did he get—?"

"From your brush, your pillow, any one of a dozen places. 'Twas only a few strands. But given the color, it was enough to convince me. So I took the risk and gave him what he wanted."

"The stone? But now you have . . . nothing to bargain with." Courtney could scarcely speak, much less think.

"'Tis time for your laudanum." Slayde had already taken up the pot of tea and poured a cup, adding the requisite dose of medicine. "If I hold your head, can you drink this?"

She attempted a nod.

"Good." He perched beside her, easing her up just enough to press the cup to her lips, offering her the tea, drop by drop, until it was gone.

It took mere minutes for the pleasant haze to settle in, surrounding the pain and holding it in faraway abeyance.

"That tasted dreadful," Courtney announced.

"I'm sure it did. But 'twas necessary nonetheless."

"The laudanum was necessary. The tea was not." Her lashes fluttered. "Do you know Papa kept a few bottles of brandy aboard the *Isobel*. For special occasions. Once 'r twice, he let me taste it. When he looked away, I finished half the goblet." A blissful sigh. "It tastes far better than tea."

A corner of Slayde's mouth lifted. "I agree."

" 'Tis also stronger. It works faster and d'sguises the bad flavor of medicine. Next time, I'd like my laud . . . laudan . . ."

"I'll make certain all your subsequent doses are served in goblets of brandy."

Her lashes drifted to her cheeks. "I'd like that."

She was asleep.

Silently, Slayde stared down at his patient, oddly moved and more than a bit unsettled.

He had time to contemplate neither.

"Lord Pembourne!" Matilda burst into the room, her eyes wide as saucers. "Come quickly!"

Whipping about, Slayde stared at the white-faced maid. "What in God's name is it?"

"It's Lady Aurora! She's home!"

Chapter 3

Slayde swooped down the staircase like a hawk.

"Aurora." Taking the hallway in a dozen long strides, he reached the entranceway door, seizing his sister's shoulders in a grip so punishing, she winced. "Are you all right?"

Indignant turquoise eyes gazed up at him. "Of course I am. Slayde, have you lost your mind?"

He blinked. "Evidently so." Slowly, he released her, his baffled gaze sweeping her from her head to toe and finding her thoroughly intact. "You weren't harmed?"

"Harmed? Certainly not. As promised, the viscountess chaperoned me everywhere." Tucking a wisp of red-gold hair behind her ear, Aurora indicated her companion. "Honestly, Slayde, it's not like you to become so emotional."

Slayde's gaze shifted from his sister to the elegant, utterly stupefied woman beside her. "Elinore?"

"Hello, Slayde," Lady Stanwyk said. Uneasily, she

assessed the tension between brother and sister, her fingers idly stroking the glittering diamond-and-emerald necklace about her throat. "Perhaps I should go."

"No, you should *not* go," Aurora declared with a vehement shake of her head. "And I apologize for my brother's rudeness."

"What do you mean, 'as promised'?" Slayde grilled her, ignoring the excess chatter as the significance of his sister's earlier words sank in.

Aurora frowned. "The note I left you. I explained where I was going, with whom, and for how long. Certainly you understood my reasoning. For heaven's sake, Slayde, I cannot remain a prisoner at Pembourne forever—"

"What note? I never received a note. Other than ransom ones," he added.

Now it was Aurora's turn to look shocked. "Ransom notes? Why on earth would you receive ransom notes?"

"Because half of Devonshire thinks you've been kidnapped, that's why. Because you've been missing from Pembourne for a week, and no one has had a clue as to your whereabouts. Word leaked out that you'd been taken. Notes began arriving posthaste."

"Oh, my God." Aurora looked positively stricken. "Slayde, I'm so sorry. I had no idea. I truly did leave you a note." Her nose wrinkled. "I can't imagine how you missed it."

"Where did you put it?"

"I propped it on my pillow. The morning I left—one week ago today."

Slayde's eyes glittered dangerously. "And where, pray tell, did you go?"

"To London." Aurora's face lit up. "It was exhilarating. Elinore took me to balls at Almack's and Carlton House. We rode in Hyde Park and shopped on Bond Street. I even peeked into White's and caught a glimpse of the gaming."

"Are you telling me you've spent the better part of the

last week traipsing about London, with no protection whatsoever?"

Her chin came up. "I'm perfectly capable of taking care of myself."

"You didn't bother mentioning this intended excursion to our staff," Slayde accused harshly. "Or is it a coincidence that not one of them reported it to me? Nor, for that matter, did they report Elinore's visit *or* your subsequent departure."

A flicker of guilt. "I met Elinore at the lighthouse. It was the only way I could leave Pembourne without being questioned or accompanied. In my confirming note, I explained to Elinore that I needed to drop something off at the lighthouse prior to our departure and asked if her carriage could collect me there. She agreed. As for our servants, they hadn't a clue of my plans. I merely strolled off in my customary direction. And, since my own wardrobe is sadly lacking in gowns appropriate for a Season, I had no reason to carry a bag. Instead, Elinore and I purchased all I needed in London. She was wonderful. And, in case you're entertaining the possibility that she was involved in my little plot, don't. This is the first she's hearing of it. So don't even consider blaming her."

"Fear not—I blame you."

"Slayde, forgive me for intruding," Lady Stanwyk murmured, inserting herself with the grace and refinement she so naturally exuded. At forty years of age, she was still a striking woman, her dark hair perfectly coiffed, her green muslin dress cut to her exact specifications. "I'm terribly sorry this dreadful mix-up had to occur. And 'tis true: this is the first I've heard of Aurora's scheme. Certainly I don't condone it; nor would I have agreed to go along with it if I had. But with regard to her safety, truly, she was quite secure and fully chaperoned. We were accompanied by two ladies' maids, a carriage driver, and four footmen. We stayed at my London Townhouse, which is fully staffed. Not to mention the fact that I was with Aurora every waking moment." The viscountess gave a delicate cough. "Other than when she darted from my carriage for that one brief dash down St. James Street to view the men's clubs. And even then, she was in my line of vision."

"I stopped only at White's," Aurora said in quick clarification. "And I raced back to Elinore's carriage the moment her footman came to retrieve me—that is, after I'd viewed White's grand bow window and squinted my way through one game of whist."

"How reassuring," Slayde bit out.

"Safety was never an issue, Slayde," Elinore repeated. "Nor was cruelty. After all—in Aurora's defense—despite the rashness of her methods, she'd assumed you'd read her note and were apprised of her whereabouts. Had either of us known otherwise, we would have rushed right home. Surely you believe that."

The helpless fury raging inside Slayde banked, and he turned to the viscountess, abruptly realizing how boorishly he was behaving. "Elinore, forgive me. This argument has nothing to do with you and should not be taking place in your presence. Thank you for taking such excellent care of Aurora and for introducing her to the fashionable world that she was evidently determined to experience."

"I'm twenty years old, Slayde," Aurora reminded him. "And you've never even brought me out. Is it so wrong for me to want to "

"We'll discuss this later, Aurora," Slayde broke in, jaw clenched in warning. "For now, I want the viscountess to know how much we appreciate her excellent caretaking."

"You needn't thank me for spending time with Aurora," Lady Stanwyk demurred, waving off Slayde's thanks. "Your parents were Theomund's and my closest friends; Aurora is like a daughter to me. Anything I can do for her—for either of you—is my pleasure."

Again Slayde brought his irritation under control, reminding himself that Elinore wasn't responsible for his sister's reckless nature. "In which case, I'll merely ask how you've been."

"For an aging widow?" A faint smile touched the viscountess's lips. "Quite well, thanks to my refreshing and delightful excursion with Aurora."

"Aging?" Slayde cocked a brow. "Elinore, you're scarcely older than I."

"How gallant of you, Slayde. However, if memory serves me correctly, you're one and thirty, nearly a decade my junior."

"You look and act like a young girl," Aurora defended at once.

Elinore patted her arm. "That's because you kept me young this week. It's been eons since I've dashed from ball to ball like a wide-eyed child fresh from my Court presentation. In fact, during the two years that Theomund has been gone, I've seldom taken part in a London Season, much less immersed myself in one." Her fingers brushed the stones of her necklace. "In truth, the excitement felt rather good."

Slayde's gaze followed her motion. "Was that a gift from Theomund?" he inquired politely.

"Yes." She glanced down at herself. "His last before he died. Lovely, isn't it?"

"Yes." Slayde's expression grew thoughtful. "Actually, it reminds me very much of a necklace Mother owned."

"It should. It's almost identical. Your father commissioned a jeweler to design your mother's as a Christmas gift. I admired it so often that, some years later, Theomund contacted the same jeweler to design one for me." A worried pucker formed between the viscountess's brows. "That doesn't disturb you, does it? That I wear something similar to your mother's?"

"Of course not. I'm sure it pleased Mother greatly."

"It did. But that's not what I meant. 'Twasn't your mother's reaction I was pondering." A slow indrawn breath. "You're away so often, I lose sight of the fact that you might still . . ." Her voice trailed off.

"My parents have been gone for over a decade now,

Elinore," Slayde supplied. "My wounds have healed, I assure you. However,"—he cast a sideways look at Aurora—"that doesn't mean I've forgotten how they died. Nor have I abandoned my intentions to shelter my sister from harm."

"Of course. I understand." Elinore turned to Aurora. " 'Tis time for me to take my leave. Clearly, you and your brother have things to discuss."

Aurora frowned, doubtless eager to forestall the inevitable. "But—"

"Thank you for understanding, Elinore," Slayde said firmly. "Good day."

"Good day."

Slayde waited only until the viscountess had gathered her skirts and gone. Then he turned to his sister. "We'll discuss the ramifications of your actions later. For now, where did you say you placed that alleged note you left me?"

"It wasn't alleged. It was real. And I left it on my pillow." Aurora headed for the stairs. "I'll show you."

Three minutes later, Slayde stood at the foot of Aurora's bed, arms folded stiffly across his chest. "Well?"

Perplexed, she shuffled her bedcovers about. "I don't understand. I put it in plain sight. Could a breeze have blown it away?"

"A breeze? From where? Miss Payne hasn't set foot in here to open a window. She's been too busy fretting over your absence."

"Well, I can't imagine—here it is!" Aurora reached between the mattress and the headboard, retrieving the note and flourishing it for Slayde's inspection. "Somehow it toppled beneath my bedding. No wonder you didn't spy it. It was wedged so tightly, not even your keen eye could discern it."

Slayde snatched the page and scanned it. "Damn," he muttered, crumpling it into a ball and tossing it across the room. "You've been frolicking about London while I've been—" He broke off.

"You've been . . . ?" Aurora prompted. Pensively, she inclined her head. "Slayde, I've never seen you so unnerved. Oh, I know how fervent you are about your role as my protector. I'm sure the ransom notes you received must have been terribly upsetting. Still, they're not the first threatening letters we've received pertaining to the diamond, nor is this the first time someone's tried to extort it from us. Obviously, just as on those other occasions, these senders were lying. I'm here. I'm fine. So why are you behaving so irrationally?"

Hands clasped behind him, Slayde regarded Aurora with the brooding, self-contained intensity she recognized all too well. "Two of the ransom notes contained locks of what I presumed to be your hair. I believed the letters were valid. I complied with the sender's terms."

"What terms?"

"An exchange—the black diamond for you."

Undiluted shock registered on Aurora's face. "So you *did* have the diamond. All these years—"

"Not all these years," Slayde interrupted. A heartbeat of a pause. "It was only recently that the stone came into my possession."

"I see. How did it come into your possession? Did you find it?"

"No. It was presented to me."

"By whom?"

"That's irrelevant. The point is, I turned it over to a man I believed was holding you prisoner, a man who obviously went to a great deal of trouble to *make* me believe he was holding you prisoner," Slayde amended. Slowly, he shook his head. "There's more here than meets the eye."

"I don't care," Aurora declared with a dismissive wave of her hand. "I'm thrilled the diamond is gone. At last we'll be rid of that horrible curse."

A dark scowl. "There is no curse, Aurora. There's only the greed of those who seek the stone, and whatever accompanies its possession. Wealth, acclaim . . . or vengeance."

Aurora sighed deeply. "You still think Lawrence Bencroft is involved. Slayde, he's too drunk to contrive some grand scheme to avenge his family's downfall. Is it so difficult for you to accept the possibility that the pirate who summoned you acted alone?"

"If he did, he's remarkably clever and thorough. Not to mention quick-thinking. He'd have to have learned about your excursion to London immediately, leapt at the chance to feign a kidnapping, and found a perfect replica for you all within a day. Quite a feat, wouldn't you say?"

"I was hardly invisible. Hundreds of people saw me in London. This pirate could have been in or about Town, caught a glimpse of me, and dispatched a missive straightaway." A flicker of bewilderment flashed in Aurora's eyes. "What replica?"

"The young woman I believed to be you when I relinquished the stone. The woman who lost her father, her home, and very nearly her life. The woman who's down the hall now, recovering from extensive injuries and severe shock. The woman who, from a distance, looks much like you and from whom that filthy pirate clearly acquired the locks of hair he sent me. *That* replica."

Aurora sank down on the bed. "You'd better explain." She listened, eyes widening as Slayde relayed the details of what had occurred two nights past. "Who is she?"

"Her name is Courtney Johnston. Her father captained the vessel that was overtaken by that blasted pirate. He was murdered at the same time that his daughter was taken prisoner. That's all I know. Miss Johnston is awake for only short periods of time. And when she is, she's still very weak, in a great deal of pain, and—much of the time—incoherent."

"And all alone," Aurora murmured. "God knows, I understand how that feels." Swallowing, she asked, "How old is she?"

"About your age, I should say."

"Does she really resemble me?"

"Yes . . . and no." Slayde studied his sister, trying to view her as a woman and not as the child he'd become responsible for ten years past. "You have the same coloring—other than your eyes—and similar builds. Otherwise, I see little resemblance."

"Is she pretty?"

"I wouldn't know," was the curt reply. "She's swathed in bandages and enveloped by bedcovers."

"How long will she be staying at Pembourne?"

"That depends on how quickly she heals." Slayde paused, frowning. "A better question is, where will she go afterward?"

Silence hung heavily in the room.

"She needn't go anywhere," Aurora put in at last. "In fact, I'd be relieved if she'd stay as long as possible. With you perpetually away, I'm virtually alone, with the exception of the army of servants you've hired to keep vigil over me. A companion would be delightful."

Slayde's eyes narrowed thoughtfully on his sister. "I realize you loathe your isolation. I always assumed it was because being confined to Pembourne made it impossible for you to gallivant beyond your lighthouse or get into some other form of mischief. In truth, I never considered the fact that you might be lonely."

"There's quite a lot you never considered." A shrug. "You're a loner, Slayde. As a result, you expect the rest of the world to follow suit. Well, not all of us are able to exist in utter solitude."

"There isn't always a choice."

"Maybe, in my case, we've just found one."

"You don't know that Miss Johnston will choose to remain at Pembourne. She's not the type to accept charity. I sense a great deal of pride beneath that broken exterior."

"You sense a great deal for a man who spends little or no time around others."

Again, silence.

"Does Miss Johnston understand all that's happened?" Aurora inquired.

"Unfortunately, yes. And she's devastated by it."

"I'm sure she is." Aurora traced the intricate pattern of the bedcovers with her forefinger. "Slayde—may I at least speak with her? I realize I was very young when Mama and Papa died. Still, perhaps there's something I could say. Something that would ease her pain—even a bit."

Slowly, he nodded. "Perhaps so. But not for several hours. She drifted off a minute before Matilda announced your arrival, and she'll probably sleep for some time now, thanks to the laudanum Dr. Gilbert left. When she awakens, I'll introduce you."

"Excellent." Aurora rose. "Now you may lecture me on my outrageous behavior and the heinous outcome that could have resulted from my joining Elinore on her trip to London."

"Would it do any good?"

"Probably not."

Slayde shook his head. "Maybe asking Miss Johnston to stay is a good idea at that, if only to divert your attention away from the outside world and all its allure."

"Or to enlighten me about it," Aurora proposed with a grin.

"Don't push me, Aurora. I'm not feeling very tolerant right now." Slayde glanced restlessly toward the bed-chamber door. "I have things to resolve before Miss Johnston awakens."

"Then go resolve them."

Slayde hesitated, feeling that all-too-familiar discomfort that accompanied his infrequent parental interaction with his sister. "Do you require anything?"

"No. But should that situation change, I'm perfectly capable of getting what I need. Remember, Slayde, while you're abroad for months at a time—doing whatever it is you do—I'm fending for myself. I hardly require an overseer."

"As your reckless little excursion to Town just proved" was the dry retort.

Aurora rolled her eyes. "I told you—"

"I know what you told me." Slayde's jaw tightened in flagrant warning. "The subject is closed. You are not to leave Pembourne without permission again. Is that understood?"

Pressing her lips together, Aurora gave a tight, though rebellious nod.

"Good." With that, Slayde dismissed the issue, striding across the bedchamber and yanking open the door. "I'll summon you when Miss Johnston awakens. *After* I've had an opportunity to prepare her for you."

It was midafternoon when Courtney stirred. She felt less disoriented this time, recalling her whereabouts almost immediately—as well as the incidents that had preceded them. The ache in her head had subsided somewhat, as had that in her ribs—whether from the lingering effects of the laudanum or the onset of the natural healing process, she wasn't certain.

She wished the wounds of her heart would be as easy to heal.

"How are you feeling, Miss Johnston?"

It was the housekeeper, Miss Payne, who entered, carrying a tray of tea and toast.

"Better," Courtney replied, her voice an unfamiliar wisp of sound.

"The slash above your eye is healing nicely. Matilda changed the bandage while you slept. She also said you're weak as a newborn babe. And she's right," Miss Payne assessed, laying out the refreshment with a purposeful air. "But it's no wonder. You've eaten nothing for days and drunk only as much as your laudanum required. Well, we're about to change that." So saying, she poured a cup of tea, then placed it on the tray next to Courtney's bedside. "Shall I help you sit up?"

"Thank you very much." Gratefully, Courtney accepted the assistance, wincing at the sharp pain in her ribs that accompanied her movements.

After what seemed like an eternity, she was sitting half upright, two pillows propped behind her back.

"Is that comfortable?" Miss Payne inquired.

"Yes, very."

"Good. Now it's time to regain your strength."

It was more an order than a statement, and Courtney almost found herself smiling. Clearly, Miss Payne was not as soft-hearted as Matilda and had therefore been chosen to administer her meal. Well, Courtney would try not to dissappoint her.

"It looks delicious." She took the proffered teacup and drank, stunned to find she was nearly parched with thirst. Twice, Miss Payne refilled the cup, and twice more, Courtney drank. Next, she attempted the toast, nibbling at the edges before taking her first normal bite.

Her insides gnawed their approval.

"Slowly," the housekeeper cautioned. "Your stomach has been empty for days. Give your body time to accept the food." Patiently, she waited while Courtney alternately ate and rested until, a quarter hour later, both slices of toast were gone. "Excellent." Miss Payne rose. "Your color has already improved."

"Indeed it has."

Lord Pembourne hovered in the doorway, watching as his houseguest licked the final crumbs from her lips. "May I come in?" he inquired politely.

"Of course." For some bizarre reason, Courtney felt a surge of nervousness, doubtless a reaction to receiving a man in her bedchamber. Despite the earl's earlier visits, this was the first time she'd been alert enough to truly consider her surroundings. And, for all her years at sea, no one but her father had ever crossed her cabin's threshold, at least not while she was within.

The earl seemed to sense her discomfort, for he approached stiffly, halting a respectful distance from the foot of her bed.

Simultaneously, Miss Payne gathered up the tray. "Miss Johnston ate her entire meal."

"So I see." Lord Pembourne's silver-gray eyes appraised the empty plates. "And without a drop of fortifying brandy. I'm relieved."

Recalling snatches of her earlier rambling, Courtney flushed.

"As for this evening's meal, I'll advise Cook to prepare some broth," Miss Payne was muttering to herself, "and perhaps a few biscuits. Yes, that should go down well." She gave the earl a quizzical look. "Will you be remaining at Pembourne for any length of time, my lord? If so, I'll need to order additional supplies and alert the staff to your extended stay."

A heartbeat of a pause. "I'm not certain. I'll advise you once my plans are made. For now, assume I'll be here."

"Very good, my lord." She swept off.

Courtney rubbed the sheet between her fingers, studying the earl's chiseled features and trying to shake off her uncustomary self-consciousness. "Are you ofttimes away from home?"

"Yes, frequently."

"For great lengths of time?"

His dark brows rose. "As a matter of fact, yes. My businesses are extensive and take me all over the world: India, the Colonies, Europe."

"How unfortunate."

He blinked. "Unfortunate? Why?"

"Because it must be very difficult—and very lonely—for you."

"Why do you assume that?"

Now it was Courtney's turn to look perplexed. "You did mention you had a sister, did you not? Before I began babbling about my affection for brandy, that is."

His lips twitched. "Yes, I did."

"Then you must miss her dreadfully when you're away. Unless, of course, you take her with you. Do you?"

"Hardly. Aurora stays at Pembourne, where she's safe and carefully watched—except on those few occasions when she's clever enough, and determined enough, to elude my staff."

Courtney frowned. "I didn't realize your sister was a child. When you spoke of my resemblance to her—well,

I was under the obvious misconception that she was a woman."

"She is." Lord Pembourne's eyes turned wintry gray. "But, as my family history will bear out, maturity does not preclude the need for safeguarding. The disaster you just survived is tangible proof of that. Had that pirate not intended to pass you off as Aurora, none of the past days' horrors would have occured."

Courtney swallowed, her anguish resurging from its private niche.

"I'm sorry." The earl's apology was immediate, regret slashing his handsome face. "That was a cruel and thoughtless statement to make. Forgive me. The last thing I intended was to upset you."

"You needn't apologize." Courtney blinked back tears, trying to steady her quavering voice. "It matters not whether we give voice to the words; Papa's death haunts me every moment, awake or asleep. Again and again, I see his face, hear his scream, feel his fear. Lord Pembourne . . . " Her chin came up. "I have a proposition for you. If you'll give me a few days to mend, I'll help you find your sister. I know the waters of the Channel as well as any sailor. I can guide you to every hidden nook, every deserted island—anywhere you wish to go. Whoever has Lady Aurora, we'll unearth him. In exchange, I ask only that once your sister is safely restored, you loan me a sailing vessel. I'll return it—intact—the instant I'm able. I'd purchase it outright, but as you know, I have no money."

"Loan you a vessel," the earl repeated quietly. "So you can seek out the pirate who killed your father and run a sword through his belly."

Courtney's jaw dropped.

"I understand what you're feeling." Lord Pembourne continued, addressing her obvious astonishment. "Only too well, in fact. I've experienced your sense of rage firsthand. But trust me; what you're planning won't erase what's happened. Nor will it ease the agony of losing your father."

"I don't care." This time the tears spilled forth of their own volition. "I'm going to find that rogue, find him and kill him. And then I'm going to travel from one ocean to the next until I recover Papa's body. He deserves a proper burial. On that grassy hill in Somerset beside Mama. Where they can be together. Oh, God . . ." Courtney dropped her face into her hands. "Why couldn't I have died with him?"

The bed sagged as Lord Pembourne sat down beside her and gathered her against him with none of the hesitation that had accompanied his previous gesture of comfort. "Because you weren't meant to die," he murmured, gently stroking her hair, "although I know how little solace that affords you right now."

"If I'm meant to live, it can only be to avenge Papa's death."

"Miss Johnston—Courtney—listen to me." The earl spoke softly, his breath brushing the bandage spanning her brow. "You're badly hurt. It will be a week before you've healed enough to stroll the grounds, much less traverse the English Channel. Also, as I just said, vengeance is not nearly as sweet as it seems." He drew a sharp breath, and Courtney had the strange feeling it was not merely she he was trying to convince. "Now that I've said all that, I offer you this promise: we'll find your father's killer, not only for your sake, but for mine."

Courtney leaned back, gazing up at him through watery eyes. "For your sake?"

"Yes. Whoever that murdering pirate was, he did not work alone. I'm certain of it. And whoever helped him devise his plot did it for more than just the black diamond."

"You're referring to the reasons behind your sister's kidnapping."

"That's the puzzle here. There was no kidnapping."

"I don't understand."

"Earlier today, mere minutes after you drifted off, Aurora strolled through Pembourne's entranceway doors. She's as intact as I. Evidently, boredom compelled her to take a jaunt to London in order to experience a taste of the Season."

Courtney blinked. "I see. No, actually I don't see."

A faint smile touched the earl's lips. "Nor do I. However, perhaps once you've met my sister, you will. Aurora is not what one would call a complacent young lady."

"But if she went willingly to London, why were you receiving ransom notes?"

"My question exactly. Further, how could a single person—namely, the pirate who killed your father—have had ample time to observe and recognize Aurora, send the appropriate letters to Pembourne, then board a ship, sail forth until he reached yours, overtake it, and hold your crew captive for several days?"

"It isn't possible." Courtney shook her head. "The *Isobel* was en route to the Colonies, three days out of port, when he made his attack. That means he had to be sailing at least that long, even if he knew our exact location and followed us. Not to mention the time it would take him to conceal his own vessel and row out to the *Isobel* under cover of darkness."

"And why would he be keeping track of your ship's whereabouts, much less following you? Even if he already knew of your existence *and* of your resemblance to Aurora—a farfetched enough idea, given that Aurora doesn't appear in public—he'd have no cause to act until he spied Aurora in London and realized she was vulnerable. And that's assuming he'd already devised his plan and was simply waiting for a chance to enact it."

"I'm still lost," Courtney murmured. "If you're right, if that pirate was working with someone, how would that someone have known of Lady Aurora's intentions to leave Pembourne and travel to London? Clearly, her decision to slip away was impulsive."

"But not unprecedented. Aurora is very creative—if not very successful—in her attempts to see the world.

Usually, she wanders only as far as the lighthouse just beyond Pembourne, by the water's edge. However, on occasion, she gets more ambitious. 'Twould be obvious to anyone watching the estate that she's eager for more freedom."

"Anyone watching the estate," Courtney repeated. "In other words, you believe Pembourne is under scrutiny."

"I do."

"By whom?"

A bitter stare. "The same man whose family has scrutinized and condemned us for generations. Ever since the quest for that bloody diamond."

"The Bencrofts? Is that the family you mean?"

"Yes. If anyone has a reason—at least in his own distorted mind—to twist a knife in my gut, it's Lawrence Bencroft, the current Duke of Morland. The hatred within that man runs deeper than you can imagine."

"Deep enough to feign a kidnapping in order to torment you?"

"Not just to torment me," Slayde amended. "To baffle, outwit, and humiliate me, and then to rob me of a treasure he considers rightfully his, a treasure that, if my guess is right, is in Morland's possession right now."

The pounding in Courtney's head had begun to intensify as the lingering effects of laudanum slowly faded. "What will you do?" she asked, unconsciously sagging toward Slayde.

"Something my family hasn't done in sixty years: go to Morland. Visit that drunken snake. And, should he be the inventor of this sick scheme, expose him for the manipulative bastard that he is." The earl looked down, taking in Courtney's drooping head. "Shall I bring you more laudanum?"

"No—please. I don't want to sleep. When I do, the nightmares return. Besides, I can't think clearly when I'm drugged. And I want to make sense of what you just said." Desperately, she battled the dull throbbing in her skull. "If what you're saying is true, if the Duke of Morland hired that wretched pirate to seize Papa's ship, then the duke must know where to find him—if only to recoup the jewel."

"I would assume so, yes." Slayde frowned. "Are you certain you're able to continue this conversation? 'Tis obvious you're in pain."

"I'm certain. Please, my lord, I need to think, to talk. Just for a while. When the pain becomes too much to bear, I'll take the laudanum. But not yet."

Lord Pembourne nodded against her hair. "As you wish." To Courtney's surprise, he made no move to release her. Instead, he eased her forward, cradling her nape and pressing her cheek to his waistcoat. "Is that better?"

"Much, thank you." In truth, it was more than better. It was wonderful. By anchoring her head in his powerful hand, the earl was releasing the pressure pounding at her skull while at the same time offering her a sturdy foundation upon which to rest. Even her ribs felt less constricted.

"They'll fade, you know."

The words rumbled through his chest to her ear.

"What will?"

"The nightmares. They won't last forever. They'll lessen, first in intensity, then in frequency. Finally, they'll besiege you only on occasion. And suddenly you'll discover they're endurable. You won't be crushed beneath their force. And you'll begin to live again."

Courtney sighed. "I hope you're right."

"I am." He hesitated. "Miss Johnston, before we resume our discussion, I have a favor to ask of you, if I may."

"A favor?" Irony laced her tone. "You saved my life, took me into your home, and are now providing both sympathy and aid, not to mention hope. You may ask anything of me you wish. And please," she added softly, "call me Courtney, as you did a few minutes past. I realize it's a bit unorthodox, but then so is the fact that you've taken a total stranger into your home and are now visiting her chambers. In addition, to be honest, I've never in my life been addressed as 'Miss Johnston'—with the exception of the one loathsome year I spent at Madame La Salle's Boarding School for Young Ladies. And that is a period of time I'd like to forget. As, I'm sure, Madame La Salle is doing her best to forget me."

The earl surprised her—and himself—by chuckling, a husky sound that rolled through Courtney like warm honey. "How ominous. Very well then, Courtney. My favor is as follows: would you consider staying on at Pembourne as Aurora's companion? Not just while you're recuperating, but afterward. Until my adventure-seeking sister drives you away. You'd be doing me a great service."

Courtney swallowed, staring at his white linen shirt front. "A service? That sounds more like a cloaked offer of charity. After all, your sister is hardly of an age where she needs a governess. No, Lord Pembourne, I cannot accept, although I thank you from the bottom of my heart. 'Tis difficult enough for me to lie here and permit your staff to wait upon me while I'm confined to bed. But the instant my body is strong enough, I'll be on my way. I won't take advantage of your kindness, avail myself of your home and your servants, when I can do nothing to repay you."

"Trust me—given Aurora's nature, 'tis I who will be in your debt, not the other way around." Roughly, Slayde cleared his throat. "Courtney, I'm going to be frank. You and I have just determined we share a mutual goal: unearthing those involved in feigning Aurora's kidnapping *and* murdering your father. Answer me this: if you were to leave Pembourne tomorrow, would it not be to hunt down that pirate?"

A small nod.

"Well, I intend to immerse myself in the task of doing just that, starting by investigating a man I believe could lead us right to your father's killer; namely, Lawrence

Bencroft. I'll delve as deep and as long as it takes to determine Morland's involvement."

"And if the duke is not involved?"

"Then I'll find out who is. Further, my resources are far more vast than yours. So why strike out on your own when by remaining at Pembourne you can benefit from my findings?"

"While contributing what in return?" Courtney asked with quiet dignity. "I won't accept charity."

"I don't think you realize just how much peace of mind you'd be affording me by keeping Aurora distracted and entertained. Translated, that means safe and accounted for, something my vast array of servants seem unable to ensure. From the reports I received upon returning from India ten days past, Aurora succeeded in sneaking out of Pembourne twice in three months, this last journey notwithstanding—a record even for my sister. And that doesn't take into account the six or seven unsuccessful attempts she made to beg, blackmail, or trick her way past the staff."

"Where is it she wishes to go?"

"I shudder to think. Fortunately, she's ofttimes content with the lighthouse as a destination. She's enthralled by Mr. Scollard, its keeper. I have no idea why, nor do I care to find out. All I know is that she dashes off to see him every chance she gets. And, eventually, one of my footmen drags her home."

Spontaneous laughter bubbled up inside Courtney, her first real laughter in nearly a week. "My lord, if you don't mind my saying so, you must have the most exhausted servants in all of England. *And* the most single-minded of sisters. I can't imagine one woman requiring a houseful of people to oversee her."

"Imagine it. You've never met Aurora."

"Evidently not. In which case, suppose I accept your terms. Has it occurred to you that if your sister is as headstrong as you say, she might not be amenable to our arrangement?"

"She's more than amenable; she's elated. She told me

so herself. You have no worry on that score. When I left Aurora, she was nearly pacing the halls, waiting to meet you."

Courtney felt strangely touched by that notion. "Very well, then. Your logic is sound, though I still question the fairness of our arrangement. Nevertheless, I'll stay at Pembourne—for the time being—and act the part of Lady Aurora's companion. Although how in the name of heaven I can counter the allure of the outside world, I haven't a clue. But I'll try, my lord."

"Thank you." The earl's fingers tightened briefly on Courtney's nape, belying his casual tone and alerting her to the significance of his next words. "By the way, with reference to given names, mine is Slayde. Not 'my lord.'"

"All right—Slayde." Reluctantly, Courtney drew back, wincing a bit at the resulting discomfort. "I assume you'd like to bring Lady Aurora in now."

"Not until you've rested." His momentary tension having dissipated, Slayde eased Courtney to the pillows.

Panic erupted inside her, screaming out that to sleep meant she would relive the dark fires of hell. "I don't want to sleep," she blurted.

"Then don't. Just rest." Astutely, Slayde studied her stricken expression. "I suggest a half-dose of laudanum, enough only to soothe the pain and make you doze. How would that be?"

"A half-dose?" Courtney breathed in a hopeful voice.

"Um-hum." His lips twitched. "In a whole dose of brandy. Much-needed brandy, I might add, to fortify you for your meeting with Aurora."

"Will you stay with me while I rest?" Mortified, Courtney realized she sounded like a frightened child. But, God help her, that's just what she felt like.

"Yes, I'll stay with you." Slayde could have summoned Matilda or Miss Payne, but he didn't. Instead, he stood, pouring a goblet of brandy and adding a small amount of laudanum to it. "Drink this," he murmured, supporting her head while she did. "All of it, as I'm sure you'll be delighted to do."

Courtney smiled, taking four or five appreciative swallows, then resting before she downed the remaining contents of the glass.

"Well done. I'm impressed." With a teasing glance at the empty goblet, he lowered her back to the bed.

"Thank you," she whispered.

"You're welcome." He gazed down at her from beneath hooded lids, his expression unreadable. "Now, let the medicine do its job. When the pain subsides, I'll summon Aurora."

Murmuring her agreement, Courtney sank into the softness of the bed. Within minutes, her body began to feel light, tingly, everything around her unfolding in slow, soothing motion. Her lashes fluttered, then fanned downward, her mind gratefully devoid of thought, her entire being blessedly absent of pain.

Slayde watched her sea-green eyes grow vague, then drift shut, and he was accosted by that same oddly bemused feeling he'd experienced earlier—odd because he wasn't a man given to emotion, nor to personal affinities of any kind. In fact, Aurora's assessment of him had been quite right. He *was* a loner, a man who relied upon only himself for constancy. Never until this moment had he ever tried so hard to convince a woman to stay with him, nor had he every truly cared if one did. Further, he'd certainly never requested that anyone— woman or man—address him by his given name. And yet he'd just done both, with a woman who was, in her own words, a virtual stranger.

Why?

Could it be the chord of memory she struck within him? Doubtful. He'd recovered from his parents' deaths years ago.

Perhaps he felt responsible for her. He had, as fate had deemed, saved her life. That idea was even more far-fetched than the first. Decency, after all, was not a forebearer of sentiment.

Then what?

Pulling up a chair, Slayde lowered himself into it, leaning forward and searching Courtney's face, as if for an answer. She was peaceful now, half asleep and unhaunted by demons, her bandaged brow unfurrowed, her breathing slow and even.

His reply to Aurora with regard to Courtney's beauty had been a lie. Despite the inhibiting bandages, Courtney Johnston was clearly lovely, her features delicate and exquisitely formed, her cheekbones high, her lips soft and full. Her figure was equally delicate, as he'd discovered firsthand—so slight he wondered how she'd withstood the hardships of the past week. Still, beneath that fragile exterior, he sensed a strength that rivaled his own, a strength that would pull her through whatever lay ahead and ensure that, somehow, she survived.

Without thinking, Slayde reached out and captured one red-gold tress, staring at it in surprise as he did. Another first-time gesture. He'd never been compelled to touch a woman's hair before. In fact, he wasn't given to touching at all, other than during a sexual liaison, and even then his urge for physical contact was rooted in carnality rather than intimacy and limited to those moments when passion dominated all else. Yet in one day, he'd impulsively enfolded this woman in his arms not once, but twice, and now had an unprecedented urge to explore the silky texture of her hair. Hair that, upon closer inspection, was not at all the fiery color of Aurora's, but a more subtle, vivid combination of warm reds, shimmering golds, and honey browns.

Slowly, he let the strands glide free of his fingers, until, one by one, they dropped onto the pillow and fanned out beside her in a blazing waterfall.

"I'm resting," Courtney announced, eyes closed, words slurred.

"So I see." A faint smile played about Slayde's lips. For whatever reason, he was drawn to this woman. And because of that—and his own longstanding suspicions— he'd help her find the bastard who killed her father, along with whoever had paid him to recover the black diamond.

God help Lawrence Bencroft if he was that man.

Sea foam trailed soundlessly into the hollow cove. Just within, the dark figure paced, then halted, emitting a savage curse and slamming one gloved fist against the stone wall.

Damnit. Where is that wretched pirate? He's had more than enough time. He was supposed to be here hours ago with the diamond—My diamond. The one I've awaited forever. Well, I don't intend to wait another day. He'd best show up. Soon. If he dares try to defy me, he'll die. Others have. Others will.

Chapter 4

"Aurora, meet our houseguest, Courtney Johnston. Courtney, my sister, Aurora."

"I'm so glad to meet you." Aurora sailed around Slayde and approached Courtney's bed. Pausing, she fingered the folds of her gown, softly adding, "I'm terribly sorry for all you've been through."

A wave of warmth pervaded Courtney's heart. "Thank you," she murmured. "And I'm delighted to meet you, too."

There was nothing average about Aurora Huntley, Courtney decided with an inward smile. She was a striking beauty, her looks every bit as vivid as the personality Slayde had depicted in his exasperated description. Her hair was a vibrant red-gold, her eyes wide, a deep turquoise blue, setting off a bold, uncompromising brow and refined, aristocratic features. In fact, delicacy and coloring notwithstanding, she looked quite a bit like Slayde.

As if reading Courtney's mind, Aurora, who had been studying Courtney in return, pronounced, "I don't think we resemble each other at all."

"I agree."

"You're what Elinore describes as the kind of woman who most other, terribly jealous women refer to as 'a classic beauty'—bandages or not."

Courtney blinked. "I? Funny, I was about to say the same about you." Her slender brows drew together. "Forgive me, but who is Elinore?"

"Aurora's connection to the fashionable world," Slayde inserted dryly.

Aurora shot him a look. "May I visit with Miss Johnston alone?"

"If she's willing." Slayde cast an inquisitive glance at Courtney.

"I'd enjoy talking with Lady Aurora," Courtney assured him.

He hesitated.

Aurora rolled her eyes to the heavens. "Don't worry, Slayde. I shan't spirit our houseguest off to parts unknown."

"How comforting." With that, Slayde opened the door and stepped out. "You have a quarter hour."

The door shut behind him.

"As you can see, my brother and I are quite different," Aurora began without preliminaries. Drawing up a chair, she settled herself beside Courtney's bed.

"Yes. You certainly are."

"Do you have brothers or sisters?"

"No." Courtney felt that now-familiar constriction in her chest. "It was just Papa and I. And now he's gone."

"Slayde told me what happened." Aurora's gaze met Courtney's. "You're very brave. I didn't think I'd survive when my parents died."

"If I recall Papa's stories correctly, you were quite young when that happened," Courtney noted. "It must have been shattering."

"I was ten. And, yes, it was. But, in truth, I don't think

there's ever an easy time to lose someone you love. Especially through a violent death."

Courtney's lashes drifted downward. "The pain is more numbing than all my injuries combined."

"Were you and your father close?"

"Very. He captained a ship. I sailed everywhere with him."

"How exciting!" Aurora's whole face glowed. "I've never been anywhere, at least not since Mama and Papa died, and even then, it was never farther than Scotland. While you—you've traveled the world, seen everything. How wondrous never to be confined to one place."

"Ironic, how different our perspectives are," Courtney replied, her voice choked. "I would have been thrilled to settle down. To live in a cottage on a hill, with my own room and a window overlooking the cliffs and the water. I used to dream that Papa would surprise me with exactly that. But my dream wasn't meant to be. Papa's life was the sea. And, since I desperately wanted to be with him, it became my life as well."

Aurora ingested Courtney's words with an intense expression that made her look all the more like Slayde. "'Twould seem there is more than one way to be lonely, wouldn't it?"

"Yes," Courtney answered, pondering the fact that beneath all the youthful recklessness Slayde had described lay a strong, insightful woman—one she was suddenly quite eager to befriend. "I believe there is."

"How old are you?" The forthright Aurora was back.

"I'll be twenty next month." Courtney smiled wistfully. "Papa's gift to me was going to be twofold: a puppy, which I've wanted since I was a tot, and one full week together as a family. On land. Just Papa, the pup, and me. Both gifts were to be presented to me later this summer, after the *Isobel* returned from delivering its cargo to the Colonies. Lexley—Papa's first mate—was going to oversee the brig so Papa and I could travel the countryside together. By carriage, not ship. But now . . ." She broke off.

Impulsively, Aurora leaned forward, seizing Courtney's hand. "Perhaps we can have a small celebration of
our own. Here, at Pembourne. That is, if you choose to
stay with us. Please, Courtney—may I call you Courtney?" She paused only to inhale, not to await Courtney's
ensuing nod. "And you must call me Aurora. Please stay.
I know Slayde can be aloof and difficult, but he's scarcely
home. And the servants, for the most part, keep to
themselves, except when they're checking up on me, of
course—which they're far less apt to do if I have a
companion to keep me from straying off Pembourne's
grounds. So you'll be allowed as much or as little
freedom as you wish. I shan't invade your privacy, or
your grief. But Courtney—" Another breath. "Sometimes grief is better shared. Else it grows larger rather
than smaller. My brother is a perfect example of that. He
keeps everything to himself. Thus, he's alone. *And*
lonely, whether he chooses to realize it or not. Well, I
won't let that happen to me. Nor to you, if you'll accept
my friendship." A dimple appeared in each of Aurora's
cheeks. "Let's see," she mused aloud, "we're about the
same size, so buying a wardrobe won't be necessary.
You'll simply wear all of my clothes—beginning next
week, when you're up and about. Shortly thereafter,
you'll be ready for long strolls. I have just the place for us
to visit. 'Tis my favorite spot in all the world, *and* the
ideal site for your birthday celebration. I'll take you
there, introduce you to the most fascinating and caring
man. His stories are mesmerizing, and the view from his
window spectacular—the very cliffs and water you've
dreamed of." Aurora's grip tightened. "Say you'll stay."

Grief temporarily supplanted by awe, Courtney stared
at Aurora, touched by her generosity, wondering if
Aurora knew just how contagious her enthusiasm was—
and how healing.

Unexpected tears filled Courtney's eyes. "Do you
know, Aurora," she managed, intentionally using the
given name she'd been requested to, "I never realized
until this minute just how bereft I was of friendship. I'd

be honored to strive to earn yours." A shaky smile. "Yes, I'll stay. And, yes, please call me Courtney. And, yes, I'd love to visit your lighthouse."

Joy—followed by surprise. "Slayde told you about the Windmouth lighthouse?"

"Not by name, no. Only that you're drawn to it, time and again."

"That's all he *could* tell you. 'Tis all he knows, or rather, all he chooses to know," Aurora added with a resigned sigh. "The lighthouse is an adventurer's dream and a wanderer's haven. Mr. Scollard, its keeper, is my dearest friend. He's a prophet and a genius. Nothing he says, or relays, is without meaning—if the listener is shrewd enough to search for it. I remember the very first story he told me. I was five years old. 'Twas about a smuggler who transported a chest of jewels to England with the intention of burying it in a forsaken cave at Cornwall. But before he could reach land, his ship was dashed on the rocks, and the jewels were forever lost at sea. Sometimes, late at night, you can still see the gems sparkling across the waters of the Channel. And—"

"That's enough, Aurora."

Slayde loomed in the doorway, his expression as dark as his tone. "I said you could meet our guest, not wear her out. You'll have plenty of time to regale her with Mr. Scollard's nonsensical yarns—if she still chooses to stay at Pembourne. A quarter hour with you might very well have altered her decision."

"Not at all," Courtney inserted. "If anything, it's reinforced it." She smiled at Aurora. "I look forward to hearing more. And to meeting Mr. Scollard—not once, but countless times."

A dazzling grin lit Aurora's face. "Cook will bake a splendid cake when your birthday arrives. We'll take it with us to the lighthouse. Maybe Elinore can join us there. Oh! You asked who she was. Elinore is the Viscountess Stanwyk. She lives in Teignmouth, less than two miles from here. She was Mama's dearest friend. But don't let her age fool you; she's as vibrant as a young girl.

In fact, she's the one with whom I spent this past week in London. Tomorrow, after you've rested, I'll tell you all about our adventures there. The important thing is, I'm sure Elinore will be delighted to partake in our birthday celebration. As will Mr. Scollard. And who knows? Perhaps he can tell you something wonderful about your future."

Her future.

Courtney felt the constriction in her chest return.

"Say good night, Aurora," Slayde commanded. "Miss Johnston is exhausted. Matilda is on her way up to change our guest's bandages and bring her some supper. Then she must sleep. You'll visit again tomorrow."

"Of course." Aurora rose. "Sleep well, Courtney." She paused, her buoyancy vanishing in the wake of solemn perception. "The grief will subside," she vowed, squeezing Courtney's hand. "And remember—you're not alone."

Courtney's lips trembled. "Thank you, Aurora. I'll keep reminding myself of that."

The grandfather clock struck midnight.

In his study, Slayde poured another brandy and paced restlessly about the room.

He'd closeted himself here to plan tomorrow's unscheduled confrontation with Morland.

Instead, he'd done nothing but think of Courtney.

There was something poignantly moving about her, something that touched a chord inside him, resonated through him like a melody he'd never heard yet somehow recognized. He'd felt it when he watched her sleep, then again when she'd been chatting with Aurora and her spirit had shown signs of revival. It was separate and apart from her beauty, even from her inner strength. The former elicited attraction; the latter, admiration. This was something different. And he was damned if he understood it.

One thing he did understand, and that was Courtney's need to strike back, to punish the bastard who'd killed her father. The more Slayde pondered the facts, the more convinced he was that the pirate in question had not worked alone. Somewhere out there was an accomplice—or, more likely, an employer—who'd paid to have the black diamond seized.

Seized—or from the viewpoint of Morland's warped mind, restored. That unstable lowlife had never ceased to believe that the jewel rightfully belonged in the hands of the Bencrofts. So if he was at the helm, it was not only to reap the wealth afforded by the black diamond, but to undo sixty years of what his distorted mind perceived as heinous injustice.

If he was at the helm.

But who else would have been twisted enough to invent Aurora's kidnapping?

Tossing off his drink, Slayde contemplated the forthcoming altercation. Confronting Morland was going to be ugly. The man was a weakling, a drunk, and a liar. He was also bitter and vindictive, hating the Huntleys with every fiber of his being. Clearly, whether he was guilty or not, he'd deny everything and throw Slayde off his estate.

Unless Slayde arrived with ammunition.

Ammunition in the form of concrete proof or, at the very least, powerful enough implications to make the duke lose his shaky composure and—given the combined effects of constantly consumed liquor and the pressure—to incriminate himself.

Raking a hand through his hair, Slayde considered that prospect. He'd have to acquire some information before bursting into Morland's home and accusing him of theft, blackmail, and, indirectly, murder. He'd visit a few of the duke's colleagues, learn a little about what the fool had been up to over the past fortnight, whom he'd seen and where he'd been.

Then Slayde would go for the kill. Through skill and cunning, he just might succeed in prodding Morland into talking a bit too much and divulging some condemning detail, after which he would ascertain the name and whereabouts of the pirate who'd killed Courtney's father and exact the revenge she sought.

As well as a semblance of his own.

The abhorrent events—and unanswered questions—of ten years past unfolded in Slayde's mind once more, in vivid, excruciating detail.

His parents, lying in pools of blood on the marble floor. The terrified servants, all shaking their heads, swearing they'd seen and heard nothing. The authorities, after weeks of futile investigation, shrugging their shoulders and abandoning their search for the murderer. And the odious, though unproven, possibility that Chilton Bencroft, Geoffrey's son and Lawrence's father, had ordered the monstrous execution, exacting the most horrible, fatal kind of revenge.

Lord, how Slayde wished he'd reached the bastard in time to learn the truth, to choke it out of him, if need be. But the old man had died a month later, succumbing to a longstanding weakness of the heart.

And the truth had died with him.

Perhaps, through Courtney, Slayde was being given another chance to see that justice was served. Tomorrow's excursion would tell.

With a weary sigh, Slayde turned down the lamp and headed for bed.

The second floor was silent.

Slayde rounded the landing, grateful that Aurora had finally retired for the night and that the servants had followed suit. He felt the need for solitude, and thankfully, all of Pembourne was deep in slumber.

A choked sound refuted that notion, reaching Slayde's ears and stopping him in his tracks. Straining, he listened, wondering if it had been his imagination.

No, there it was again. Someone was crying. And, judging by the direction of the sound, that someone was Courtney.

All thoughts of solitude having vanished, Slayde retraced his steps, turning the door handle without pausing to knock.

Shadows washed the room, broken only by the dim glow of a single lamp. It was enough. Slayde could easily discern Courtney's slight form, huddled in the center of the bed, weeping as if her heart would break.

"Courtney?" He shut the door, crossing over.

Her head came up, and she stared at him, her eyes damp pools of jade. "I'm sorry," she whispered. "I didn't mean to awaken anyone."

"You didn't. I was already awake." The agony on her face was unbearable and, without thinking, Slayde perched on her bedside, reached out for her.

She went into his arms with a heartbreaking whimper, burying her face against his shirt as harsh sobs wracked her body.

"Shhh . . . it's not the wounds, is it?"

"No."

"I thought not." Tenderly, he stroked her hair, his lips brushing the satiny tresses.

"It was . . . a dream."

Slayde could well imagine what, or whom, she'd dreamed of. "It's all right. You're awake now."

"I wish I weren't," she wept. "Oh, God, I'm trying so hard to be strong, but I'm just not sure that I can be, nor that I even want to be. I'm sorry . . . I don't mean to sound childish and irrational. I can't seem to help myself."

"You're neither irrational nor childish." His palm caressed her back, feeling her agitated tremors even through the thin barrier of her nightrail. "You've endured a brutal shock, not only to your body, but to your life. You must give yourself time to heal."

"And what if I can't heal?"

"You will."

"I don't think so. My dream . . ." With a shaky sigh, Courtney drew back, gazing up at Slayde with haunted eyes. "What would you say if I told you I think Papa's alive—that he didn't drown when he went overboard? Would you think I was mad?"

"I'd think you were mourning. Denial is part of that process."

"No. My dream was too real." She dashed away her tears. "He was calling out to me. Not in a spiritual sense, but in an actual one. He was reassuring me that he lived."

"You're emotionally drained and physically depleted. Not to mention the fact that you have a concussion, which very often jumbles thoughts. Believe me, you're not mad. You're perfectly normal."

"Am I?" Her breath came in sharp pants, and when Slayde eased her toward the pillows, she clutched at his shirt, terror slashing her delicate features. "Talk to me," she pleaded softly. "Stay with me. Just for a while. Don't leave me alone with this horrible, gripping emptiness."

"I won't," he promised, reversing his motion and bringing her against him. "I'll stay as long as you need me. I wasn't leaving. I was just helping you to lie back and rest."

"I don't want to lie back—or to rest. I want to talk. Please."

How well he understood. "By all means." Shifting a bit, Slayde eased her onto her side, cushioning her head in the crook of his arm. Then, he stretched out beside her, his back propped against the headboard. "How's that?"

A deep, contented sigh. "Thank you."

"My pleasure. Would you like a fire?"

"No. I'm fine—as long as I'm not alone."

"You're not. I'm right here." He waited until his words had sunk in and he felt the panic ease from her muscles. Then he sought to distract her. "Did I hear Aurora mention something about your birthday being imminent?"

A tentative nod. "Next month." She swallowed. "Papa's gift was to be a puppy."

"Any specific kind of puppy?"

"No. Just one who needed me—and, of course, one who was a natural sailor."

"As you are, I presume."

An ironic sound escaped Courtney's lips. "I? Hardly. I dreaded every moment of our journeys. That's why the second part of Papa's gift meant so much. He planned to spend one full week with me. On land. Funny—" Her voice quavered. "At the time, it seemed too short an interval. Now, one week seems like the most priceless of gifts."

Slayde felt a wave of compassion—and a surge of confusion. "If you dreaded your journeys, why in God's name did you go? Surely your father didn't insist that you remain—"

"He didn't," she interrupted. "Papa never knew of my feelings. No one did. In fact, you're the first person I've ever told. Had I confessed the truth to Papa, one of two things would have happened: either he would have given up the sea, which I couldn't abide—'twas his life—or he'd have restored me to boarding school, which would have been akin to thrashing me. I'd spent months pleading with him to withdraw me and equally as many months upending the school so they were more than happy to comply."

Slayde's lips twitched. "It sounds like you were a terror."

"I was." He felt her smile faintly against his shirt. "Trust me, Aurora is a lamb in comparison."

"What a harrowing thought." Slayde's brows knit. "When we first spoke of your father, you referred to the *Isobel* in affectionate terms—as your home."

"It was. Because Papa was there. But every night, I prayed for the impossible: that he would tire of the sea on his own and choose for us to settle down. To make a real home, together."

"I see." Slayde stared off into space, wondering why he, the most circumspect of men, was asking so many intrusive questions, and more importantly, why he felt compelled to know as much as he could about his beautiful houseguest. "Is your mother alive?"

"No. Mama died just after I was born. I never knew her. But I knew a great deal *about* her. Papa spoke of her constantly: her beauty, her warm-hearted nature, her enthusiasm for life. Of course, he was more than a bit subjective. He adored her."

"Did she live near the docks? Is that where they met?"

A soft breath of laughter. "She lived in a mansion. They met when Papa's ship was docked and Mama happened to be strolling near the water's edge. Mama's parents were blue bloods—titled and affluent. Needless to say, they were less than thrilled with her choice of husbands. But it didn't matter, not to her or to Papa. They were very much in love. The fact that she was an aristocrat and Papa a sea captain mattered not a whit. Eventually, their devotion triumphed. They procured her parents's blessing and were married that very week."

Courtney rose up, inclining her head in question. "Do you recall the timepiece you rescued? The one you placed in the nightstand drawer?"

Slayde nodded. "I remember."

"It's the finest of captain's watches. *And* Papa's most treasured memory of Mama. She gave it to him as a wedding gift, a symbol of their lives and their love. Not only is the craftsmanship exquisite, the scene within—" Courtney broke off, her eyes widening eagerly. "Would you like to see it? *Really* see it, in detail?"

The glow on her face was worth the cost of a dozen timepieces combined. "Yes, I would. Very much."

Gingerly, Courtney twisted about and extracted the piece of silver with a familiarity that made Slayde suspect she'd done this repeatedly over the past two days. "I realize you must already have glanced at it," she said, "but 'tis far too beautiful for a cursory look." Lovingly, she caressed the gleaming case, extending the watch for Slayde's perusal.

He took it, noting the intricacy of the pattern etched on the outside. "It's lovely."

"Open it," Courtney urged. "Hold it to the lamp so you can see the scene inside."

Slayde complied, studying the enchanting picture that greeted him.

A solitary ship graced the center of the watch's face. The vessel appeared to be paused on a course to the lighthouse depicted on the right—no, not paused—unmoving. Cushioned by peaceful sea waters, the ship remained as it was, halted midway to its destination, suspended in time.

"According to Papa, Mama claimed he was the ship and she, the lighthouse," Courtney elaborated, her voice choked. "That's because, until a few days past, the picture moved. The lighthouse beam appeared, beckoning, and the ship sailed toward it, hastening toward its welcoming light just as Papa always did to Mama. He took the watch with him wherever he traveled, kept it with him all these years—even after she died. It was his way of having Mama beside him, always." A shuddering breath. "He gave me the timepiece just before he was forced overboard, told me to keep it as a memory of them both. I clutched it long after that animal locked me in my cabin. I was afraid to open the case, because I knew what I would find. At last, I relented, needing to see I was wrong—only to discover I was right. Just as I dreaded, the watch had stopped." Hollow emptiness returned to Courtney's eyes. "It won't start again until Papa is home where he belongs."

"Courtney—"

"Don't tell me he's dead," she refuted in a strangled whisper. "I refuse to accept that." Two tears slid down her cheeks. "I can't explain it, but while I realize up here"—she touched her brow—"the implausibility of what I'm saying, in here"—she lay her palm over her heart—"I believe otherwise." Valiantly, she struggled for control. "So let's not discuss it, all right? Let's speak of something else."

With a wordless nod, Slayde snapped the watch case shut and replaced it in the drawer. "The timepiece is exquisite. Your mother had exceptional taste." A heartbeat of a pause. "And an exceptional daughter."

Warm color tinged Courtney's cheeks. "Thank you."

"You're welcome." Unsettled by his own sense of imbalance, Slayde sought a safer ground. "Tell me, why did you hate sailing? Was it the lack of privacy?"

Courtney shook her head, capturing a tear with the tip of her tongue. "No. I had all the privacy I wished for. In fact, I spent long hours alone in my cabin. Only Papa visited me there. The men were given strict orders—by Papa—never to enter my quarters."

"I don't blame him. A beautiful woman, together with a shipload of men? Were I your father, I'd have locked you in."

A twinge of amusement. "I was hardly compromised. The men treated me with the utmost respect. After all, my father was their captain."

"Where did your ship journey?"

"To the Colonies. We carried furniture and other English goods to New York and Boston."

"Did you dislike visiting the Colonies?"

"Actually, I found them quite fascinating. Why?"

"I was only wondering if perhaps that was the reason you disliked your trips aboard the *Isobel*."

"No, it wasn't."

"Very well, then; was it the food you so detested?"

Courtney's lips curved. "In truth, the meals served at Madame La Salle's Boarding School were far more apt to cause fatal illness than those served aboard the *Isobel*. I also had less privacy, more restrictions, and far more unsavory companions at school than at sea. No, 'twas none of those things that deterred me."

"I'm mystified, then. What caused you to loathe sea travel?"

"The fact that the moment the ship left the wharf, I became violently seasick and remained so for the duration of each and every trip. Which, incidently, is why I spent so much time in my cabin. 'Tis difficult to walk about the deck with your head in a chamber pot."

Laughter rumbled in Slayde's chest. "I should think it would be."

"I truly hoped I'd outgrow the weakness with time," Courtney murmured ruefully. "But after twenty years, that possibility seems unlikely."

"Twenty. Is that how old you're turning next month?"

"Yes."

The lighthearted moment vanished as ugly memories lanced Slayde's heart like a knife. "I was only a year older than that when my parents died."

Tilting back her head, Courtney studied his expression. Then, tentatively, she reached up, her fingers brushing his jaw. "I can't begin to imagine how agonizing that must have been. At least I was spared seeing Papa—" She broke off, drew a sharp, unsteady breath.

"I was the one who found them," Slayde replied tonelessly. "I returned to Pembourne late that night. I knew something was amiss when I found the front door slightly ajar. They were in the library on the floor. They'd been run through by a sword. The whole area surrounding them was covered in blood. No matter how many years go by, I'll never forget that image. It's ingrained in my mind forever."

"The authorities never unearthed the murderer?"

"They stopped looking as swiftly as they possibly could. Officially, the crime was declared the unfortunate result of a burglary, since the strongbox containing my mother's jewels was missing. That was the *official* report. The truth is another story entirely." Seeing Courtney's puzzled expression, he stated flatly, "To be blunt, Bow Street was terrified. Lest your father have neglected to mention it, the world believed—*believes*," Slayde amended in a bitter tone, "that the Huntleys are condemned to an eternity of hell. A hell spawned by some bizarre, nonexistent curse, one that is perpetuated by the very greed of those who seek its source."

"The black diamond."

"Yes. The black diamond."

"Slayde—" Courtney's voice was soft, her fingers

gentle on his face. "You've understood—and eased—my pain. Let me ease yours. Share it with me."

That familiar wall went up. "That won't be necessary. My parents were killed over a decade ago. I've long since come to grips with the pain."

"Have you?"

Their gazes locked—and the wall toppled.

"My great-grandfather and Geoffrey Bencroft were partners in a joint venture." Slayde was astounded to hear the story emerge from his lips. "Their quest was to locate the world's largest black diamond, stolen centuries earlier from a sacred temple in India and never recovered. Once it was found, their intentions were to deliver the gem to a Russian prince who was offering an outrageous fortune in exchange for the diamond. Dozens of mercenaries had already tried—and failed—to find the stone. My great-grandfather and the late duke were determined to succeed, and they agreed that after they had, they would divide the fortune equally. The only dark cloud threatening their crusade was the mythical curse accompanying the stone, a curse that, according to legend, went 'He with a black heart who touches the jewel will reap eternal wealth, while becoming the carrion upon whom, for all eternity, others will feed.'"

Courtney shivered. "How menacing. Papa never relayed the exact wording of the curse. All he told me was that your great-grandfather supposedly returned to England without the Duke of Morland, but with the stone. And that your family has endured the consequences of the curse ever since."

"I don't believe in curses," Slayde bit out. "Only in those who perpetuate them, and those who effect them by virtue of their greed."

"You think whoever killed your parents wanted the diamond for the wealth they'd derive from it?"

"Of course. 'Twas no secret that the jewel is worth a king's ransom. Nor that my great-grandfather was the last known man to possess it, and that he never delivered it to the Russian prince. The mystery was, where did he hide the stone? *That,* no one knew. So, for four generations, thieves and barbarians have done all they could—including commit murder—to uncover the whereabouts of the wretched gem."

"Did your great-grandfather die before he could tell anyone the truth?"

"Yes. According to my father, he died less than a week after returning to England."

"How?" Courtney murmured. "How did he die?"

"He was dashed on the rocks at the foot of Dartmouth Cliffs."

Courtney tensed, and Slayde anticipated her next question even as she uttered it. "Was he . . . alone?"

"If you mean, was he pushed, no one knows. There were no witnesses." Unconsciously, Slayde tightened his arms about Courtney. "Each successive generation of Huntleys has endured bloodshed. We've also enjoyed a sizable, ever-increasing fortune. So, according to those who believe in myths, the curse has come to pass."

"But two days ago, you turned the black diamond over to that despicable pirate, so the curse should end for you."

"Should it? Not when the true curse is the hatred spawned generations ago and furthered by the Bencrofts. Trust me, Courtney, that hatred will never end."

"'He with a black heart . . .'" she recited thoughtfully. "The Bencrofts think of your great-grandfather as such for deceiving Geoffrey Bencroft and disappearing with the stone."

"Yes. And they despise us because of it. You see, from the moment the diamond left Geoffrey's hands, the Bencroft fortune began dissipating. Each successive loss they suffered heightened their resentment. And there wasn't a bloody thing we could do to alter that. True, my great-grandfather cheated Geoffrey out of his half of the diamond's worth. But he also never sold the stone or reaped any actual profits, so after his death, we had no tangible fortune to share with the Bencrofts. Further, we couldn't turn the stone over to them even if we'd wished to; we hadn't a clue where it was hidden. Consequently, we had no way of righting his wrong."

"And they didn't accept that as truth?"

"Not for a minute. And any hope my family had of appeasing their hatred was quickly snuffed out. Less than a fortnight after my great-grandfather's demise, word reached England that Geoffrey Bencroft had succumbed to a fever and died on his journey home. From that moment on, the Bencrofts' enmity intensified to the point of obsession—violent obsession. Of course, at the heart of that obsession lay Geoffrey's son, Chilton, the new Duke of Morland. New to his title, but not his role," Slayde clarified. "Chilton had been the acting head of his family for years, running the estates and businesses while his father gallivanted about the globe. By the time Geoffrey died, Chilton's reputation amongst members of the *ton* was notorious. He was ruthless in his dealings—and the Huntleys became his prime target. He used every opportunity to malign our name and thwart our business ventures. It maddened him beyond reason when each attempt not only failed, but resulted in further gains for us and more abject poverty for them.

"One month before my parents' deaths, Chilton's mind snapped. He and his only son Lawrence—the current Duke of Morland—forced their way into Pembourne and invaded my father's study. Lawrence hung back, enraged but willing—no, more than willing, grateful—to leave the verbal assault to his father, while he himself tossed off a bottle of madeira and paced sullenly about the room. In contrast, Chilton raved like a madman, shouting accusations about how my family had destroyed the Bencrofts and how it was time for him to even the score, to make the Huntleys pay. The servants and I threw them out. But I remember Chilton's expression vividly: there was murder in his eyes."

"You think he—or they—killed your parents?"

"Just Chilton," Slayde corrected. "And, yes, I do—although the authorities were never able to prove it. As for Lawrence, he's too weak to kill anyone, although

Lord knows, the intensity of his hatred is more than sufficient to incite murder. And he's certainly clever enough to manage it—when he's sober. But he isn't strong enough to wield the weapon; he'd sooner hire another to do it for him, someone like the bastard who seized your father's ship. Now *that* is the type of method Lawrence would employ. In fact, the more I consider it, the more convinced I am that he is the orchestrator of that entire plot. Tomorrow, I intend to learn the truth. And when I do, a segment of justice will have been served. Generations of Bencrofts may have gone unpunished, but the *current* Duke of Morland will pay—he and his pirate conspirator."

Slayde felt a tremor run through Courtney's body. Blinking, he jerked back to the present, staring down at her face and seeing tears gather in her eyes.

"I'm sorry," he murmured, his thumbs capturing the moisture as it trickled down her cheeks. "I don't know what possessed me. The last thing I wanted was to frighten you with my family history."

"I asked for the details," she managed to choke out. "And you didn't frighten me. At least no more than I already was. All you did was make me aware of the extent of your hardships. Dear God, Slayde, you've endured so much—far more than I." Her voice dropped to a whisper. "Yesterday, you said you would undo my loss if you could. Well, right now, all I wish is that I could undo yours."

The earnest proclamation of empathy was the last reaction Slayde had expected and the most impacting one he'd ever endured. Although he'd never discussed his family history before tonight, he was nonetheless acutely aware of the ugly speculation the Huntley name inspired. In the past, those with whom he associated fell into one of three categories: the few who were blessedly ignorant, the handful who were perversely intrigued, and the predominant group, who were altogether terrified—of the Huntleys and their demonic curse.

Not so Courtney. Here she was, gazing up at him with

a wealth of hurt in her eyes—hurt not for herself, but for him. She wanted to undo his suffering, to eradicate his pain. And why? Simply because she cared.

Something profound moved in Slayde's chest, soothing his remembered anguish in a rush of warmth. "That's the most selfless offer I've ever received," he heard himself mutter, realizing even as he said it that it was true. "Thank you, sweetheart."

The endearment, uttered in a tender, husky voice, was more intimate than a caress . . . and just as pivotal, given the heightened emotion spawned by the past few minutes.

An invisible barrier was traversed.

Their gazes met and held, Courtney's eyes widening as awareness flickered in the sea-green depths, her lips parting as if in question—and invitation.

Slayde's heart began slamming against his ribs, a compulsion like none he'd ever experienced propelling him forward. Acting on that compulsion—and on a pure instinct he'd never known he possessed—he lowered his head and captured her mouth under his.

The world shifted—permanently.

It was Slayde's first coherent thought as he tasted her, molded the delicate contours of her lips to his, warmed and stilled her trembling with his mouth. She tensed, quivered, then melted against him, her small fists knotting in his shirt, her soul seeking whatever replenishment he could offer.

He offered—but was it for her sake, or his?

The question vanished, unanswered, lost beneath the extraordinary feeling building between them. Slayde slid down on the bed, twisted about until Courtney lay supine, caged between the strong columns of his arms. Tangling his hands in her hair, he fused their mouths, deepening the kiss with equal measures of need and restraint. *Her injuries,* his dazed mind cautioned. *Don't forget her injuries.*

Courtney herself had forgotten them.

Lost to the moment, she welcomed the miracle of their

kiss as a wondrous balm to her agony and a startling awakening of her senses. Like a tantalizing aroma, it assuaged one need, slowly kindled another. "Slayde," she heard herself whisper. "Hold me."

He shuddered, his arms contracting around her with a will all their own. Parting her lips, his tongue took hers, caressing it in a way that made tremors of sensation shiver down her spine. She complied with his unspoken request, opening her mouth wider, deepening his presence as their tongues tasted, touched, melded, and withdrew, only to begin again.

Time ceased to exist, seconds blending into minutes, minutes converging into an immeasurable eternity. Courtney's fingers relaxed, her palms opening, gliding up Slayde's shirt to the breadth of his shoulders, her arms entwining about his neck. In turn, he lowered himself until his shirt just brushed the soft swell of her breasts, balancing himself on his elbows so as to carefully avoid her ribs. His own hands, unable to remain still, roamed up and down the silken skin of her arms, her shoulders, her neck, savoring the quivers of response his touch evoked.

"Courtney." He said her name in a reverent whisper, his lips leaving hers to feather across her cheeks, his tongue absorbing the tears still glistening there. He kissed her nose, her lids, the corners of her mouth, before returning to her lips, brushing them in a slow, eloquent wisp of motion. "Don't cry."

"I won't," she promised, her voice breathless, swamped in sensation.

Her innocence, her honesty, intensified Slayde's rampaging emotions almost beyond bearing. With a strangled groan, he buried his lips in hers once more, tugging her closer, giving in a way he'd never given, taking in a way he'd never longed to take.

Later, looking back on this unprecedented madness, Slayde wondered what would have happened had Courtney not, at that precise moment, winced with pain. But she did—and the motion was like a slap to his unfocused senses.

"Courtney?" He raised up, searched her face. "Is it your ribs or your head?"

"My ribs." Her lids lifted, her eyes still dazed with wonder. " 'Twas only a sting. I'm fine. Truly." Hesitantly, her fingertips brushed Slayde's mouth, and she gazed up at him as if to verify the events of the past few minutes. "Did this really just happen?"

He felt as incredulous as she. "I think it did, yes." He inhaled shakily, lowering himself beside her, drawing her closer until her head was tucked beneath his chin. "I should apologize."

"Don't."

"Are you all right?"

Courtney nodded. "A bit dizzy, but fine. More than fine, actually. I feel as if I'm floating. What's more, I'm not at all sure I want to descend to the ground. Or to reality, for that matter. I'd rather stay on this extraordinary cloud you've given me."

What in God's name was he allowing to happen? "Courtney—"

"I must sound absurd," she interrupted self-consciously. " 'Tis just that this was my first kiss. And while I've ofttimes tried to imagine what it would be like, nothing prepared me for the deep, sweeping magic—" She broke off, and Slayde could feel her face flame against his throat. "Did you ever notice that in the darkness you can say things you could never say in the light? 'Tis almost as if time is suspended until dawn."

Slayde swallowed, staring at the ceiling. "That applies not only to words, but to actions as well."

"Yes, I suppose it does."

The hurt in her voice tore at his heart, but he was helpless to alleviate it. Still reeling from his own unfathomable behavior, he saw that one thing was glaringly obvious; he had to leave her—now—before things got out of hand. Courtney Johnston was a beautiful, unspoiled young woman who was alone, vulnerable, and untouched, not only physically, but emotionally as well. Despite the severity of her personal loss, her exposure to the world and all its ugliness was nil. He could not, would not, immerse her in the hell that was intrinsically tied to his life as a Huntley—despite the staggering feelings she inspired in him.

Or, perhaps *because* of them.

'Twas one thing to permit her to exist on the periphery of his existence, as Aurora's companion, as a houseguest. But a deeper, more poignant involvement? When she had a world of pain behind her and a wealth of life ahead? No. Whatever unprecedented sensations were stirring to life within him, whatever bizarre transition was propelling him toward her, he owed it to her to fight it—before it truly began.

Before it was too late.

"Go to sleep, Courtney," he murmured, coming to his feet and easing her head to the pillow. "You need rest. And so do I. I'm leaving for Morland in the morning."

For a moment, she said nothing, just staring at him in the semidarkened room. Then she nodded, settling herself amidst the bedcovers. "I pray you learn something—something that will give us both a measure of peace. And Slayde?" She raised up on her elbows, her hair sweeping the pillow in a shimmering, moonlit waterfall. "Thank you—for the comfort *and* the cloud."

Chapter 5

The wind whipped about the Red Cliffs.

Miss Payne shivered, drawing her shawl higher around her shoulders as she eased into the alcove and approached the formidable figure awaiting her.

"You're late," the icy voice pronounced. "I instructed you to be here at nine. It's twenty minutes past."

"I know—and I apologize. But I had to be certain no one at Pembourne saw me leave. As it is, the earl wasn't yet abed when I slipped away. 'Twould have been better if I'd lingered until he was. But I didn't want to detain you."

The glittering gaze bore into hers. "What did you learn?"

Miss Payne drew a sharp breath. "From the snatches of conversation I've managed to overhear, 'twould seem that Armon took matters into his own hands. The second ransom note arrived at Pembourne a day earlier

than your orders specified. That very night, his lordship
dashed off to comply with the kidnapper's terms. The
girl he returned with is the daughter of the sea captain
whose ship Armon seized—and she bears a striking
resemblance to Lady Aurora. Apparently, there was a
struggle, during which time the girl—Miss Johnston—
toppled overboard. Lord Pembourne dived in after her
and—"

"I don't give a damn about the girl. What about the
diamond?"

Like a fatal dagger, the demand sank into Miss Payne's
gut. Inadvertently, she took a step backward, dreading
the reaction she was about to elicit. "Lord Pembourne
turned it over to Armon."

Silence.

Nervously, the housekeeper wet her lips. "I've never
known Armon to do anything quite so stupid."

"On the contrary—his plan was brilliant." A rustle of
motion as the dark, cloaked figure emerged from the
shadows. "Quite brilliant. 'Tis a pity he'll never enjoy
the fruits of his labor."

With that, the black cloak brushed by and was swallowed up by night.

Dartmouth was silent, the crude road adjacent to the
wharf deserted.

Uneasily, Armon glanced behind him, reassuring himself that the cove where the *Fortune* awaited him was
nearby, safely within view. All he had to do was hand
over the diamond, pocket the three hundred thousand
pounds, and sail off to his new life—far away from
England.

He hurried toward the alley that was his customary
meeting place. Grimes would be waiting. He always was,
whenever Armon sent word ahead that he'd be coming.
And in this case, the fence had probably slept in the alley
the night before. Just knowing he'd soon be receiving the
black diamond—a treasure worth more than a hundred

times his customary exchange—hell, Grimes's beady little eyes had probably bugged out of his head when he'd read the message.

Armon's fingers slipped inside his coat, closing around the bulky shape of the diamond, as if for comfort. The bloody stone was enormous—over two hundred carats, if memory served him right. Well, whoever wanted it was welcome to it. As for him, all he wanted was the money being offered in exchange.

With a relieved sigh, Armon reached his destination. Rounding the wall, he eased halfway down the alley, noting the dark silhouette fifty feet away. "Grimes?"

"Sorry, Armon." Slow, purposeful footsteps. "I had some urgent business for Grimes. Thus, he was detained."

All the color drained from Armon's face. "I . . ."

A bitter laugh as the footsteps closed in—and halted upon reaching their prey. "Why, Armon, if I didn't know better, I'd say you were disturbed by my visit."

The barrel of a pistol glinted in the night.

Armon backed against the wall, his mind racing for a nonexistent means of escape.

Lying would be futile. Fleeing, impossible.

Dying, inevitable.

"I have the stone." Wildly, he groped inside his coat, tearing open the lining—and praying for a miracle.

"I assumed you would."

"Here." He extended his shaking hand, the diamond clutched tightly in its grasp. "Take it. It's yours."

"It most certainly is." His fingers were unpried. The gem disappeared. "Our business is now complete. *Adieu,* Armon."

He hadn't time to reply.

The pistol fired. Its single shot, issued at point-blank range, struck Armon's chest with a quiet thud. He crumpled and fell.

With but a cursory glance at the dead body, his assailant turned triumphant eyes to the priceless jewel, studying its shimmering facets. "Finally. After all these years, justice is served."

The clip-clop of horses' hooves permeated Courtney's consciousness, rousing her from half-slumber. Eyes flickering open, she took in the pale glints of dawn as they tentatively brushed the room. Her first thought was that it was far too early for those on land to be traveling.

Her second thought was that it was Slayde, leaving for Morland.

Automatically, she pushed herself up to a sitting position, relieved when her head and ribs retaliated with only a mild protest. Moving aside the bedcovers, she eased herself to her feet. Her legs wobbled but held. She took one step, then another, making her way over to the window and peering out.

The phaeton had rounded the drive and was traversing lush acres of greenery, heading away from the manor, its sole occupant the powerful man holding the reins.

Slayde.

Leaning against the wall, Courtney watched him until he disappeared from view, fervently wishing she were going with him to confront Lawrence Bencroft—her injuries be damned.

Hands balling into fists, Courtney said a silent prayer that Slayde would learn something, that his trip to Morland would yield results. That, upon his return, they'd be one step closer to finding the pirate who'd seized her father's ship, and one step closer to peace and resolution.

Unsteadily, she made her way back to the bed, lifting her father's timepiece from the drawer and clasping it in her hands. Was it madness to believe he was alive? Or, if not madness, then irrational faith? Last night, the idea had seemed so plausible. But today, in the cold light of day, the events of last night were distant and dreamlike.

All the events of last night.

Propping up her pillows, Courtney leaned back, her fingertips brushing her lips as mists of memory laced her thoughts. Pensively, she reflected on those unexpected moments in Slayde's arms.

Unexpected, but unsurprising, given the intensity of the conversation that had preceded them, the revelations and emotions that had been roused.

What *was* surprising was how natural it had felt— being close to Slayde, having his mouth touch hers, teach hers, take hers. She, whose romantic ideals, transient life, and protective father had precluded even the most innocent of courtships, had welcomed a man to her bed and participated in the most exquisite awakening of the senses imaginable.

She was overreacting, she reminded herself silently. After all, it had been only a kiss, not a coupling. Then again, perhaps that made it all the more poignant, her heart argued back. True, nothing had happened, and yet . . . it had felt so incredibly right, having him beside her, sharing their pain, their pasts, and ultimately their embrace.

With a pang of emptiness, Courtney contemplated the man whose teachings had spawned her overreaction: her father. 'Twas he who'd assured her, time and again, that her heart was meant to be awakened but once, that her tremendous capacity to love was destined for but one— the right one. She was meant for a man who needed her as much as she did him, one whom destiny would bring into her life when the time was right.

Had that time just arrived? Or was last night merely a case of one human being reaching out to another? *Papa,* she mourned silently, *how can I recognize that man without you here to guide me?*

Her throat tight with unshed tears, Courtney gazed down at her father's timepiece, torn by grief and confusion. It was the same confusion she'd seen mirrored in Slayde's eyes, not during their kiss, but after. He'd been as affected as she. And given her newly acquired knowledge of his past, she understood why. Emotional involvement was not something Slayde would permit. What was it Aurora had said? *He keeps everything to himself. Thus, he's alone. And lonely, whether he chooses to realize it or not.*

But last night he hadn't kept everything to himself. He'd opened up to her, discussed his grief in a way that both startled and unnerved him. And, in the process, he'd discovered something about himself he hadn't known existed and didn't intend to tolerate: vulnerability. So he'd done the safe thing, the *only* thing he could—he'd retreated.

The creak of the bedchamber door interrupted her musings.

"Courtney? Are you all right?" Aurora poked her head in, relief flooding her face as she saw Courtney reclining against the pillows. "I was on my way to the lighthouse. I heard shuffling noises from your room and thought you might be in pain."

"Thank you." Once again, Courtney felt deeply touched by Aurora's concern. "I'm fine. What you heard was my feeble attempt to move about. I crept to the window and back, which is as much as I'm able to do. 'Tis so frustrating—" She broke off.

"I understand. Confinement is dreadful." Aurora crossed over and perched on a chair. "Had I known you were awake, I would have visited earlier. I thought only the servants were up."

"Earlier?" Courtney blinked. "It can't be much past dawn. What time do you generally arise?"

A grin. "I have little patience for sleep. Shocking, isn't it? For a noblewoman to loathe her rest?"

Courtney grinned back. "No more shocking than a sea captain's daughter who loathes the sea." She arched a brow. "Am I to presume that your friend the lighthouse keeper also awakens at first light? You did say you were on your way there."

"Truthfully, I don't think Mr. Scollard ever sleeps. In fact, 'tis difficult to imagine his having a home—other than the Windmouth Lighthouse. All the times I've burst in, uninvited, he's always been at his post. And I've done that frequently, at hours ranging from dawn 'til midnight."

"I don't doubt that you have." Courtney bit back laughter. "This Mr. Scollard sounds fascinating."

Aurora leaned forward. "I believe he has the ability to see things most of us do not. 'Tis a gift; call it insight, wisdom, or something more. Whichever it is, it's astounding. I can't wait for you to meet him."

"Nor can I." Courtney sighed in exasperation. "I feel so miserably helpless—for many reasons. I need to be up and about."

"And you will be. By week's end, you'll be strolling with me to the lighthouse, you'll see." Aurora glanced up, the sound of clinking china announcing Matilda's imminent arrival with Courtney's breakfast. "What if I asked Matilda to serve my breakfast up here as well? That way we'd be able to continue our chat. Or did you wish to be alone?"

"That's the last thing I wish. But what about your excursion?"

"It can wait until later. The only reason I was hurrying off so early is that I hoped to leave Pembourne before . . ." Her voice drifted off.

"Before your brother spied you," Courtney finished for her. "Well, fear not. Slayde left Pembourne a few minutes ago. He'll be gone all day—maybe longer."

"Where did he go?"

Courtney chewed her lip, wondering how much Aurora knew, then deciding that dishonesty was no way to begin a friendship. "To Morland."

"Morland?" Aurora nearly toppled off her chair. "The Huntleys haven't been welcome there for six decades."

"Nor are they now. But Slayde intends to meet with Lawrence Bencroft."

Aurora frowned. "He thinks the duke is involved with my feigned kidnapping."

"Yes, he does."

"Do you?"

"Aurora, I've never even met Lawrence Bencroft. I'm certainly not qualified to judge his guilt or his innocence. But I do trust Slayde's opinion, which is obviously based on years of firsthand experience. So given what he's told me, yes, I believe it's possible that the duke is involved." Courtney drew a slow, inward breath. "To be frank, I'm clinging to the hope that he is—for Slayde's sake and for mine. I intend to unearth the filthy pirate who captured the *Isobel*. And if Lawrence Bencroft isn't the man to lead me to him, I'll find the one who is."

The bedchamber door opened, admitting Matilda and an aromatic tray of food. "Lady Aurora—I didn't know you were here." A twinkle. "Although I should have guessed."

"You know me well." Aurora smiled. "Matilda, would it be too much trouble for you if I breakfasted here with Courtney?"

An approving glint lit Matilda's eye. "Not at all. I'll just have a quick look at those bandages. Then I'll leave this tray and arrange for another to be brought up." She bent over Courtney, lips pursed as she scrutinized the young woman's forehead. "How are you feeling this morning, Miss Courtney?"

"Much better" was the grateful reply. "Thanks to your ministrations, the pain is nearly gone. Now, if only I could overcome this weakness."

Matilda straightened. "Eat every morsel on this plate and you will." With that sage advice, she hurried off to order Aurora's breakfast.

"Well?" Aurora teased. "What are you waiting for? You'd best have eaten at least half your food by the time Matilda returns, else you'll get quite a scolding." Sobering, she glanced at the timepiece still clutched in Courtney's hand. "That's lovely. Would you like me to hold it so you can eat?"

Courtney blinked, having momentarily forgotten her beloved treasure. " 'Twas Papa's," she murmured, turning the watch over in her palm. "My mother gifted him with it on their wedding day. He gave it to me—rather like a legacy—right before he . . ." She swallowed. "It hasn't moved since then. But I'm sure you'd enjoy looking at it. There's an image of a lighthouse that probably resembles your Windmouth Lighthouse." She snapped it open. "You're welcome to—" Abruptly, she sat up, staring at the watch's face.

"Courtney? What is it?"

"The timepiece. It jumped ahead."

"I thought you said it had stopped."

"It had. At half after six, the precise time Papa went overboard. But just now, as I was looking at it, the time—and the scene—moved. Only once. Then it froze again. But it definitely moved." She looked up, a dazed expression in her eyes. "Maybe Papa really is alive."

Aurora stared. "Courtney, what are you talking about?"

"I had a dream. Papa was calling out to me, telling me he was alive. I know it sounds insane, but do you think what just happened with the timepiece was some kind of sign to that effect?"

Rather than dubious, Aurora looked intrigued. "You didn't actually see your father go down?"

"No." Courtney shuddered. "I heard his scream. That sound will haunt me forever. But when he was being thrown overboard, I was in the midst of being dragged below and locked in my cabin."

"And obviously his body was never discovered." Aurora was becoming more fascinated with each passing moment.

"But he was bound," Courtney felt compelled to reason aloud. "Weighed down by the huge sack of grain Lexley was forced to tie to his leg. To survive such an ordeal would be virtually impossible. Still—"

"Mr. Scollard." Aurora came to her feet. "We must bring you—and your timepiece—to Mr. Scollard. If anyone is able to discern the unknown, 'tis he. The instant you're well, we'll head for the lighthouse and discover if the watch's motion and your dream really are signs."

"You don't think I'm mad?"

"Of course not. Mr. Scollard has taught me that every belief, every legend—no matter how farfetched—has shards of truth to it. 'Tis up to us to unearth those truths, to discern fact from fiction."

"That's not always easy," Courtney mused, half to herself. "Nor, in all cases, is it practical. There's merit to Slayde's contention that my dream was merely a reaction to Papa's death, or rather to my inability to accept it."

"You told all this to Slayde? Why? And when?"

Hearing the stunned bafflement in Aurora's tone, Courtney desperately wished she could call back her words. Despite Slayde's justifiable, utterly proper reason for visiting her bedchamber last night, the outcome had been anything but proper. And to discuss even the innocent prelude to that outcome, especially with Slayde's sister, was going to be exceedingly difficult.

Courtney's voice quavered as she grappled with her self-consciousness, opted for brevity. "Slayde heard me crying and came to check on me. I blurted out my dream."

Aurora rolled her eyes, exasperation rendering her oblivious to Courtney's discomfort. "You blurted to the wrong person. While my brother is perhaps the most decent, responsible man on earth, he is also the most pragmatic and unemotional. He believes in nothing, least of all that which he cannot see."

"You're referring to the Huntley curse."

This time Aurora's brows did go up. "Slayde spoke of that?"

Much safer ground. "Yes. But actually, he didn't need to. Papa has mentioned it, as have his crewmen. Your family—and the black diamond—are renowned at sea."

"Renowned? You mean notorious." Aurora folded her arms across her chest, her palms rubbing the fine muslin as if to warm away her trepidation. "I'm so relieved the stone is gone, together with all the ugliness it embodied.

It's destroyed our family, whether or not Slayde chooses to believe it."

"Oh, he believes it. The only difference is, he believes the curse is not the diamond itself, but those who seek it."

Aurora's gaze grew speculative. "You've been at Pembourne for but a few days. Yet my brother has shared more with you than he has with anyone, including me."

"Aurora, he hasn't—"

Swiftly, Aurora waved away Courtney's protest. "You don't understand. I'm not upset. In fact, I'm elated that Slayde has allowed someone to venture past those bloody walls of his. Perhaps he's finally recognizing that none of us can survive alone. If so, there just might be some hope for him after all, but only if he accepts the fact that needing others is not an affliction but a blessing."

Slayde would not have welcomed Aurora's proclamation.

A mile from Pembourne, he steered his phaeton into its fourth circular trip around the picturesque country road, berating himself yet again for departing from Pembourne at the absurd hour of six A.M.

Absurd because, even with the stops he intended to make, the ride to Morland—just six miles inland of the small town of Dawlish where Pembourne was situated— would take no more than an hour. Plus, the businessmen he meant to visit prior to descending upon the duke would hardly be at their establishments at the first light of dawn.

Which meant he could do naught but drive aimlessly for hours.

Nevertheless, he'd needed to get away.

The need itself was unsurprising. Most of his return trips to Pembourne were brief, characterized by a restless unease that took him away almost as soon as he arrived. He'd stay only long enough to ensure Aurora's well-being, then depart on another business journey— abroad and as far from the past as possible.

Not this time.

This time, he'd been troubled not by restlessness or even unease, but by a myriad of conflicting emotions, the result of which was an unprecedented combination of tenderness, determination, and guilt. All of which pertained to Courtney—Courtney and whatever had transpired between them last night.

What had *transpired* was merely a kiss, he amended silently. What had *happened* was another story entirely.

He'd never forget the look on her face when he'd left her: not distress or guilt or even regret, but wonder. There had been wonder in her sea-green eyes, an exhilarated awe that both humbled and terrified him.

Because he'd felt it, too.

This whole situation was insane. He'd rescued the woman from death, taken her into his home. 'Twas only natural that she reach out to him for comfort, that he reach out to offer it.

Comfort, hell. That kiss had been deep, consuming, underscored by an unknown, but no less profound, emotion that shook him to his soul. Not to mention desire, desire as unfamiliar as it was intense, simmering beneath the surface like the first embers of a fire about to blaze out of control.

For a man who'd lived one and thirty years and who, despite his solitary existence, was no stranger to passion, it was sobering to feel more shaken by a kiss than he'd felt as a result of his most ardent sexual joining.

His behavior prior to that kiss was even more unsettling.

Never had he gone to a woman's bed without the mutually agreed-upon decision to couple. Yet last night, long before their embrace was even a thought, much less an action, he'd stretched out alongside Courtney as if it were the most natural thing in the world to do, held her without a shred of discomfort, talked with her—not as an overture to coupling, but as an entity unto itself.

And told her things he'd never told another.

Oh, his recountings could hardly be described as great

revelations, not when half of England was privy to the details of the Huntley curse. Still, he'd never shared his thoughts, his feelings, with anyone. Like his life, they were his and his alone.

Until last night.

Moreover, it wasn't only their talk that unnerved him, or even their kiss—although God help him, he couldn't forget the taste of her mouth, the softness of her skin, the delicacy of her frame. It was the aftermath that shook him.

Never had he carried memories of a woman with him, much less wanted to slay her dragons the way he did Courtney's. He was determined to find the pirate who'd killed her father—regardless of whether Morland was involved—and drive a sword through his heart, just to give her back a semblance of what she'd lost.

All in all, Slayde concluded, his fingers tightening about the reins, he'd just enumerated far too many *nevers* to suit him. Consummate realist that he was, he forced himself to acknowledge the truth: not only did Courtney Johnston have an amazing effect on him, but after a matter of days—or perhaps right from the start—she'd touched something inside him he hadn't known existed and would will away if he could.

Ironic that he would do so more for her sake than for his own.

'Twas true, he was a loner. He'd been that way all his life—from Eton to Oxford. How much of that trait was inherent and how much a result of the alleged curse and its ramifications, he hadn't a clue. The fact remained that, since childhood, he'd relied only upon himself. His parents' murder had heightened that independence and inner strength, because from that day forward, he had no longer been a man unto himself. He was needed—by Aurora, by the enormous responsibilities left to him as the Earl of Pembourne. *And* he was determined, having endured the profound devastation rendered by those who sought the black diamond, to retain his autonomy, not only emotionally, but in fact.

Thus, on the day he discovered his parents' bodies, he vowed to himself that the last generation of Huntleys had suffered the hatred and greed spawned by his great-grandfather's theft, that the last drop of Huntley blood had been spilled.

That the family name would die with him.

It wouldn't be difficult to accomplish. He and Aurora were the last remaining Huntleys. Aurora would marry—he'd see to it—and her children would bear her husband's name. After which, if Slayde died without wife or issue, Aurora's offspring would inherit the Pembourne estates and fortune while remaining immune to the Huntley curse.

If Slayde died without wife or issue.

Accordingly, his responsibility was to relinquish any thought of marrying or siring a child. And he'd fulfilled both aspects of that responsibility—the former by undisputed decision, the latter by discipline and by choosing seasoned bedmates who were equally as adamant about avoiding conception as he.

Hardly a description of Courtney.

No, a woman like Courtney was destined for a loving husband, a houseful of children, and a lifetime of untinged tomorrows, none of which he could offer her. So attraction or not, wonder or not, she had no place in his life. And since she was clearly too naïve to recognize this, it was up to him to protect her.

To save her—again. Only this time, from himself.

Jaws tightly clenched, Slayde urged the horses toward the town of Newton Abbot—and toward the meetings that would culminate in a confrontation with the Duke of Morland.

It was just past ten o'clock when Slayde steered his phaeton around the bend leading to Morland Manor.

Grimly, he contemplated the tactics he would take in light of what he'd learned from those of the duke's colleagues with whom he'd spoken.

His findings had been most surprising.

Evidently, Morland had changed considerably over the past few months—not in his finances, but in his behavior. According to two local merchants and the local innkeeper, he'd emerged from his estate, not once but several times, using the inn to meet with colleagues whose descriptions Slayde recognized as belonging to a prominent Devonshire banker and an equally respected solicitor.

Meetings he'd been sober enough to conduct.

Seeking out the two men in question, Slayde had been blocked by a wall of professional ethics, gleaning nothing save his own inference that Morland was re-emerging into the business world.

Why? More importantly, what could have prompted this sudden and drastic transformation?

Slayde intended to find out.

A wry smile twisted his lips as he passed through Morland's iron gates and regarded the desolate structure looming ahead. First, he'd have to get inside, push past the servants, and get to the duke. Needless to say, he didn't anticipate a particularly warm welcome.

His assumption was confirmed five minutes later by the pinch-nosed butler who answered his knock. "Yes?" he inquired, his bland tone telling Slayde he had no idea of his caller's identity. But then, why should he? Slayde had never so much as crossed Morland's threshold.

"Good day," he replied, equally aloof. "Kindly advise His Grace that the Earl of Pembourne is here to see him."

Comprehension struck.

All the color draining from his face, the butler sputtered, "D-did you say . . . ?"

"Indeed I did. Now that we've confirmed that I am indeed Slayde Huntley, go tell Morland I'm on his doorstep, with no intentions of leaving until we've spoken."

Forcibly, the butler restored his composure. "His Grace is out."

" 'Out' as in away? Or 'out' as in passed out—drunk?"

A haughty sniff. "Away, my lord."

"Fine. Then I'll wait for him to return."

"That could be hours."

"I'm in no hurry." So saying, Slayde shrugged off his coat and slung it over the astonished butler's arm. "Is the library down this corridor?" he inquired, already heading in what seemed to be the logical direction. "I'll pass the time reading."

"But, Lord Pembourne, you can't—"

"Thayer, whose phaeton is that around front?" The voice at the front door brought both men up short. Turning, they watched Lawrence Bencroft step through the entranceway. "I'm not expecting anyone."

"Ah, but someone is expecting you," Slayde said, his tone ominously quiet.

Morland's head came up, like a wolf scenting danger, his eyes narrowing on his guest. "Pembourne."

"Ah, you're sober enough to recognize me. An impressive feat, considering the fact that we haven't seen each other in—let's see, how long has it been since you shut yourself up in here with only a bottle as company? Eight years? Or is it nine? I believe it was nine—a mere year after my parents' deaths."

"What the hell are you doing in my home?" Morland nearly flung his coat into Thayer's arms, heading toward Slayde with angry—but steady—steps. "Get out. Or I'll have you thrown out."

"No, Morland, you won't. Because you know damned well why I'm here. And you can't risk tossing me out without first hearing what I have to say—and discerning precisely how much proof I have of your guilt. So cease this heroic display and let's get to the matter at hand. Shall we adjourn to the library? Or do you want me to air my accusations in front of your entire staff? The choice is yours."

Morland drew a harsh breath, his eyes narrowing on Slayde as he mulled over what had been said as well as what had been implied. "You haven't changed a bit, have you Pembourne? Still as callous as ever. Very well.

Unlike the members of your family, I'm not a monster. Although I cannot imagine what you're raving about or why you think I know the purpose of your visit." A swift glance at Thayer. "The earl and I will be in the library. No refreshment is necessary. Knock on the door in precisely ten minutes. Bring three or four footmen with you, lest Lord Pembourne prove difficult. Either way, he will be escorted from the manor at that time."

"Very good, sir." Thayer rushed off like a mouse who'd been freed from a trap.

Silently, Morland led the way to the library, shutting the door firmly behind him and removing his timepiece for a quick glance. "Your time is short. So get to the point. What is it you want?" He furnished Slayde with only an icy but unglazed stare.

Slayde perched against the mantel, averting his gaze as he took a minute to calm himself. He hadn't expected the rush of fury that accompanied coming face to face with Lawrence Bencroft after all these years. Suddenly, it was a decade earlier, and he was back at Pembourne, discovering his parents' lifeless bodies on the floor, hearing the droning voices of the authorities as they concluded that it was obviously the work of a burglar. And, most infuriating of all, seeing Morland's cloudy expression when Slayde had stormed into Almack's and publicly accused him—or rather, his now-dead father—of committing the crime. Hands shaking so badly his drink had sloshed onto the polished floor, Morland had slurred out some less-than-convincing, intoxicated denials—denials that, at least for Slayde, had fallen on deaf ears.

The only thing that had kept him from choking the life out of Lawrence was the possibility that the inebriated fool might have been unaware of Chilton's plan.

But now Chilton was dead. Which made this current plot Lawrence's alone.

"Pembourne, did you invade my home just to scrutinize my library shelves?" Morland was demanding.

Slayde's gaze snapped back to his prey. "No," he

managed, thrusting the past from his mind, supplanting it with the present. "I've invaded your home to unearth the truth about your blackmail scheme. And I *will* unearth it, using whatever means are necessary."

The implicit threat hung heavily between them, and Slayde saw a vein begin to throb at Morland's throat. The bastard had deteriorated, he noted abruptly. Time had taken its toll, as had bitterness and alcohol. Morland's hair, once raven black, was now predominantly gray, his broad shoulders stooped, his face lined and puffy. In short, he'd become an old man.

"What blackmail scheme?" Morland questioned warily.

"The one that involved Aurora's alleged kidnapping. And the name—and whereabouts—of the pirate who assisted you."

A flicker of emotion—was it trepidation or surprise?—registered on the duke's face. "I haven't the slightest clue what you're babbling about."

"Don't you? Then let's disgress for a moment. When last I saw you, you were being tossed out of White's, for the third and final time. Even their gracious members lose patience with an unruly drunk who owes thousands of pounds to each of them. As I recall, you were livid, resentful, and barely able to hold your head up. A week later, I heard you'd withdrawn to Morland, supposedly for good. Now, some nine years later, you've evidently relinquished the bottle and rejoined the world—specifically by taking productive jaunts into Newton Abbot. Am I correct thus far?"

Morland swallowed, angry spots of color tingeing his cheeks. "Why the hell have you been checking up on me?"

"We'll get to that in a minute. For now, tell me, are my facts correct?"

"Yes." The answer was unexpectedly straightforward. "I've spent years in a perpetual stupor. And, yes, I've spent that time sequestered here at Morland, where I retreated for what I intended to be forever. What you failed to mention, however, is that my incessant drinking and ultimate seclusion stemmed from losses caused by the Huntleys."

"We didn't put the bottle in your hand nor relegate you to self-imposed isolation. We also didn't squander your money or undermine your business ventures. How long are you going to blame us for your own weaknesses?"

"My so-called weaknesses didn't cause my son's death."

Slayde's jaw unclenched a fraction as he recalled the pale young man who'd attended Oxford when he did—and died before ever completing his education. "Hugh was very frail, Morland."

"He was also my firstborn, the heir to my title and to whatever funds remained in my estate. And with his mother gone, he was all I had left."

"You still had—*have*"—Slayde corrected himself—"Julian."

A harsh laugh. "Julian? Don't insult me, Pembourne. You know very well my younger son hasn't returned to Morland Manor in years. He has as little use for me as I do for him. He's my grandfather all over again: irresponsible, self-centered, always abandoning his duties to dash off on one adventure or another. Hardly someone for a father to rely upon in his old age. Hubert was my life, my future. And because of the Huntleys, he's dead."

"Hugh died from a fever, not a curse."

"I disagree. Every heinous incident that's plagued my family began the day your great-grandfather stole that black diamond and kept it, rather than delivering it as he and my grandfather had originally promised. That piracy spawned a curse that, unless the wrongs he committed are rectified, will poison our lives forever."

"Rectified?" Slayde leaped on Morland's pointed statement, perceiving the chance to elicit the confession he'd come for. "Is that what you're in the process of doing—rectifying the past to obliterate the curse?"

"You're talking in riddles again."

"Am I? Then I'll be direct. What incited you to relinquish your seclusion?"

A shrug. "Perhaps it was the realization that I'm getting old, the desire to seize whatever fragments of my life are left. Not that it's any of your concern."

"Oh, but it is my concern. Because, you see, I've had some interesting chats with the village merchants this morning." Slayde pressed on with his charade. "As well as with your solicitor and your banker. It seems that you've been conducting a little financial business of late, discussing some upcoming investments and reallocation of funds. Quite impressive for a man of supposedly paltry means. One would almost think you were coming into money—a great deal of money. Of course, that would be impossible for a man with only an estranged son for family and no dealings with the world, wouldn't it?"

Morland's fist struck a side table. "How dare you intrude into my affairs!"

"In this case, they're my affairs, as well." Slayde went in for the kill. "Because the crime you committed to procure your new-found wealth was a crime against me—*and* one that affected the lives of innocent people. Don't even consider absolving yourself with the fact that it was your accomplice who carried out the sordid plan. *You* invented it. Through *your* orders, that filthy pirate blackmailed me, captured a ship, killed its captain, and severely wounded his daughter. All of which I've vowed to avenge." Slayde's eyes glittered dangerously. "And being the callous animal you've accused me of being, I'll begin by thrashing a confession out of you."

Rather than shrinking in terror, Morland seemed to visibly relax, the pulse in his throat slowing to normal. "In other words, with regard to whoever's orchestrated this crime you're raving about, you have no proof."

Damn the bastard for being sober. "How much are you getting for the diamond, Morland?" Slayde demanded in a final attempt to render Lawrence off balance, to pressure him into letting some small detail slip. "How much did you pay that pirate to get it?"

Morland's eyes narrowed. "Are you telling me the stone is missing? The stone whose whereabouts you supposedly never knew?"

"You know damned well it's missing. I turned it over to your cohort in exchange for the woman I thought was Aurora. And, incidentally, that woman—the captain's daughter—is staying at my home. Because of you, she's injured and orphaned. So for her sake and mine, you can begin by telling me where I can find your accomplice. I have a score to settle with him." A lethal pause. "I have an even bigger one to settle with you."

"Well, you won't be settling it today," Lawrence said icily. "Because I have nothing to tell you. I applaud the fine work done by this pirate—whoever he might be— but I fear I've never met the man, much less ordered him to extort the diamond from you. However, when you find him, let me know. I'd like to be the first to offer my congratulations—and to convince him to restore the stone to the royal family who paid for its recovery. Then perhaps my luck really will change." In a sudden, impatient gesture, Morland extracted his timepiece, cast a swift glance at it. "I fear your ten minutes are up. Further, since I am—according to your own intrusive investigations—a busy man, and since I've only just walked through my own entranceway . . ."

"From where?" Slayde interrupted, seizing the unanticipated opportunity Morland had just provided. "That was to be my next question. Where is it you just returned from? Not the village; I've just come from there, spoken with all your colleagues. So precisely where did you go and with whom did you meet?"

The pulse in Morland's throat accelerated again. "Get out, Pembourne."

"What's the matter? Did I strike too close to the truth? 'Tis an innocent enough question. When put to an innocent man, that is."

Morland flung open the library door and stepped out,

just as Thayer and four footmen approached. Gesturing for the butler to proceed with fulfilling his orders, Morland turned his frigid stare on Slayde. "Get out," he ordered. "Now. Of your own volition or with the aid of my staff. Either way, this conversation is at an end. Permanently. You're never to set foot in my home again. Is that clear?"

Unmoving, Slayde glared back, hate coursing through his blood like an untamed river. "Very clear. As is the answer you've just provided. You were meeting with that pirate, weren't you? Paying for his services. Has he given you the diamond yet?"

Shaking with rage, Morland turned and stalked down the hall.

This time, Slayde moved. Reaching the doorway, he shoved by the unsettled servants, calling out, "Don't become too complacent, Morland. I'll see you in Newgate yet."

A bitter laugh. "And I'll see you in hell, Pembourne."

Chapter 6

Courtney was sitting in a chair by the window, pushing a half-eaten scone about on her plate, when Slayde's phaeton rounded the drive. Instantly, she tensed, fingers gripping the chair arms as she fought the impulse to dash from her bedchamber and down the stairs in order to learn what information Slayde had wrested from the Duke of Morland. Pragmatism restrained her. If she reaggravated her wounds now, Lord alone knew how long she'd be bedridden. And whatever she intended to do—based on Slayde's findings—it didn't include being an invalid.

Impatiently, she shifted in her seat, wondering why it was taking Slayde an eternity to alight from his carriage and make his way to the second floor.

What if he weren't coming directly to her chambers?

That untenable possibility incited action.

With a slight grimace, Courtney pushed herself to her

feet and sidestepped the end table. Waiting only until her ribs had finished clamoring their protest, she tied the sash of her wrapper and maneuvered her way across the room. A brief respite to steady herself. Then, she gripped the door handle and eased open the door.

She nearly collided with Slayde in the hallway.

"What are you doing out of bed?" he demanded.

Courtney tilted back her head until she could meet his disapproving gaze. In truth, she hadn't realized just how tall he was until now. Then again, this was the first time she'd been on her feet in his presence. "I was on my way to speak with you," she replied. "I knew you'd returned; I saw your phaeton round the drive beneath my window. I had to know what you'd found out."

He scowled. "Very little." Reflexively, he grasped her elbows, urged her to retrace her steps. "You shouldn't be up."

"But I am. I have been since noontime. I intend to be until dusk. So don't bother escorting me back to that prison of a bed. I want to hear everything that's happened. And I want to hear it in an upright position."

Slayde's dark brows lifted, a twinge of amusement easing the taut lines about his mouth. "Evidently, you're healing. I begin to see signs of the tyrant Madame La Salle rejoiced in bidding good-bye."

"I am."

"You are—which? Healing or a tyrant?"

Courtney smiled in spite of herself. "Both." She pointed at the mahogany end table. "See how much better I am? I was enjoying my afternoon refreshment in a chair."

"Then let's restore you to it and we'll have our conversation."

"All right." She allowed herself to be eased back into the seat, unable to deny the incredible relief her body experienced as it relinquished the burden of standing.

"Better?" Slayde drew up a second chair and joined her.

"Much. Thank you."

"You're welcome."

Their gazes locked, and Courtney felt a jolt of awareness rush through her, memories of last night darting dangerously close to the surface. Slayde was remembering, too; she could tell by the intensity of his gaze, the tension suddenly pervading his powerful frame.

With a visible effort, he looked away, clearing his throat and surveying the bedchamber. "I'm surprised my sister isn't glued to your side. I rather expected she'd spend the day regaling you with Mr. Scollard's fanciful tales."

"She was. She did." Following Slayde's lead, Courtney complied with the change in subject. "Aurora was with me all morning. Just before noon, she left to . . ." A delicate pause.

". . . To visit the Windmouth Lighthouse," he supplied. "Her customary destination. Courtney, your loyalty is commendable. But you needn't worry about betraying Aurora's confidences. My staff is well paid and equally well instructed. All of my sister's actions are reported immediately upon my return to Pembourne."

"Don't you think that's a bit restrictive?"

Slayde's jaw tightened. "Restrictive, but not excessive. Given the situation, it's the way things must be."

Courtney bit her lip to stifle the argument she felt coming on. Slayde's overseeing of Aurora was none of her business. Further, she understood that his overprotectiveness was rooted in love, love and concern for Aurora's safety.

Which reminded her of the pressing issue: Slayde's trip to Morland.

"Did you see the duke?" She leaned forward to ask.

"Oh, I saw him all right." With a brooding expression, Slayde stretched his legs out in front of him. "But the visit was far from what I expected."

"What do you mean?"

Courtney listened intently as Slayde relayed the entire

day's events to her, from his subtle questioning of the merchants in Newton Abbot to his ugly and unresolved confrontation with Morland.

"You think he's hiding something," Courtney deduced, when Slayde had finished.

"I damned well do. Why else would he suddenly and conveniently be resurrecting his life?"

"Maybe for the reason he gave you—to reclaim whatever's left."

"Which is nothing, according to him."

"He didn't react at all when you mentioned that pirate, or Papa?"

Slayde's lips thinned into a grim line. "Only by gloating."

"Then we're right back where we started." Even as she gave voice to the untenable truth, an emotional dam—too overpowering to keep intact—burst inside her. Ignoring the warning twinges that accompanied her actions, she vaulted to her feet, crossing over to the wardrobe and pulling out one of the gowns Aurora had provided. "I can't wait another minute."

Slayde was beside her in a heartbeat. "What in God's name do you think you're doing?"

Gripping a blue day dress, Courtney turned, regarding Slayde with anguished determination. "What I should have done from the onset: go to search for Papa—*and* that filthy pirate who hurt him."

"Courtney." Slayde's hands were gentle on her shoulders. "You're going nowhere. You can scarcely stand up, much less leave Pembourne."

"I'll manage. Anything is better than this inactivity. I can't lie here, doing nothing, for another minute." She punctuated her words with adamant shakes of her head, fighting back tears of anger and frustration. "Don't you understand? I'm wasting time. If Papa *is* still alive, he needs me. I can't just lie in bed, day after day, waiting for some miraculous occurrence to resolve things. I've got to do something—now." She clutched Slayde's waistcoat.

"Please, lend me a vessel. I'll return it, I swear. But I must . . ."

The effects of her taxing flurry of activity and her vehement shakes of the head struck all at once. Wildly, the room began to spin, her limbs turning to water, pain lancing through her skull in quick, sharp bites. She knew she was going to faint, just as she knew—somewhere in the far reaches of her mind—that Slayde was going to catch her.

A flash of darkness; a brief snatch of time. Then she was on the bed, and Slayde was pressing a cool compress to her forehead.

"All right?" he murmured.

Her lashes fluttered, then lifted. "All right," she managed gratefully, feeling the room right itself as Slayde applied the cool cloth to her neck and wrists. "I'm sorry. 'Tis just that—"

"You needn't explain. Or apologize." His hard hand closed around her trembling one. "Helplessness is a terrible feeling. How well I know that. But Courtney . . ." He tipped up her chin. "You must be realistic. You're too weak to sail. You haven't a clue about where to search for this pirate or his ship." A weighted pause before Slayde pressed on, almost as if he was forcing the words to emerge. "And the odds that your father survived the Channel—bound, gagged, and weighted down—are nil. So stop torturing yourself with the notion that you should be doing something to recover him."

Her heart wrenched, logic combatting hope, causing it to flicker and ebb. "The watch moved today," she whispered. "That, and my dream—couldn't they be signs?"

"They *are* signs—signs that you're mourning a terrible loss and want desperately to undo it."

"But the watch . . . ?"

"That was a mechanism, not a miracle." A spasm of pain crossed Slayde's face. "I wish I could make it otherwise."

His strangled tone penetrated Courtney's grief, and she scrutinized his face, realizing that he was enduring his own inner turmoil, berating himself for failing to resolve things today. "Slayde." She lay her palm against his jaw. "Thank you for going to Morland. It must have been terribly difficult for you. I know you did it, at least in part, for me. You'll never know how grateful I am."

"Grateful for what? I went to get the name and whereabouts of the man who killed your father. I came away with nothing. Damnit." Slayde's fist struck the mattress. "I never expected Morland to be sober, much less vital. He hasn't been either in over a dozen years—ever since his son died."

"He had a son?"

"Two. Hubert was the elder. He died of a fever while attending Oxford. Morland, of course, blames the Huntleys and that blasted curse—yet another misfortune he holds against us. In any case, Morland's never recovered from Hugh's death."

"What about his other son?"

"Julian? He's a year younger than Hugh. He and Morland are about as compatible as a fox and a hen. Morland believes in home and hearth; Julian believes in challenge and adventure. The one thing Morland *doesn't* believe in is compromise. So the two of them went their separate ways long ago. From what I recall, Julian hasn't been home in over five years."

"He's been abroad all this time?"

"No, he shows up in England for a Season now and again—between exploits. But he doesn't visit Morland Manor. Nor does his father send for him."

"The duke sounds like a very inflexible man."

"He's a black-hearted bastard. Not as cruel as his father was, but nearly."

Courtney's fingers drifted lightly over Slayde's jaw. "Confronting the duke—just seeing him after all this time—must have been dreadful for you. Especially given your suspicions that he was connected with your parents' murders."

An excruciating silence. "It was hell," Slayde admitted at last in a rough, gravelly voice. "All the images came pouring back, as vivid as if they'd just occurred. It's been years since that nightmare happened; I really thought I'd put it behind me. But I haven't."

"You don't ever put something like that behind you, Slayde. You simply tuck it away, and pray each time that it doesn't resurface until you've gathered enough strength to face it again. And you say a prayer that maybe, just maybe, each 'next time' will hurt a little bit less."

A trace of awe softened Slayde's expression. "You're extraordinary, do you know that? Here you are, suffering an unbearable loss, but rather than seeking comfort, you're attempting to comfort me."

"Were my attempts successful?" she whispered.

"That's the most astounding part of all—yes."

"I'm glad. You're a wonderful man, Slayde. You've spent your whole life being strong for others. 'Tis about time you allowed someone to be strong for you. Thank you for letting me be that someone—even for a fleeting moment."

"Courtney." Slayde's knuckles grazed her cheek, his fingers sifting through the loose strands of her hair. His eyes darkened from silver to slate, and Courtney knew—probably before he did—that he was going to kiss her. She watched an internal battle wage across his face, and her heart skipped a beat as he relented, lowering his head to hers.

Tenderly, her hand slipped to his nape, telling him without words what she wanted, urging his mouth down to hers.

Their lips met, clung—and all resistance shattered. It was just as it had been last night: deep, consuming; even daylight's clarity was unable to mute the maelstrom of emotions they evoked in each other.

With rough desperation, Slayde's mouth seized hers, circling once, twice—hardening abruptly as he sought a deeper joining, urged her to accept the penetration of his tongue.

She opened to him with the same pure joy she'd felt last night, only this time without the safety of darkness to retreat behind when the madness subsided. She was rewarded with a harsh, inarticulate sound as Slayde's tongue mated with hers, his hands cradling her head as if to soften the voracity of his kiss.

Courtney needed no softening. Unfurling like a flower to sunlight, she sought more of the magic, wrapping her arms about Slayde's neck, her tongue returning his caresses, entwining with his.

Slayde shuddered, a new tautness pervading his body, one Courtney found unfamiliar but wildly exciting. His hand shifted, moved beneath her wrapper, and her breath caught as he cupped her breast, his thumb tracing the nipple through the fine silk of her nightrail.

"Slayde." She uttered his name on a shiver, stirring restlessly beneath a flicker of white-hot sensation. Her nipple hardened, throbbed, awakened to a touch it had never experienced but nonetheless knew. Slayde's thumb circled, paused, brushed the aching tip until she whimpered. Again and again, he repeated the heated caress, each time more intimately, his urgency a palpable entity that blazed through her like fireworks.

A groan vibrated in Slayde's chest, and his fingers swept over the curves of her body, his touch unbearably erotic, even with the layer of silk between them. His hand was shaking when it returned to her breast, this time easing not merely beneath the wrapper but beneath the nightrail as well.

Courtney cried out at the sensation of his warm palm on her naked flesh. Unconsciously, she arched upward, pressing her breast more completely into his hand, melting as he began caressing her in the same exquisite ways he had before, only now with nothing between them.

The kiss burned out of control, Slayde's mouth devouring hers with a hungry rhythm that matched the strokes of his fingertips. On and on it went, a heart-stopping eternity elapsing, interrupted by nothing save their pounding hearts and escalating desire.

By the time Slayde tore himself away, forcibly lifting his body from hers, his breathing was ragged, and Courtney was trembling so badly she was grateful to be lying down. Her knees would never have supported her.

"God," Slayde rasped, not even pretending to deny the magnitude of what had just happened. His lids were hooded as he stared down at her, his eyes a glittering silver, alight with awe. "Courtney . . . I . . ."

"Don't." Courtney could scarcely speak. Instead, she pressed her fingers to his lips, tracing the lingering warmth of their kiss. "Words like *I'm sorry* or *this should never have happened* would be too painful to hear."

Mutely, he nodded.

"Just answer one question for me, and we'll never speak of this again," Courtney continued, searching his face. "What I felt—the intensity, the wonder—did you feel it, too?"

Slayde swallowed, then kissed her fingertips before easing them away. "Yes, Courtney. I felt it, too."

"Good."

"No. Not good."

A tremulous smile curved Courtney's lips. "We weren't going to speak of it again, remember?"

"We also weren't going to repeat it."

"That, my lord, was your vow, not mine."

Exhaling sharply, Slayde scowled, preoccupied by his own troubled thoughts. "Promise me you won't do anything as stupid as you did just before you fainted," he said abruptly. "Promise me you'll stay put, let your body heal."

All levity having vanished, Courtney shook her head. "I can't promise you that. I can't simply sit by and let that animal get away with what he did to Papa."

Slayde's scowl deepened at her reply. "Before I returned to Pembourne, I made one other stop. I hired an investigator. He and his associate will scrutinize Morland Manor twenty-four hours a day—unless Bencroft leaves the estate, in which case they'll follow him wherever he goes, report back on whomever he meets. Between their efforts and mine, we'll unearth that bloody pirate, I promise you."

"*If* he's Morland's accomplice," Courtney amended softly. "Slayde, your decision to hire an investigator was both sound and incredibly generous, and I thank you for it. But what you've just described fails to take one thing into account: what if Morland is innocent? What if, despite your gut instincts, he's not involved in the theft of the black diamond? You yourself said that dozens of others have tried, and failed, to spirit the stone away. What if, this particular time, it was another person who orchestrated the theft? Then you're watching the wrong man while the real criminal walks free. Please. Put your personal feelings aside long enough to be objective."

Thoughtfully, Slayde weighed the credibility of Courtney's words. "All right," he conceded at last. "I see your point. Although my convictions haven't lessened," he added quickly. "So far as I'm concerned, Morland is guilty."

"I understand. But if he's not . . ."

"Very well, if he's not . . ." Slayde paused, an idea sparking in his eyes. "What if I were to travel to London, seek out Bow Street and ask them to track down that pirate? I'm willing to bet he's still on English soil. Think about it. He'd never leave the country until he'd turned over the diamond and extracted his payment. In order to accomplish that, he'd have to first sail from our meeting place on the Channel to shore, then make the transaction—not to mention the fact that he'd need time to reclaim his own ship and transport his crew and whatever cargo he pilfered from the *Isobel* to his vessel. All those tasks together would consume at least several days. Which means he's probably still in England. And who better to unearth him than Bow Street?" Slayde gave a decisive nod. "I'll ride to London first thing tomorrow and supply them with your excellent physical description of the culprit. They can begin at once. This way, if Morland really is innocent, we'll have professionals conducting an investigation that's separate and apart from him, one that should yield results whether or not he's involved. Would those steps be enough to keep you from dashing off and worsening your wounds?"

Courtney resisted the urge to fling her arms about Slayde's neck—partly because it was too soon after the devastating encounter they'd just shared and partly because of the battle she knew was about to ensue. "Those steps would be more than enough. 'Tis a splendid idea. Except for one slight modification. I'm accompanying you to London."

"You're what?" he thundered, looking as if she'd just suggested walking into a lion's den. "Absolutely not."

"Why?"

"Why? Have you any idea how long the carriage ride is from Devonshire to London? How many hours you— and your wounds—would be bounced along bumpy roads?"

"I presume you'd stop overnight at an inn."

"After a full day of travel, and prior to another one, yes."

"Then I'll sleep soundly and recoup my strength."

"No."

"Please, Slayde." She couldn't stop herself; she seized his hands. "I told you, I'm nearly healed. And I've seen many carriages owned by the nobility—I eye them whenever the *Isobel* is docked—and they're more luxurious and comfortable than this bed. I promise to rest on your cushioned seats throughout the entire trip. As for the uneven roads, at worst they'll cause me a twinge or two. Believe me, the motion will be minor in comparison to that of a storm-tossed sea. And twinges will be heaven compared to seasickness."

"Courtney—"

"Slayde." Her fingers closed around his. "You've confronted your nightmare. Now I must confront mine. Let me come with you."

Her final words found their mark.

For a long moment, Slayde stared down at their clasped hands. Then, he gave a slow, reluctant nod. "All right. 'Tis against my better judgment, but I'd be an utter hypocrite if I refused you. Further, I have the distinct feeling that if I don't relent, you'll find a way to get to London on your own."

"I'm very resourceful," she concurred softly. "Just ask Madame La Salle."

A corner of Slayde's mouth lifted. "And to think I viewed Aurora as difficult."

Courtney smiled. "I warned you."

"Indeed you did. Very well, Miss Johnston. Tomorrow we journey to Bow Street—both of us."

As it was, Bow Street journeyed to them.

Matilda had just finished removing Courtney's last bandage—and delivering her fifth lecture on the dangers of traveling so soon after being injured—when the sound of an approaching carriage reached their ears.

"Isn't it a bit early for visitors?" Courtney inquired.

"Indeed it is." Matilda angled Courtney's chin so she could study her forehead. "Splendid. The gash is nearly healed. Now 'tis only an ugly cut." She paused. "However, your ribs are still tender and you're as weak as a kitten. If you ask me—"

"Who would come to Pembourne before seven A.M.?" Courtney interrupted, walking slowly toward the window.

A shrug. "Probably the Viscountess Stanwyk. She visits Lady Aurora now and again." Matilda sighed deeply. "Very well, if you insist on traveling to London with Lord Pembourne, then I shall accompany you."

"You?" Courtney turned, her brows arching in surprise. "Whatever for?"

It was Matilda's turn to look amazed. "To chaperon you, of course. You can't very well journey alone with the earl. You're a single young lady with a reputation to consider."

"A reputation?" Courtney's shoulders began to shake with laughter. "Oh, Matilda, I have no reputation, nor do I care a whit about one. The sole year I spent as a proper young lady was at a boarding school that would rather endure a plague than readmit me. The remainder of my life, I've been at sea. I'm hardly in danger of being compromised by traveling with Lord Pembourne."

"Still, I'll . . ."

Strained male voices drifted up through the open window.

"That can't be Lady Stanwyk," Courtney murmured, peering out. "Oh, God." All the color drained from her face. "Matilda, Slayde is talking to a gentleman in uniform. The uniform looks like one of those worn by Bow Street."

Ignoring her physical discomfort, Courtney gathered up her newly donned skirts and made her way to the door. "I'm going downstairs," she announced in a tone that precluded argument.

"I'll assist you." Matilda scurried to her side.

By the time they reached the foot of the stairs, Slayde and his visitor had entered the manor and were conversing heatedly. Slayde's expression was grim, while the stocky uniformed gentleman looked decidedly uneasy, shifting from one foot to the other and hanging near the entrance like a scared rabbit longing to bolt. Courtney paused, not merely to study the men, but to clutch the banister in an attempt to still her swimming head and trembling limbs.

"Are you all right, Miss Courtney?" Matilda asked with a worried frown.

"Fine, Matilda. I'm just regathering my strength."

Hearing their voices, Slayde glanced up, his dark scowl growing darker. "Courtney."

She braced herself for what she assumed would be an admonishment about overexerting herself.

It never came.

Without another word, Slayde walked rigidly toward them, taking Courtney's arm and nodding a curt dismissal at Matilda. "I'll take over from here."

"Very good, m'lord," the lady's maid replied. "I'll pack Miss Courtney's bag for your trip."

"No. Don't."

Courtney started at the harshness of Slayde's tone.

So did Matilda. "But I . . . that is—"

"Forgive my rudeness, Matilda," Slayde interrupted, clearly trying to make amends, at the same time ending the conversation. "But packing is no longer necessary."

"As you wish, sir." With a bewildered curtsy, the maid hastened off.

"Slayde?" Courtney searched his face, a tight knot of dread forming in the pit of her stomach. She could both feel and see the tension emanating from him—tension that told her something significant had occurred. "What is it? What's happened?"

"Come with me." Looping his arm firmly about her waist—whether for physical or emotional support, Courtney wasn't certain—Slayde led her down the marble hallway to where the uniformed gentleman hovered. "Rainer, this is Miss Johnston. The matter on which you've come to Pembourne concerns her as well." Glancing at Courtney, he added, "Mr. Rainer is from Bow Street."

"Mr. Rainer." Courtney could hear her voice quaver.

"Miss Johnston." The square-shouldered man scarcely acknowledged her. He was too busy gauging his distance to the front door.

Icily, Slayde gestured across the hall. "The yellow salon is comfortable and nearby. Let's talk in there."

Rainer froze, then retreated two steps backward. "That won't be necessary. I've given you the information and the note. There's nothing further—"

"I beg to differ with you." Slayde's eyes blazed silver sparks. "There's quite a bit yet to discuss, as I'm sure Miss Johnston will agree once she's heard the reason for your visit. Five minutes of your time is all I require." A bitter pause. "Rest assured, the yellow salon is quite safe. In my experience, curses afflict people, not homes. Further, unlike illness, curses are not contagious."

The Bow Street man had the good grace to flush . . . although he made no move to advance farther into the manor. "My instructions were to deliver the note and return to London at once."

Slayde's jaw tightened. "To further investigate the matter?"

A surprised blink. "What matter? The death of a noted scoundrel? Frankly, my lord, we have real crimes to deal with—crimes against the innocent."

"Like my parents, you mean."

Rainer sucked in his breath. "That was a terrible tragedy, the earl and countess being killed in their own home. Unfortunately, the thief who committed the murder left no trace of his identity. Bow Street did all it could."

"Of course you did," Slayde mocked. Releasing Courtney, he strode around and flung the front door wide. "Go, then. You've done all you could—once again."

Ignoring the sarcasm, Rainer nodded, nearly knocking Slayde down in his haste to comply. "Good day, my lord."

He darted from the manor into his waiting carriage.

Seconds later, it disappeared around the drive.

Courtney walked over, watching the play of emotions cross Slayde's face. Gently, she touched his sleeve. "Why was Mr. Rainer here?"

Slowly, Slayde turned, gazing down at Courtney's hand and blinking as he recalled her presence. "He saved us a journey." With a weary sigh, he took her arm. "Let's sit down. You're weak, and this conversation is going to take some time. Despite Rainer's ludicrous claim to the contrary, the reason for his visit was anything but perfunctory."

"All right." Courtney bit her lip to keep from blurting out a million questions. But once she was settled on a cushioned settee in the yellow salon, she could no longer contain herself. "Slayde, please. My imagination is reeling. Tell me what's happened. Why was Bow Street here and why aren't we going to London?"

Slayde lowered himself beside her, gripping his knees and meeting her gaze. "Because the pirate we were hoping to unearth is dead."

"Dead?"

"Yes. The description Rainer gave me matches yours exactly—right down to the ring on his finger."

Courtney swallowed, trying to absorb this unexpected development. "Who was he?" she asked woodenly. Abruptly, the questions began spilling forth on their own. "How did he die? Who found him? Where? Did he say anything before he died, give us a clue to the *Isobel's* fate?"

"He was Sewell Armon, long known as a privateer. He and his ship, the *Fortune,* were evidently notorious for seizing vessels all over the world, taking prisoners and booty. His body was found in a deserted alley in Dartmouth, about thirty miles from here—by a group of urchins scrounging for food. He was already dead; he'd been shot in the chest."

"I see." Courtney rubbed her temples, a twinge of relief instantly supplanted by the horrible realization that with Armon dead, her hopes of learning anything about the fate of the *Isobel* were extinguished.

Coming to his feet, Slayde crossed over and poured two goblets of brandy, pressing one into Courtney's hand. "Drink this."

Feeling oddly dazed, she accepted the glass, taking two healthy swallows. "Now I'll never find Papa," she whispered.

"Courtney, that bastard hadn't an inkling of what might or might not have happened to your father after he'd been thrown overboard. His only thought was to procure the black diamond."

"But he did know what happened to our ship, our crew."

Roughly, Slayde cleared his throat. "From Rainer's

description, Armon wasn't known for leaving evidence in his wake."

"Evidence. Do you mean vessels or people?"

"Both."

Courtney's eyes squeezed shut, everything inside her going cold at the image of her home, her friends, being destroyed. "Then it's over." Her lashes lifted, the pain of loss swamping her in great, untamed waves. "No, actually it's not. You were right. It will never be over."

Placing their glasses on a side table, Slayde gathered her against him, pressing her cheek to his waistcoat and gently stroking her hair. "The grief will dim. It won't consume you forever. Nor will the hatred—not with Armon dead."

"Retribution is a poor substitute for having my life back. But you knew that already, didn't you?"

"Only because I spent years forcing myself to remember it, to think rationally. In truth, with or without proof, I hungered to tear down Morland's doors and choke the life out of him. But what good would it have done? I'd be in Newgate, and my parents would still be gone."

Slayde's explanation prompted a thought. "What about the black diamond?" Courtney demanded, leaning back to scrutinize his face. "Did Bow Street recover it when they found Armon's body?"

Silence.

Realization struck. "It wasn't there, was it? The stone was gone, seized by whoever killed him." Courtney's racing mind didn't await a reply. "I heard Mr. Rainer mention something about a note. Did they find that note on Armon's person?"

"Yes."

"What prompted them to deliver it to Pembourne?"

"The fact that it was addressed to me." Slayde reached into his pocket, extracting an unsealed envelope marked *The Earl of Pembourne, Pembourne Manor, Dawlish, Devonshire.* Deftly, he removed the single sheet of paper within, unfolding it and offering it to Courtney.

She scanned the contents, which read:

Pembourne:
 The exchange will be made tonight. Eleven P.M. Ten miles due south of Dartmouth—in the open waters of the English Channel. Take a small, unarmed boat. Come alone, accompanied only by the diamond. Heed these instructions or your sister will die.

"A ransom note," Courtney murmured.

"Indeed. What puzzles me is that it's identical to the one that brought me to your ship."

Courtney inclined her head quizzically. "I don't understand."

"Do you recall my telling you that the week Aurora disappeared, I received several ransom notes?"

"Yes. You said only two were credible, accompanied by locks of what you assumed to be Aurora's hair, but were, in fact, mine."

"Exactly. And this message is a replica of the second of those notes."

"Are you sure?"

"I committed every word to memory. Yes, I'm sure. Even the hand is the same." He frowned. "The only difference is the date. The one I received was dated one day earlier than this one."

"That makes no sense." Courtney's brow furrowed as she examined the page again. "Why would this Armon write two identical notes directing you to do the same thing on two different days? For that matter, why did he keep this note at all, rather than send it? Slayde, are you sure the notes are the same? Can we check?"

"Of course." Slayde rose. "All the threatening letters I received are in my study." He hesitated. "Will you be all right here for a moment?"

A slow nod. "Actually, I think I need a minute to myself." She attempted a smile. "I'll be fine."

With a probing look, Slayde complied. "I shan't be long."

Once alone, Courtney leaned her head back on the sofa cushion, trying to assimilate the day's developments, allowing her rampaging thoughts to unravel at will.

The pirate who'd taken all she loved was dead. Abruptly, the need to unearth him, to vent her anger and fury until they were spent, was gone. Gone also was her life—at least the one she'd known—together with the comforting semblance of stability it had contained. Her existence was in shambles, as was her emotional well-being. At the same time, physically, she was greatly improved and, thanks to Matilda's excellent care, nearly ready to venture out.

Out—to where? To what?

Before she could embark on a future, she had to come to terms with her present, relinquish her past.

Her father was gone.

Even as she formed the thought, her heart rejected it. The fact was that acceptance had yet to supplant grief, and each unresolved question—plus her own nagging, unrealistic hope—further complicated the healing process.

The only way to stop the past from haunting her was to find a truth she could live with. But what truth was that and how in God's name could she find it?

Mr. Scollard.

With a surge of hope, Courtney recalled Aurora's enthusiastic depiction of the lighthouse keeper. Perhaps so wise a man could help resolve her doubts as to whether her father lived, advise her on how to proceed from here, guide her toward an answer—be it action or acceptance—so she could move ahead with her life.

Her next challenge was the present. Pembourne. She was needed here. And not only as Aurora's companion, although she didn't take that commitment lightly and was, in fact, looking forward to befriending Slayde's sister. But Aurora's scars were minimal, worn close to the surface, thereby making them easier to discern and to heal. Slayde's scars were another matter entirely.

How long had it been since he'd allowed another person to so much as approach his walls of self-protection? Had he never before offered any part of himself other than the cursory, even prior to his parent's horrid demise? Was it possible that she was truly the first to sense, to see the emotional depth he guarded so fiercely, the vulnerability he refused to accept?

And if so, hadn't she been offered a wondrous opportunity to show him what he'd been missing?

To show *him?* Courtney's conscience intruded skeptically. *Very well then,* was her silent admission, *to show us both.*

The truth was undeniable. She *wanted* to stay close to Slayde, to explore—to rekindle—the extraordinary sensations he evoked inside her. To understand the basis for those feelings and to discover where they might lead.

A shiver of anticipation ran up her spine. Were these the incredible emotions her parents had experienced when they met? Was this the man destined to need her love, to give her his? Was this miraculous connection between them real or just an ephemeral wisp of magic conjured by mutual pain and understanding?

Why in the name of heaven was there such an abundance of questions and such a frustrating lack of answers?

"Courtney?"

She hadn't heard Slayde return.

Her head came up, and she blinked, giving him a weak but reassuring smile. "I haven't fainted. I was just thinking."

"Well, we certainly have something to think about," he replied, his expression grim. "Take a look." Crossing over, he sank down beside her, drawing the table closer and placing the three notes side by side upon it.

Abandoning her philosophical musings, Courtney peered over Slayde's shoulder and scrutinized the sheets of paper. "You were right. Other than the date, the second note you received and the one just delivered by Bow Street are identical."

"No, *you* were right. They're not." He pointed at the first ransom note he'd received, then the undelivered one found on Armon's body. "Study these two closely." He waited for her nod. "Now inspect the middle one again. Carefully. Tell me what you see."

For a long moment, Courtney was quiet, eyes narrowed on each individual page. Then she gasped. "The one in the middle is written in a different hand than the other two."

"Exactly. It's a near-perfect copy. Someone worked very hard to replicate the handwriting. But the curves of the letters, the angles—they're slightly off, not enough to notice, unless you're examining them together, up close, comparing one to the other, but the difference is there. Someone else wrote this second note."

"Wait." Courtney shook her head, then frowned as it began to throb. "You're saying that whoever wrote the first and third notes were one and the same person— someone other than whoever wrote the second note."

"Yes. And stop shaking your head. You'll aggravate whatever's left of the concussion."

Courtney scarcely heard the admonishment. "If Armon kept the final note, never sending it, I presume he substituted the second note in its stead."

"And had that substitute delivered to me on the day I sailed out to the *Isobel.*"

"Then who penned the others?"

"Whoever orchestrated this scheme. My guess is he gave them to Armon with orders to have the first note delivered just after Aurora left Pembourne, the next on the day before her return."

"But Slayde,"—Courtney frowned—"that presumes this other person knew of Aurora's plans to travel to London."

"Indeed it does."

"How? Who?"

"We'll have to put that question to Aurora. My immediate response would be that Elinore must have been aware of the upcoming trip; after all, Aurora sought her out as both transport and chaperon. And since Elinore hadn't a clue that the whole excursion was Aurora's little secret, she might have mentioned the forthcoming trip to anyone." Slayde's expression hardened, his eyes glittering dangerously. "Of course, there could be another explanation. The orchestrator of this scheme could have been someone seeking vengeance badly enough to scrutinize Pembourne, not only over the past fortnight, but continuously. Someone who studied Aurora's restless comings and goings and deduced that it was just a matter of time before she performed a foolhardy stunt like dashing off to London with Elinore. And when she did, he jumped on the opportunity, giving Armon the first ransom note and following Elinore's carriage to London. There, he had only to stay close enough to Aurora to learn how long she intended to stay in town, then dispatch the next note to Armon while remaining in London to ensure that Aurora's plans didn't change."

Courtney's brows arched in response to Slayde's far-fetched explanation. "I needn't ask who you believe that 'someone' is."

"No. You needn't."

"'Tis very little fact and much speculation."

"All of which makes sense."

"Not completely. Putting aside Morland's involvement—or lack thereof—let's say you're right and Armon penned the second note as a way to subvert the third. Why, then, didn't he destroy the latter? Why was he keeping it?"

"I suspect he didn't pen the second note himself but had it copied. Probably by a damned good forger who used the third note as a prototype before returning the original to Armon, who then paid him to send the well-crafted replacement to me after the *Fortune* had gone in pursuit of your ship. Which would explain why the undelivered note was still in Armon's possession."

"By predating the replacement by a day, Armon managed to seize the stone while his colleague was still in London," Courtney mused aloud. "Giving Armon time to bolt before his actions were discovered."

"But it didn't work that way. Armon underestimated his partner's intelligence—or perhaps his sobriety. The bastard caught up with him, confiscated the jewel, and killed him."

"Which brings up another question. Once Armon had the jewel, why did he remain in England? Surely he realized he was a walking target. Why didn't he flee the country?"

"He probably intended to—after collecting his money. Remember, Courtney, the stone was worth a fortune. I'm sure Armon preferred pound notes to a huge, cumbersome jewel."

"So he was en route to his monetary connection when he was overtaken—and murdered." She inclined her head. "Underestimated 'his sobriety,' you said. We're back to the Duke of Morland again."

"He had the motive and the opportunity. Remember, he's no longer in seclusion. These past few months, he's made a miraculous *and* convenient re-emergence into the business world."

"We could easily discern if he traveled to London last week."

"We could and we will. But that alone isn't enough. We must determine where he was when Armon—" Slayde broke off, realization darting across his face. "Armon was murdered either early yesterday morning or late the night before—in Dartmouth, which is a two- to three-hour carriage ride from Morland. I arrived at Morland Manor late yesterday morning. The duke returned to his estate immediately thereafter. When I asked where he'd been, he refused to answer. I know he wasn't in the village; I'd have seen him there when I was questioning the merchants. So where was he?" A fierce glint lit his eyes. "And doing what—killing his accomplice?"

"Slayde." Courtney struggled to remain calm. "Your theory is plausible. But we haven't a shred of evidence."

"Then we'll have to find some." Slayde averted his head, staring icily across the room. "If Morland is the man Armon worked for, then he's indirectly responsible for your father's death and the fate of your ship."

"I know." Courtney swallowed, hard. "Slayde, what about the *Fortune,* Armon's ship? Did Mr. Rainer mention if Bow Street was pursuing it?"

Slayde's laugh was harsh. "He didn't need to mention it. They're not. Bow Street is terrified of the Huntleys. You saw how fast Rainer bolted—he's afraid to so much as cross my threshold. No, Courtney. Any further investigating, we'll have to do on our own."

"Then we shall." Courtney sat bolt upright, battling the surge of dizziness that immediately claimed her. "We'll begin by riding to Dartmouth. From there, we'll sail out in search of Armon's ship. Doubtless, it's heading as far and fast from English waters as possible. I suspect the crew fled long before Armon's body was discovered. They must have waited in a nearby cove for his return, and when hours passed without a sign of their captain, they probably panicked and set sail. They couldn't have traveled more than fifty or sixty miles. We'll find them." She bolted to her feet. "We *must* find them. Some of Papa's crewmen might still be—" Abruptly, she swayed, clutching the table for support.

"Courtney." Slayde leapt up and caught her elbows, easing her back to the sofa. "As we've discussed, you're in no condition to traverse the seas. Further, we haven't a clue in what direction the *Fortune* is traveling. To go after it would be to waste precious time, time that could be spent gathering evidence and proving Morland's guilt—or unearthing whoever really is guilty. Think about it. I agree with you that the *Fortune* must be found. But 'twould be far easier for the investigative firm I've hired to send an experienced navigator after it, while you and I delve into the crucial matter of unmasking Armon's accomplice."

Fists knotting in the folds of her gown, Courtney willed away the damnable weakness that thwarted her every move. "I hate this," she bit out.

"I know. Take deep breaths and sit quietly. The lightheadedness will subside."

A minute later, she nodded. "I'm better now." Soberly, her gaze met Slayde's. "I'll agree to your suggestion, but only if this delving includes my efforts as well as yours."

He scowled. "You've been out of bed for an hour and you're barely able to stand. Resting on a carriage ride to London was one thing. Dashing about Devonshire doing what I intend—hunting down unsavory jewel contacts and interrogating any other lowlifes who might have known Armon and who might lead us to his accomplice—is quite another."

"I see your point." Courtney chewed her lip. "Very well," she conceded. "I'll remain at Pembourne, spend the day with Aurora—perhaps even find out who knew of her plans to go to London." A pause, as Courtney fought to still the pounding in her head. "You do what you just described: probe the wharf near Dartmouth to learn who Armon's associates were, hire an investigator to go after the *Fortune.*" Her chin set stubbornly. "But before that investigator begins his search, bring him to Pembourne. I want to talk with him. He'll need the facts I can supply: descriptions of the *Fortune*'s crewmen who accompanied Armon onto the *Isobel,* snatches of conversation I overheard, and most importantly, names and descriptions of Papa's crew, in case any of them were taken prisoner and are still alive. None of this should delay your investigator's search by any considerable amount of time. I'd be willing to wager a thousand pounds—if I had it—that as a result of their successful retreat, Armon's crew has been lulled into a false sense of security and has, by now, slowed their ship's frantic pace, reasonably convinced no one is pursuing them. Which no one was. Until now. So—" Courtney concluded, hearing her own voice waver, a clear warning that her energy was rapidly diminishing—"is my plan acceptable?"

Slayde studied her, brow furrowed. "The idea seems sound enough. As you pointed out, the *Fortune* can't have ventured far. One extra day won't give them much more of an advantage, especially if we counter that advantage by spending the time gathering information to hasten our search. Moreover, your idea appeals to me for another reason. The knowledge that my investigator will accompany me home tonight should serve to keep you at Pembourne—you *and* Aurora."

"Aurora? How does she factor into this?"

"Aurora factors into anything that involves trouble," Slayde retorted dryly. "She thrives on adventure, or hadn't you noticed the way she glows when she's relaying one of Mr. Scollard's tales? She accepts every word as absolute truth—and not only those in *his* stories. She believes in every farfetched legend she gets wind of, including the one surrounding that wretched black diamond. Although, in that case, I must admit I was relieved as hell to discover she feared the jewel and its curse, else she probably would have escaped from Pembourne and combed all of England to find the bloody stone."

"Probably," Courtney concurred, recalling the sparkle in Aurora's eyes when she'd recounted one of Mr. Scollard's yarns.

"And now?" Slayde continued. "With a mystery such as the one you and I are embarking upon? Right here in her own home? 'Twould awaken every reckless impulse she possesses." He cast a knowing look out the window. "By now, she's undoubtedly on her way home from the lighthouse—where she's been since dawn—eager and ready, having noted Bow Street's carriage round our drive. Unfortunately, Rainer's visit cannot be kept secret from her; the lighthouse provides a superb view of Pembourne. You can see the entire estate from its tower."

Courtney frowned, an unwelcome possibility inserting itself in her mind. "If you're asking me to lie to Aurora about the reason for Mr. Rainer's visit, I won't. 'Tis my intention to earn your sister's friendship. In order for that to happen, there must be honesty between us. I know no other way. Deceit has no place in a caring relationship."

An odd expression crossed Slayde's face. "No, it doesn't. Not unless there's just cause to employ it. Which in this case, there is not." Roughly, he cleared his throat. "I wasn't suggesting you lie to Aurora. I only meant to point out that once she learns why Bow Street was here, she'll be ready to plunge right into what she'll view as a grand adventure. You'll need to pin her down to keep her from following my carriage to Dartmouth. And trust me, pinning Aurora down is like trying to catch a firefly. Even *I* know that."

Even you? Courtney wanted to blurt out. *As her brother, it should be* especially *you.* Wisely, she refrained from speaking her opinion aloud. It was too premature, too intrusive. But someday—soon, if she had her way— Slayde would allow Aurora into his heart.

Storing away that inspiring possibility, Courtney replied, "Fear not, my lord. I'll pique Aurora's interest by telling her about the investigator's imminent visit. In the interim, I promise to keep her occupied."

Occupied. Now *that* spawned another interesting notion, one that sent Courtney's thoughts spinning in an entirely different direction. Hadn't she, mere minutes ago, determined that she *must* put her past to rest? Well, why not start today? With a bit of help, she could seek some answers *and* keep Aurora amused at the same time.

If only she could combat this intolerable weakness long enough to do so.

"Courtney? Are you in pain?"

"No." In truth, she was fading fast, but she wasn't about to reveal that to Slayde—not in view of the plan she'd just formed. "I'm a bit tired, but I'm fine." She drew a shaky breath, trying to regain a semblance of strength. "Are we in agreement, then? I'll stay behind; you bring the investigator to Pembourne tonight."

"Agreed."

"Good." Courtney rose—slowly, this time—accepting Slayde's proffered hand in order to sustain her balance. "Then I shall return to my chambers at once, to rest up for Aurora's arrival. You leave for Dartmouth now."

Slayde wrapped his arm around her waist. "I will. *After* I've escorted you to your room and made certain you don't swoon." His meaningful look told Courtney her false bravado hadn't been the slightest bit convincing. "I'm glad you prefer honesty. You're a deplorable liar. Now lean against me or you'll never manage the stairs."

With a wave of gratitude—and something more, Courtney complied. "A deplorable liar? Admittedly so, my lord." She paused, tilting her face up to his. "You, on the other hand, are a far too accomplished one. You've not only fooled the world, you've even fooled yourself. Thank goodness, you've just met someone you can't fool—me."

Stunned disbelief flashed across Slayde's features.

Courtney gestured toward the doorway. "Shall we attempt the stairs?"

For a long moment, Slayde remained silent, and Courtney could actually feel the tension rippling through him.

Abruptly, he nodded. "Yes. You're exhausted."

Without another word, he guided her from the salon, up the stairs to her room. There, he turned her over to Matilda's able care. "Rest" was all he said before turning on his heel and leaving the bedchamber.

Perhaps she'd overstepped her bounds after all, Courtney mused a half-hour later, sinking gratefully into the bed's softness. But instinct told her she'd done the right thing. Slayde needed awakening . . . and awakened he would be.

Yawning, she snuggled under the covers, fatigue descending upon her like a heavy blanket. Her limbs felt weak as water, her eyelids drooping, half closed. In the distance, she heard Slayde's phaeton round the drive, then head away from the manor—toward the answers they sought, she hoped.

She wouldn't fight sleep. She'd give in to it, restore her strength.

Then later, she'd relay her intentions to Aurora, who would be unquestionably diverted and eager to assist in a venture she herself had proposed: getting Courtney to the lighthouse.

And to Mr. Scollard.

Chapter 7

"Courtney? Are you awake yet?"

Stirring from a half-sleep, Courtney lifted her head from the pillow and blinked. "I think so, yes." She brushed tendrils of hair from her face and gestured for Aurora to come in. "What time is it?"

"Half after eleven." Aurora entered, shutting the door with a guilty expression. "You've been asleep since I arrived home at nine. And Matilda will never forgive me if she knows I awakened you."

"Half after eleven!" Courtney pushed herself into a sitting position, glancing at the clock for confirmation. "That's impossible. The last time I looked it was twenty past eight."

"Evidently, you were wearier than you realized." Crossing over, Aurora perched in a nearby chair. "From all the activity that took place at Pembourne this morning," she prompted meaningfully.

Courtney began to laugh. "Aurora, you look like a

hopeful pup awaiting a treat. Has no one filled you in on anything yet?"

"No. Slayde is nowhere to be found, and not one of the servants can—or will—provide the answers I seek." Another expectant look. "Can you?"

"What would you like to know?"

"To begin, why was Bow Street here? What did they want? Did it pertain to your father? Your ship? The black diamond? Were they here to meet with you, or Slayde? How did they hear of your whereabouts? Did you learn anything? Will they be back?"

"Only that?" Courtney teased. "Very well, I'll answer your questions." Recalling Mr. Rainer's fleeting but critical visit, she sobered. "Bow Street was here because they found the pirate who took over my father's ship. And 'twas Slayde they came to see; they didn't even know of my existence."

"But if they found the pirate . . . didn't he confess?"

"He couldn't. He was dead—shot in the chest."

Aurora sucked in her breath. "Dead . . . where did this happen?"

"In Dartmouth. Some local urchins discovered his body in a deserted alley."

"Dartmouth is right here in Devonshire, not thirty miles from Pembourne." Aurora frowned. "Even so, I don't understand. If he is dead, what prompted Bow Street's visit to Pembourne? They certainly didn't come to elicit Slayde's help. They'd rather consort with the devil than seek out the Huntleys."

"So I observed. The reason they came to Pembourne, albeit reluctantly, is because they found a note in the scoundrel's pocket. It was addressed to your brother." Slowly, leaving nothing out, Courtney relayed all the details they had thus far.

"My God," Aurora murmured when Courtney was through, "this becomes more complicated by the minute." Compassion softened her features. "No wonder you slept so long. You must be spent. What can I do to help?" Abruptly, she glanced toward the closed bed-chamber door. "And where is Slayde?"

"He's gone to Dartmouth to try to unearth this Armon's contact. He's also hiring an investigator to go after Armon's ship."

"To go after Armon's ship—without us?" Aurora's reaction was so much what Slayde had depicted that Courtney nearly grinned. "You're the one who saw this Armon's men firsthand and can identify them. Not to mention—"

"Wait." Courtney held up a restraining palm. "Before you plunge into the same tirade I myself did not four hours past, let me put your mind at ease. Slayde has promised to bring this investigator to Pembourne so that I might speak with him—*prior* to the onset of his search."

"Here?" Aurora sat straight up. "When?"

"Tonight."

"Excellent. The only thing better would be if you were well enough for us to accompany him on his explorations."

"Us?"

A grin. "Certainly, us. That's what being my companion is all about. We must become inseparable."

"Especially when it means delving into an enticing mystery," Courtney put in dryly.

"Especially then," Aurora agreed without the slightest attempt at pretense. "Nevertheless, since you're not up for traveling, 'tis our responsibility to use today to our full advantage. We must amass all your knowledge and devise all our questions prior to this investigator's arrival, so that we can make full use of his visit and he can swiftly unearth Armon's accomplice."

"I agree," Courtney replied, reminded of the promise she'd made to Slayde: to probe the matter with Aurora and determine what light she could shed on the possible identity of Armon's accomplice. "Aurora, you just asked if you could help. There's one thing you can do, something that might make all the difference in the world.

Think—who did you tell of your intentions to travel to London last week? Who might have known you'd be leaving Pembourne?"

Aurora pondered Courtney's question. She propped her chin on her hand, clearly racking her brain for answers. "I see the direction in which you're heading. You're wondering if someone used my departure from Pembourne to feign a kidnapping in order to extort the black diamond from Slayde. The idea is sound. The problem, however, is I told no one of my plans. No one, obviously, other than Elinore, who was my intended chaperon, and Mr. Scollard, who is my sole confidant and would never repeat a word I divulged."

"I assume that trustworthiness applies to the viscountess, as well, that she would have kept your secret."

"Yes and no," Aurora replied frankly. "And the 'no' part is why I didn't tell her it was a secret."

"You've lost me."

"Had Elinore known my trip to London was confidential, she would indeed have kept it from the world. But, had she known it was unsanctioned by Slayde, she would have canceled the entire trip, which is why I didn't dare tell her the truth. She believed I had Slayde's blessing, that he knew everything other than the dates of my journey—and those I specified in the note I left him. So, in answer to your question, yes, Elinore is entirely trustworthy—when her silence is solicited. In this case, it was not."

"I see." Courtney chewed her lip. "How long had you two been planning this trip?"

"Nearly a fortnight."

"So 'tis possible she mentioned it to others."

"Entirely possible. Slayde was away until just before I left, so I really didn't worry over who knew of my plans. So long as Slayde didn't know . . ." Aurora shrugged. "In truth, he's my sole obstacle." A thoughtful pause. "What I can do is summon Elinore to Pembourne. She'll gladly recount who she might have spoken with about my impending arrival in London."

"That's a good idea." Courtney nodded. "Perhaps she can come by tomorrow, if she's not otherwise engaged."

"I'll send her a missive at once." Aurora shifted restlessly. "I wish we could sail with that investigator. Unfortunately, you're not yet well enough."

"True. But perhaps I am well enough for a stroll."

Aurora's eyes narrowed. "Meaning?"

"Meaning I want to attempt the lighthouse today." Courtney leaned forward intently. "Aurora, I must determine whether Papa is alive. And if Mr. Scollard is as perceptive as you say . . ."

"He is," Aurora confirmed. "I've told him all about you—just this morning, as a matter of fact. He's looking forward to meeting—and to helping—you."

"Then let's go." Courtney shoved back the blankets and swung her legs over the side of the bed. Gingerly, she stood, clutching the bedpost until her lightheadedness subsided. "If you'll help me dress, we can avoid alerting Matilda to our plans." A tentative step, then another. "She'll hear about our excursion later, of course. But we needn't worry her in advance."

So saying, Courtney crossed the room and tugged open the wardrobe, her motions tentative, unsteady.

Aurora watched, indecision warring on her face. After a moment, she rose, walking over and offhandedly extracting clothing from the wardrobe. "Courtney, I'd like nothing better than to take you to the lighthouse," she stated, fingering one of the soft muslin gowns she'd loaned Courtney. "But are you sure you're ready for this? Mr. Scollard isn't going away. And you're still so weak. We could spend the day preparing for our chat with the investigator, then traipse to the lighthouse in two or three days, when you're stronger."

Courtney's hands balled into fists. "Please don't mollify me like a child. You and I both know we can 'prepare,' as you put it, in less than an hour. As for waiting two or three days to visit Mr. Scollard . . ." Her voice choked. "I can't bear lying abed, hour after hour, accosted by fear and uncertainty. So, able or not, I must try. Today."

Her desperation must have conveyed itself, because Aurora turned to her, brows raised, and nodded. "All right. Then try we shall. We'll leave the manor through the rear entrance. That way, neither Matilda nor any of the other servants will see us—except those appointed by my brother specifically to scrutinize my actions, of course. But most of those men are posted about the grounds, not in the manor. And they'll give us no trouble; they're quite used to my trips to the Windmouth Lighthouse."

Courtney flashed a grateful smile. "Then it appears our goal is as good as attained."

An hour later, she felt otherwise.

"I never imagined your estate was so vast," she managed, leaning weakly against an oak tree, one that was but a third of the way to their destination, and peering across the endless acres of greenery stretching before her. "We've been walking for an eternity." She brushed damp tendrils of hair off her forehead, her breathing rough and shallow.

"Courtney, I think we should go back." Aurora abandoned all attempts at tact. "You're on the verge of collapse. Come, let me help you." She grasped Courtney's arm, adding lightly, "If you don't care for yourself, care for me. Slayde will have my head if I'm responsible for worsening your injuries."

"You're not responsible—I am." Courtney took another half-hearted step. "As I said earlier, I'm not a child. I'm a grown—" Her knees gave out and, with a broken sound, she sank to the grass.

"Courtney!" Thoroughly alarmed, Aurora squatted down beside her.

"I'm conscious," Courtney murmured, pressing her face against the cool ground and wishing she could just go to sleep until the weakness and dizziness faded. "But I suspect . . . you're right. We . . . should return to . . . the manor."

That did it.

Aurora bolted to her feet. "Cutterton!" she called,

waving earnestly toward a cluster of trees nestled in the eastern corner of the estate. "I need you."

An instant of silence. Then, the rustle of trees as a stocky man of middle years emerged. With an incredulous stare, he made his way toward Aurora.

"Hurry," she urged.

"Lady Aurora," he began upon reaching her, his tone rife with disbelief, "how did you know to call me?"

Aurora looked equally amazed. "Who else would I call?"

"How in the name of heaven did you know I was behind those trees?" he demanded.

She rolled her eyes. "Don't be ridiculous, Cutterton. This entire section of the estate is your domain. Just as the western corner is Plinkert's. You have men stationed at healthy intervals between you, precisely as Slayde commanded."

The poor man couldn't seem to recover. "All this time, you knew we were there?"

"Of course. Now, please, I need your help. Miss Johnston is unable to walk on her own. We must carry her back to the manor."

"Yes, certainly, my lady."

Still muttering, Cutterton bent down and scooped Courtney effortlessly off the ground. "Forgive me, Miss Johnston, but I don't think your legs will hold you."

A weak smile. "Thank you, Cutterton."

She was only minimally aware of their return trip to the manor, until Siebert, the butler, summoned Matilda from her duties.

"What were you thinking of?" the distressed maid asked as she tucked Courtney back into bed. "And you as well, Lady Aurora. Surely you didn't imagine Miss Courtney could traverse the entire estate, in her condition?"

"Matilda, don't blame Aurora," Courtney murmured weakly. "She tried to discourage me. I refused to listen. The fault is mine, and mine alone." She smiled faintly. "But I shall be duly punished by having to endure the

130

earl's bellowing later tonight. So, please, have pity on me."

Matilda stifled a smile. "If you're trying to procure my silence, don't bother. Even if I agreed to say nothing to Lord Pembourne, Cutterton would make quick work of exposing our deception. He's doubtless poised and waiting for Lord Pembourne's return, prepared to enlighten him the instant the earl's phaeton passes through Pembourne's gates. So my soft heart cannot prevent the earl's furious tirade."

"Nor should it." Miss Payne swept into the room, her uniform as crisp as her tone. "I'll take over from here, Matilda. Evidently, a firmer hand is needed to ensure that Miss Johnston makes a full and rapid recovery."

A flicker of surprise crossed Matilda's face. "Very well."

"Thank you for your concern, Miss Payne," Courtney inserted, unable to bear the embarrassment and hurt she saw in Matilda's eyes, "but, in truth, 'twould take an army to confine me for this length of time. Matilda has done a wonderful job; after all, according to Lord Pembourne, Dr. Gilbert believed me to be so badly depleted, he expected a week or more to pass before I was strong enough to stand on my own two feet. Instead, in half that time, my wounds are nearly healed, I'm out of bed for long periods of time, and I'm impatient to end my prolonged period of confinement." A smile. "Matilda's skillful ministrations and Cook's mastery in the kitchen are responsible for that miracle. Unfortunately, their abilities cannot extend to remedying my lack of common sense. So, please, don't condemn anyone for my own foolhardy actions."

Miss Payne seemed to thaw a bit. "Matilda knows better than to think I was reprimanding her." A nod of approval in Matilda's direction. "She is every bit as fine a caretaker as you've just described. I only meant that perhaps she needed some assistance from someone with a slightly less tender heart."

"Only if that someone also has a fleeter foot," Aurora

put in cheerfully. "As you know, Miss Payne, I'm quite adept at escaping confinement, even when it's a foolish thing to do. Well, evidently my new companion is equally as adept. I fear the staff at Pembourne is going to have their hands full."

"Companion?" Miss Payne inclined her head.

"Yes. Slayde has asked Courtney to stay on." Aurora's lips twitched. "To help keep me in line."

"Lord help us." Matilda rolled her eyes.

"I see." Miss Payne busied herself with the curtains, half closing them to limit the afternoon sunlight as it spilled into the bedchamber. "Matilda, why don't you fetch Miss Johnston a tray? She should eat something before she naps."

"Of course." With a grateful smile in Courtney's direction, Matilda hastened from the room.

"Siebert tells me you were on your way to the lighthouse," Miss Payne remarked conversationally, checking the pitcher to ensure it had fresh water. "Why?"

"To visit Mr. Scollard; why else?" Aurora answered. "I wanted Courtney to meet him."

"So badly that you risked her health?"

"As I said, that was my fault," Courtney repeated. "I'd hoped Mr. Scollard could supply me with some insight—insight that would grant me a measure of peace. I begged Aurora to take me. She had little choice, other than tying me to the bed."

"Well, try to remember that your body is not always able to do what you command it to."

"I will."

Miss Payne smoothed her uniform. "I'll go assist Matilda. But I'll be back," she added pointedly, "to ensure you're still abed."

The moment the housekeeper's footsteps disappeared down the hall, Aurora dissolved into laughter. "Poor Miss Payne. She takes her job so seriously. She's worked for my family for over two decades. Papa hired her before I was born. I don't think she's ever adjusted to my unpredictable behavior, try as she might."

"Then I doubt she'll fare well with mine." Courtney gave a faint smile, which quickly faded. "I'm sorry if my stupidity yields unpleasant consequences for you. 'Twas never my intention to get you in trouble."

Aurora shrugged. "I'm always in trouble. I've learned to ignore it. And now that you're here, I have someone to ignore it with."

"None of this is going to make Slayde very happy," Courtney murmured, half to herself. "He was reluctant to take me to London because of my weakened state. I think he was quite relieved when the trip became unnecessary. And this morning, he virtually ordered me to remain at Pembourne until he returned with the investigator tonight—which I led him to believe I would."

Aurora's eyes had widened. "*You* convinced Slayde to take you to London? When?"

"We were to leave this morning in the hopes of finding Armon. But Bow Street's visit—"

"I didn't mean when were you leaving," Aurora interrupted. "I meant when did you convince him to take you?"

Warning bells. "Yesterday. When he returned from Morland."

"Amazing." Aurora shook her head. "In twenty years, I've never 'convinced' my brother to do anything." A pause. "Other than to persuade you to stay."

A faint blush crept up Courtney's neck. "Aurora . . ."

"Please don't apologize. I think it's quite extraordinary. I can scarcely wait to see where it leads."

"Where it leads?" Courtney's throat grew so tight she could scarcely speak. "Aurora, you're making far too much of this. Your brother is a fine man. That, combined with his own tragic experience, has rendered him very compassionate, with regard to me and my loss. He's trying to help me. And, yes, on some level, we understand each other." Seeing the skeptical lift of Aurora's brows, she added, "Very well, we're drawn to each other. But that's the full extent of it. There's nothing more."

"*Yet,*" Aurora qualified.

"What makes you think there will be?"

"The way your eyes light up when you speak Slayde's name. The fact that he's shared confidences with you he's firmly vowed never, ever to discuss—with me or anyone." Aurora gripped the bedpost, meeting Courtney's gaze with her own candid one. "Courtney, I don't profess to knowing my brother well. He spends more time abroad than he does at Pembourne. But I'm smart enough to understand the reason for that. He's running away from something. 'Tis only a matter of time before he realizes that something is himself and therefore cannot be escaped. If you're the one destined to help him perceive that, to give him a reason to stay, I'm elated."

Swallowing, Courtney lowered her head, staring intently at the bedcovers. "Do you believe that's possible?"

"Do you care for him?" Aurora countered.

"Yes." It was a breath of a whisper. "I know it's been less than a week. But when we're together, I feel . . . Yes."

"Then you have your answer."

"Not quite," Courtney reminded her with a rueful smile. "I think it's necessary for Slayde to return my feelings in order for your assumptions to become fact. And, given how strong his desire for autonomy is, I'm afraid I have a formidable task ahead of me."

"I agree. You're fighting a lifetime of solitude, plus Lord knows what else. But from what I've seen, you're an exceedingly good fighter."

Courtney's smile widened. "I am indeed. I'm also a dreadful loser."

"Then don't lose," Aurora replied with a conspiratorial twinkle in her eyes.

"I'll do my best."

"And you'll succeed. Because, in addition to your feelings and your determination, you'll have a wealth of opportunity. Provided by the best cohort of all—me."

Courtney leaned forward and squeezed Aurora's hand.

"Despite the tragedy that brought me to Pembourne, I'm very glad we met."

"As am I."

Aurora fell silent as Miss Payne sailed back into the room, a steaming tray in her hands. "I shooed Matilda off for some rest," she announced, setting the tray on the nightstand. "Cook prepared two portions of everything, so you two young ladies can chat while you eat." Straightening, she cast a warning glance at them both. "But once your meal is complete, Miss Johnston must rest. Is that clear?"

"Perfectly," Aurora replied. "Thank you, Miss Payne."

"You're quite welcome." The housekeeper turned to Courtney. "Eat everything on your plate. You're thin as a reed. Good food will speed your recovery."

"Yes, ma'am."

Brushing a few imaginary specks of dust from the furniture, Miss Payne took her leave.

"I'll serve us." Aurora rose, fetching the two plates of food and handing one to Courtney. "Every morsel now," she teased, dropping back into the chair. Spearing a piece of mutton, she paused, giving Courtney a quizzical look. "Does Slayde truly believe someone learned of my trip to London by pure chance and seized that opportunity to extort the black diamond?"

Courtney stopped chewing. "No."

"I thought not," Aurora replied, resuming her meal. "He believes the Duke of Morland is responsible."

"Yes, he does. In Slayde's opinion, the duke was aware of your restlessness, having had Pembourne watched long enough to determine your behavior, and was therefore awaiting just such an opportunity as the one you gave him when you dashed off to London. At which point, he acted." Courtney regarded her plate. "To me, the theory sounds a bit farfetched. On the other hand, I do agree that the duke is the most logical suspect. He loathes your family and has coveted the black diamond for years. Not to mention the fact that he was away from his estate at the time Armon was murdered."

"And sober when he returned," Aurora added, recalling the details Courtney had relayed earlier. "Maybe the idea isn't quite as extreme as it sounds. Especially given the irrational intensity of the hatred the Bencrofts have sustained for us for generations. Oh, 'tis true I never gave as much credence to Lawrence Bencroft's potential for retaliating as Slayde did—not so long as he was drunk and in seclusion. But now that all that's changed, Slayde's suspicions are more than justified."

Courtney cleared her throat. "Aurora, do you believe the Bencrofts were involved in your parents' murder?"

A flash of grief. "Honestly? I don't know."

"Forgive me," Courtney inserted at once, distressed that she'd caused Aurora pain. "I didn't mean to upset you with my question. 'Tis not my intention to hurt you. Forget I asked."

"No. Truly, it doesn't hurt to talk about it. Lord knows I rehashed it for Bow Street, and then countless times with Slayde. 'Tis only that I spent months, years, racking my brain for some detail I might have forgotten, something that could have identified their killer. The problem is, I was scarcely ten years old when it happened and was therefore sound asleep in my room, which, as you know, is one landing and half a house away from where the murder took place. I heard no commotion. The question is, was that because none occurred—that Mama and Papa knew their killer and willingly admitted him? Or is it because the murderer caught them by surprise and committed his crime so swiftly and silently that he didn't disturb the rest of the house? I simply don't know. But I *can* tell you this: I do believe that Chilton Bencroft was capable of murder."

"You remember him?"

A shiver. "I saw him but once, on that horrible day he exploded into Pembourne. 'Twas enough. Chilton Bencroft was not a man to forget. Especially if one was a child. He's the sort that leaves a lasting, terrifying image in a young mind. His eyes burned with a rage that bordered on insanity. His voice could smother the sound of thunder, and the threats he hurled at Papa were heard throughout the entire first floor of the manor—by me and the servants. And, of course, Slayde, who physically threw him out."

"What about Lawrence? Do you remember him?"

"Vaguely." Aurora frowned. "I remember only a tall, black-haired man with a drink in his hand. Chilton was so overpowering, I hardly noticed his son. Was Lawrence capable of murder? I simply don't know."

"Well, Slayde believes he was—on some level then; on all levels now. Chilton is dead. If Lawrence hired Armon to kill my father, steal his ship, and blackmail Slayde into delivering the black diamond, then he did it on his own."

"How does Slayde plan to prove this?"

"He's investigating all Lawrence's activities since his sudden re-emergence from Morland, as well as all his business dealings. If the duke is in possession of the black diamond or connected to Armon in any way, Slayde will uncover that information—and use it to condemn Morland to Newgate."

"And both your father and my parents' murders will be avenged," Aurora concluded fervently.

"Avenged, yes. Altered, no." Courtney traced the pattern of her napkin. "When I first regained consciousness, Slayde warned me that vengeance wouldn't ease the pain. He was right. If Papa is dead, no amount of retribution can bring him back. That's part of what Slayde has been grappling with all these years. He yearns for justice, yet he knows it cannot alleviate the sense of loss he's felt since your parents' deaths." She swallowed. "God, how I wish I could help him."

"I think you are—more than Slayde knows." Aurora studied Courtney's face. "Perhaps more than either of you knows." With that, she leaned forward, gesturing toward Courtney's plate. "Eat. You need your strength—to talk to the investigator and to endure being berated by my brother when he learns you attempted the lighthouse." Grinning, she cut another piece of mutton. "I don't envy you."

Both women's soft laughter trailed into the hallway, where Miss Payne hovered, ostensibly reviewing her list of the day's chores. Slipping the page into her pocket, she glanced about, confirming that the corridor was deserted. Reassured, she hurried off, acutely aware of the pressing responsibility that had just presented itself.

It was imperative that she report all she'd learned. Immediately.

Chapter 8

"Aurora, I want to speak with you—now."

Rising from her writing desk, Aurora picked up the missive she'd just addressed and tossed Slayde an unruffled look. "Of course you do." She crossed over, ignoring his formidable presence in her doorway and stepping past him into the hall. "Constance?" she called to a passing maid. "Would you mind asking Siebert to have this letter delivered to Lady Stanwyk before dark?"

"Certainly, m'lady." The girl took the note, curtsied, and went to do Aurora's bidding.

"Planning another excursion?" Slayde inquired dryly.

Aurora's smile was pure sunshine. "If I were, I'd have been smart enough to do so while you were in Dartmouth." She re-entered her chambers. "Please, do come in."

Slayde complied, shutting the door behind him. "Damnit, Aurora, what were you thinking?"

She faced her brother, arms folded across her chest, not even pretending to misunderstand the cause of his unrest. "What was I thinking? That Courtney was desperate to *do* something, to find some degree of resolution that would put her life in order. That had I refused to accompany her, she'd have attempted the lighthouse on her own—in which case, I wouldn't have been there to summon help, and she might have suffered a relapse."

"You're trying to convince me this stroll was Courtney's idea?"

"I'm not trying to *convince* you of anything. As I told Courtney, I haven't managed to do so in twenty years, so I've all but given up. I'm simply speaking the truth."

Slayde sucked in his breath. "Courtney mentioned nothing of her intentions to me—and I saw her this morning just before I left."

"I suspect she knew what your response would be and chose secrecy over warfare."

"I'm not amused."

"No, I can see that." Aurora inclined her head. "Did you hire an investigator? Is he here with you?"

"Yes. He's in the library with Courtney," Slayde bit out. His gaze probed Aurora with carefully measured concern. "Is she all right?"

Aurora nearly smiled at the unprecedented vulnerability in his tone. "Didn't you see her?"

"Only in passing. I introduced her to Mr. Oridge, who wanted to spend some time chatting with her. I'll go down and join them in a few minutes."

"But first you had to lambaste me."

"I'm not lambasting you. I'm questioning you."

"Accusing me, you mean." Aurora pressed on, not awaiting a reply. "I don't think you realize how strongminded Courtney is. She needs no one to instill ideas in her head. She does quite well on her own."

"So she tells me." The silver fire in Slayde's eyes banked a bit. "If I've been unduly harsh, I apologize." He cleared his throat. "Now, if you'll excuse me, I'll join Oridge in the library."

"Of course." Aurora watched her brother's retreating back, a smug smile curving her lips. *An apology,* she mused. *Slayde's second unprecedented act of the day.*

Perhaps it was time to stop seeking adventure outside Pembourne's iron gates. 'Twould seem that life here was about to become far more interesting.

The library was deserted when Slayde arrived. Puzzled, he walked through the hall, glancing into each room and finding them empty.

"Is something amiss, m'lord?" Siebert inquired from the entranceway.

"I was under the impression Miss Johnston and Mr. Oridge were in the library. Evidently, I was mistaken."

"I believe they were there for ten minutes or so, sir. Then they each retired to their respective chambers."

"I see." Slayde was already in motion, retracing his path up the stairs, this time taking them two at a time.

"Come in," Courtney responded to his knock.

Slayde stepped inside, immediately spying Courtney where she stood by the open window, gazing out across the drive.

"Are you all right?" Slayde shut the door behind him.

"Yes," she murmured without turning. "I was just thinking that this window does not provide a full and proper view of your estate. The grounds of Pembourne are far more extensive than I ever anticipated." Sighing, she pivoted, facing Slayde as a prisoner would a firing squad. "But then, I suspect my encounter with your grounds is precisely the subject you've come to address."

"First tell me why your conversation with Oridge was so brief."

Courtney fingered the folds of her gown. "Your investigator is a most insightful man. I think he realized I was not myself. And since he intends to remain here most of tomorrow, gathering whatever information he can, he suggested we postpone our in-depth discussion until morning, after which he'll take one of your ships and leave directly from Devonshire."

"A sound idea."

"'Twas Mr. Oridge's." Courtney tucked a loose strand of hair behind her ear, her mouth curving impishly. "But, given you think the suggestion is sound, I'm sure you guessed whose idea it was. I have the distinct feeling you don't think much of my ideas at the moment."

Slayde didn't return her smile. "So Aurora *was* speaking the truth. You *did* initiate this afternoon's foolhardy stunt."

"You've already spoken to Aurora?" Courtney shook her head in exasperation. "I wish you had more faith in your sister. She's neither an idiot nor a child. And she's certainly not a liar. I hope you didn't vent your rage at her."

"I started to. She stopped me."

"Good. Because she truly tried to dissuade me from going. I wouldn't listen."

"Why not?"

Courtney's lashes fanned her cheeks. "You know the answer to that. I need to *do* something. I thought perhaps a conversation with Mr. Scollard would provide some sort of sign."

Slayde crossed over, gripped her shoulders. "A sign of what? Whether your father is alive? Courtney, Mr. Scollard is just a man, not a god—regardless of what Aurora has told you."

A painful silence.

"Courtney . . ." Slayde wanted to recall his words and shake some sense into her all at once.

"Slayde, this is a futile argument. Besides, we have more important things to discuss." Tilting back her head, Courtney searched his face. "Did you learn anything in Dartmouth?"

"Not much." Slayde's gaze fell immediately to her lips. Damn. What was there about this woman that reduced every ounce of his resolve, his long-standing vows to ashes? He'd spent the entire carriage ride to Dartmouth reminding himself why he had to keep away from her, to disregard the pull between them. Yet here he was, home not an hour, and all he could think of was holding her in his arms, tasting her mouth.

"Slayde?" Courtney's expression was quizzical. "Are you keeping something from me?"

"No." He forced himself to remember the fundamental issue at hand. "I asked a lot of questions, got the names of three merchants who were reputedly adept at forgery and were rumored to handle disreputable business transactions. However, two of them are in prison and one has relocated to Paris to bleed fresh prey. None of them was in Dartmouth this past month and therefore none could have been Armon's contact. There was a fourth fellow mentioned, a John Grimes, an unsavory merchant who apparently sells everything from valuable paintings to gems. Unfortunately, he has conveniently been out of town since yesterday, not due to return until next week. I didn't leave my name, only the fact that I'm in search of a particular painting and that he was mentioned as a possible source. This way, he won't be forewarned and try to bolt. But when he returns from his little holiday, I'll be waiting.

"As for Armon's known contacts," Slayde continued with a disgusted frown, "I was in and out of every pub in Dartmouth, handing out pound notes by the dozens. The lowlifes that frequent the places took my money, admitted to knowing Armon, then proceeded to tell me precisely what we already knew: that Armon captained the *Fortune;* that he and his men were notorious for the booty they obtained at sea; that of late, Armon had taken to bragging that very soon he'd be coming into a huge sum—enough to keep him fat and happy for life. None of which is any great revelation. So, effectively, I have nothing concrete to report."

"I see." Beneath his hands, Slayde could feel Courtney's shoulders tense.

"We've just begun," he told her quietly. "We *will* unravel this mystery. Remember, I gave you my word."

That wrenching smile. "I haven't forgotten. 'Tis what keeps me going when all else seems hopeless."

"Cutterton said you'd collapsed." Slayde's voice sounded hoarse, even to his own ears. "That he carried you back to the manor."

"'Tis true. He was extremely kind."

"And *you* are extremely weak." Slayde's hands glided up to frame her face. "What must I do to keep you from jeopardizing your recovery? Lock you in your room?"

"That depends. Would you stay locked in with me?" The instant the words were out, Courtney looked positively mortified, as if she wanted to sink through the floor and die. Her face grew hot beneath Slayde's palms, twin spots of crimson staining her cheeks nearly as red as her hair. "Forgive me . . . I . . ."

"Yes," he heard himself say, touched by her heartfelt candor, propelled by something far stronger than his resistance. "Yes, I'd stay with you." With that, he lowered his head and covered her mouth with his.

It was as natural as it was overpowering, their hearts and bodies hurtling to life, clamoring simultaneously for more. The kiss sizzled, burned, exploded, and preliminaries were cast aside, unwanted, intolerable.

With an inarticulate sound of joy, Courtney flung herself into the embrace, opening to Slayde's penetration, rising onto her toes to give him better access.

Ardently, Slayde seized what she offered, frantic to hold her, to taste her, to absorb the miraculous balm she provided, to fill the unknown void within him that seemed suddenly endless, unendurable. "Courtney." His fingers clenched in her hair, handfuls of rich, cool silk, his tongue possessing her mouth, melding with hers. He felt a shiver run through her, her arms entwining more tightly about his neck, deepening a kiss that was already out of control.

Control be damned.

Slayde pulled Courtney against him, his lips leaving hers to blaze a heated trail down her neck, her throat, the upper swell of her breasts. He could still remember the way her naked skin had felt against his palm, her nipple hardening, her breast swelling to his caress. God, he'd driven himself half crazy remembering, fervently wishing he'd never touched her, more fervently wishing he'd never stopped.

"Oh, Slayde." His name was a breath of a whisper, vibrating against his lips as they traced her bodice. "That feels so . . ."

"I know." His mouth returned to hers, devouring her with an urgency that precluded all else. With shaking hands, he unbuttoned her gown, finding the smooth skin of her back and shuddering at the unbearable agony of desire spawned by even the simplest, most innocent contact.

Unthinking, uncaring, Slayde swept Courtney to the bed, followed her down, desire coursing through him in wide, hot rivers of need. "I want you," he rasped against her mouth. "God, Courtney, I've never wanted like this."

If she answered, he didn't hear. Having slipped her gown from her shoulders, he tugged down her chemise, nearly insane with the need to see her, taste her, touch her again. He could scarcely breathe past the pounding in his chest, a pounding that intensified at his first glimpse of her utterly flawless beauty. For an endless moment, he just stared, transfixed by the soft, delicate mounds, the pale pink nipples that were hardening beneath his gaze.

"Slayde?"

Somewhere in the dim recesses of his mind he heard her. "What?" He virtually tore his gaze away, forced himself to meet her shy, uncertain look.

"Am I all right?" she whispered.

"All right?" He could scarcely speak. "You're . . ." How in God's name could he find the right words when they had yet to be invented? "You're a miracle."

Courtney's eyes filled with tears. "So are you."

A stab of guilt lanced Slayde's heart. "No, sweetheart, I'm not." He lowered his head, kissed the hollow between her breasts, steeling himself to stop at that. "I'm anything but a miracle."

"You saved my life," she whispered, her fingers sifting through his hair. "And awakened feelings inside me I never knew existed. If that's not a miracle, what is?"

Her poignant declaration gave Slayde the strength he'd lacked.

Slowly, he raised up, met her misty gaze. "I'm a Huntley, sweetheart. That's a curse, not a miracle."

"I don't believe in curses. Neither do you. You told me so yourself."

"I said I didn't believe the black diamond was cursed," he corrected. "Unfortunately, the search for it is. And my family is right in the middle of that search."

"The search is over."

"No. It's not."

"As far as the Huntleys are concerned, it is. You delivered the diamond to Armon."

"No, I didn't."

A shocked silence, broken only by the ticking of the clock.

"What did you say?" Courtney asked at last.

Slayde sat up, torn between emotion and pragmatism, protection and candor. "We need to talk."

"Evidently we do." Courtney pushed herself to a sitting position, tugging up her gown in awkward, self-conscious motions.

"Let me." Slayde readjusted her clothing, wishing he could recall his frank outburst. Damn. He never involved anyone in his decisions, never divulged his thoughts or his actions, least of all now, when there was so much at stake. Why the hell had he suddenly become unable to keep his mouth shut? Was he losing his heart *and* his mind?

"I can't reach the buttons. If you would just fasten them, I'll manage the rest." Courtney's head was bowed, her voice muffled as she struggled with the back of the gown.

Studying the lustrous crown of red-gold hair, Slayde experienced a wave of shame and regret. He was responsible for Courtney's self-censure, her humiliation. He'd acted selfishly, incited by his unprecedented, burgeoning feelings—something he'd had no right to do. For although she obliterated his control, his reason, his sanity, he'd taken advantage of her, knowing there could be no future between them, knowing he'd cause her naught but pain. And now, what in God's name could he say to ease the confusion and self-doubt she was feeling?

Ease them? Hell, he was about to intensify them.

"Courtney." He hooked his forefinger beneath her chin. "Before I delve into what I suspect will be a very complicated explanation, it's important to me that you know I meant every word I said a few minutes ago. You're beautiful. And I've never wanted anyone the way I want you."

"I believe you." Courtney raised her head, and Slayde was startled to see none of the shame and remorse he'd expected. To the contrary, the sea-green eyes that searched his face were soft, not with contrition, but with concern. "You needn't convince me. Nor console me. I don't regret a moment of what just happened—*almost* happened," she amended. "What I do regret is your reasons for pulling away."

"You don't know what those reasons are."

"Perhaps not. But I suspect they stem from your notion of protection. Protection *and* self-protection."

Her assessment diverted Slayde from the disclosure he was about to make. "Self-protection?"

"Of course." Courtney sighed. "You're even more accomplished at that than you are at protecting others. The latter you're aware of; the former, you're not."

Her depth of insight was staggering, and—if the constriction in his gut was any indication—accurate. "Tell me, since I'm unaware of it: what is it I'm protecting myself from?"

"Hurt. Allowing someone into your life, your heart. Allowing that someone to penetrate thirty-one years of solitude—solitude reinforced by the pain of your parents' deaths." She lay her palm against his jaw. "I don't blame you, Slayde. 'Tis far easier, far safer, to remain detached."

"Safer, yes," he said with an ironic shake of his head. "Easier? Not since I met you."

A tremulous smile. "I feel it, too, you know."

"I know you do. And, self-protection notwithstanding, it can't happen. *We* can't happen." Slayde wrenched away, stalking the length of the bedchamber, halting at the window.

"Where is the diamond, Slayde?"

"I haven't a clue." He grasped the curtain, crushing the fine material in his fist. "I've never laid eyes on it."

Another heartbeat of silence.

"Then what did you give Armon?"

"A fake. A damned good one, created by the best and most discreet jeweler in England."

Slayde heard Courtney's sharp intake of breath. "I don't understand. How could a jeweler craft a replica of something no living soul has seen? What did he model it after? And how could he make it authentic enough to fool a discerning eye?"

"A never-before-seen gem is far and away the easiest one to duplicate. After all, there's no one to contradict the authenticity of its form. Its worth? Ah, that's another thing entirely. So, in answer to your last question, my copy *wouldn't* fool a discerning eye. Fortunately, Armon didn't possess that eye; nor, for that matter, does the man he worked for—unless he happens to be an authority on jewels. More likely, only the expert who eventually purchases the stone will be proficient enough to discern the truth." Slayde stared, unseeing, across Pembourne's lawns. "I was in an unthinkable quandary. So far as I knew, Aurora had been kidnapped. The bastard who had her was demanding something the whereabouts of which I knew nothing. My only choice was to convince him I could produce the stone in exchange for Aurora's life. Oh, I suppose I could have ransacked the caves of

Cornwall, praying I'd stumble upon the diamond. But, given that generations of men have done so and failed, the odds and the timing were against me. I had mere days to come up with an alternative. So I did. I sought out a brilliant jeweler who happens also to be a colleague—a trusted one. He fashioned a makeshift diamond for me. It was easy enough. After all, we weren't concerned about the accuracy of each and every facet; as I said, no one alive today has ever seen this gem, and descriptions of it are as legendary as they are varied. In terms of color, onyx made a fine substitute. The damned fake was so good, I myself half believed it was genuine."

"Why did you lead everyone, including Aurora and me, to believe you'd conveyed the actual diamond to Armon?"

Slayde's lips thinned into a determined line. "That protective instinct you just referred to. Aurora is terrified of the curse. If you recall, she believes it to be fact. I had no intention of destroying her peace of mind with the truth. And you? You have the same active mind as Aurora. Had I told you the truth, you would have immediately begun contemplating the possible ramifications: would Armon discover the switch? If so, would he retaliate? And how? No, Courtney," Slayde gave an adamant shake of his head. "You needed no further worries to hinder your healing process." A pause. "Moreover, I'm not in the habit of confiding in others."

"I realize that," Courtney replied softly. "And I'm grateful you decided to make an exception. You have my word: I will never breach your trust."

A hard lump formed in his throat. "I know that."

"Then why, Slayde? Why can't we happen?"

He released the curtain still clenched in his fist, watching it unfold and float back into place. "I made a vow to myself the day my parents died," he revealed, his voice low and rough. "I vowed never to permit another soul to be hurt by that bloody curse."

"What has that to do with—" Courtney inhaled sharply. "You're afraid that if you let me become part of your life, I, too, will be endangered?"

"Precisely. 'Tis only a matter of time before my hoax is discovered. Then, we'll be right back where we started, with every fortune-seeking vulture on earth pursuing the black diamond—and the Huntleys."

"But how could they possibly reach—much less hurt—me? You keep Pembourne guarded like a fortress."

"And living within the walls of a fortress would please you?"

"I'm doing so now."

"You're injured and weak now. Moreover, Aurora needs you. None of those situations is permanent. When they change, you'll be able to leave Pembourne, unafraid and unconnected to the Huntleys."

"Slayde . . ." He heard the rustle of her gown as she rose and came to stand beside him. "I can never be unconnected to the Huntleys. Not after all that's happened." She touched his sleeve. "Physical joinings are not the only type that bind people together. In fact, I suspect they pale in comparison to other, more profound types of joinings, such as those of the mind, the heart—"

"Stop." Slayde caught her elbows, dragging her close enough to see the torment in his eyes. "Don't you understand what I'm telling you? I intend the Huntley name to die with me. There will be no wife, no children, no legacy to keep the curse alive. There will be only generations of greedy men, casting themselves into a living hell as they ransack the globe for the diamond, breeding others to do the same. But there will be no more Huntley prey upon which to feed."

Courtney gasped as she realized the implication of Slayde's assertion. "You'd do that to yourself? Live and die alone just to protect those who might not seek such protection if they were asked?"

"Yes."

"What about Aurora? She's a Huntley. And, as you

just said, you can't chain her within Pembourne's walls forever."

"I don't intend to. My goal for Aurora is to see her safely wed—to a man who will give her *his* name and *his* protection—after which she'll cease to be a Huntley."

"So that's what you meant when you said Aurora's need for me is temporary."

Slayde nodded tersely. "Soon Aurora will leave Pembourne, move on to her own life—one of security and freedom. And wealth. In addition to whatever affluence her future husband can and will provide, she'll also inherit the entire Huntley estate."

"After you die," Courtney qualified.

"After I die," he repeated.

"Damn you." Golden sparks ignited Courtney's eyes. "How can you speak of your life as if it were nothing more than an extraneous but necessary evil, a mere steppingstone for others? You're a wonderful man. You will *not* condemn yourself to a lifetime of loneliness just to stave off a tragedy that might never occur." She raised her chin a notch. "I won't let you."

"You won't let—" Slayde broke off, staring in astonishment. Whatever reaction he'd expected, it hadn't been this. Actually, now that he considered it, the reaction he'd expected, knowing how tender-hearted Courtney was, was aching compassion followed by saddened acceptance. Or, given the intensity of their recent physical encounter, maybe even disenchantment that he'd allowed things between them to progress so far when there was virtually no hope for a future.

Instead, she was renouncing his decision and vowing to resurrect his life, intent on saving him from himself.

His autonomous heart yielded a bit more. And his precarious resolve intensified.

"Thank you," he murmured solemnly, brushing his knuckles across Courtney's cheek. "I'm humbled. No one has ever . . ." He cleared his throat. "I'm also adamant about my vow. Now more than ever." He silenced her protest by pressing a gentle forefinger to her lips. "Don't. I won't change my mind. And I assure you, not even your will is strong enough to bend mine." With an excruciating effort, he released her and walked away. "I'll be leaving Pembourne first thing in the morning."

"Tomorrow?" Courtney sounded shaken, whether from his pronouncement or their discussion, Slayde wasn't certain. "But Mr. Oridge is here," she added.

"I realize that, but 'tis you he needs to speak with, not I."

"In other words, you're running away."

Slayde pivoted, his eyes narrowing on her face. "No. I'm riding to Morland. Or at least to the outskirts of the estate where my investigator is posted. I want to ascertain if he's learned anything of interest. If Morland has made any unexpected trips, met with anyone of import or means, I'll ride back into the village, seek out Morland's banker and solicitor, and exert more pressure—I hope enough to unnerve one of them into divulging even the smallest of incriminating details. As for Oridge, I'll return in ample time to meet with him before sending him off in one of my ships to pursue the *Fortune.*"

"I see." Courtney's tone told him she still believed he was running away.

Hell, she was right. He was.

"Slayde?"

"What?" He watched her cross towards him, and he battled the urge to drag her into his arms, vows be damned.

"The duke might be dangerous," she murmured, laying her palm against his jaw. "Be careful."

"I will."

Tension crackled between them.

Abruptly, Courtney rose on her toes, wrapped her arms about Slayde's neck, and tugged his mouth down to hers.

He made a rough sound deep in his throat, pulling her to him and burying his lips in hers for one long, unendurable—and final—moment.

At last he broke away, feeling a tangible emptiness as

their bodies separated, fervently wishing he were anything but a Huntley. God, he didn't want to let her go. All he wanted was to lose himself inside the gift she offered.

But he couldn't. He cared too damned much, more than he himself had realized until this very moment.

With a muttered oath, he turned on his heel, leaving the embrace, the bedchamber, and Courtney behind.

Because he had to.

Chapter 9

Aurora scooted up the path leading to the manor, glancing at the position of the sun. It couldn't be much past seven, she decided. It had been dark when she'd left for the lighthouse at half after five. But now the household was up and about, and she was eager to return in time for Courtney's meeting with Mr. Oridge and for Elinore's impending visit.

The drive came into view, and Aurora halted, startled to see Slayde's phaeton, ready to go, and her brother, who was in the process of climbing into the front seat and taking up the reins.

"Slayde?" She called his name, taking the remaining distance between them at a dead run.

Slayde's head snapped about, and he scowled, looking as cantankerous as his guards did after one of her escapes. "What is it, Aurora?"

"Where on earth are you going? Isn't Mr. Oridge speaking with Courtney this morning?"

"To Newton Abbot. And yes. Now, does that satisfactorily answer your questions?"

She blinked, taking in the deep circles under his eyes. Clearly, he hadn't slept a wink. "What's the matter? Is something wrong?"

"Nothing's wrong," Slayde snapped, fingers tightening about the reins. "I'm just eager to be on my way. And, lest you forget, I'm not required to give you a schedule of my comings and goings. If I recall correctly, 'tis the other way around—not that you adhere to that principle. Good day."

With a slap of the reins, he was gone.

Aurora stood, gaping after him, wondering what had inspired his black mood. Had he and Courtney argued? 'Twas possible, especially if he'd given Courtney an especially bad time of it during his lecture about her attempted walk to the lighthouse. Or was it something else, something to do with the mystery?

This did indeed require investigation.

Bursting through the front door, Aurora nearly knocked Siebert over.

"Oh, forgive me, Siebert," she apologized at once. "'Tis just that I'm in a frightful hurry."

"Of course you are, m'lady." With a resigned sigh, Siebert recovered his balance and his dignity.

"Where is Courtney? Is she awake? Abed? At breakfast? She hasn't begun her meeting with Mr. Oridge yet, has she?"

"No, m'lady, she has not. Miss Johnston is taking breakfast in her bedchamber in order to conserve strength for her conversation with Mr. Oridge."

"I see. Thank you." Lifting her skirts, Aurora fairly flew up the stairs, rapping soundly on Courtney's door. "Courtney? May I come in?" she asked, pressing the latch and stepping inside.

Seated at the table by the window, Courtney had her head bowed over an object clutched in her hands. Looking up, she gave Aurora a tolerant smile. "It appears you're already in."

"I'm sorry." Aurora glanced from the tears on Courtney's lashes to the timepiece in her grasp. "I shouldn't have burst in like an unruly child. 'Twas very rude of me. I'll come back later."

"No, please stay." Courtney beckoned to her. "I'd welcome the company, truly."

"If you're sure." Aurora hesitated, torn between compassion and eagerness.

"I'm sure."

"Good." That settled, Aurora shut the door and came to sit beside Courtney. "You were thinking of your father."

"Yes." Courtney stroked the timepiece. "I was wishing he were here to advise me. I'm too much a novice, I'm afraid."

"A novice? At what? Perhaps I can help."

"No, somehow I don't think you're in a much better position than I to offer advice. Not in this area, that is."

"You might be surprised. Try me."

Silence.

"Slayde," Aurora pronounced. She grinned at Courtney's surprised expression. "Don't look so shocked. I may be, as you so aptly put it, 'a novice' at matters of the heart, but one needn't touch a flame in order to know it burns. Besides, I saw my brother as he prepared to leave Pembourne. 'Twas a first, to say the least."

"What do you mean?"

"I mean he would have cheerfully run me down, that's how out of sorts he was. In fact, he was downright irrational. And, trust me, Courtney, Slayde is *never*, *never* irrational. Intense, yes. Detached, definitely. But irrational? No. He simmers beneath the surface, churns with emotions he'd never permit himself to express. But outwardly, he remains composed—even when I know he'd like nothing better than to thrash me. He simply doesn't do things like explode or lose control—until now." Aurora's grin widened. "In my assessment, only two instigators could have provoked my brother into losing his unshakable control: Lawrence Bencroft or you. Bearing that in mind, I came to your chambers, only to find you misty-eyed and upset. If I add the two incidents together, it doesn't take a genius to guess which of the two instigators it was."

"I suppose not."

"Did the two of you argue?" Aurora pressed.

"Not really, no. An argument would have been welcome compared to the discussion we had."

"What kind of discussion?" Seeing Courtney shift uncomfortably in her chair, Aurora added, "I realize I'm prying. But I can't very well help you overcome the obstacles if I don't know what those obstacles are."

Courtney sighed, laying her father's timepiece on the table. "The only obstacle I see is also the most difficult to surmount: Slayde himself."

"Are you in love with him?"

A faint smile. "Didn't you already put that question to me?"

"No. The question I put to you was 'Do you care for him?' To which you replied, 'Yes,' Now I'm asking something more. Are you in love with my brother?"

"Yes," Courtney heard herself whisper, startling as the fervent affirmation left her lips. *'Tis true,* she thought, the realization flooding her heart. *The very answer I've sought has found me—just as Papa predicted.* "Unbearably so," she added softly.

"Are you sure?"

"Extremely sure."

Aurora looked fascinated. "I've never been in love."

"Nor I."

"Then how can you be so certain? And in so brief a time?"

Courtney's lips curved. "A very intelligent friend of mine once said, 'One needn't touch a flame in order to know it burns.'"

"Ah. A wise friend indeed." Aurora's eyes sparkled. "Very well, in light of your answer, we must bring Slayde around without delay."

All humor vanished from Courtney's face. "You have no idea how formidable a task that promises to be."

"Don't underestimate my brother's feelings for you, Courtney. I believe he's equally as smitten as you. Which, for a man like Slayde—one who's accustomed to depending only upon himself—is akin to drowning."

" 'Tis more than Slayde's emotional independence at stake," Courtney revealed. "It's . . ." She paused, weighing her words carefully. She'd vowed to Slayde not to divulge the truth about his fraudulent diamond, and she intended to keep that vow. "He fears for my safety. Not only my safety but the safety of anyone he cares for. He's sworn to preclude any potential danger by forsaking any future ties."

Aurora frowned. "The black diamond is gone from our lives, along with its horrifying curse. I gather, therefore, that what you're telling me has something to do with the Bencrofts and Slayde's belief that they're determined to punish us and forever exact their revenge."

"That's exactly what I'm telling you. Slayde doesn't believe the curse lies with the diamond, but with the men who vie for it. Most especially, with the Bencrofts, whose hatred he's convinced will never be extinguished. You of all people know how staunchly he believes that. 'Tis why he's so watchful of you and your whereabouts. Well, his protective convictions go far deeper than that." Courtney met Aurora's questioning gaze. "To put it bluntly, Slayde refuses to carry on the Huntley name, either through marriage or by siring a child. He's determined to let the hatred die with him."

Aurora sat bolt upright. "He told you this? That he intends never to marry or father children?"

"Yes."

To Courtney's amazement, Aurora clapped her hands together in glee. "This is even more wonderful than I thought."

"Aurora, did you hear what I just said?"

"Of course I did. The question is, did you?"

"Did I what?" Courtney was beginning to think she'd lost her mind.

"Did you hear what you just said—or rather, implied?" With an impatient shake of her head, Aurora rushed on. "No, evidently you didn't, or you wouldn't look so morose. Courtney, why would Slayde be telling you something so pointed, so intimate, if he weren't falling in love with you? The answer is, he wouldn't." She jumped to her feet, nearly dancing about in joyful anticipation. "This task is going to be easier than I thought."

"The man intends never to marry or sire children," Courtney repeated—for her own sake as well as Aurora's. "You don't find that a bit daunting?"

A shrug. "Not particularly. It doesn't surprise me; as you yourself just said, I know how certain my brother is that the Bencrofts orchestrated every tragedy the Huntleys have ever endured. Also, given Slayde's propensity for solitude, I suspect he never envisioned needing anyone, much less loving her, enough to alter his decision. But all that's changed now. He's in love. He's vulnerable."

"And he's going to fight it every inch of the way," Courtney reminded her.

"Indeed." Aurora's face lit up. "But then it wouldn't be a challenge if he didn't, now would it?"

Unbidden laughter bubbled up inside Courtney. "You're astonishing."

"Nothing like Slayde, am I?" Aurora quipped back.

Sobering, Courtney refuted her friend's statement. "To the contrary, you're a great deal more alike than I originally surmised. You're both strong-willed, loyal, and stubborn, with enormous hearts and brilliant minds. The difference is in the way you express those traits, not in your intrinsic characters."

"I don't understand my brother," Aurora said frankly. "And he understands me even less."

"I realize that," Courtney murmured. *I also intend to change it,* she vowed silently. *'Twill be my special gift to you both; perhaps the only one I can offer to sufficiently thank you for what you've given me.*

"In any case, each of our tasks is clear," Aurora concluded. "You must seize every opportunity and use it to make Slayde see the truth: that his love for you is far more pivotal than any foolish vow he made to himself before the two of you met. And that together you can overcome anything, even the Bencrofts."

"Only that?" Courtney teased. "Tell me, is your task equally as simple?"

"Not simple, but creative. 'Tis my job to ensure that you have innumerable opportunities to do your job."

"Ah. Need I remind you that Slayde is a skilled and seasoned loner who's adamant about remaining so?"

"No, you needn't." Aurora's grin was impish. " 'Twould seem, my friend, that two novices are about to undo one expert."

"Very well, Miss Johnston." Oridge scribbled down a few additional notes, then raised his head and leveled his keen investigator's gaze on Courtney. "We've gone over all the events you can recall from the time this Armon seized the *Isobel* to the time Lord Pembourne rescued you from the channel. You've given me detailed descriptions of the pirates who accompanied Armon onto your ship. And you've provided me with a list of names of the entire crew of the *Isobel*."

"That's correct, sir." Courtney massaged her temples, wishing the throbbing in her head would subside. Then again, how could she expect that it would? After all, she and Mr. Oridge had been ensconced in the library for what seemed like an eternity, hashing and rehashing the events that had brought her to Pembourne.

Inadvertently, her gaze wandered to the library's grandfather clock. Half after three. With the exception of a thirty-minute meal in the adjoining salon and one much-needed hour-long nap in her chambers, she'd been seated on the sofa since nine o'clock this morning, reliving the most harrowing experience of her life. She felt utterly drained and physically spent. And her concussion had little to do with it.

"Are you all right, Miss Johnston?"

Her head jerked around and, seeing the genuine concern on the investigator's face, she felt a stab of guilt. "Forgive me, Mr. Oridge. Yes, I'm fine."

"No apology is necessary." He closed his portfolio. "I realize how difficult this must be for you—in more ways than one." He cleared his throat, speaking in a low, reassuring tone. "Answering countless questions is exhausting. Far more exhausting, in fact, than asking them."

Courtney gave him a weak smile, grateful for his attempt to put her at ease. "I have little patience for these lingering injuries of mine. If only my strength were back, I'd go after the *Fortune* myself."

"Then how fortunate your strength hasn't cooperated," Oridge returned curtly, all semblance of compassion having vanished. Leaning forward, he gripped his knees, an intense expression on his face. "Miss Johnston, I'm going to be blunt. Traversing the ocean as a sea captain's daughter does not make you a seasoned navigator. You might think you know a great deal about ships. Trust me, you don't. Not when it comes to dangerous matters like pursuing a pirate ship *and* dealing with the pirates once you've found them. So if you have any heroic notions of striking out on your own, forget them. I'm good at what I do. If Armon's ship can be found, I'll find it. And you'll stay alive in the process. Am I making myself clear?"

"Perfectly clear."

"Good. Then I have only one more question for you. What kind of cargo was the *Isobel* carrying?"

"If you're asking if our cargo was valuable enough to pilfer, the answer is yes. We transported furniture and other manufactured goods to the Colonies."

"Furniture? Unlikely," Oridge muttered. "Other goods . . . such as what?"

"Pardon me?"

"Was there anything on board your ship that would

bring a nice sum but was less cumbersome to transfer than furniture?"

"Why, yes." Courtney had no idea what avenue Oridge was pursuing, but she followed nonetheless. "I wasn't privy to a full list of our cargo, but I do recall there were silver pieces, vases, and several expensive wooden clocks aboard. Are those the type of things you mean?"

"Those are exactly the things I mean." Oridge came to his feet. "Thank you, Miss Johnston, you've been a great help. I suggest you go to your chambers now and rest."

Courtney rose as swiftly as he. "What is it I helped you with? What prospect are you entertaining?"

"As I said, you're pale and weary." He crossed over, pulled open the library door and gestured for her to pass. "I'm sure the earl will fill you in on whatever you need to know."

Slowly, Courtney walked toward him, halting only when she'd reached the open doorway. "You're not going to tell me anything, are you, Mr. Oridge?"

"No, Miss Johnston, I'm not."

She nodded, frustration screaming along every nerve ending in her body. "I don't like your answer. But I respect it. The earl is your employer. Any conclusions you reach, you must first discuss with him."

"Thank you for your understanding," Oridge said with businesslike formality.

"You're welcome." Courtney stepped into the hallway, feeling baffled and weary and far too stimulated to rest. Until Slayde returned to answer her questions, she feared sleep was out of the question.

"Pardon me, Miss Johnston."

Courtney turned to see Siebert standing a few feet away. "Yes?"

"Lady Aurora asked me to give you a message when you'd finished speaking with Mr. Oridge. Which I presume you have?" Receiving Courtney's confirming nod, he continued. "She asked if you'd join her and the viscountess in the yellow salon. That is, if you're not too fatigued. Lady Aurora did specify that she'd understand if you preferred to retire to your chambers." The tone of Siebert's voice clearly stated that Lady Aurora would understand no such thing.

With a glimmer of humor, Courtney replied, "Thank you, Siebert. I'll join them at once."

Recalling the location of the yellow salon, she made her way there, knocking politely before entering.

"Come in," Aurora called out. Her eyes brightened when she saw who her visitor was. "Oh, Courtney." She jumped to her feet. "I'm so glad you're able to join us. At long last, I can introduce you to Elinore."

The elegant woman seated alongside Aurora rose, a smile of welcome on her face. "Miss Johnston, I'm delighted. Aurora has spoken of you with such enthusiasm."

"As she has of you," Courtney reciprocated, feeling suddenly shy. Lady Stanwyk was not at all the plump, gray-haired, motherly figure she'd expected. She was exquisite: all rose-colored silk and glittering jewels, her dark hair upswept and curled just so, her demeanor polished, regal.

"Please, dear, sit down and have some tea." Evidently, the viscountess sensed her unease, for she beckoned Courtney in, pouring a cup of tea and offering it to her along with a plate of scones. "Aurora has been filling me in on the past week's dreadful events. Please accept my condolences. Your loss must be very painful. Not to mention how difficult today must have been, between answering endless questions and reliving your harrowing experience. I appreciate the fact that you were kind enough to join us when I'm sure you'd much rather be abed."

"I . . . thank you." Courtney accepted the proffered refreshment, lowering herself gratefully to the settee. Beneath Lady Stanwyk's warmth and compassion, she could feel her shyness wane. "Actually, I'm glad for the company. When Siebert found me, I was contemplating what to do, given that I felt too drained to do much of anything, yet far too awake to lie down. Tea and pleasant conversation are precisely what I need."

"Perfect," Aurora proclaimed. "Because tea and pleasant conversation are precisely what Elinore and I are indulging in." Helping herself to another scone, she sat down beside Courtney. "Elinore received my missive. She was generous enough, as always, to respond immediately."

"I had no idea what was transpiring at Pembourne, else I would have been here sooner." The viscountess resettled herself and took up her cup, sipping her tea gracefully. "I'm still having trouble digesting all this. When Slayde said he'd received ransom notes during your absence, I had no idea he meant anything of this magnitude."

"Why would you?" Aurora turned to Courtney. "We get threatening letters on a steady basis. Or rather, we *did,*" she corrected herself, relief evident in her every word. "Because of that wretched black diamond. Thank God it's gone."

Courtney felt a stab of guilt, one she firmly squelched by reminding herself that Slayde's deception had been effected with Aurora's well-being in mind. "I can understand your feelings."

"And *I* can understand why that dreadful pirate chose your father's ship to attack," Elinore put in, studying Courtney before glancing briefly at Aurora. "There is a striking resemblance between the two of you. A cursory one, to be sure. But more than enough to fool Slayde on a dark night at sea. The poor man must have been beside himself. No wonder he was so irate when we arrived home from London."

"Speaking of London . . ." Aurora leaned forward. "That brings us to the reason for my missive. Elinore, I awaited Courtney's arrival to address the subject, because we have an important question to ask you—one that affects Courtney as much, if not more, than it does me. I pray your answer will help shed some light on whoever, if anyone, was working with this Armon."

Elinore's brow furrowed. "Of course, anything. How can I help you?"

Aurora sighed. "At the risk of bringing up a sore point, it concerns my trip to London—the one you and I just made."

"What about it?"

"During the fortnight we were making our arrangements, do you recall discussing them with anyone? Or if not discussing them, mentioning the possibility that I might be arriving in Town?"

An affectionate gleam lit Elinore's eyes. "Of course I mentioned it. I was far too excited to keep the news to myself. Further, how else would I ensure the deluge of invitations that awaited us upon our arrival? When Lady Southington and Lady Hucknell came to tea the previous week, I made certain they understood the situation—how important it was for the right people to include us on their guest lists. After all, this was your first trip to London; I wanted it to be everything you craved. I emphasized that very thing to my staff when I assigned two dozen of them to go on ahead and open the town house. I wanted everything perfect for you: your room, your social calendar." Seeing Aurora slump down on the sofa, Elinore paused, the sparkle extinguished from her eyes. "I assume that's not what you wanted to hear."

"No," Aurora replied. "But the fault lies with me, not you. I never told you I intended the trip to be kept secret—most probably, because I wanted just the opposite: for the *ton* to welcome me with open arms. In truth, I'd have been thrilled if the whole bloody world knew—so long as Slayde didn't."

Elinore gave her a stern, measured look. "Then Slayde was right. You really did intend to go without his knowledge."

"No, I intended to *ride off* without his knowledge," Aurora corrected. *"And* to travel too far for him to drag me back. After which I assumed he'd find the note I left him and accept my decision, however unwillingly. Had I any clue . . ." Her voice trailed off.

"I'm not sure I understand your line of thinking." Elinore shook her head in puzzlement.

"Forgive me, Lady Stanwyk," Courtney put in. "All this is my idea. I wondered if perhaps someone else was involved in Aurora's feigned kidnapping, someone who learned ahead of time that she'd be in London and therefore arranged with Armon to send the notes and seize the *Isobel* during her absence."

"I see." Comprehension dawned on Elinore's face. "And you were hoping I could shed some light on who that someone else might be."

"Exactly."

Aurora shook her head in disgust. "The answer to that is any one of five hundred people, thanks to me."

"Stop it." Courtney squeezed Aurora's arm. "You had no way of knowing about Armon or his plan. You were simply planning a pleasurable trip with the viscountess."

"I, too, feel dreadful," Elinore murmured, lowering her cup and saucer to the table.

"Please don't blame yourself, my lady," Courtney said. "Neither you nor Aurora did anything wrong. I didn't expect this avenue to lead us anywhere; the whole idea was farfetched. I merely wanted to leave no stone unturned. The last thing I wish is for the two of you to feel guilty. So, please, let's just drop the subject. All right?"

"All right." For a moment, Elinore fell silent, assessing Courtney's dejected state. "I have a suggestion," she said at last. "'Tis late, and you're exhausted. Why don't I return tomorrow and the three of us can spend a lovely afternoon together. In fact, I'll speak to your cook and ask her to prepare a picnic lunch. We'll sit in the garden, eat, chat, and relax. How does that sound?"

Courtney felt her last filaments of shyness evaporate. "Thank you, my lady. Aurora didn't exaggerate when she spoke of your kindness."

"Then perhaps you'll agree to call me Elinore. As I

intend to call you Courtney. This way, I'll feel you're not only Aurora's friend, but mine as well."

"I'd like that . . . Elinore." Courtney smiled, coming to her feet, a wave of weakness reminding her just how tired she really was. "I think I'll take your advice and go rest. But I look forward to our picnic with great anticipation."

Elinore's smile was as dazzling as her jewels. "Wonderful. Until tomorrow, then. Good night, Courtney."

The silence awakened her. Courtney sat up, realizing by the darkness and the quiet that it was late—very late.

Swinging her legs over the side of her bed, she turned up the lamp, frowning when the hands of the clock announced that it was past midnight. Not only had she slept through dinner, she'd undoubtedly slept through Slayde's arrival *and* his conversation with Mr. Oridge.

Well, she was now wide awake. And she had no intention of remaining unenlightened.

Donning her day dress once again, she quickly ran a brush through her tangled curls before leaving her chambers. The hallway was dark, most of the servants obviously having retired for the night.

Where was Slayde?

Before she attempted ransacking a manor she still didn't know her way around, Courtney decided to ask.

"Miss Payne?" She wasn't surprised to find the housekeeper still up and about, standing just outside the library door, apparently compiling a list of the next day's chores. "I'm glad I found you."

"Miss Johnston." The housekeeper nearly dropped her quill. "You startled me. What are you doing up at this hour? Are you ill?"

"No, I'm fine. I apologize; I didn't mean to frighten you. Nor will I detain you, as I can see that you're quite busy. I only wanted to know where the earl is."

"Why, abed, I assume. He returned to Pembourne before dark, and I haven't seen him since."

"Could you tell me which chambers are his?"

This time the quill hit the floor. "Pardon me?"

"Lord Pembourne's chambers," Courtney repeated patiently. "Where are they?"

"Why, I . . ." Miss Payne cleared her throat several times. "The ones at the far corner of the east wing."

"That's the wing my chambers are in, is it not?"

A nod.

"Good. Then I'll find him myself and not trouble you further. And as it is imperative that I speak with him immediately, I'll be on my way. Thank you, Miss Payne. Good night."

"Good night," the housekeeper managed.

So much for the reputation Matilda is so desperate to protect, Courtney thought with an inner smile. *By tomorrow, I'll be labeled a fallen woman.*

Ah, well, there was no one she'd rather fall with than Slayde.

Her smile vanished as she neared his door. The purpose of her visit tonight had little to do with their blossoming feelings for each other.

She knocked.

"Yes?" Slayde's response was muffled, but too quick on the heels of her knock for him to have been asleep.

"May I come in?" Courtney stepped into the semidark room, uncertain what his reaction would be to her presence. With a surge of relief, she noted that he was both up and dressed, standing by the open window, brow furrowed in thought.

"Courtney." He looked more surprised than anything else. "Of course." He walked over, lines of fatigue etched on his face, his gray eyes dark with concern. "Is something wrong?"

Abruptly, something was.

Courtney's throat tightened as her body became achingly aware of Slayde's proximity. There was something extraordinarily intimate about being in his chambers, even though they were both fully clothed and her purpose was virtuous. She leaned back against the closed door, gazing up into his hard, handsome face, trying to still her body's trembling, to remind herself why she'd come. "No. 'Tis just that after Mr. Oridge and I spoke . . . he suggested . . . I wondered—" She broke off, not even remotely aware what she was saying.

Later, she wondered who reached for whom. Now, it didn't matter.

She was in Slayde's arms, where she belonged, crushed against his body, her heart pounding against his. His mouth devoured hers, took possession without asking, savored every tingling surface. His hands swept over her, cupping her breasts, stroking her nipples until they hardened against his thumbs.

"I can't keep my hands off you," he muttered thickly, tangling his fingers in her hair, tilting it back to give him access to her throat, her shoulders, the pulse in her neck. "Every time I'm near you, this is all I want." He felt her shiver and raised his head, frowning. "Am I hurting you? Your ribs?"

"No." She caressed his jaw, the soft hair at his nape. "You could never hurt me. Slayde, I—"

"Listen to me," he interrupted, his features hardening with determination. "I'm going to answer all the questions you came in here to ask. Then, you're going to turn around and leave—before I lock that damned door and take you to bed. Do you understand?"

A surge of heat shot through her. "I understand. Whether I comply is another story."

"You must comply. I won't let this happen, Courtney. I will *not* do this to you."

"You wouldn't be doing this to me. *We'd* be doing it to *each other."*

Slayde smiled faintly. "Trust me, sweetheart; it's not the same thing."

"Why? Because your reputation doesn't matter and mine does?"

"Because of all the reasons I enumerated yesterday. Because I want you to know only happiness for the rest of your life." A spasm of pain crossed his face. "Because I'm so bloody in love with you that it staggers me." He released her, turned away. "Don't say anything. Just let me talk. Then walk out of here. After that—" He swallowed. "I'll be leaving for London at first light. I'll be away from Pembourne for nearly a week, time enough to regain my damned self-control."

"You're going to London?" Courtney was still reeling from the impact of his declaration. He loved her. *He loves me.* 'Twas the greatest miracle of her life. "Why?" she asked, squelching the joy she longed to express. "Why are you going? Because of me?"

"No—although, Lord knows I can't seem to be around you without behaving like a callow youth. I'm going to London because of what I learned today from my Morland investigator. Apparently, Bencroft made a trip into Newton Abbot yesterday. He met with his banker and solicitor, who, I soon discovered, left for London immediately following that meeting. I intend to find out why."

"Do you think there's a connection between their actions and the black diamond?"

"I'm sure of it." Slayde pivoted to face her. "Consider all the facts—which you now have—and suppose for the moment Morland is guilty. If he'd made an attempt to trade the diamond for money, he would have discovered it to be a fraud. Word would have reached us. Morland would have reached us. So, obviously no exchange has been made. My guess is that Morland intends to fulfill his grandfather's original objective: to turn the stone over to Russia—to the royal family who paid for its recovery, thereby accomplishing two ends: reaping his family's share of the payment *and* ridding them of the curse."

Courtney's brow furrowed. "Where do the duke's banker and solicitor fit into this?"

"Provisions must be made. Specifically, the stone must be shipped, requiring someone to make the necessary arrangements with a discreet shipping company. A huge sum of money would then arrive in Morland's name. Someone must receive it, place it carefully and quietly in the bank, perhaps transfer a portion of it to Newton Abbot."

"I see," Courtney breathed. "So you're traveling to London to make inquiries, to see about any unusual, last-minute shipments leaving for the continent."

"Or any unusual meetings taking place between Morland's banker and other bank officials," Slayde added. "As for Oridge, he'll be traveling with me. He thought of a likelihood neither you nor I did: the prospect of Armon's men sailing to London to sell the booty they stole from the *Isobel* before they bolted to parts unknown."

"Wouldn't that be risky?"

"They're pirates, Courtney. Their priority is the money they make off their pillaging. If they can line their pockets with silver before leaving English waters, they will. Besides, as Oridge reminded me, why would they assume they were being tracked down? When Armon left the *Fortune,* he had the black diamond in his possession. If he was intercepted, 'twould be the interceptor who had the stone, not the crew. Thus, they wouldn't feel the least bit threatened."

"Then my whole theory about their fleeing like the wind is wrong." Courtney's eyes lit up. "Perhaps they can be readily apprehended after all."

"Oridge's hope exactly. He intends to make several visits in London in the hopes that the pirates will still be about. If not, he'll determine when they left and sail after them straightaway."

"And you?" Courtney asked softly. "What will you do once you've gotten the answers you seek? Return to Pembourne? Or continue to run away from something you can't escape and shouldn't want to?"

Slayde tensed. "I think I've answered your questions—at least those for which I have answers. Now go to bed."

"You have," she replied, remaining perfectly still, holding him with her gaze alone. "All but the last. You even answered the wondrous question that's plagued me for days." She raised her chin, willing him to see the magnitude of her feelings. "Now it's my turn. I love you, Slayde. With all my heart. And no matter how hard you fight it, how far you travel, that love will be here when you return." She rose on tiptoe, kissed him softly. "Godspeed."

Chapter 10

The rest of the week passed in startling contrasts; as Courtney's body healed, her heart ached.

Days were lovely, filled with visits from Elinore, long talks with Aurora, and strolls about the grounds that increased in number and duration as the week progressed.

Nights, however, were endless, plagued by worry, filled with nightmares in which her father was calling out to her, needing her, his image rapidly changing to one of Slayde, doing the same. Time after time, Courtney would awaken in a sweat, huddling in the center of the bed until her breathing slowed and her pulse stopped racing. Then she'd turn up the lamp, fumble for her timepiece, and cling to it desperately, wondering why the dreams were intensifying rather than diminishing.

Was it an indication that her father was alive? Or simply a manifestation of her internal turmoil over Slayde? Either way, by week's end, her nerves were stretched to the breaking point. There was no longer any excuse. Her body was almost fully recuperated. 'Twas time to act.

Her mood was one of staunch determination when she arose on the sixth day following Slayde's departure. She'd slept not a wink, alternately planning the upcoming day and tossing about in a futile attempt to rest her cluttered mind.

This was to be the day; she'd decided that somewhere between three and four A.M. Aurora didn't know it yet, but right after breakfast, they were going to make the long-awaited trek to the lighthouse—only this time they would succeed.

Courtney frowned, brushing disheveled strands of hair off her face and crossing over to the dressing table. What she truly wanted was to leave for the Windmouth Lighthouse immediately, and breakfast be damned. But Elinore was joining them for their morning meal, and she'd be terribly hurt if Aurora and Courtney were absent when she arrived, so the conversation with Mr. Scollard would have to wait a few more hours.

Pensively, Courtney poured cool water into the basin. If things went well, she could visit with Elinore, meet with Mr. Scollard, and be back at Pembourne by midafternoon—just in case the other cause of her upheaval returned.

Slayde.

Instinct told her he'd be home soon. The very thought made her pulse race, triggering several different reactions, each one as powerful as it was conflicting. She wanted to fling herself into his arms and welcome him home. She wanted to hang back and see if he could really keep his vow and restrain his feelings for her. She wanted to interrogate him about whatever he'd learned in London.

And she wanted to do these things all at once.

Courtney rolled her eyes. 'Twas no wonder she couldn't sleep. She could scarcely manage her thoughts when she was awake.

A songbird outside her window trilled, reminding her that the morning was ticking by. Well, whether or not the new day was ready for her, she was ready for it. Purposefully, she splashed some water on her face, just as her bedchamber door opened.

"Courtney?" Aurora poked her head in. "Finally, you're up. Did I forget to tell you Elinore was coming to breakfast?"

"You told me four times," Courtney assured her, grinning as she plucked a lime-green day dress from her wardrobe. "And each time I was delighted."

"But you're not ready." Still hovering in the doorway, Aurora frowned.

"The viscountess is not due at Pembourne for over an hour," Matilda announced, sailing into the room. "I'm certain we can have Miss Courtney dressed and ready in that amount of time. That is, *if* we have no interruptions." She arched an affectionate—though pointed—brow at Aurora.

"Very well," Aurora said with a sigh.

"I'd planned to find you before breakfast anyway," Courtney told Aurora with a meaningful glance. "If it's acceptable to you, I'd like to take that walk we discussed—just as soon as Elinore leaves."

Aurora brightened at once. "Of course. I know just the walk you mean."

"So do I," Matilda inserted dryly. "Are you certain you're up for it, Miss Courtney?"

"I'm certain," Courtney replied. Grinning, she did a mock pirouette in place. "See? I'm as good as new."

"Almost," Matilda qualified.

"Excellent!" Aurora turned to go, infinitely more cheerful than when she'd arrived. "I'll see if Cook needs help."

"And I'll be on time for breakfast," Courtney called after her. Still smiling, she turned to Matilda. "If I'd been blessed with a sister, I'd want her to be just like Aurora."

"Perhaps that blessing will come to pass," Matilda replied, readying the gown as Courtney slipped out of her nightrail and into her undergarments.

Courtney's fingers paused on the ribbons of her chemise. "What do you mean?"

A knowing smile. "Here, lovey, step into this." She eased the dress up Courtney's torso, carefully avoiding the tender area where her ribs had recently healed. "I mean that you and Lady Aurora might become sisters, after all. If not through blood, then through marriage."

The very word made Courtney's mouth go dry. "What makes you think that could happen?"

"Really, Miss Courtney, I've worked at Pembourne since before the earl was born. I'm aware of everything that occurs here—as well as things that don't. And one would have to be blind not to see the way you and Lord Pembourne look at each other. If ever there were two people in love, it's you."

"You're very insightful," Courtney murmured. "But Matilda, love in one thing; marriage is quite another."

"The earl hasn't a snobbish bone in his body. So if you're fearful of the class difference . . ."

"It has nothing to do with our social standings. Nor with our feelings. 'Tis just that—" She stopped, not sure how much to reveal.

Matilda fastened the final button on Courtney's gown. "Lord Pembourne is a complex man. He's been a loner all his life. That tendency intensified over the last decade—for obvious reasons. But in my opinion, he has a tremendous capacity to love and be loved, a capacity that was buried deep inside him and that awaited only the right woman to coax it out." She beamed, smoothing Courtney's bodice, then lifting her chin with a gentle forefinger. "I believe that woman is standing right before me. What's more, so does she. Now, shall we arrange your hair before the viscountess arrives?"

Sparks of anticipation danced in Courtney's eyes. "We shall. All at once, I find myself ravenously hungry."

* * *

"You're looking splendid. Why, there's color in your cheeks I haven't seen until now." Elinore studied Courtney over the rim of her coffee cup, nodding her approval as she spoke.

"I'm feeling much better," Courtney replied, biting into a biscuit. "And I have you and Aurora to thank."

"Not to mention the fact that Slayde will soon be home," Aurora added.

Courtney shot her a look. "I'd sooner think it's Elinore's visits and Cook's meals that sped my recovery."

"Then let's just say my brother's arrival will complete the process."

Elinore cleared her throat. "You're fond of Slayde, I take it?"

"He's been generous and heroic, from saving my life to opening the doors of his home to me," Courtney answered carefully. "We also have a great deal in common. So, yes, I'm fond of him."

"And he's fond of you as well," Aurora said cheerfully.

"How wonderful." Elinore smoothed her strand of pearls, eyes alight with interest. "When did this happen?"

"Nothing's happened." Courtney wondered if the prospect troubled Elinore. After all, Slayde's mother had been her best friend. Perhaps she wanted more for him than a sea captain's daughter.

"Nothing's happened *yet,*" Aurora qualified again. "But it will."

"I certainly hope so," Elinore surprised Courtney by saying. "Lord knows, it would give him a new purpose, something that should have happened long ago."

"What do you mean?" Courtney inquired.

Elinore glanced at Aurora.

"Courtney knows all about Mama and Papa's murders," Aurora answered her unspoken question. "Slayde filled her in, given the fact that he believes the Bencrofts were responsible for both that crime and the one just committed against Courtney's father."

"I see." Elinore's gaze flickered to Courtney. "Then

you understand the way Slayde thinks, how preoccupied he's been since his parents' deaths. I've tried, over and over, to convince him to bury the past, to get on with his life. But it's been more than a decade, and he's only withdrawn deeper and deeper into himself. If you can give him something else to care about, a future to look toward, you'll have repaid his heroism and generosity threefold."

Courtney's misgivings abated. "Have you known Slayde since he was a young boy?"

A nod. "I was sixteen when Theomund and I wed, and I came to live at Stanwyk. Aurora wasn't yet born and Slayde was about six. He was quiet and serious even then, spending most of his time on his studies or out sailing his skiff. Whatever he undertook over the years— be it reading and writing, or sailing and hunting—he always excelled at them. And he always did them alone."

"Did you see him often?"

"Not really. Soon after my marriage, Slayde was off to Eton, and he returned only on holidays. Then, it was Oxford, Europe, India." Elinore sighed. "Slayde rarely stayed at Pembourne for any length of time, especially after his parents died. It was as if the horrible memories drove him away."

"I'm sure they did," Courtney murmured, automatically reaching into her pocket and extracting her father's timepiece. "Memories can sometimes be unendurable."

"What is that?" Elinore asked, brows raised in curiosity.

"My timepiece. I customarily leave it in the drawer of my nightstand, but today"—a quick glance at Aurora— "I needed it with me. It belonged to my father. He gave it to me just before he was thrown from our ship." Courtney snapped it open to show Elinore the scene within. "'Twas at that moment it stopped. It hasn't resumed, other than once, when—" With a sharp sound, she broke off, her gaze riveted to the watch's face.

"Courtney?" Elinore pressed. "What is it, dear?"

"The watch. It moved again. Just now. Like the last

time. 'Tis as if Papa . . ." Abruptly, she bolted to her feet. "I must know." Her distraught gaze shifted to Aurora. "We've got to leave for the lighthouse. Now. Please, Aurora. If Papa's alive . . . if there's anything I can learn . . ."

Aurora rose at once. "Elinore, will you excuse us?" she asked, already following Courtney toward the door. "Courtney and I must make a trip to visit Mr. Scollard. She's well enough now. And if anyone can help her, he can."

Elinore stared after them, looking utterly bewildered. "Why, certainly. Is there anything I can do?"

"Just understand," Aurora called over her shoulder as she disappeared into the hallway. "We don't mean to be rude. 'Tis just that—"

The rest of her sentence was cut off by the sound of the entranceway door as it shut behind them.

The Windmouth Lighthouse was nestled at the foot of the hills, beckoning them like a warm, familiar friend.

"How lovely," Courtney whispered, pausing to regain her strength, tilting back her head in order to admire the stone tower from its base.

"It's fifty-seven feet high," Aurora informed her, as proud as if she'd built the structure herself. "And over a hundred years old. But Mr. Scollard keeps it looking new. He not only operates the light, he maintains the entire building himself; there's not one chipped or broken stone, or a spot on the balcony that's not freshly painted. Come—let's go in." She tugged at Courtney's arm. "Your strength is all but sapped."

"You're right about that." Briefly, Courtney leaned her forehead against the cool stone, watching as Aurora walked through the unlocked door. "Shouldn't we knock?" she murmured, following along, then hesitating at the threshold.

"It's not necessary. Mr. Scollard knows we're here. See? He's prepared a fire and some tea. Why don't you sit down and rest a bit."

"How on earth did he know . . . ?" Courtney's voice drifted off as she entered the lighthouse, blinking in surprise as she did. Whatever she'd expected, it hadn't been this quaintly decorated room with watercolors hanging over a settee, twin armchairs perched on either side of a brick fireplace, and a glorious fire, before which sat a tray containing a steaming pot of tea and three cups.

"Isn't this room perfect?" Aurora demanded.

"Perfect," Courtney echoed, still staring at their refreshment. "How did Mr. Scollard know we'd be coming?"

Aurora shrugged. "The same way he knows everything. Look back there." She pointed toward an alcove at the rear of the room. "That leads to Mr. Scollard's chambers. I've never seen them, but I know he built them himself so he'd be able to man his post at the blink of an eye, without the hindrance of traveling. Every evening, at the first sign of sunset, he heads up to the tower to light the lamp. He's never been late nor skipped a night. Whenever I visit—be it morning, noon, or night—he escorts me to the tower. I adore watching the ships and the waves and listening to him spin his yarns. They're filled with adventure and excitement." A fond smile. "I've been visiting the lighthouse since I was a child. And in all these years, Mr. Scollard has never run out of legends or patience."

"He sounds wonderful." Totally intrigued by Aurora's description, Courtney lowered herself to the settee, catching sight of the endless spiral staircase that led to Aurora's haven. "Is Mr. Scollard in the tower now?"

"Customarily, he would be. He spends most mornings polishing the lanterns, making certain all the apparatus is in perfect working order for sunset. However, given our visit, I suspect he's in his chambers."

"Did you tell him we might be coming by today?"

"No. I never need to tell Mr. Scollard anything. He foresees things on his own, which is why he's doubtless on this level rather than in the tower. He realizes you're too weak to make such a steep climb." Seeing Courtney's baffled expression, Aurora grinned. "Trust me. Mr. Scollard will be joining us in a few minutes. Then you can form your own opinion."

Even as Aurora spoke, a light tread sounded from the rear, and Courtney twisted about expectantly.

A minute later, an elderly man emerged, wiping his hands on his apron. His weathered face, beneath a mop of snow-white hair, was lined with age, but his keen gaze was sharp as a tack, his eyes the brightest blue Courtney had ever seen. Fascinated, she stared at him.

"Welcome, Miss Johnston," he said, his gruff voice devoid of surprise. "See, Rory? Your friend healed quickly. Almost quickly enough to suit you."

"Nothing is ever quick enough to suit me, Mr. Scollard," Aurora returned with a grin.

"True." He gave a disgusted grunt. "No patience. Not a whit. Even after all these years." His glance fell on the teapot. "Why haven't you had your tea?"

Somehow Courtney found her voice. "We were waiting for you."

"Don't. You need your strength. Or else you'll undo all Matilda's hard work." He poured a cup and handed it to Courtney, his hand as steady as a lad's. "Here. Strong. Too strong for Rory, but she'll have to make do. You're the guest today. So the tea is just the way you like it— strong and dark. That's what happens when you live among sailors. You learn their habits. Never met a sailor who took his tea weak." He glanced about the room, his vivid eyes searching. "You could actually use some of that brandy you like so much. I've got a bottle around here somewhere." A shrug. "Maybe later. Yes, later would be better. Spirits make you too groggy. And if you're not clear-headed, we won't be able to examine that watch of yours." He arched a brow at Courtney, whose mouth was still hanging open. "Drink the tea now while it's hot," he advised. "You can stare at me later."

"I'm sorry." Instantly, Courtney lowered her gaze. "I didn't mean to stare. I just . . ." What in God's name could she say? That until now she'd believed visionaries existed only in books?

"The tea," Mr. Scollard reminded her.

Nodding, she took a sip, then another. It was by far the best tea she'd ever tasted—and the most fortifying. Already, renewed strength was beginning to pervade her body.

"That fool pirate," Mr. Scollard muttered, pouring two additional cups. "You don't look a bit like Rory. But I guess at night, the coloring could fool someone, especially someone who looks but can't see. At least then, he couldn't. He sees now. Good for you." Mr. Scollard nodded his approval. "Here, Rory." He turned, handing Aurora her tea. "Drink up. I planned to have those little iced cakes you like so much, since, as it turns out, Miss Johnston likes them, too. But given the fact that neither of you is hungry—besides the fact that Miss Johnston's unsettling experience this morning has left her too anxious to eat—I decided to postpone the cakes for another time. Maybe for her birthday. Good idea. For her birthday." He nodded at his own superb alternative. "Now, shall we have a look at that timepiece?" He pulled up a chair, extended his hand.

Wordlessly, Courtney extracted it, placed it in his palm.

"Hmmm." He turned it over, studying the engraved case. "Nice workmanship. Costly, too. Doesn't surprise me, given how much your mother loved him."

"How did you know . . . ?" Courtney gave it up, snapping her mouth shut. Something told her that to continue asking Mr. Scollard where his knowledge came from was not only futile but a senseless waste of time—time she'd squandered too much of already. "Can you tell me anything?" she asked.

Mr. Scollard raised his head and scowled. "I can tell you you're as impatient as Rory. And, in your case, it's even more a hindrance. Patience is an ally you'll need in the weeks to come. Patience of the head *and* the heart. So learn some."

"Yes, sir." Courtney didn't know whether to laugh or cry. The only thing she *did* know was that Mr. Scollard was correct. In his assessment *and* his cure. Patience. After almost twenty years, she'd have to acquire some. "Take your time," she requested. "I'll have another cup of tea."

"Good idea." Those penetrating blue eyes bore into her, watched her refill her cup, then drain it. "You're a brave girl. It's good your strength is nearly renewed, because you're going to need it. Every bit of it."

The saucer struck the table with a thud. "Are you saying Papa is gone?"

"Gone? An interesting term. Gone he is—from eyes, from ears. But from mind? From heart? Not gone. Some ties can be broken. Others cannot. Your job is to discern the difference."

"Ties?" Courtney leaned forward. "What ties? Are you referring to physical bonds or spiritual ones?"

"If memories can't be silenced, spiritual bonds can't be broken. Not so with physical bonds. *If.*" Mr. Scollard snapped open the timepiece, studying the unmoving scene. "The ship seeks the lighthouse, yet it's thwarted."

"The watch stopped," Courtney explained. "Then it moved—twice. What does it mean?"

"You're confused. Don't fight confusion. It usually gives way to enlightenment. What we see, what we hear, it all means something if we look long enough, patiently enough to fathom its purpose. Most difficult of all are the times we must wait for that purpose to find *us.* Those times require all the patience I just mentioned."

"And is this one of those times?"

"Yes."

"Mr. Scollard." Courtney inhaled sharply. "Please tell me. Is Papa alive?"

"That you'll have to discover for yourself. My vision alone can't help you. But another can."

"Another? Another person? Who?"

"Listen with your heart. It won't fail you." So saying, Mr. Scollard snapped the case shut, handed the watch back to Courtney. "That tea should have done its job by now. You'd best be getting back to Pembourne. To prepare. For the end of one journey and the beginning of another." He rose, reaching over to ruffle Aurora's hair. *"You,* I'll see tomorrow."

Aurora's brows knit in puzzlement. "Can't I bring Courtney with me?"

"You may. But you can't." Mr. Scollard turned, studying Courtney with a far-reaching gleam in his eyes. "I won't be seeing Miss Johnston for a time." He lay a gentle hand on her shoulder. "Go with strength. Return with wisdom."

For some unknown reason, tears filled Courtney's eyes, a flash of insight telling her that the next time she sat in this room all would be changed.

"Change is essential in order to grow, Courtney," Mr. Scollard said quietly. He inclined his mop of white hair. "I can call you Courtney, can't I? Given that you prefer it."

"You can and you may," she responded, attempting a smile.

His gaze delved deep inside her, as reassuring as it was perceptive. "Don't doubt your strength, Courtney. Call upon it. It will serve you well." So saying, he turned away, gathering up the china and replacing it on the tray. "Time to polish the lanterns. Before you know it, sunset will be upon us. Good day, ladies."

Wiping his hands on his apron, he ascended the stairs to the tower and disappeared.

Courtney shifted in her garden chair, inhaling the fragrant scent of roses and lilacs, staring out across the darkening grounds of Pembourne. She clutched the timepiece in her lap, only minimally aware that the sun had long since faded, casting the garden in which she sat in shadows.

She'd been here for hours—ever since she and Aurora had made their silent trek back from the lighthouse— her mind besieged by questions. Aurora had somehow understood her need for solitude, merely squeezing her hand in unspoken support and leaving Courtney to her contemplations.

Other than Aurora, no one knew her whereabouts, a fact for which she was grateful. She had much to ponder, an abundance of soul-searching to conduct, a need triggered by Mr. Scollard's profound assertions and equally profound implications.

Patience, he'd said. Strength. Ties that were able to be broken; others that were not. The end of one journey and the beginning of another.

Like wisps of smoke, fragments of Courtney's intended course began unfurling inside her. At last, one piece of the puzzle—that which pertained to the onset of her impending journey—fell into place.

Her fingers tightened about the watch.

Papa. Two tears slid down her cheeks. *You'll never truly be gone. But 'tis up to me to make peace with myself, to discern physical from spiritual. Thus, I must take the first leg of the journey Mr. Scollard spoke of, to return to the spot where the nightmare began. Perhaps therein my answers will lie.*

Gripping folds of her gown, Courtney sat forward, staring off toward the Channel as her purpose found her, just as Mr. Scollard had predicted. She'd leave right away, seek her truths.

But how could she reach them? In one of Slayde's ships.

Swiftly, she rose, gathering her skirts, preoccupied with one goal: to rush down to the wharf and be gone.

You owe it to Slayde to tell him first, her conscience warned.

Impossible, her urgency argued. *Slayde is in London. I haven't a clue when he'll return. And I haven't the time to wait.*

Her common sense tried next. *But it's nearly night, the worst time of day to sail off to parts unknown.*

I can't let that—or anything else—deter me. I must go.

She'd taken but three steps when another internal

voice resounded, this one halting her in her tracks. *Patience, Courtney.* It was Mr. Scollard, speaking as clearly as if he stood beside her. *You must learn some. Now more than ever—you must.*

"Mr. Scollard?" She looked about in bewilderment. Nothing but the gardens and trees met her scrutiny.

Listen with your heart, Courtney, the gruff, omniscient voice persisted. *It won't fail you.*

With a resigned sigh, Courtney retraced her steps, sank back down into the chair. "Very well," she acquiesced, somehow unsurprised by Mr. Scollard's unseen presence. "I'll try."

She could almost see him smile.

She must have dozed.

Firm hands gripped her arms, shook her awake with gentle, but insistent motions. Disoriented, she cracked open her eyes and shivered, wondering why so cold a breeze permeated her bedchamber. "Matilda, would you mind closing the window?" she murmured. "It's so chilly in here."

"I'm not surprised," Slayde's deep voice replied. "It's one A.M. and you're sleeping in the garden wearing only a thin muslin gown."

"Slayde?" Courtney blinked. "You're home?"

"For hours." He eased her forward, wrapping his coat about her shoulders. "Hours spent searching the manor for you. Everyone thought you were abed, which my visit to your chambers rapidly disproved. Everyone but Aurora, who wouldn't divulge a bloody thing. I nearly bellowed her walls down before she finally told me your whereabouts. Evidently, you've been out here since midafternoon. Let's get you inside before you become ill."

"No." Courtney shook her head, suddenly quite awake. "I need to talk to you. Alone."

"If it's about what I learned in London, trust me, it can wait until morning." He scooped her into his arms.

"Please," she whispered, with another shake of her head. "It's not. It's about . . . something else."

Slayde paused, searching her face. Whatever he saw there made him comply. "All right." He lowered himself to the chair, enfolding her in his coat—and his arms.

Besieged by weariness, Courtney nestled against him. "I missed you," she murmured, abandoning any notion of remaining aloof. "I'm glad you're home."

He swallowed, audibly. "I thought of you a great deal. And I worried. You and Aurora together . . . I half expected my staff to have resigned during my absence."

Courtney smiled. "I was under the impression you considered me a good influence on Aurora."

"A wonderful companion. A good friend. But a good influence? Hardly. Remember? You filled me in on your past antics." He smoothed her hair from her face. "You're troubled. What is it? According to Matilda, you've been a model patient: visiting with Elinore, strolling the grounds with Aurora, and—oh, yes—Cutterton mentioned today's trip to the lighthouse."

An exasperated sigh. "Is there anything Cutterton doesn't know?"

"No. Now, tell me. Did Mr. Scollard upset you in some way? He's harmless enough, if a bit eccentric."

"He's extraordinary. So is his tea, which I'm convinced has healing powers. And, no, he didn't upset me. But he did cause me to think." She inhaled sharply, meeting and holding Slayde's gaze. "I want to borrow a ship—a small one—preferably with a crew of one or two. I'm a fairly good navigator when my head isn't thrust in the chamber pot. Unfortunately, that's not very often. So I can't go alone. But go I must. At first light." Her fingertips brushed Slayde's jaw. "Please. Don't say no."

Slayde's features had grown harsher with each passing word. "Armon is dead," he answered roughly. "What is it you're seeking?"

"The spot where he boarded the *Isobel*. I need to be

there again, to see where Papa went down. I'm not sure why, but it's the only way I can find peace. Perhaps, since I never actually saw Papa go overboard, it's easier for me to deny the inevitability of his death. I don't know. I only know I must go. I considered doing so before you returned, but something Mr. Scollard said . . ." She wet her lips. "In any case, I waited. Please don't make me sorry I did."

Conflicting emotions warred on Slayde's face. "Very well," he said at last. "We'll leave at first light."

"We?" She sat bolt upright.

"We," he repeated. "I'll be damned if I'll let you go alone. You need a crew? I'll supply one: me. I'm one hell of a good navigator and I don't require a chamber pot." His silvery gaze narrowed in uncompromising decision. "That had best be acceptable, because it's the only way I'll lend you that ship."

At that moment, Courtney loved him more than she'd ever believed it was possible to love anyone. " 'Tis more than acceptable, my lord," she breathed, pressing her lips to the hollow at the base of his throat. " 'Tis another miracle."

Chapter 11

Their ketch left Devonshire along with the last vestiges of darkness.

Courtney leaned against the railing, drawing her mantle more closely about her as the wind picked up, snapping the sails to life and propelling their small vessel toward its destination. She watched the Red Cliffs recede into a panoramic view, marveling at how beautiful this section of England was—how perfect for a cottage, a garden.

A home.

With a lump in her throat, she turned away, wondering if she dared any longer hope that dream could become a reality.

This trip would tell.

"Are you all right?" Slayde asked, glancing over from the helm.

"Fine." She forced a smile. "My stomach has yet to begin lurching. When it does, you'll see me dash below."

"Maybe you should go to the cabin now," Slayde returned soberly. "You look exhausted; did you shut an eye last night?"

"No." There was no point in lying. "I couldn't." She walked over to stand beside him, clutching the mast and gazing out to sea. "Be careful maneuvering into the Channel. If I recall correctly, there are limestone sheets and sandtraps somewhere in this area."

Slayde arched a brow. "Thank you. But you needn't worry. We're heading south, away from Portland and the more precarious waters of Lyme Bay. I promise not to dash us on the rocks."

Catching the teasing note in his voice, Courtney smiled—a genuine smile this time. "Forgive my interference. 'Twould seem you know the waters better than I."

"Only those surrounding Devon," he corrected. "By afternoon, I'll be relying upon your knowledge of the Channel as it moves farther from the English shore."

"I only hope I recall the spot where Armon attacked the *Isobel.*"

"You will."

Courtney inclined her head, gazing up at him. "Elinore said you sailed a great deal as a youth."

"I did. I enjoyed the utter solitude of being on my skiff."

"And now?"

"Now?" He shrugged. "Mostly I travel as a passenger, to conduct business."

"And to escape, just as you did then."

His handsome features hardened. "Ofttimes escape is essential."

"Other times it's impossible."

Silence.

"Will you tell me what you learned in London?" Courtney asked, wisely changing the subject.

"Not much. From the inquiries I made, no questionable shipments to any large European port have been arranged, nor have any large sums been reportedly deposited or transferred. Of course, that doesn't mean either of those two events didn't occur. My contacts can't ascertain the private dealings of every bank in London or the cargo of every vessel entering or leaving the city's docks. Still, instinct tells me that had the black diamond been shipped from England, word would have leaked out. Between the huge sum involved and the age-old legend, 'tis too fascinating an occurrence to have transpired without a shred of gossip being spread."

"What about the duke's solicitor and banker?"

"Ostensibly, they did nothing other than meet with other prominent businessmen who are in London for the Season."

Courtney chewed her lip thoughtfully. "Slayde, you yourself alerted Morland to the fact that you were delving into his activities. Is it possible he was aware you'd followed his colleagues to London and advised them to await your departure before taking action?"

"I suppose. In truth, it's difficult for me to attribute such cunning to a weak drunkard like Morland. Then, again, he's no longer the man I recall. And he is Chilton's son." Slayde gave a frustrated shake of his head. "Honestly, Courtney, I just don't know."

"What about Oridge?"

"Ah, Oridge. He's the only one who's managed to yield some results. We went our separate ways once we reached London, then met at an out-of-the-way pub on the day I left for Pembourne. According to his sources, a few disreputable men matching the descriptions you'd given him were seen peddling silver near London Bridge."

"When was this?" Courtney demanded. "Is Mr. Oridge certain the men were Armon's crew?"

"Two days before Oridge's arrival, and yes. He confirmed it several times over. Which means his theory was right; Armon's men didn't immediately flee the country. Conceivably, they could still be in England or, at worst, they've traveled a short distance. Either way, Oridge will find them—and their ship. Of that, I have no doubt. The question is, what peace will that bring you? Who of your father's crew might those filthy pirates have allowed to live?"

"I've asked myself those same questions, especially with regard to Lexley." Courtney swallowed past the lump in her throat. "And the answers will doubtless be painful. But I must face them nonetheless."

"I know." Slayde stared out over the gently rolling waters. "In addition to the avenues my investigators are pursuing, I still want to check out that unsavory merchant, Grimes, to see if he was the contact Armon was en route to on the night he was killed. After you and I return from this excursion, I intend to head back to Dartmouth. Perhaps Grimes has slithered his way home from wherever the hell he was. If he knows anything, I'll *urge* him to cooperate."

Courtney's insides surged, whether in reaction to their conversation or as the onset of her customary seasickness, she wasn't certain. "I think I'd best go below," she said shakily, her voice as unsteady as her stomach.

Slayde cast a swift glance at her. "Do you need my help?"

"No." She was already on her way. "I just hope you had the good sense to provide a chamber pot in the cabin."

The next hour was one Courtney would have liked to forget—just as she'd liked to forget the dozens of other times she'd spent crouched on a cabin floor heaving until her muscles ached. She was thankful she'd eaten very little the previous night, although her body seemed not to care, protesting the motion of the ship with wrenching spasms that went on long after her stomach was empty.

At last, the torment ended and she collapsed in an exhausted heap, too spent to even attempt sitting up. As if from a distance, she heard Slayde come in, and she murmured gratefully when he carried her to the berth, gently wiping her face and neck with a cool cloth.

"Rest," he urged softly.

"But I have to . . . direct our way." She felt as weak as a rag doll.

"You will. Soon. For a while, I'll head in the general direction the *Isobel* would have taken—toward the Colonies. I'll awaken you when I need you."

"Slayde?" Courtney's eyes drifted shut.

"Hmm?"

"Thank you." With that, she slept.

She jolted awake, a shaft of sunlight reminding her that the afternoon was well under way and her input would be needed in order to reach their destination. On wobbly legs, she arose, sagging with relief when she spied the basin of water Slayde had left. She drank and washed, then crept from the cabin and climbed topside, rejoining Slayde at the helm.

"Hello," she greeted him, grateful to see the water was calmer.

His head jerked about, his eyes narrowing on her face. "I was just about to check on you. How do you feel?"

"Better." A rueful smile. "As I said, I'm not much of a seafarer, although I've never before been quite *this* sick—not to the point where I fell into a dead sleep after being ill."

"You've never before been recovering from severe injuries, body depletion, emotional turmoil, and physical fatigue," he reminded her darkly. "Perhaps that had something to do with your reaction."

"Perhaps." She peered out to sea, trying to get her bearings. "What time is it?"

"A little past one. We're lucky; the winds are with us and we've gone a lot farther than I anticipated." Slayde rubbed his jaw. "You said the *Isobel* was three days out of port when Armon overtook you. How much of that time were you sailing along at a rapid pace?"

"If you're asking what portion of those days were spent in open waters, not very much. 'Twas foggy when we left London. Halfway down the Thames, the winds turned against us. I recall Papa having a difficult time navigating the Downs, trying to avoid the Goodwin Sands. It wasn't until we'd cleared the Strait of Dover that we began picking up speed."

"The Goodwins can impede the very best of sailors. However, in this case, the fact that it inhibited the *Isobel*'s progress works in our favor. That, together with Devonshire's western location and the beneficial winds now propelling us, convinces me we have very little westerly distance to cover before we reach the spot where your ship was attacked."

"Yes, I can see you're heading almost due south," Courtney murmured thoughtfully. "I only pray my recollections come through when I most need them."

Even as she spoke, Mr. Scollard's voice sounded from somewhere inside her. *Your memory will prevail, Courtney. Now call upon your strength. And remember to listen with your heart. It won't fail you.*

Three hours later, Mr. Scollard's prophecy was confirmed.

The waters had grown rough over the past few miles. Now, harsh waves pounded at the ketch, rolling it from side to side, yet Courtney's stomach went oddly and abruptly still. With a hoarse cry, she flew to the railing, her heart threatening to pound its way out of her chest. "Papa," she whispered, staring into the inky depths of the Channel. She groped for her timepiece and clutched it, seeing fragments of a vision unfold in her mind's eye: Armon boarding with his crew, Lexley fighting valiantly for his captain, her father, bound and gagged, weighted down, dragged toward . . .

"Papa," she whispered again, hearing his scream, feeling his fear as he struck the water and went down. "Oh, God—Papa."

A sudden wind whipped about her, reached inside her with an icy chill that had little to do with the temperature.

Slayde abandoned the helm, came to stand beside her. "This is the spot." It was a statement, not a question.

"Yes." She swallowed, pain lancing through her like a knife as she focused on the eddying waves. "The currents are strong."

"Very strong." Slayde's fingers closed around hers.

"I knew they were," she whispered. "But somehow I remembered them rushing in the opposite direction— toward England rather than away. Had that been the case, Papa might have been hauled closer to shore. As it is . . ." She squeezed her eyes shut, feeling her father's presence in her heart, her soul—but nowhere she could touch. "He's not here," she stated simply, her lashes lifting. Reverently, she cradled the timepiece in her hands. "We can go back."

Courtney didn't speak the whole way home, nor did she cry. She simply stood on deck, feeling naught but a vast swell of emptiness and a profound sense of isolation. It was over. She'd made the trip, sought her answers, and excruciating though they might be, found them.

Later, she'd feel. But for now, there was nothing.

She blinked in surprise when twinkling lights came into view, alerting her to the fact that not only had night fallen, but their ship was nearing land.

"Where are we?" she managed, her voice sounding thin to her own ears.

"Cornwall." Slayde veered the ketch inland. "It's after midnight. We'll spend the night at an inn and go on to Pembourne at dawn."

Dazed, she glanced up at him. "Why?" Even as the word left her lips, she visualized the worried, well-meaning homecoming that awaited them. "Never mind," she countered hastily. "An inn would be fine."

She went through the motions, helping Slayde bring in the ketch, then accompanying him to a small local inn, where he took two adjoining rooms. She bid him good night, not even noting her surroundings as she woodenly undressed down to her chemise, sinking into the bed in the hopes that it would warm the chill permeating her body.

It didn't.

Pressing her face into the pillow, Courtney willed herself to cry. Anything would be better than this hollow ache. It was unbearable.

The adjoining door opened, then shut. She didn't have to look to know it was Slayde. The bed gave beneath his weight as he sat beside her. "Courtney." He smoothed her hair from her brow. "Don't be afraid. The emptiness is part of the loss. It won't last forever."

"Won't it?" She raised up on her elbows, searching his face. "It has with you."

Agony slashed across his features. "You're wrong."

"I hope so." She drew a shuddering breath. "I don't think I can bear to live this way—so hollow, so cold."

He reached for her, drew her into his arms. "You're not cold, sweetheart. And you won't stay hollow."

Desperation seized her and cried out for relief. "Slayde, I can't endure this," she said in a broken whisper. "Make the emptiness go away."

His silver eyes darkened with suppressed emotion. "I wish to God I could." His lips brushed her cheeks, the bridge of her nose. "I'd absorb the pain and the cold, fill every shred of emptiness, if I could. But trust me. You're far too extraordinary, too warm and giving, to remain hollow. In time, your very nature will fill the emptiness." A fervent pause. "Just as it's filled mine."

Courtney blinked, a tinge of joy seeping through the void, wrought by something more potent than the emptiness. Never had she expected Slayde to make such an admission, one that, for him, was akin to an admission that he needed her. That, combined with his declaration last week . . .

"Slayde," she murmured, voicing the question that had plagued her since she'd visited his chambers. "The night before you left Pembourne, you said you loved me. Did you mean it?"

He never averted his gaze. "I meant it."

"Then say it again. If it's possible for my love to fill your emptiness, perhaps yours can fill mine."

Tenderly, Slayde framed her face between his palms. "I love you," he stated simply. "Your pain is mine."

Tears dampened Courtney's lashes. "Stay with me. Don't go."

"I won't."

"I need you."

A harsh tremor ran through him. "I need you, too."

Slowly, their gazes met . . . and locked. Silent seconds ticked by as the full impact of what was happening, where they now hovered, sank in.

Without a trace of doubt, Courtney reached up, untying Slayde's cravat and shoving it away. She leaned forward, kissed the hollow at the base of his throat. "Make love to me," she breathed.

"No." The word vibrated against her lips, more surrender than refusal. Fervently, he battled the inevitable, tugging her away, even as his fingers tangled in her hair, tilted her face toward his. "Courtney . . . no," he refuted hoarsely, his body trembling, his stare fixed on her mouth.

"Yes." Courtney's arms entwined about his neck. "Oh—yes."

Slayde's mouth was on hers before she'd finished speaking, the struggle lost beneath the powerful feelings that surged between them, commanded him to take what was already his.

Her lips parted, welcoming what was already hers.

And the world exploded.

The kiss was frantic, urgent, pain and emptiness melding, clamoring to be assuaged by something far more potent. Slayde pressed Courtney back against the pillows, devouring her mouth with an unappeasable hunger.

"I've dreamed of you every night, burned for you every day," he muttered. "God, I want you more than I want to breathe."

"I want you, too." She was equally urgent, bringing him closer, her fists knotting in the folds of his coat and attempting to push it aside. "So much that I ache with it."

Slayde responded to her unspoken plea without pause or question. Impatiently, he shrugged out of his coat, nearly tearing his shirt and waistcoat in his haste to remove them. Bare-chested, he brought his torso back to Courtney's.

They both moaned at the contact, a sensation too unbearable to withstand—even through the barrier of her chemise.

"More. I need more of you." Planting burning kisses down her neck and throat, Slayde made quick work of her undergarment, untying the ribbons and dragging it away, flinging it to the floor. "You're so bloody beautiful," he rasped, his lips discovering all he'd been denying himself for weeks. "God, so beautiful."

Courtney cried out when his lips surrounded her nipple. Heat poured through her in drenching waves, singeing her blood and filling every empty niche inside her. Her hands came up to cradle Slayde's head, to prevent him from stopping the wondrous havoc he was wreaking on her senses.

Stopping wasn't even a remote prospect.

Slayde was lost, beyond thought or reason, drunk on Courtney's scent and taste, the warmth of her skin, the miracle of her response. Again and again, he drew the tight peak into his mouth, circling with his tongue as if to memorize her flavor. Finally, he moved to her other breast, lavishing it with the same exquisite torture, making Courtney twist restlessly on the sheets and cry out.

His hunger goaded him on. Lifting his head, he wrenched the bedcovers away, his greedy stare feasting on the remainder of her beauty. Tenderly, he traced the bruises on her ribs, pressing soft kisses against each one. "Not even these could mar such perfection," he murmured, his lips shifting lower, to the hollow of her abdomen, the silkiness of her thighs. His palm covered the auburn curls between her legs, warming and possessing her all at once. "You're a miracle," he breathed, his fingers sliding lower, slipping into the warm wetness that beckoned him. "A miracle I thought didn't exist."

A dark roaring pounded in Courtney's head, and she responded instinctively and without embarrassment, opening herself to the magic of his touch, her hips lifting in silent invitation. She heard his groan, felt the heat of his breath.

And then, his mouth.

Her eyes flew open, a wild shudder rippling through her at the first stroke of his tongue against her heated flesh. She whimpered his name, her fingers clenching in his hair, her thighs parting wider with a will all their own.

His possession was absolute, more consuming than she could bear. It scorched through her, sent streaks of lightning up her legs and into her core, made her scream and arch and beg for more. She blazed beneath his every caress: his tongue, his lips, and then his fingers, gliding into her, opening a passage that ached for him to fill it.

Slayde's heart was thundering so savagely, he feared it might explode from his chest. His breath was coming in harsh gasps, his senses filled with Courtney's scent and taste, the incredibly tight, hot feel of her. He was a stranger to this blinding, devouring passion, never imagined it existed. At this moment, nothing and no one mattered but Courtney—Courtney and what was happening between them.

His breeches were an unendurable barrier.

Tearing himself away from her, he vaulted to his feet, shoving his breeches off, kicking them aside.

Courtney's lashes lifted slightly, and she drank in his nudity, her cheeks flushed with newly discovered, escalating passion. "Slayde." She opened her arms to him.

He covered her in a heartbeat, kissing her with a ferocity they both craved. "Your ribs . . ." he managed.

"I don't feel them, just you," she panted, wrapping her

arms about him, exploring the muscled planes of his back. "There's nothing but you."

His gaze darkened to near-black. "Open for me. I need to be inside you."

Instantly, she complied, parting her thighs until they cradled his hips. "Like this?"

"Yes," he ground out, teeth clenched to retain a semblance of self-control. "Now wrap your legs around me. Oh . . . God." A hard shudder wracked his body; sweat broke out on his brow.

"That feels so right," she whispered, lifting her legs to hug his flanks, easing him into her tight, wet warmth.

"Courtney." His mouth seized hers, his tongue delving deep in an overwhelming need to possess her everywhere at once. Slowly, his hips pressed forward, pausing, circling, readying her for his penetration. "Tell me if it hurts," he commanded. "If it does . . . I'll stop." Even as he uttered the vow, he wondered if he'd be able to keep it. Already, he felt reason slipping away, lost in a roaring deluge of sensation. He was shaking, drenched in sweat, teetering on the brink of climax—and he was yet to be fully inside her.

"It doesn't hurt," Courtney soothed. "It feels—" She broke off, gasping as he pushed deeper, stretching and invading her as he reached the thin barrier of her maidenhead.

Forcibly, Slayde raised his head, braced himself on his elbows. "Courtney?"

She drew his mouth back to hers. "I love you," she whispered. "Don't stop."

It was too much.

With a hoarse growl of need, Slayde thrust forward, tearing the fragile membrane and burying himself to the hilt. He heard Courtney whimper, felt her tense, and his hands balled into fists, making deep indentations in the pillow as he battled for sanity. "Sweetheart?"

She didn't answer at once and, in that instant, Slayde cursed himself a hundred times over for causing her pain. He was just about to withdraw—no matter what the cost to him—when she shifted, the tension easing from her delicate frame.

"Slayde." She murmured his name reverently, and it was the most exquisite sound he'd ever heard. Like a precious flower, she opened to him, melted all around him, drew him deeper into her breath-taking warmth. "There's no more pain," she breathed. "Just . . . heaven."

"Heaven is where miracles belong," he said huskily, rocking slowly against her. "Move with me. Touch heaven in my arms."

"I already have."

Groaning softly, Slayde cupped her face, holding her gaze as he withdrew partway, then thrust back inside her—deeper this time—before beginning a heart-stopping rhythm that took their breath, their souls, creating a bottomless yearning that gnawed harder with each escalating stroke.

"Slayde . . ." Courtney's eyes widened as her body responded on its own, undulating frantically as it sought relief from the welcome agony Slayde was lavishing upon it.

"Yes," he whispered, quickening his thrusts, feeling her inner muscles tighten around him, clenching him in a way that made the climax he'd been fighting to suppress ignite in his loins. Warning bells sounded—and were silenced, drowned out by the roaring in his head, the shards of heat that streaked through him in scalding, relentless waves. "Courtney," he rasped, taking her to the pinnacle with him, teetering at its excruciating edge. "Look at me. Let me watch your face when it happens."

"Oh . . . God." She arched wildly, her nails digging into his back, her body unraveling in a series of frenzied spasms that clasped at Slayde's length, gripping him again and again—plummeting him into sensual oblivion.

"Courtney!" He shouted her name, lunging into her

with all the urgency in his soul, erupting in a scorching, bottomless release, his seed exploding from his body, flooding hers.

They collapsed in a tangle of arms and legs, Slayde's head dropping into the crook of Courtney's shoulder, his entire being dazed from the magnitude of what had just occurred. He dragged air into his lungs, realizing—with whatever fragments of sanity he possessed—that his weight was too much for her—certainly too much for her ribs.

Summoning a modicum of strength, he shifted, only to feel the wetness of his seed inside her, a tangible reminder of his unprecedented loss of control—and its potential results.

He rolled away, gritting his teeth, all too aware of the dark cloud of guilt and trepidation that loomed ahead, poised and ready to engulf him, render its punishing aftermath.

But, God help him, that dark cloud hadn't been enough. No curse, no vow, no iron will had managed to tear him away, to stop him from pouring his entire being into hers.

"Slayde?" Courtney moved beside him, a sleepy question in her voice.

"I'm here." He reached for her, enfolded her against him, cradling her gently in his arms.

"Mmm." She snuggled closer, already half asleep. "It *was* a miracle, wasn't it?"

Slayde swallowed, pressing his lips into her hair. "Yes, sweetheart. A miracle—and more."

"I love you." With that, she slept.

Wide awake, he held her, staring across the room and watching the one tiny window as it transformed night to dawn, berating himself all the while.

What in God's name had he done? What had he been thinking? The answer to the latter was obvious: he *hadn't* been thinking. He'd been wanting, feeling, and—the biggest miracle of all—needing.

And, in the process, taken something from Courtney he had no right to take.

If Arthur Johnston *were* alive, he'd call Slayde out in a heartbeat, defend his daughter's honor—and with every right.

The irony was that, were Slayde anything but a Huntley, no defense would be necessary. He loved this woman and, by the very miracle that brought them together, he'd give his soul to escort her down the aisle, place a ring on her finger and, before God and man, claim her as his.

Thereby condemning her to what—a lifetime of solitude and imprisonment?

And if he relinquished her? his heart argued back. What would he be condemning her to then? A lifetime of loneliness and despair? Unthinkable. He'd known both those emotions for years, and he'd never subject Courtney to either. Her glowing heart would be extinguished, her spirit crushed.

Which left—what?

Courtney was a woman who could love but once. Slayde knew that as surely as he knew the timeless certainty of his own feelings. She could never give herself to another man—physically or legally—not after what they'd just shared; not even before, having blessed Slayde with the one-time gift of her heart.

And her old life was gone—her father murdered, her home destroyed. So what could the world offer that would strengthen Slayde's conviction to set her free, obliterate the urgent voice that commanded he bind her to him forever, make her his wife and the black diamond be damned?

"Papa!"

Slayde jolted from his musings with a start, all his attention focused on Courtney, who was now struggling to free herself, shoving at his chest as if he were the obstacle that stood between her and her father. "No . . . let me go . . . Papa!"

"Courtney." Slayde shook her, first gently, then more firmly until her eyes snapped open. "Sweetheart, wake up."

"Slayde?" She looked totally disoriented, her entire body trembling with memory.

"Shhh, yes." He caressed her back until the trembling stopped. " 'Twas only a dream."

"A dream," she repeated, sagging weakly against him. "It seemed so real."

"It always does." Slayde's jaw set. How well he remembered those hellish nights following his parents' murders: awakening in an icy sweat, reliving those inescapable moments of discovery again and again.

Drawing a shuddering breath, Courtney leaned back, searched Slayde's face. "Was it like this for you?"

"Yes."

"What did you do?"

"The very worst thing possible: submerged it. Somehow I believed that by burying the memories, I could make them vanish. I was a fool. It wasn't until I met you that I realized pain can be shed only by sharing it."

She smiled faintly through her fear. "You really have changed."

His thumbs caressed her cheeks. "I owe that to you."

"And to Aurora," Courtney amended. "She's been attempting to coax you out of solitude for years."

"Perhaps I wasn't listening."

"Perhaps you should. Your sister understands you better than you think. She's not a child anymore, Slayde. She's a woman—a very special woman. Isn't it time that you got to know her?"

Tenderness surged anew. "Another gift, my beautiful miracle?"

"No, my lord. Merely a suggestion."

"Very well. Suggestion taken. But in return, you must accept one from me." He framed her face between his palms, his gaze holding hers. "Tell me about your dream—and the memories you saw when you stared into the waters. They were one and the same, weren't they?"

Courtney's lips trembled. "Yes."

"Tell me."

"'Twas mostly what I've already told you," she whispered. "I was beside Papa at the helm. I heard someone shout. When I turned, Armon and his pirates were boarding our ship. Two or three of them dashed below to overtake whichever members of our crew were on the berth deck. Armon and two others leapt onto the quarter-deck. One held me, while Armon and the other seized Papa, bound and gagged him, then shoved him at Lexley, who was being held at gunpoint, and ordered him to tie a weight to Papa's leg and thrust him from the *Isobel*." Courtney began to tremble again. "I remember Lexley's stricken expression as he complied. Dear God, how I wanted to spare him and save Papa. I tried. I fought and kicked, but those monsters dragged me below and locked me in my cabin. I was on the stairway when I heard Papa's scream." Tears slid down her cheeks. "Yesterday, when we reached that spot in the Channel and I gazed into the water, I could actually feel his terror. 'Twas agonizing, almost as if I were living through it with him."

"You were." Slayde gathered her against him, warming the chill from her soul. "You still are," he added softly, stroking her hair, even as his mind began to race.

Something about her recounting troubled him, struck a note of discord. He frowned, wondering what it could be and why he hadn't perceived it the first time she relayed the specifics to him. Probably because he'd been preoccupied with Aurora's safety, hearing only those things that could provide a clue as to his sister's whereabouts. But now . . .

Silently, he reviewed Courtney's story, beginning with Armon's seizure of the *Isobel* and culminating in Johnston's horrible demise, his screams as he fell to his death . . .

Screams?

Slayde tensed. If the man was securely bound and gagged, how could he scream? Whimper, yes. Choke out a cry, perhaps. But scream? Hardly.

Had Johnston somehow managed to loosen his gag? Or, more plausibly, had Lexley found the opportunity to loosen it for him? And, if so, could the first mate also have loosened the bonds and the sack of grain about Johnston's leg? Was it actually possible that Lexley had found ample time to try to save his captain's life?

Caution warned Slayde that his premise was far too obscure and unlikely to risk upsetting Courtney with. Moreover, even if his notion had merit, even if Lexley had aided Johnston, severed all his bonds when no one was looking, the currents would still have hauled Courtney's father out to sea. Survival was virtually impossible.

Virtually.

But what if, by some stroke of luck, Courtney's earlier premonitions were right? What if Arthur Johnston was alive? What if, futility be damned, there was a filament of a chance that Courtney could have her old life back?

It was the most unlikely prospect Slayde had ever entertained, much less acted upon. He was a man who believed in absolutes, never in dreams and signs and implausible hopes.

And never in miracles.

Reverently, Slayde gazed down at the miracle in his arms, casting all his former principles to the wind, and making a new, unspoken vow—one more decisive than any that had preceded it.

If Arthur Johnston was alive, he would find him.

Chapter 12

Courtney felt almost as helpless now as she had when Armon attacked the *Isobel*.

Sighing, she rolled onto her back, staring at the ceiling of her bedchamber. She was anything but tired. Yet, feigning exhaustion was the only way she could be alone with her thoughts. Not that she wasn't grateful for the cluster of concerned faces that had accompanied her arrival. Never had she felt so much a part of a family as she had when Aurora had hugged her fiercely and said, "Your home is here now. We'll help you heal." Or when Matilda's compassionate eyes had filled with tears—which she'd quickly dabbed away with her apron—and she'd clucked over how worn out Courtney looked, how badly in need of hot food and sleep. Even Siebert had taken special pains, ordering the footmen to assist Miss Johnston to whatever room she preferred and then insisting they make her thoroughly comfortable. And when she'd chosen the yellow salon, Miss Payne had herself delivered the refreshment, hovering about like a bee poised over a flower.

The caring reception meant more to Courtney than she could ever express.

If only Slayde hadn't disappeared into his study the instant they arrived, summoning Siebert once or twice to dispatch messages to parts unknown, not emerging even to join her for dinner.

Relinquishing all attempts to rest, Courtney rose, crossing to her window to watch the sun set. Halfway there, she caught a glimpse of her reflection in the looking glass, and paused, stepping forward for closer inspection.

The same face looked back at her, thinner perhaps, and a great deal more strained, but otherwise unchanged. And her nightrail-clad body looked pristine, revealing nothing of the metamorphosis that had taken place.

Funny, how false appearances could be.

Slowly, Courtney's hand came up, fingers brushing her lips, her cheek. The emptiness inside her still lingered, yet it was eclipsed by the glory of what had taken place in that simple inn at Cornwall.

Never had she imagined making love could be so beautiful, so all-encompassing. Never had she envisioned being so utterly one with another human being. Those hours in Slayde's arms had changed her life, magnified her love threefold, and she wouldn't trade them for anything on earth. She ached for the pain that had brought them together, but, in her heart, she knew their joining had been inevitable, as natural as dawn melding with day.

If only Slayde weren't suffering.

Courtney's arm dropped to her side, and she continued her path to the window.

Slayde loved her. There wasn't a doubt in her mind of that fact, nor of the fact that he knew, as well as she, that they belonged together. Yet, he was fighting that knowledge, fighting it every inch of the way.

The irony of it all was that what he was fighting was not his feelings, but hers. After years of solitude, Slayde was accepting the fact that he needed someone other than himself, that his heart was no longer his own.

What he couldn't accept was her need for him.

Damn that bloody curse.

Courtney slammed her fist against the sill. What could she do to convince Slayde that his efforts to protect her were for naught? How could she make him believe that she felt safe here, that she belonged nowhere else, that she'd gladly live under lock and key rather than sacrifice the chance to share his life?

She couldn't.

The only way Slayde would not only relent, but welcome the prospect of her commitment, was if the black diamond were gone from their lives forever.

Well, she had no idea where the stone was. Then, again, neither did anyone else.

Courtney's head came up, her mind racing with a budding idea. No one knew the gem Slayde had surrendered to Armon was a fake. In fact, no one knew much of anything, other than generations of escalating hearsay. Everything concerning the black diamond was whispered nervously behind closed doors, snatches of rumor being passed from gossip to gossip.

Wasn't it time to alert the world to the truth? That the infamous black diamond was no longer in the Huntleys' possession?

A small smile curved Courtney's lips. If there was one thing she'd learned from years of pretending to be an ardent sailor rather than a seasick passenger, it was that perception was ofttimes more important than reality. 'Twas time to put that principle to work.

"Courtney?" 'Twas Slayde's voice outside her door. "May I come in?"

"Of course." She turned to greet him, her heart wrenching at the lines of torment on his face. Determinedly, she reminded herself that she was about to alleviate them. "You weren't at dinner."

"I wasn't hungry." He shut the door behind him, eyes searching her face. "How do you feel?"

"My emotions are mixed," she answered honestly. "I'm still in shock over Papa, torn between grief and denial. But I'm no longer empty—thanks to you."

Emotion darkened his gaze. "Are you in any discomfort?"

"No." She shook her head, touched rather than embarrassed by his concern. "I soaked in a hot bath. I feel fine."

"Good." He cleared his throat. "I wanted you to know I'm riding to Dartmouth tomorrow, to see if Grimes has returned."

"You mentioned your intentions to do that while we were on the ketch."

"I hope he'll turn out to be Armon's contact. If he does, I'll ensure that he gives us whatever information he has: where the stone was headed, to whom—maybe even who wrote the ransom notes."

Pensively, Courtney studied Slayde, pondered the fervor of his quest. "You're still hoping it's Morland. And that by proving he orchestrated this scheme, you'll avenge not only Papa's death, but your parents' as well."

Slayde nodded stiffly. "Yes. I'd be lying if I said otherwise. But it's not hope I feel, it's conviction. I truly believe the Bencrofts are murderers, twice over."

"I know you do." Courtney's earlier surge of hope wavered in light of the realization that, by publicly announcing the Huntleys' forfeit of the black diamond, she was giving Slayde only a portion of what he craved. She'd be ensuring his family's safety, yes, but what he truly lacked, what he needed to make him whole, was peace—a peace he could acquire only by resolving the past and letting it go.

Which meant finding his parents' killers.

So be it. Ever so slowly, Courtney's chin came up. She was well now, with no one to answer to and no responsibilities, other than serving as Aurora's companion. In light of that, why couldn't she do for Slayde precisely what he was trying to do for her?

She could and she would.

Hope resurged, full force, along with the second part of her decision. Not only would she eliminate the stigma of the Huntley curse, she'd do her damnedest to learn who killed Slayde's parents.

And she'd begin with the Duke of Morland.

"Courtney?" Slayde was frowning. "Have I upset you?"

"No. Not at all." She gave him a reassuring smile. "I appreciate what you're doing for me. When did you intend to leave for Dartmouth?"

"After breakfast."

"And after you speak with Grimes, will you be home straightaway?"

"Unless he gives me reason to stay, yes." Slayde's eyes narrowed quizzically. "Why?"

A casual shrug. "Only because I thought perhaps Aurora and I might visit Mr. Scollard tomorrow; he has a way of taking my mind off my pain. But I do want to be at Pembourne when you return, in case you have something significant to report."

"I see. Very well, why don't you plan your walk for the morning. I don't expect to be home before midafternoon."

"Excellent." Courtney could hardly wait to get started.

"I should let you rest." Slayde hesitated, wrestling with his own internal conflict. "Courtney," he tried, his voice hoarse with strain. "Last night—you gave me a gift more precious than I could ever imagine. I feel undeserving and grateful—and so much more. My feelings—" He broke off.

"You gave me the same," Courtney replied with quiet insight. "You needn't assign words to what we shared."

"There are none to assign. It defied words."

A heartbeat of silence.

With a sharp breath, Slayde crossed the room and pulled Courtney into his arms, kissing her with more aching emotion than either of them could bear. "Sleep well, my beautiful miracle. And know that I'm reliving every moment, just as you are."

Eyes closed, Courtney heard the quiet click of the door as he took his leave. She stood, unmoving, savoring his touch, his declaration—all of which strengthened her resolve twofold.

Her lashes lifted, and she waited, biding her time, ensuring that she gave Slayde ample opportunity to retreat to wherever it was he was going.

A quarter hour later, she slipped from her room and headed down to Aurora's, praying that her friend would be in, rather than taking one of her restless evening strolls through the gardens, or worse, to the lighthouse. The last thing Courtney needed was to have to prowl through the manor and beyond—and risk running into Slayde.

"Aurora?" She knocked. "Are you in?"

The door opened instantly, and Courtney was greeted by Aurora's concerned face. "Courtney . . . come in." Tugging her inside, Aurora shut the door and assessed Courtney from head to toe. "You look better. Did the rest help?"

"No—and yes." Courtney dropped into an armchair. "No, the rest did nothing. I didn't shut an eye. But, yes, I look better. That's because I feel better." She sat up straight, her eyes glowing. "I have a plan."

"A plan? I thought you were in your room grieving over the finality of what you and Slayde discovered on the search you just made."

"I was—in part." Courtney gripped folds of her nightdress. "But grief was only one of the emotions I was experiencing. There was . . . so much more."

Aurora studied Courtney speculatively. "Why do I feel as if something else occurred on this trip?"

"Because you're very astute." Courtney leaned forward. "Will you help me?"

"Help you with what?"

"My plan. If I'm successful, Slayde will be a new man, freed from the chains of the past, and ready for a wondrous future—I hope with me."

Aurora blinked. "'Help you'? To achieve what you just described, I'd move mountains." She perched at the edge of her bed. "I'm a captive audience."

"To begin with, we must convince the world that the black diamond is no longer in the Huntleys' possession."

"Which it isn't."

Courtney had to bite back the truth. "The point is, no one knows that. The *ton* thrives on rumors; 'tis time we gave them one to savor, one that will eliminate the danger and the black cloud shrouding your family's name."

"But my great-grandfather stole the gem. How can we disprove that?"

"We can't. Nor do we have to. Aurora, my mother was a blue blood—at least by birth. Papa's told me numerous stories about the *ton*. He used to say that if scandals decided which aristocrats were to be embraced and which were to be shunned, the fashionable world would consist of an empty ballroom. 'Tis not your great-grandfather's crime that causes the world to ostracize you, 'tis everyone's fear of the curse. If we set the record straight, the stigma of your past will remain, but the fear will be extinguished. You'll be admitted, if not welcomed, by the *ton*. Truthfully, however, that's not the end result I'm striving for. My goal is to eliminate the threat to our safety—along with Slayde's obsession about maintaining his solitary life. Both of these things would be accomplished by convincing the world that the Huntleys and the black diamond have parted company."

"And how do you propose to convince them of that?"

"That's where you come in. Tell me, do you know where in his study Slayde keeps his important papers?"

A baffled nod. "In his upper right-hand desk drawer."

"Excellent. Then that's where he must have placed the three ransom notes he received from Armon. I want you to sneak in and take them. Also, find a blank sheet of Slayde's personal stationery. Take that, too."

"What on earth for?"

"Because you and I are going to pen a letter outlining the circumstances that led up to the surrender of the black diamond. Then you're going to prevail upon Cutterton to send one of his most trusted men to ride into London and deliver our letter and the three ransom notes." Courtney frowned. "It must be someone thoroughly trustworthy, who will bring those notes back the instant they've been read and copied. As it is, we'll have our hands full, keeping Slayde from finding out before I choose to tell him. We'll have to steer him far away from his study for three or four days. Also, whoever Cutterton selects can't be someone whose absence Slayde would notice; tell him to choose a guard who's not terribly visible. Invent whatever explanation you need to. Tell Cutterton it's a matter of life and death, if that's what it takes. Just persuade him to cooperate. Can you?"

Aurora was still gaping. "Go to where in London? And what good will it do for *us* to write this letter?"

"To the *London Times*. And so far as the newspaper is concerned, *Slayde* will have written the letter. 'Twill be his signature—albeit forged—they see at the bottom, his explanation they'll read, and his ransom notes they'll have as proof. They'll publish them all with great pleasure for the world to pore over and believe. And that will be the end of the perils associated with being a Huntley." Courtney inclined her head. "Now, can you or can you not persuade Cutterton to go along with this?"

A radiant smile erupted on Aurora's face. "Even if I have to feign an attack of the vapors. I'm on my way." She leapt up, heading for the door. "This is more exciting than trying to escape from Pembourne."

"And equally as rash," Courtney called out pointedly.

Aurora turned. "Do I detect a note of censure?"

"Indeed you do. I know you're impatient. So am I. But bursting into Slayde's study tonight would be a mistake. Should he walk in, it would destroy all our well-laid

plans." Her eyes twinkled. "On the other hand, I know
for a fact he's leaving for Dartmouth right after breakfast
tomorrow, which would eliminate the threat of discovery and make your task that much easier. *I'll* distract the
servants, while you get the notes and paper. Agreed?"

"Agreed." Aurora walked back reluctantly.

"There's more," Courtney baited.

Her lure had the desired effect. Aurora's face brightened with curiosity. "Tell me."

"The first part of my plan will succeed only in silencing Slayde's worries about the threat from the world at
large."

"But it does nothing to ease his apprehension over
Lawrence Bencroft," Aurora finished for her.

"Exactly. Not only does Slayde believe the duke hired
Armon to attack the *Isobel,* he believes the duke's late
father killed your parents. And *I* believe it's time to
resolve that matter once and for all."

"How?"

"Tomorrow, while Slayde is away, I am going to pay a
little call on the Duke of Morland. I'm going to confront
him with evidence and perhaps elicit a reaction."

"But you have no evidence."

"I'll feign otherwise. I'll pretend to be emotionally
overwrought, determined to vent my rage at the duke.
I'll tell him who I am, that I know he hired Armon to
seize my father's ship. Then I'll blurt out how Armon
gloated over his intentions to cheat his employer out of
the stone. Too witless to control my tongue, I'll let it slip
that I've recovered Armon's journal, which specifies
everything—and everyone—who was involved in the
plot, *in writing.* And I'll conclude by informing the duke
that I've delved deeply into his past and have proof that
he and his father did, indeed, murder the late Earl and
Countess of Pembourne. I'll give him an ultimatum:
either he confesses to his connection to Armon, or I'll go
to Bow Street about both crimes, the latter of which was
cold-blooded murder, punishable by hanging."

Aurora listened to Courtney's story with an awed

shake of her head. "You're amazing. I never realized you were so . . . so . . ."

"So much like you?" Courtney teased. "Remember, I was ill when you met me. I'm healed now. And I'm every bit as resourceful—*and* as much trouble—as you are."

"Where do I fit into all this?" Aurora demanded. "I'm not letting you go to Morland alone."

"I never imagined you would. Your job there will be to distract Slayde's investigator, a needed precaution in the event Slayde told him our names. If that's the case and the man hears my name announced, he'll doubtless rush forward to stop me, thus ruining everything. I need enough time to get into the manor and confront the duke. I don't care if I'm spied on my way out—Slayde is going to hear about this visit soon enough—from the duke himself, if he reacts according to plan. But I want the chance to do what I came to do before I'm dragged off."

"Courtney." Aurora paled. "What if Lawrence Bencroft really did kill my parents? What if he's dangerous? You could get hurt."

"Slayde believes Chilton was the truly dangerous Bencroft, and he's dead. Besides, Lawrence wouldn't assault me in front of his entire staff." Courtney chewed her lip thoughtfully. "You and I will set a time limit. If I'm not out in, say, a half hour, alert Slayde's investigator and rush to my rescue. How would that be?"

"Fine." Aurora looked equally thoughtful. "Do you realize we could avenge your father, unearth Mama and Papa's murderers, *and* give Slayde a real life all at once?"

"I'm praying for exactly that."

A brief pause. "There's one thing we haven't discussed."

"Which is?"

Aurora sighed, torn between eagerness and honesty— honesty winning out. "The *ton*'s reception. You touched on the subject before, then dismissed it—possibly without considering what you were dismissing. Courtney,

I've heard equally as much about the fashionable world as you have. According to Elinore, they can be quite vicious. During my sole foray into the London Season, she served as my chaperon, thus preventing a wealth of pointed fingers and icy stares. But I don't delude myself. Despite my elation at attending so many grand balls, I knew people were whispering behind my back. After all, I'm a Huntley. Were I to truly make my debut, be brought out on Slayde's arm, I'd be subject to blatant rejection and snubbing—even *after* you and I have successfully enacted all we just discussed. As you yourself pointed out, your plan—though positively brilliant—will eliminate the *ton*'s fear, but 'twill do nothing to erase the age-old scandal. For myself, I don't care. I'll withstand the less-than-kind reception, just to be among people, to see the world. But for you, who's already seen and done so much, there's nothing to be gained and a great deal of potential hurt to endure. Remember, once you and Slayde are wed, the Huntley whispers will extend to you. Are you sure you're ready for that?"

Courtney's eyes glowed. "I'm sure I love your brother. As for the world, I don't care a whit about what they say or don't say about me. Let them gossip. Nothing would make me prouder than to stand beside Slayde—as his wife and your sister." Rising, Courtney walked over to squeeze Aurora's hands. " 'Tis not an issue—honestly. But I appreciate your worrying about me."

A current of understanding ran between the two women.

"Now, back to our plan," Courtney continued. "Tomorrow morning, we'll all breakfast together. Once Slayde leaves, I'll stand guard while you get the papers. Then I'll head off to the stables and fetch two horses while you plead our case to Cutterton." A worried pucker. "I'm not the best of riders, but for the relatively short distance to Morland, I'll manage. We'll ride to the lighthouse, wait a prescribed period of time, then head out from there. I'll tell Matilda I'm eager to see Mr. Scollard, but too peaked to walk. That will explain why we're not on foot."

"Perfect."

Courtney gave Aurora's hands another squeeze. "Again, thank you."

"No, Courtney, 'tis I who thank you," Aurora murmured, gazing at her friend. "I believed fate brought you to Pembourne for my sake. Which it did—in part." An insightful nod. "But the more amazing part . . ." She smiled. "My brother is a very lucky man."

"Ah, I've been expecting you." Mr. Scollard made his way down the last three steps from the tower, greeting Courtney and Aurora as they bustled through the lighthouse door. "Actually, you're a bit early," he amended, glancing at his timepiece. "Given Courtney's limited riding ability, I assumed you'd need some extra time." He shrugged. "No matter. Tea is prepared."

Courtney laughed, unfastening her mantle. "You were right. I did need that time. Unfortunately, my mount did not. He descended the hill like a bullet. He galloped; I prayed."

Nodding his white head, Mr. Scollard poured three cups of tea. "Prayers are invaluable—as you're fast finding out." He offered her a cup, assessing her with those probing blue eyes. "I didn't anticipate another visit from you so soon. I'm glad you found your way."

"As am I." Courtney knew they were referring to more than today's jaunt.

"The journey continues," he apprised her, handing Aurora her tea. "You and Rory are entering a dark segment, but one you must embark upon—carefully. Drink up."

Aurora took a huge gulp, then broached the subject that had plagued her the past hour. "Mr. Scollard, I asked Cutterton to dispatch one of his men to deliver our letters to London, and he agreed. No questions asked."

A knowing nod. "He's a good man, Cutterton. Very dedicated."

"But intolerably overprotective, as you know from my constant complaints. His attitude this morning was completely out of character. I expected to have to beg and plead, fall at his feet, pretend to be violently ill, concoct some extravagant lie. Yet all I did was make my request—stipulations and all—and off he went to find Mathers, who he assured me was the right man." Aurora's eyes narrowed. "Did you have anything to do with Cutterton's sudden and inexplicable agreeability?"

"I?" The lighthouse keeper's brows rose. "I haven't spoken a word to the fellow."

"Your powers are far-reaching."

A chuckle. "So is your determination."

Aurora sighed. "As usual, you're not going to answer me, are you?"

"I thought I had."

"Mr. Scollard," She tried another, equally important, tactic. "What advice can you offer Courtney and me? I know you can't—or won't—foresee the outcome of our venture, but what glimpses can you share?"

A fond smile. "Twenty years will be celebrated. Just as we celebrated yours, Rory."

"My birthday," Courtney murmured. "'Tis in a fortnight I'd forgotten."

"You've been preoccupied." His eyes sparkled. "And very inventive, as well. I commend you on your plan."

Eagerly, Courtney leaned forward. "Will it succeed?"

"Just as it is with me, you see much—and much, you don't." Abruptly, the lighthouse keeper frowned. "Danger," he murmured, an odd light coming into his eyes. "'Tis only now emerging to take form. Terrible danger. Look deep within. It's festering close at hand."

"Danger close at hand?" Courtney repeated. "Do you mean the duke? Will he thwart my plan? Will it fail?"

Mr. Scollard's gaze was wise, but troubled. "Sometimes we must fail in order to succeed."

With a thoroughly exasperated sigh, Courtney replied, "I wish I understood the meaning of your words."

"If you did, I wouldn't be speaking them." His sober mood lifted as quickly as it had descended. "Now drink up. Both of you. Fortify yourselves, then hurry and take your leave. The earl will be home by midafternoon. You have much to accomplish before then." Another glance at his timepiece. "Goodness. It's even later than I realized. You'd best take the phaeton. I'll bring it around. Courtney, you drive. If I recall correctly, your father taught you how during one of your stays in the Colonies."

Courtney nodded, beyond surprise. "He did."

Beside her, Aurora's cup clattered to its saucer. "Phaeton? What phaeton?"

"Why mine, of course," Mr. Scollard supplied.

"When did you acquire a phaeton?"

Thoughtfully, he pursed his lips. "I don't recall. I only know it's on hand when I need it."

Incredulous hurt filled Aurora's eyes. "Then all these years, all the times I've wept to you about how desperately I longed to escape Pembourne's walls, you could have helped me—and you didn't?"

Mr. Scollard went to her, placed his work-worn hands on her shoulders. "Ah, but Rory, I did help you. You just have yet to realize it." He patted her cheek. "But you will. Soon, I'm happy to report. Very soon."

With that, he hastened off.

Ten minutes later, Courtney's and Aurora's horses were pulling the phaeton along the quiet country road at a healthy clip as Courtney steered them decisively toward Morland. "Papa would be proud. Evidently, his lessons did sink in. Which is a relief, given how pathetic I am on horseback."

"You were awkward, not pathetic," Aurora protested. "Remember, you spent most of your life on a merchant ship, where riding is not exactly a priority." She pointed southwest. "Morland's estate is six miles inland. If we continue on this road, we'll reach Newton Abbot, the village on the outskirts of Morland. From there, we take the right fork and follow it directly to Morland."

Courtney blinked. "I intended to follow this road inland, but only because I've heard Papa's crew describe Newton Abbot as being set back from the shore. After that, I feared we'd have to rely upon our wits."

A grin. "Sometimes, though rarely, I'll admit, knowledge surpasses wits. This is one of those times."

"How did you come by such specific instructions?"

"I took the liberty of questioning Siebert—casually, of course. He's a wealth of information, privy to everything. Except, this time, my intentions. Even *he* never imagined I'd actually invade Bencroft's home. He thought it was just my insatiable curiosity piping up. And he willingly supplied me with what he assumed to be theoretical directions."

"And you think *I'm* resourceful."

Aurora's grin vanished. "Speaking of being resourceful, where does a lighthouse keeper store a phaeton?"

"That's but one of a thousand questions about Mr. Scollard that we'll never know the answers to." Courtney glanced at her friend. "You're not still upset with him, are you?"

"I suppose not. If he says he acted in my best interests, then I must have faith and believe he did."

"I agree." Courtney gripped the reins more tightly. "It occured to me that if Slayde is right and Morland has been scrutinizing Pembourne for some sinister purpose, your racing off in a phaeton and *truly* escaping could have exposed you to Lord knows what. Consider that."

"You're right," Aurora conceded. "Perhaps that's what Mr. Scollard was alluding to." She cast a worried look at her friend. "Which doesn't exactly make me feel at ease about your marching into the duke's home."

"I have no choice. I must see him." A pause. "Can you tell me anything about him that might help?"

"Nothing. I don't even remember what he looks like, other than his coloring and the fact that he was clutching a goblet. I know from Slayde that he's a recluse and a drunk. I'm afraid that's all I can tell you."

Courtney's jaw set. "Well, perhaps *I'll* soon be able to tell *you* more."

The iron gates appeared in front of them thirty minutes later.

"A formidable dwelling," Aurora commented, as Courtney maneuvered the horses down the drive.

"It looks neglected." Courtney assessed the thick woods and uninviting manor. "And somber."

"Stop just before the drive bends around the house so we can hide the phaeton in the woods. You go in; I'll conceal myself among the trees, looking very covert. That should arouse the suspicions of Slayde's investigator—and call attention to me and away from you, allowing you ample time to get to the duke. After that, well, I'll think of something to keep the investigator's concentration riveted on me. For a half-hour. That's it. Any later, and I begin shouting for help."

"Agreed." Courtney squinted as the manor loomed closer. "The house looks deserted. I hope the duke didn't pick this particular time to go out."

"Doubtful. It's too early to conduct business." Aurora waited until Courtney had veered the phaeton off the road and hidden it behind a thick clump of trees. Then, she turned toward her, grim-faced. "Good luck."

A wan smile. "Thanks."

Climbing down from the phaeton, Courtney walked the remaining length of drive, her step decisive, her heart hammering in her chest. She mounted the two stone steps and knocked.

"Yes?" A haughty-looking butler answered the door.

"I'm here to see the duke."

One brow rose. "And who, might I ask, are you?"

Courtney's chin came up. "A woman who has business with your master, not with you." She pushed past him, crossing the threshold into the hall. *Excellent,* she commended herself. *You got in without announcing yourself.*

Now, even if Slayde has provided his investigator with names, the man will have no clue as to your identity.

She could almost hear Aurora's applause.

"Now where can I find His Grace?" she demanded, resuming her performance.

"Madame, you cannot just barge in here and insist on seeing the duke. I must know—"

Pivoting about, Courtney regarded him with blazing eyes. "Does the duke seek your approval on all his women? If so, he's a poor excuse for a man."

Courtney wondered who was more shocked by her brazen comment, the butler or she.

"I . . ." He wet his lips. "His Grace told me nothing about . . . wait here." His mouth snapped shut, and he stalked off, rigid as a drawn bowstring.

The instant Courtney saw the direction he was taking, she followed behind, silently and with enough distance between them so he wouldn't sense her presence.

"Your Grace?" she heard him ask, once he'd veered into a room. "There's a young woman here to see you. She says you summoned her."

"A woman?" the duke sounded perplexed. "What kind of nonsense—"

"I never claimed to have been summoned," Courtney interjected, shoving past the butler into what looked to be a study. "I merely said I had business with the duke. Which I do."

Lawrence Bencroft rose to his feet, his dark eyes baffled. "Who are you? What business do you have with me?"

"Private business." Courtney gave him what she hoped to be a suggestive look, then inclined her head pointedly at the butler.

A thoughtful silence, then a nod. "You may leave us, Thayer."

Thayer needed no second invitation. He was gone in a heartbeat, the door shut in his wake.

"Now." The elderly duke walked around his desk,

giving Courtney a solicitous smile, one she imagined that had once been charming, on a face that had once been quite handsome, but was now lined with bitterness and age. "You're very lovely. Please enlighten me. Which of my colleagues was kind enough to send you to me?"

"No one sent me. As I said, I'm here on personal business."

An amused look. "Really? Then, I'd be delighted to hear what sort of business we have to discuss."

"The business of my father and how you killed him."

Morland stopped in his tracks, his smile fading, his eyes narrowed on Courtney's face. "Who are you?"

"Courtney Johnston." She gripped the back of a chair to still her body's trembling. "Arthur Johnston's daughter."

"Who the hell is Arthur Johnston?"

"He *was* the captain of the *Isobel,* the ship your pirate accomplice Armon seized in order to blackmail Slayde Huntley into relinquishing the black diamond."

Morland's lips thinned into a grim line. "Did Pembourne send you?"

"No," she countered, intentionally amplifying her voice to a shrill pitch in order to suggest rising hysteria—although, God help her, she didn't have too much pretending to do. *"I* came on my own. I'm the woman Armon passed off as Aurora Huntley so he could steal that wretched stone." Courtney met Morland's gaze, her heart slamming so hard against her ribs she could scarcely breathe. "There's no point in denying it. Armon himself told me you'd paid him to confiscate the diamond. He also gloated to me, again and again, that he had no intentions of sharing the stone with you, that he meant to sell it and flee the country. He called you a stupid old fool."

Morland's expression remained unchanged. "You're obviously deranged," he assessed calmly. "Either that, or you're working with Pembourne in some sick attempt to malign me. He, too, burst into my home raving about a pirate I supposedly paid to extort the black diamond from the Huntleys. Now that I reflect upon it, he bellowed something about housing the daughter of a murdered sea captain at Pembourne. You, doubtless, are that homeless chit. Very well, I'll play along with your amateur theatrics and tell you precisely what I told your cohort, or your keeper, or whatever role Pembourne has assumed in your life. I never met this fellow, 'Armon.' However, if he did manage to wrest the jewel away from the Huntleys in order to restore it to its proper owner, I commend the man. And if escape is what he seeks, I certainly hope he finds it."

"He's dead," Courtney spat. "But you know that. After all, you killed him."

A stony silence. Then: "I killed no one."

"Liar," Courtney accused, her voice shaking as she delivered her final blow. "You killed my father. You killed Armon. And ten years ago, you killed the Earl and Countess of Pembourne."

That got a reaction. Morland turned three shades of red, his eyes ablaze with hatred, his fists clenching violently at his sides.

At that moment, he looked every bit the murderer.

"What did you say?" he ground out through clenched teeth.

"I know everything," Courtney blurted, mentally gauging her distance to the entranceway door. Lord, she hoped Aurora was standing vigil. "I found Armon's journal. Your entire plan to blackmail Lord Pembourne out of the diamond is outlined—fully—including your name and the extent of your involvement." Perceiving Morland's escalating rage, she sought the courage to continue. She pictured her father's face, the anguish in Slayde's eyes, thereby finding the incentive she needed. "The moment I read that journal, I vowed to make you pay for Papa's death. So I delved into your activities, your past, your family—and I found precisely what I needed, with little effort, I might add. Obviously, Bow Street didn't conduct too thorough an investigation. Else they, too, would have found the irrefutable evidence I did."

"What irrefutable evidence?" Morland thundered.

"Proof that you and your father cold-bloodedly murdered the late Earl and Countess of Pembourne." Courtney took two subtle backward steps toward the door, her palm raised. "Don't bother denying it. My proof is as conclusive as if you'd been caught standing over the bodies, sword in hand." She retreated until her fingers closed around the door handle. "Here's my ultimatum, Your Grace,"—she spat out the formal address— "either you publicly admit that you paid Armon to commit his crime, which would convict you only of being a thief and an indirect accomplice to Papa's drowning, or I'll provide Bow Street with every shred of evidence I have. At which point, you'll be arrested and hung for murder."

Morland made a harsh sound deep in his throat, then took two steps in her direction.

It was more than enough.

Courtney flung open the door and bolted.

Tearing down the hall, she nearly plowed through Thayer, yanking open the entranceway door and dashing down the steps and across the drive.

"Courtney! Over here, by the phaeton!"

Her head jerked in the direction of Aurora's voice, and she rushed toward it. Shoving tree branches aside, she retraced her steps at a dead run, praying she'd recall the spot where they'd hidden the carriage.

She collided with a solid chest and a pair of muscular arms.

"Don't scream," Aurora advised hurriedly as Courtney struggled to free herself. "Rayburn is Slayde's investigator."

Courtney ceased her struggles. Still gasping for breath, she tilted back her head, meeting the grim stare of a stocky, square-jawed man.

"Are you all right, Miss Johnston?" he asked tersely.

"I think so." She glanced over her shoulder. "Morland could still be following me."

"Then let's not take any chances." Rayburn hoisted both women into the phaeton, then climbed in and took up the reins. "We'll be at Pembourne in record time."

Rayburn was true to his word.

Twenty-five minutes later, they sped through Pembourne's gates and raced up the drive.

The phaeton halted at the entranceway door.

Aurora glanced at the manor, then uneasily at Courtney. "I'm suddenly not terribly eager to go in."

"Nor am I." Courtney had finally stopped shaking about ten minutes past. Now, visualizing Slayde's reaction to the news of where they'd been, she wondered if she'd been safer at Morland.

Rayburn swung down from the phaeton. "Despite your reservations, we'd best get inside. Just in case Morland did decide to follow us." He squinted toward the gates. "Although I saw no indication of such."

That convinced both women.

Scrambling down, they abandoned the carriage and scurried up the steps and through the door, Rayburn at their heels.

"Lady Aurora? Miss Johnston?" Siebert's brows drew together at their harried state. "Is something amiss?"

"Yes, something is very amiss," Rayburn answered. "These young ladies needed an escort home. I provided one—me." With that, he turned to the butler. "You must be Siebert. My name is Rayburn. The earl has engaged my services on a particular business matter. I know he left Pembourne early this morning. Has he returned yet?"

"No." A glint of understanding lit Siebert's eyes. "His lordship alerted me to the fact that he'd employed you— and in what capacity. He also advised me that it was possible you might, at some point, need to come directly to Pembourne to meet with him. I presume that occasion has arrived. Please make yourself comfortable in the earl's study. He's due back within the hour."

"No!" Courtney burst out.

Both men stared at her.

"What I meant was, why not show Mr. Rayburn into the yellow salon. 'Tis far more comfortable than the study. And we can provide him with some refreshment until the earl's return. Don't you agree, Aurora?" Courtney gave Aurora a not-the-study look.

"Absolutely," Aurora concurred. "The yellow salon would be ideal."

"Except for the fact that the viscountess is already occupying that room," Siebert inserted, gazing at Courtney and Aurora as if they'd gone quite mad.

"Elinore is here?" Aurora asked.

"Indeed—for the better part of an hour."

"Splendid. Then we can all take tea together." Aurora seized Mr. Rayburn's arm. "Please, won't you join us? I still have many questions. For example, how did you know who I was? When you accosted me behind that tree, I assumed you thought I was an intruder. Then you called me by name, demanded to know what we were doing at Morland, and, more specifically, what Miss Johnston was doing in the manor. I'm terribly impressed."

"Don't be," Rayburn replied with a flicker of amusement. "Your brother provided me with the names and descriptions of both you and Miss Johnston. It's fairly routine for me to familiarize myself with the potential victims of the subject I'm scrutinizing."

Siebert had turned positively green. "You went to Morland?" he managed.

Aurora rolled her eyes. "Yes, Siebert, we did. And we're back, safe and sound. Now, please, I beseech you not to lecture us. As it is, Slayde will probably choke us with his bare hands." She turned to Courtney, her face alight with interest. "Tell me again how Morland looked just before you bolted. Do you really think you provoked him into revealing his guilt?"

"I certainly hope so," Courtney muttered. "If not, I took ten years off my life and am about to be choked for naught."

"Perhaps you'd best show Mr. Rayburn into the yellow salon," Siebert croaked. Turning, he headed down the hall. "I'll arrange for the tea."

"No need." Miss Payne scurried out of a nearby anteroom at that moment. "I was about to bring some refreshment to the viscountess. I'd be happy to provide enough for Lady Aurora, Miss Johnston, and . . . forgive me, sir . . . ?" She inclined her head quizzically at the investigator.

"Rayburn," he supplied.

"Mr. Rayburn."

"Thank you, Miss Payne." Siebert took out a handkerchief and mopped at his brow. "Then I'll maintain my post." He cast a sidelong glance at Aurora. "And await the duke's return."

Elinore rose gracefully when Courtney and Aurora escorted Rayburn into the yellow salon. "Good afternoon," she said with a smile. "I see you've brought a guest."

"Hello, Elinore." Aurora indicated for Rayburn to have a seat on the sofa. "This is Mr. Rayburn. He's an investigator. Slayde hired him to scrutinize Morland's estate." Seeing the investigator start with surprise, she explained, "Elinore is like part of the family. We have no secrets from her."

Reluctantly, he nodded.

"Rayburn, this is the Viscountess Stanwyk."

"My lady." He bowed, politely waiting until all the women had been seated before perching at the edge of the sofa.

"Mr. Rayburn." Elinore folded her hands in her lap, turning her concerned gaze on Aurora. "I take it Slayde is still as adamant as ever about proving Lawrence Bencroft's guilt."

"So are we," Aurora responded.

"*If* he's guilty," Courtney inserted.

Aurora blinked. "Given the way he reacted to your threat, you're not convinced?"

"He *was* menacing," Courtney admitted. "Still, all he did today was to disclaim any knowledge of Armon or his scheme."

"That could be cunning, not innocence."

"Of course it could. His anticipated reaction to my accusations should decide which of the two it is."

"You went to Morland?" Elinore looked horrified. "Both of you?"

"Yes." Aurora answered proudly." 'Twas Courtney's idea. She was incredibly brave, confronting that monster face to face."

"But, why, for heaven's sake?"

"Why indeed." Slayde's livid voice lashed through the room like a whip.

Four heads jerked about, gazes riveted on the open doorway.

Rage emanating from every inch of his powerful frame, Slayde made his way across the salon, his steps taut with the control he was exerting to keep from exploding. Reaching the sofa, he nodded curtly at Rayburn. "Thank you for your diligence." He walked on.

Alongside Rayburn, Aurora held her breath, waiting.

For the first time, Slayde bypassed his sister, pausing directly before Courtney. His composure disintegrating, he seized her elbows, yanking her from the sofa to meet his gaze.

"What the hell were you thinking of?"

Chapter 13

"Did you honestly believe Morland was going to unburden himself and confess to his crimes?"

Slayde was pacing about the sitting room, tossing infuriated looks at Courtney, who was perched on the settee, calmly watching him.

"No," she replied. "And when you stop lecturing me as one would a small child, I'd be happy to provide explanations for both your questions—the one you've just asked and the one you fired at me prior to our discreet withdrawal to the sitting room." Her lips twitched. "Poor Elinore. She looked as if she were trying to memorize the number of stones on her bracelet, that's how intently she was staring at it. You might not erupt often, my lord, but you're quite formidable when you do."

"I'm not laughing, Courtney."

"I know you're not." She sighed. "Very well. What was

I thinking? I was thinking that Morland needed a good, old-fashioned scare. That if he believed someone—other than you—had tangible evidence of his crimes, it would induce him to act."

"Act how? By harming you, too?"

"He'd hardly shoot me down in the middle of his home amidst a flock of servants," Courtney reasoned. "No, I hoped he'd panic, rush over here, and react to my ultimatum."

"Ultimatum?"

A nod. "I warned Morland that unless he made a full confession about his connection to Armon, the extortion of the black diamond and, indirectly, Papa's death, I'd give Bow Street written evidence that he and his father murdered your parents."

Slayde's jaw dropped. "You warned . . ." A swallow, as he again sought control. "What evidence?"

"With regard to Armon, an alleged journal outlining names and details. With regard to your parents, I didn't stay long enough to enumerate. Once I delivered that final blow, Morland lost his composure, and common sense insisted I bolt. But he knows who I am *and* at whose home I'm residing. I fully expect him to explode into Pembourne and do something irrational, something that could give us the very evidence we seek." Courtney's smile was impish. "I was extraordinarily convincing."

With a muffled oath, Slayde sank down beside her. "I'm sure you were. Convincing and reckless. Damn it, Courtney, if anything had happened to you—"

"I wasn't alone. I had an exceptional cohort."

"How reassuring—Aurora," he muttered dryly. "When I asked you to stay on as Aurora's companion, I'd hoped you'd reform her, not outdo her."

"I'm fine, Slayde," Courtney said softly, slipping her hand into his, understanding far better than he that along with loving and needing came the fear of losing. "I'm sorry I caused you pain. But maybe, just maybe, my plan will work."

His fingers tightened around hers. "How did you get by that sentry, Thayer?"

Courtney braced herself. "I implied I'd been . . . sent." She licked her suddenly dry lips. "To tend to the duke's needs."

Slayde's head whipped around. "'The duke's needs,'" he repeated in utter disbelief. "You masqueraded as a . . ."

"Yes," she interrupted hastily. "More or less. Morland seemed pleased enough, until he learned my true purpose in coming."

"I'm sure he did." Slayde looked positively stricken. "I don't know whether to shake you senseless, applaud you, or simply thank God that you escaped unscathed."

"I'm not partial to the first choice. A combination of the second and third would be lovely."

Groaning, Slayde pulled her to him, pressed her head to his chest. "You're aging me. Miracles aren't supposed to do that."

She smiled, listening to the strong, steady beat of his heart. "I love you. Miracles *are* supposed to do that."

She felt him tense. *God,* she prayed silently, *let me help him. Let me heal him so we can have our future. Please.*

"I found Grimes."

Drawing back, Courtney studied Slayde's taut expression. "And?"

"And he did his damnedest to avoid me. I literally had to corner him in his disgusting excuse for an establishment, then grab him as he tried to get by me."

Courtney sat up straight. "Then he was Armon's contact?"

"Not only his contact, but his forger. Evidently, Mr. Grimes is a man of many talents, all of them unlawful ones. But with enough coercion and two hundred pound notes, he gave me the information I sought. It seems that he and Armon did a great deal of business together. Several weeks ago, Armon approached him, saying he'd soon be getting his hands on the infamous black diamond and that he was looking for a buyer. Grimes is no fool; he knows how much that bloody stone is worth. So he agreed to pay Armon three hundred thousand pounds—a mere fraction of what the stone would bring—no questions asked. Armon told him there was one more catch to the arrangement; he needed Grimes to copy a note for him."

"The ransom note," Courtney supplied.

"Right. Well, Grimes didn't mind—hell, it was the easiest catch to fulfill, given his skill at forgery. He copied the note, altering only the date, and gave both notes back to Armon. Oh, and he suggested to Armon that he not destroy the original, just in case it was needed again, such as if I didn't comply with the terms of the note Armon did send, compelling Grimes to forge another."

"That explains why the third note—the one Grimes calls the original—was in Armon's pocket when he died."

"Exactly. He probably intended to wait until the transaction was complete and the diamond in his possession before destroying the note Grimes used as a model."

"Did Grimes tell you who his buyer for the diamond was?"

"According to him, he'd had several bites. Also, he had yet to contact his most promising potential buyer: the royal family who'd originally offered a fortune for the gem's restoration. Believe me, Grimes knew what he stood to gain. But he never had the opportunity to reap that enormous profit. On the night he and Armon were to make the exchange, he arrived at the designated alleyway to find Armon dead and the diamond gone."

Courtney drew a slow, inward breath, asking the most vital question of all. "Had Grimes any idea who Armon was working with? When they made their arrangements, when they exchanged the forged ransom note, did Armon ever mention the name of his mysterious employer?"

"Not according to Grimes," Slayde replied. "He swore

Armon never referred to his employer by name. And, trust me, I pressured him for answers—a dozen times, with my arm against his throat. Either he was telling the truth or he's more afraid of the man he's protecting than he is of me."

"It could be the truth. Remember, when Armon was aboard the *Isobel*, he spent a great deal of time in my cabin, gloating. Yet never once did he use his employer's name. Perhaps he was too shrewd to do so, even to Grimes."

"Perhaps." Slayde didn't look convinced. "I could have persisted, but Grimes was sheet-white and trembling like a leaf as it was. If I knew for certain he was hiding something, I would have beaten him senseless, but my conscience refused to permit me to bodily harm a man I wasn't sure knew any more than he'd already revealed. Moreover, I didn't want him to flee to parts unknown. So I backed off, lulled him into a false sense of security. This way, he'll remain in Dartmouth, should we need to question him at a later date." With a resigned sigh, Slayde leaned back against the cushions.

"You look tired," Courtney observed softly.

He gazed at her from beneath hooded lids. "Weary, not tired. I aged ten years when Siebert told me where you and Aurora had gone." A regretful look. "I wish you'd have more faith in me. I vowed to find Armon's accomplice, and I shall."

Courtney leaned toward him, shaking her head. "I never doubted you, Slayde," she countered, knowing it was time to reveal her true reason for descending on Lawrence Bencroft, to share with Slayde what she'd hoped to accomplish—and why. "Avenging Papa's death wasn't my motivation for confronting the duke. Nor was determining if Morland was, in fact, Armon's accomplice. What I'd hoped was to provoke—"

"Lord Pembourne?" Siebert's purposeful knock interrupted Courtney's revelation.

Slayde came to his feet, recognizing the urgent note in his butler's voice. "Yes, Siebert, come in."

"Forgive me for intruding, sir. But you did advise me to summon you immediately if you received word from Mr. Oridge." He held out an envelope. "This missive just arrived."

"Maybe he's found something." Courtney, too, was now on her feet.

Swiftly, Slayde took the letter and tore it open, scanning its contents. "Oridge located the *Fortune*. The ship made its way down the Thames, rounded the coast, and passed Sandwich, heading south through the Downs. Evidently, Oridge waited for the right moment, then crowded the *Fortune* until it fell victim to the Goodwin Sands. The ship is being hauled back to London. Oridge wants me to meet him there."

"I'll pack." Courtney headed for the door.

"Courtney." Slayde caught up with her in the hallway.

"Don't even consider asking me to stay behind," she cautioned.

A twinge of amusement. "I had no intentions of doing that. I was merely going to suggest we leave for London today, rather than wait for morning. I know it's after two, but we could travel five or six hours before darkness falls and, as a result, be that much farther on our way when we stop for the night. We'll stay at an inn in Somerset and be refreshed and ready to begin anew at daybreak. Is that acceptable?"

"My bag is as good as packed." Courtney turned to go.

Abruptly, she realized they had an audience.

Aurora, Elinore, Rayburn, and Siebert hovered nearby, all of whom, upon hearing Courtney and Slayde, began talking at once, beginning with Rayburn's "Shall I return to my post, sir?", followed by Siebert's "I'll summon Matilda to assist Miss Johnston," which was simultaneous with Elinore's tactful "Courtney, might I be of some assistance?" and Aurora's resounding "Why are you going to London?"

Slayde stared amazedly at all four of them. "You're awaiting our emergence like a pack of sentries. Did you think I'd done Courtney bodily harm?"

Characteristically, it was Aurora who answered. "Can you blame us for being worried?" she demanded, planting her hands on her hips. "Slayde, you very nearly assaulted poor Courtney before dragging her from the salon—after having bellowed so loudly upon arriving that you doubtless incited a stampede in the stables. For a man who prides himself on his self-control, you behaved like a wild boar."

There was a chorus of sharp inhalations as everyone awaited Slayde's response.

To the amazement of all, he began to chuckle. "You're right, Aurora. Although I find your analogy most unflattering. Still, I do see the similarities, now that you've called them to my attention." Sobering, he shifted his gaze to Rayburn. "Yes. Return to your post. I want to know if Morland so much as blinks in the direction of my estate."

"Yes, sir." The investigator hurried off.

"Siebert, Mr. Rayburn will need some means of travel," Slayde prompted. "A carriage perhaps?"

"Hmm?" The butler was still staring at Slayde as if he were a stranger. "Oh. Mr. Rayburn. Of course, sir." He nodded crisply and complied, although he paused once or twice, glancing over his shoulder as if to confirm that the man who'd just successively shouted and laughed was indeed the earl.

"Slayde," Elinore inserted, "has something significant happened? Is that why you're leaving for London?"

"Armon's ship was located," Slayde answered tersely. "Courtney and I are going to London to recover whatever members of her father's crew are aboard." He frowned. "Will you excuse me? I must speak with my guards to prepare them for the possibility that Morland might make an appearance while we're gone." His silver eyes darkened, his gaze hard as steel as it fixed on Aurora. "I want you inside the manor until we return. No strolls, no lighthouse, nothing. Is that thoroughly understood?"

Seeing the familiar mutinous expression that flashed

on her friend's face, Courtney added her voice to Slayde's. "We stirred up a hornet's nest today, Aurora. If Morland is the criminal we suspect he is, my instigation will have rendered him more dangerous than ever. Please, don't argue with Slayde or do anything foolish. Not this time. Your life could be at stake."

Aurora's anger cooled somewhat. "You're right. Very well, I'll stay snug—and bored—in the manor until your return. Unless," she added hopefully, "you want me to accompany you on your trip?"

"Absolutely not." Slayde shot that notion down at once. "As it is, I'll have my hands full keeping Courtney out of trouble. At least knowing you're safe will afford me some peace of mind."

A resigned nod.

"Go, Slayde," Elinore urged him. "I'll assist Courtney until Matilda appears to take over."

"Thank you."

"I wish you luck," she called after him. Brows drawn in concern, she watched his retreat, then took Courtney's hands in hers. "Are you certain this ordeal isn't going to be too painful for you, dear? You have no idea which of your father's crew have survived, nor what kind of condition they'll be in. Moreover, seeing them will doubtless evoke devastating memories."

"I'm sure you're right," Courtney conceded. "But 'tis something I must do." Her chin set. "Not only do I want to rescue Papa's crew, I intend to search every inch of Armon's ship until I find a clue as to the identity of his accomplice. Surely there must be something: a note, a journal, a letter. I told Lawrence Bencroft I had written proof. Well, by week's end, perhaps that boast will become a reality."

The tiny Somerset village was shrouded in newly settled darkness when the Huntley carriage rolled in.

The ride from Pembourne had been quiet, both occupants preoccupied with the anticipation of what lay ahead. During the last few hours of travel, Courtney had dozed, her body protesting the grueling day to which it had been subjected. First Morland, then Slayde, now this.

Lord, she was tired.

"I'll have my driver post the horses and find out where the nearest inn is," Slayde announced once they'd come to a halt. "We'll eat, get some rest, then travel all day tomorrow."

"All right." Courtney stretched, her muscles cramped and achy.

Frowning, Slayde traced the circles beneath her eyes. "You're exhausted."

"I have no reason to be. I dozed throughout the entire carriage ride."

"Exhaustion isn't always cured by sleep, nor caused by lack thereof." Slayde's knuckles brushed her cheek.

The tenderness in his voice, his touch made Courtney's chest tighten, as did the realization of why Slayde was making this trip—and for whom.

For the first time since leaving Pembourne, her thoughts returned to the truth she'd been about to share with him when Siebert's knock had intruded, shattering the intimacy of their mood, a mood that had been further eclipsed by Oridge's message, then forgotten during the long, tense carriage ride to Somerset.

'Twas time to recapture it.

Pensively, Courtney gazed into Slayde's handsome face. She needed him to understand her true motivation for going to Morland, to realize that what she'd done was inspired by love, not lack of faith. Her faith was unconditional; she knew he'd succeed in bringing Morland, or whoever Armon's accomplice was, to justice.

For *her*.

But the person for whom Courtney was pursuing Morland was *Slayde*. 'Twas *his* past she sought to resolve, *his* future she longed to ensure, *his* heart she was determined to grant peace.

And, danger or not, she would.

Abruptly, her fatigue vanished.

"What is it?" Slayde was studying her quizzically.

"Nothing. I'm just glad we're stopping for the night. I want to finish the conversation we were having earlier."

"So do I." Slayde looked like he wanted to say more, then checked himself. "I'll make the necessary arrangements. I won't be more than a few minutes." He opened the carriage door and swung down. "You rest."

Rest? Hardly.

As Slayde headed off, Courtney alit as well, stretching her limbs and wondering how Slayde would react when she told him that barging in on Lawrence Bencroft was but one of the steps she'd taken to silence the echoes of the past.

Then there was the other step.

She grinned, savoring the fact that by tomorrow, Cutterton's man would reach London, turn the letter and notes over to the *Times* and see that they were copied, then reclaimed and returned to Pembourne. Within days, the entire world would be buzzing with the news that the black diamond was no longer in Huntley hands.

And Slayde's future would be his.

Shaking out her skirts, Courtney strolled away from the carriage, too restless to remain confined a moment longer. She inhaled deeply, infused with hope and excitement, a prescience that something life-altering was about to occur. The night was misty, a light wind playing through the trees, and she wandered along the roadside, letting the cool air waft across her face and breeze through her hair.

She never heard her assailant.

One minute she was meandering about the road, daydreaming, the next, Slayde was shouting her name, the pounding of his footsteps alerting her to the oncoming danger.

Her head jerked around, a scream freezing on her lips as, out of nowhere, a masked rider bore down on her, the glint of a pistol leaving no doubt as to his intentions.

The shot rang out, whizzing past Courtney's face just

as a powerful force struck her body, knocking her breath from her lungs as it catapulted her sideways, tumbling her to the cold, hard ground.

The hoofbeats thundered by and disappeared.

"Courtney?" Slayde eased away from her, his face stark with fear. "Sweetheart, are you all right?"

She raised her head, numb with shock, and nodded, unsure what had happened, not quite able to catch her breath. She glanced at Slayde, then down at herself, realizing on some obscure level that he had managed to take the brunt of the fall, cushioning her weight with his.

"Answer me," he commanded, cupping her face, scanning her body for visible signs of blood. "You weren't hit, were you?"

The bullet. He meant the bullet. Someone had tried to shoot her.

Tremors of reaction shuddered through her. "No," she managed. She pointed to her chest. "My . . . breath . . ."

"Shhh, I know." Slayde nearly sagged with relief. "'Twas just the fall." Slowly, he rubbed her back. "Relax. Your breathing will return to normal on its own." Another concerned look. "Your ribs—I tried to shield them as best I could."

"They're . . . fine." The trembling began to subside as Courtney's breathing evened out. "Slayde . . . that man tried to kill me." She went ashen even as she said it.

"Yes." The expression in Slayde's eyes was positively murderous. "He did."

"Was it Morland?"

"I don't know. He wore black clothing and a mask that covered his head and face. I couldn't even make out his build—the darkness made it impossible to distinguish." A muscle worked in Slayde's jaw. "But given your excursion to Bencroft's estate this morning . . ."

"M'lord! M'lord!" Seaford, the Huntley driver, rushed over. "Are you hurt?"

Slayde rose, hoisting Courtney to her feet, assessing her carefully. "I don't think so, Seaford." He hooked an arm about Courtney's waist. "But we'd best get Miss

Johnston to the inn." For a split second, he averted his head, searching the now-deserted road before them, a lethal look flashing across his face.

Alongside him, Courtney shifted.

His head whipped around. "Can you walk?"

She nodded. "Nothing is broken." An anxious glance at Slayde. "What about you? You fell harder than I did."

"I'm fine." His tone was harsh, clipped. "Let's go."

Neither of them spoke until they reached the inn, both still in shock at what had happened. Slayde took two adjoining rooms, then arranged for hot baths to be brought up shortly.

It seemed like an eternity, but thirty minutes later, Courtney sank gratefully into a steaming tub, letting the warmth soak away her fear and discomfort. She washed herself hastily, eager to banish the memories of what had just occurred, more eager to be finished so she could simply drift, do nothing.

Think nothing.

Rinsing her hair, she relaxed, sliding down until her head rested against the side of the tub, shutting her eyes and emptying her mind.

God, this is heaven, she thought, lulled into a delicious half-sleep. *Heaven.*

"You look like a beautiful mermaid." Slayde's deep voice resounded in her ear. "But the water's growing cold. Besides, we've got to get you to bed."

Courtney blinked, wondering when Slayde had come into the room. She'd certainly never heard him enter, but there he was, crouched beside her, tucking damp strands of hair off her face.

"I'll sleep here," she mumbled.

A chuckle. "Not unless you want to shrivel away to nothing." He lifted her from the tub, enfolding her in towels and carrying her to the bed.

His warmth felt wonderful. Courtney murmured a protest when he placed her on the sheets, then sighed with contentment when he followed her down, enveloping her against his solid strength. Instinctively, she snuggled closer, rubbing her face against what she discovered to be his bare, damp chest. "That's right," she announced, half to herself. "You had a bath, too."

"Um-hum." The husky sound tickled her ear. "Then I donned my breeches and came in to check on you. I needed to make sure you were all right." He swallowed, hard, his voice growing oddly choked. "Are you hungry?"

Awareness won out over fatigue, and Courtney's lashes lifted, her eyes luminous with emotion as they gazed into his. "No." She lay a trembling palm against his jaw. "That's twice you've saved my life," she whispered.

Torment slashed his features. "I didn't think I'd reach you in time." His fingers threaded through her damp, tangled hair. "In that split second when I saw the pistol barrel gleam and you standing in its path, the only thoughts that kept running through my mind were that I couldn't reach you . . ." He drew a deep, shuddering breath. "And that without you, there's nothing."

"Slayde." She caressed the warmth of his skin, twined her arms about his neck.

"Nothing, Courtney." He kissed her, first tenderly, then with an urgency like none he'd ever known. "God help me if I'd lost you. God help me . . ."

Fiercely, Courtney returned Slayde's kiss, tears burning behind her eyes as she felt, and shared, his desperation. Their love for each other was a miracle—a miracle that, but for the grace of God and the space of a heartbeat, could have been snatched away.

Making it all the more precious.

With shaking hands, Slayde flung Courtney's towels aside, staring worshipfully down at her before lowering his head, his mouth burning kisses down her throat, her neck, the upper swell of her breasts. He shifted, nuzzling her nipple into a damp, hardened peak, then drawing it into his mouth, first slowly, then repeatedly, powerfully, until Courtney was whimpering with need and Slayde's breath was coming in harsh, painful rasps. Still, he didn't stop, moving to her other breast, rendering the same exquisite torture until Courtney was sure she would die.

"God, I need all of you," he muttered thickly, his fingers gliding down, parting her thighs, finding and penetrating her all at once.

"Slayde." Courtney sobbed his name, opening to his touch, her hips lifting in silent plea when his finger slid inside her, began an unbearable rhythm of plunge and retreat. "Slayde," she managed, undulating to meet his caresses. "I'm dying."

"So am I." He rose, cast his breeches to the floor and knelt between her parted thighs, his gaze hot, wild.

He needed more.

Drowning in desire and emotion, Slayde lifted her legs over his shoulders, burying his mouth in her sweetness.

Courtney unraveled at the first lash of his tongue, the feelings too strong to fight, the climax too essential to delay. She heard herself scream, felt the clawing release erupt inside her, spasm after shuddering spasm gripping her, hurling her into a sensual oblivion too beautiful to experience alone.

"Slayde," she gasped, tugging at his arms as he raised his head, gazed at her with a wealth of yearning in his eyes. "Please . . . I need you inside me."

With a groan of surrender, Slayde complied, fitting his body to hers and burying himself to the hilt in one perfect, inexorable thrust. Her contractions clasped at his length, shattering his control, instantly propelling him over the edge of intoxicating sensation. "Courtney." He pounded into her, his thrusts wild, uncontrollable, his fingers biting into her hips as he worked them to meet the frenzied motion of his. "Courtney." He went rigid, his entire being focused on that highest pinnacle of sensation.

He toppled over the edge, crushing her against him, pouring into her in bottomless, scalding bursts, seeking her womb in an inherent need to give her everything— his love, his soul.

His child.

"Yes." Fervently, Courtney held him, feeling the same reckless need as he, her body opening to receive his seed. She shuddered, her own spasms heightened by the euphoric knowledge that she and Slayde were one, that he was a part of her and she of him.

Slayde collapsed, tremors still vibrating through his powerful frame as he blanketed Courtney, dragged air into his lungs. Eyes shut, he savored the lingering filaments of sensation, acutely aware of the warm wetness of his seed, not spilled on the sheets beside him, but buried deep inside Courtney.

He awaited the onslaught of guilt.

It never came.

Worry, however, did—the instant he felt Courtney go limp beneath him.

Shifting his weight to his elbows, Slayde brushed damp tendrils of hair off her face, panic streaking through him in lightning waves when she remained unmoving, eyes closed. Had he hurt her? She was so slight and delicate and, Lord only knew, there had been nothing delicate about the way he'd just taken her. He'd been a wild man, frenzied with his need to possess her, to reassure himself that she was alive and whole and here in his arms. He'd been lost to his own raw emotions, oblivious to her ribs, her head, her brush with death— the second in a fortnight—everything but the hollow aching in his soul.

"Courtney." He uttered her name with hoarse urgency. "Look at me."

Her lashes fluttered and lifted slightly, providing Slayde with a quick glimpse of dazed, sea-green eyes.

"Did I hurt you?"

A faraway smile. "Hurt me?" She sighed, shifting slightly. "Oh, no."

Relief flooded through him in great, untamed waves. Reason intruded, reminding him that, whether or not she was aware of it, his weight was too much for her. He began to lift himself away, only to discover that to do so was a sheer impossibility—not because he was physically unable, but because he was emotionally unwilling. To separate his body from Courtney's was an intolerable option.

He solved the problem by rolling to one side and taking her with him. Gently, he cradled her in his arms, her head tucked beneath his chin, his body still imbedded in hers.

"How's that?" he murmured.

"Ummm," Courtney mumbled, snuggling closer.

Myriad emotions—vast, extraordinary—knotted in Slayde's chest, and tenderly, he kissed Courtney's disheveled crown of red-gold hair. "Sweetheart, I'm sorry. I lost my mind entirely. Are you all right?"

She tipped back her head, her lips softly parted, her cheeks flushed with the lingering effects of their passion. "'All right'? No. Overwhelmed, exhilarated, dazed, awed—yes. But 'all right'? No. Never again." With a tremulous smile, she brushed her fingertips across his chin. "And you? Are you all right?"

"No." Slayde pressed her palm to his lips. "I'm humbled." He kissed her wrist, her forearm, her shoulder. "I'm drunk with discovery." He raised his head, gazed into her eyes. "And I'm so in love it astounds me."

"As am I." Courtney grew sober. "So in love I could never leave you, even if you sent me away."

His eyes darkened. "God help me, I don't have the strength to send you away."

"That wouldn't be strength; 'twould be stupidity."

"With regard to *my* future," Slayde qualified, voicing his fears aloud. "But what about *yours?*"

"My future is with you. Regardless of what that entails."

Slayde groaned, pressing his forehead to hers. "I want that so desperately, it terrifies me. Because I have no right. No right to feel what I'm feeling, want what I'm wanting. But, God, how I need you. I, who have never needed anyone in my life. I need you to fill my life, to fill *me*—in all the ways I never knew I was empty." An abrupt swallow. "When I went so berserk just now, it was because I was frantic, frantic to meld us into one, to merge all of you with all of me. Frantic to give you—" He broke off.

"Your child," Courtney finished softly, tears glistening on her lashes as she gazed into Slayde's tormented eyes. "I was just as frantic—to conceive your child, to carry it, to bear it." She gave him a watery smile. "I want all your children. An estate full of Huntleys with spirit and fire and strength. Oh, Slayde, how could babes born of our love be anything but blessings?"

His resolve was shattering, and he knew it. Or perhaps it had shattered the moment he'd pulled Courtney from that sack, held her while she cried, bared all his scars for her to see. She was indeed a miracle—a miracle who deserved a life, not of fear and isolation, but of freedom and security. Damn it, why couldn't he offer her that?

"Courtney." His grip tightened, holding her to him as if to negate the potential outcome of his words. "There's so much I can't give you."

"You, my darling, have given me all I've ever dreamed of," she countered, her expression so beautiful and earnest Slayde wanted to enfold her in his arms and never let her go. "You've given me passion and tenderness. You've given me comfort, love—a piece of heaven." She glanced down, slipping her palm between them to lay it against her abdomen. "And who knows? Perhaps you've given me something more than either of us can yet discern."

Slayde's gut wrenched with the impact of her words. "I love you," he said fervently. "But I'm so bloody afraid . . . for you, our children . . ."

Courtney kissed the damp column of his throat. "I know you are. And I refuse to permit it. So I've taken steps to relegate that fear to the past—along with the events that incited it."

"What?" Slayde's question vibrated against her lips. She felt him tense, draw back. "Courtney—" He gripped her arms. "What steps?"

Filled with a sense of rightness that not even Slayde's

tone could dispel, she replied, "You already know about my visit to Morland, although you misconstrued its purpose. I wasn't trying to goad Morland into revealing the name of Armon's accomplice, though I would have welcomed the information had he provided it. What I hoped to do—what I might very well have *succeeded* in doing—is frighten him enough to give himself away, to prove, once and for all, that his family was responsible for your parents' murders. What you don't know," she pushed on, determined to tell Slayde everything, "is that I also loaned the three ransom notes you received, plus a forged letter allegedly written by you, to the *Times*. In turn, the *Times*, through its vast number of copies, will soon notify everyone that the black diamond is no longer in the Huntleys' possession." Courtney smiled at Slayde's stunned expression. "There. I've spoken my piece."

"Well, I haven't spoken mine," Slayde retorted in amazement. "You did *what?* When?" His mind was racing, absorbing the implications of her revelation. "How did you manage this?" A scowl. "I needn't ask with whom."

"No, you needn't. Aurora was the most splendid of accomplices. I composed the letter. She penned it. She copies your hand and signature beautifully. And I did a fine job of explaining how you traded the stone for her life. Our parcel should be arriving in London late tomorrow. Thus, in a matter of days, all those seeking the black diamond will know to seek it elsewhere— putting an end to your worries over our safety and the safety of all future Huntleys." Courtney leaned forward, pressed her lips to Slayde's chest, nuzzling his warm skin, trailing her tongue over the hair-roughened contours.

His muscles tightened at her touch. "You did all this . . . for me?"

"No, I did all this for us."

A hard swallow. "But as we know, the diamond is

still—" Slayde's breath expelled in a hiss when Courtney lapped at his nipple.

"*We* know that," Courtney concurred, reveling in his utter masculinity, his involuntary response to her as he throbbed and hardened, filling and awakening her body, causing it to soften, melt around him. "But no one else does." She pressed hot, open-mouthed kisses down his chest, then up again, giving the other nipple the same attention she had the first. "You've spent far too much time dwelling on the truth and not enough time thinking up a diversion. I merely provided one for you."

"Oh, you're quite a diversion," Slayde assured her thickly. His fingers curved around her nape, tugging her head back until he could bury his lips in hers. "The full impact of all this has yet to sink in. Once it does, I'll have a hundred questions—all of which I intend for you to answer." His hands slid down to her bottom, lifting her and melding their loins in one unyielding motion. "Later." He groaned as she wrapped her legs around him, arched to take him deeper. "Much later."

They made love all night, hungrily at first, then, slowly, deeply—murmuring to each other in heated fragments, exploring the dizzying rapture their joined bodies made, discovering all the facets of the miracle that was theirs.

The culmination of that miracle came at dawn.

"I love you," Courtney was whispering as Slayde moved on her, in her, their gazes locked, their fingers intertwined overhead.

Slayde's grip tightened, his eyes growing fiercely gray. "Marry me," he demanded hoarsely, pressing his hips to hers with an urgency that transcended the physical. "Courtney—marry me." It was both command and appeal, torn from his chest, wrenched from his soul. "No matter what the future brings. I can't live without you. Be my wife."

Courtney raised up, brushed her lips softly across his. "Yes." Her eyes filled with tears, but she didn't blink or look away. "I can't live without you either. I didn't live until we met. Yes. I'd face anything to be your wife."

He climaxed, gritting his teeth against the unexpected surge of pleasure, pouring into her in a torrent of feeling more profound than words could express.

He expressed them nonetheless.

"I love you," he ground out, convulsing yet again. "God, I love you."

Slayde's response triggered hers, and Courtney shattered, drenching spasms rippling through her, dissolving her into a million fragments of light and love.

Afterward, they didn't speak, just lay together quietly, watching the sun rise.

"It's never looked so beautiful before," Slayde murmured, Courtney curved against him, his chin atop her head.

With a smile, Courtney recalled Mr. Scollard's words. "That's because before, you looked but couldn't see."

"Hmm?"

"On my first visit to the lighthouse, Mr. Scollard declared Armon a fool for substituting me for Aurora since, in his opinion, we look nothing alike," Courtney explained. "But he said that at night, the coloring could fool someone. 'Especially,' to quote his exact words, 'someone who looks but can't see.' Then he added, 'At least then, he couldn't. He sees now.'" She twisted around to see Slayde's face. "After which he nodded and told me, 'Good for you.'"

Slayde blinked. "Scollard actually said all that?"

"Every word."

"He was talking about me. About us." Slayde grinned. "Perhaps he really is a visionary."

Thank you, Mr. Scollard, Courtney offered silently, snuggling into Slayde's arms.

"We haven't finished discussing your delivery to the *Times,*" Slayde reminded her.

A smile. "What would you like to know?"

"How you managed it: collecting the notes, transporting them to the newspaper."

"A simple task for two resourceful women like Aurora and me. Aurora pilfered the notes and stationery from your desk. I conjured up the letter, explaining exactly what had happened and why you'd been forced to hunt for the diamond, then surrender it to Armon. I made you sound positively heroic—" Courtney's grin turned impish. "Heroic, but humble. Between that and the outrage the notes will evoke, the compassion over what you've been forced to endure, you'll probably be knighted."

"I doubt it," Slayde returned dryly. "By the way, just where *did* I find the gem?"

"I never specified. Pick your hiding place."

Slayde rolled his eyes. "And who carried this parcel to London?"

"Mathers."

"Mathers?" Slayde's head shot up. "Who authorized him to—"

"Cutterton did. He instructed him to deliver the papers, wait for them to be copied, then bring them immediately back to Pembourne. And before you blame Cutterton," Courtney added quickly, "I believe Mr. Scollard's wizardry had something to do with Cutterton's uncustomary agreeability. He consented to Aurora's request without a single question or comment."

"You're right. Scollard is a wizard." Gently, Slayde turned her toward him, framed her face between his palms. "Courtney—thank you. No one has ever . . ." He struggled for the right words. "What you did for me . . ."

Courtney pressed a silencing forefinger to his mouth. "I love you, too, Slayde," she whispered.

A pained expression crossed his face. "So now that you've rendered me safe, how do I do the same for you? Or have you forgotten last night's episode?"

"No. I haven't." She sighed. "I wish we knew for certain that rider was Morland. But we will, once we return home. Rayburn will tell us if the duke left his estate."

"Unless Rayburn wasn't at his post at the time. Remember, Morland could have followed you, Aurora, and Rayburn to Pembourne, then waited and followed us here."

"Even if that's so, Rayburn restationed himself outside Morland hours ago. If the duke tried to shoot me, then rushed back to Morland, Rayburn would have witnessed his arrival." Courtney's eyes sparkled. "If so, we'll have more of the ammunition we seek. Further, I intend to make full use of our time aboard the *Fortune*, to search it from top to bottom. Armon might have left something about—a missive, anything—that mentions his employer's name. And if that name happens to be Morland, the duke will be well and duly implicated. *That* knowledge should be enough to push him over the edge."

"Courtney, if Morland is the one who just took a shot at you, he's already over the edge," Slayde said grimly. "We're not pushing him any further."

"We must. The whole purpose of this plan is to pressure him into confessing to your parents' murders."

"Not anymore, it's not." Slayde's grip on Courtney tightened. "Didn't you hear what I said? Without you, there's nothing. I need you, damn it. And I intend to keep you safe. If Morland is guilty, the son of a bitch *will* pay. For the past, yes. More importantly, for the future he almost robbed us of—a future I never imagined having and don't intend to forfeit." A muscle worked in Slayde's jaw. "So we'll find a way to unmask him prudently, without endangering your life. *Our* life," he added, his voice thick with emotion. "Sweetheart, don't you understand? Before, there was retribution. Now there's you."

The magnitude of Slayde's pronouncement sank in, bringing tears to Courtney's eyes. "Thank you," she breathed. "That was the most beautiful declaration of love I could ever hope for."

A brooding expression clouded Slayde's gaze. "There's something I must ask you," he said abruptly. "And I want you to consider the question carefully before you answer it."

"All right."

"If your father were still alive, would that affect your decision to marry me?"

Courtney stared. "What?"

"Were your father here, alive and well, were you able to have your old life back rather than take on the ardors of mine, would you choose to? I want the truth."

"Then here it is: no." She wrapped her arms fiercely about Slayde's waist. "You, Lord Pembourne, are a wonderful and compassionate man. You're also a dolt. Do you honestly believe I accepted your marriage proposal because I'm alone? Slayde, I accepted because I love you. Yes, I wish to God Papa were alive. But if he were, the only thing about our wedding that would change is the fact that he could officially give me away, share in the joy I'll feel when I become your wife." Her lips trembled. "And, Slayde, he *would* share that joy. He's the one who told me, time and again, that I'd know when I met the right man, a man who needed me and my love as much as I needed his. I'd give anything if Papa could have lived to see his prophecy become a reality—and to meet you. He'd think so highly of you, and you of him." Courtney drew a shaky breath. "In my heart, though, he'll be here to bless our union. I wish he could be here in fact. But even if he were, I'd still be bidding my old life good-bye. Because never have I wanted anything as much as I want to become your wife. Does that answer your question?"

Slayde made a rough sound deep in his throat. "Not only my question, but my prayer."

"Then will you answer an equally difficult question for me?"

"Anything."

Courtney wet her lips, summoned her courage. "Your proposal came on the heels of my recounting what I'd done with the ransom notes. What if I hadn't told you of my plan? What if I'd never thought of it to begin with? What if, in the worst case, my plan fails, if we were never to learn the truth about your parents' murderers and if the dangers associated with the black diamond were to somehow seep back into our lives?" She searched

Slayde's face. "Would you regret asking me to marry you?"

"Not in a thousand years," he answered instantly.

"But what about—"

"My vow?" he finished for her. "To hell with it. I made that vow in empty ignorance, before I knew what it meant to love. My feelings for you . . ." With trembling hands, he gathered her closer. "These feelings dwarf everything: my vow, the diamond and its fabricated curse, even the past and all its agony. I'll never let anything harm you. I'll protect you with my life. And I'll make you happy—happier than you ever dreamed possible." Lowering his head, he brushed Courtney's lips with his. "Does that answer your question?"

An aching smile. "Not only my question, but my prayer."

Chapter 14

"My lord." Oridge greeted Slayde at the door of the warehouse he'd specified as their meeting spot. "I'm glad you're here." A flicker of surprise as he glimpsed Courtney. "Miss Johnston accompanied you, I see."

"I insisted on coming, Mr. Oridge," Courtney answered for herself. "I can't be shielded. 'Twas my father's ship Armon seized. Because of him and his men, I lost my home, my father, and very nearly my life. If any of Papa's crew is still alive, I want to see them firsthand. Further, I want to be allowed to board the *Fortune* after it's been emptied, to look around for possible clues that could lead us to Armon's accomplice. Oh, and I'll be more than happy to identify any members of his crew I recognize from the *Isobel*'s capture. That will give Bow Street additional leverage to hang them."

Oridge glanced at Slayde, who nodded.

"Miss Johnston is right," he told his investigator. "She

is directly involved in this mystery—even more so than you're yet aware."

"Sir?"

Slayde frowned, recalling for the umpteenth time the recent attempt on Courtney's life. "I'll explain later. For now, fill us in on whatever you've learned thus far."

"Very well," Oridge agreed. "Armon's first mate did a fair amount of talking, once he was properly persuaded." A subtle flexing of his muscles left little doubt as to what method of persuasion Oridge had used. "Evidently, most of the *Isobel*'s crew were transferred to the *Fortune,* as per Armon's instructions."

"Were they hurt?" Courtney demanded anxiously.

"No. To the contrary—they were ignored. Once Armon's crew realized their captain was gone for good, chaos erupted. His men were preoccupied only with getting to London and pawning the booty they'd pilfered from the *Isobel,* then sailing off to parts unknown. Your father's crew was imprisoned aboard the *Fortune* solely during those hours when Armon's men disembarked to hawk their goods. Otherwise, they were free to move about at will, so long as they didn't make trouble. Which none of them did. Consequently, they are now alive and unharmed—at least those crewmen who were transferred to the *Fortune,* that is."

" 'Those who were transferred to the *Fortune,*' " Courtney repeated. "Who wasn't?"

"Ten men in all—one of whom, as you know, was your father."

"What about Lexley—Papa's next in command?"

"He, unfortunately, was another of the ten. It seems Armon viewed him unfavorably; he said Lexley had given him too much trouble to be spared."

"He did." Courtney's throat tightened. "Poor Lexley battled Armon every step of the way. Especially when he commanded him to hurl Papa overboard." She bowed her head. "The only time Lexley complied without resistance was when Armon ordered him to transfer me to Lord Pembourne's fishing boat. *That* order he embraced, realizing it would afford me my sole chance of survival. Lexley was decent and loyal—too loyal to serve a pirate. And, because of that, he died."

"We don't know that for a fact."

Courtney's head came up. "What do you mean?"

"Lexley wasn't killed on the spot. He and the eight other crewmen I mentioned were shoved into longboats and taken beyond Cornwall to Raven Island."

"They were left there . . . alive?"

"Yes." Oridge held up a restraining palm, trying to temper Courtney's eagerness. "I must caution you, Miss Johnston, that the odds of surviving Raven Island are very slim. No ships travel there, not with the harsh currents and jagged rocks, so the prospects of a chance rescue are nil. There is also little to eat and nothing in the way of shelter."

"Then what hope is there?"

"The fact that I've arranged a *planned* rescue. The instant I wrested the details of what had occurred from Armon's first mate, I sent word to a colleague of mine, who, along with five associates of his, happen to be among the most extraordinary and seasoned navigators in England. I didn't receive word back from my colleague until just before you arrived, as he lives far west in Cornwall. In any case, he and his men departed for the isle instantly, equipped with longboats, food, and medical supplies. They left from Falmouth, so they'll probably have reached Raven by now. Let me repeat, the chances of recovering your crew alive are remote but, in their favor, it's been a rather mild May. And, should Lexley and the others have discovered any source of food—be it nuts, berries, or an unlikely fish or two—there is a slim chance they could be alive. We'll soon know."

"Thank you," Courtney said gratefully. "I pray your efforts, and the efforts of your men, are successful."

"As do I." Oridge gestured for her and Slayde to follow him. "Armon's men are in the rear of the warehouse, under guard. Once you're finished with them, they'll be taken away. As for *your* crew—" Oridge grinned. "I took the liberty of providing them with a few rounds of ale at the local pub. By now, they must be feeling quite renewed."

"I hope I can make the same claim once I've faced Armon's men," Courtney muttered, suddenly shaken by the fact that she was about to confront the fiends who'd destroyed her home and killed her father.

"You will." Tenderly, Slayde enfolded her fingers in his, his warmth a welcome balm to her distress. "I'm right beside you."

Courtney could actually feel his strength seep through her, renew her faltering courage. "Thank you, my lord," she replied, love shining in her eyes. "Although I must warn you that once this ordeal is over, I'll want to join my father's crew at that pub, where I intend to consume one—perhaps two—full goblets of fortifying brandy."

Slayde's smile wrapped itself around her. "My pound notes are ready."

It was like reliving a nightmare, Courtney thought, scrutinizing the cluster of surly, foul-smelling pirates, meeting the cruel gazes of those who'd boarded the *Isobel* with Armon. She'd caught mere glimpses of them during those horrible days of her imprisonment; in fact, the only ones she'd viewed up close were the two who'd joined Armon in besieging the quarter-deck. Yet it mattered not. Their bristled faces, filthy hair, and arrogant sneers had engraved themselves in her mind forever—an indelible horror that no amount of retribution could erase. Just looking at them now was enough to make her gut clench and her blood run cold.

And, God help her, to remember.

Slayde was watching her unsteady breathing, her ashen expression. "Oridge, I have nothing to say to these bastards," he pronounced. "So far as I'm concerned, you can take them away and hang them all now. But let's allow Miss Johnston to identify those who seized her father and her ship, just to eliminate any chance that the magistrate might be generous in his sentencing. Then, get the scum out of here."

"Certainly, my lord." Oridge turned to Courtney. "Miss Johnston, do you recognize any of these thugs?"

With a shudder of revulsion, Courtney nodded. "Those two." She pointed at the last two men on the left. "They guarded the *Isobel*'s berth deck. I saw them outside my cabin door whenever Armon opened it. The scarred one in the rear I recognize as well. He preceded Armon onto the *Isobel*." Courtney's heart lurched as her eyes found the most painful memory of all. "The stout one on the right and the grizzled-looking one beside him are the ones who invaded the quarter-deck with Armon." She felt their icy, unrepentant stares, and a violent surge of hatred shot through her—so intense that, at that moment, she wondered if she, too, were capable of murder. "The latter one held me; the former aided Armon in wresting Papa from the helm." Her voice broke, and she turned away, literally shaking with rage.

"Oridge?" Slayde questioned instantly.

"That's more than enough," Oridge assured them. "We can now add murder to their list of crimes." He nodded at the guards. "Take them."

Even with her back to them, Courtney could still see their faces. She squeezed her eyes shut, desperately trying to block out the memories flooding through her.

"Let's adjourn to that pub." Slayde wrapped a strong arm about her waist, leading her away—from the warehouse and the past. "I could use a drink myself. Then we'll head back to the inn and rest. Later today, we'll board the *Fortune* and have a look around."

"No," Courtney whispered, shaking her head. "Although I thank you from the bottom of my heart. But I can't rest until I've searched Armon's ship. I need to go there now."

Slayde stared down at her for a long moment. Then, he

nodded. "Oridge," he said quietly. "Lead us to where the *Fortune* is docked. While we're searching, I'll fill you in on all the events preceding—and during—Miss Johnston's and my trip to London."

An hour later, having scoured Armon's quarters inch by inch, Courtney had all but given up. For the third time, she delved through his desk, hunting for a journal, glancing up occasionally to see if Slayde was having any better luck searching Armon's trunk, or Oridge, through his bedding.

Hadn't the bloody pirate kept any written records at all?

She was about to scream in frustration when, from a kneeling position beneath the berth, Oridge made a triumphant sound of discovery. "This looks promising."

"What?" She was beside him instantly, holding her breath as he extracted his discovery, then eased back on his haunches to examine it.

It was a single sheet of paper that had been folded into a tiny square, then jammed beneath the leg of Armon's bed—so carefully placed it was almost invisible.

Courtney gasped as Oridge smoothed out the page and came to his feet. "That's the Huntley family crest," she pronounced. "'Tis the same stationery on which Aurora and I penned our note to the *Times.*"

"It is indeed," Slayde concurred, reaching Courtney's side. "The crest is faded, but nonetheless distinguishable." His brow furrowed. "Who wrote the letter? What does it say?"

"'Tis a diagram, sir. And a note." Oridge turned his attention to scanning the contents.

Abruptly, Slayde went rigid. "My God," he breathed, snatching the paper from Oridge's hands. "A sketch of Pembourne Manor. Or at least a portion of it, from the entranceway to the library. I don't understand." He squinted. "The bloody note at the top is faded."

"Bring it closer to the light," Courtney urged, rushing to the porthole. She waited until Slayde had complied, then peered over his shoulder and read the message aloud:

A: I was instructed to prepare this sketch for you. Use the passage to the library for both coming and going. You'll find it unbolted when you arrive. I'll secure it once you've gone. The strongbox is concealed in the top drawer of the library desk. The jewels are in it. Take it. Just before you leave, unlock the entranceway door and leave it ajar. Don't fail.

The library. The strongbox. The jewels. The faded letters. Dear Lord, it couldn't be.

Courtney's gaze darted to the upper corner of the page, finding and confirming her worst suspicions. The date on the note read *27 March 1807.*

Beside her, Slayde made a strangled sound, and she turned, searching his agonized face, finding her answer even before he spoke.

"My parents died four days after this note was penned."

"Oh, Slayde." Instinctively, Courtney reached for him, clasping his taut forearms.

"Armon killed them." Slayde's throat was working convulsively, his stare now fixed on the sketch. "No wonder Bow Street couldn't find any clues on or near the manor—Armon didn't break in, nor did he exit through the front door. That also explains why my parents never suspected there was an intruder inside when they returned home that night. If he came and went through the library, the entranceway door was still properly locked upon their arrival. He didn't open it until after . . . after . . ." A hard swallow. "Bow Street checked the passage—a mere formality, given the front door was ajar—but it was secured at both ends."

"Who knew of its existence?" Oridge asked quietly.

Slowly, Slayde turned toward the investigator, his eyes bleak with realization. "Only those at Pembourne: my family, the servants. We never used the bloody thing. My great-grandfather was the last Huntley to have need of a passage for secret comings and goings."

"Perhaps the last *Huntley.* Evidently not the last *person.*"

Again, Slayde's stare returned to the sketch, as if needing further confirmation that the atrocity he was beholding was indeed real. "Someone living at Pembourne drew this sketch," he said, giving voice to the unfathomable truth. "Someone I *trust,* someone *my father* trusted. Whoever that someone is helped Armon break in and kill my parents."

"I doubt murder was part of their original intention, sir," Oridge interceded gently. "More likely, they meant to snatch that strongbox and bolt. Unfortunately, your parents surprised them by returning."

"What the hell's the difference?" Slayde shot back, his fist striking the wall of Armon's cabin so hard it shook. "The end result is the same. Armon murdered my parents, aided either firsthand or indirectly by a trusted resident of Pembourne."

"Both of whom were receiving orders from whoever ordered this sketch to be drawn," Courtney murmured, once again studying the note. "Do you think he was seeking the black diamond?"

"It would stand to reason that he was." Oridge rubbed his chin. "Given that Armon blatantly extorted the diamond from Lord Pembourne scant weeks ago, my suspicions are that his motivation *and* his employer have remained the same. So, I would think, has his coconspirator."

Silence, as the implications of Oridge's conjecture sank in.

"You're saying there's a traitorous bastard living at Pembourne," Slayde bit out. "Not only then, but now." He sucked in his breath. "It makes a world of sense, now that I think of it. That's how Armon could so cleverly plan Aurora's alleged kidnapping and coincide it with his ransom notes. He had a wealth of information close at hand: his Pembourne accomplice. He had only to confer with that faithless bastard to know my sister's intentions—and to act on them."

"Close at hand," Courtney murmured. "Of course—that's what Mr. Scollard meant." Intently, she searched her memory. "'Danger,' he said. ''Tis only now emerging to take form. Terrible danger. Look deep within. It's festering close at hand.'"

"Scollard said that?" Slayde demanded.

Courtney's grip tightened. "Yes, the morning I left for Morland. At the time, I thought he was warning me to be careful during my upcoming confrontation. But he wasn't. He was talking about the traitor at Pembourne. Now that I reflect on it, he became terribly agitated as he spoke the words aloud, almost as if he were sensing something for the first time, as if the danger were just now becoming powerful enough for him to perceive."

"And the next day, someone tried to kill you."

"Who, may I ask, is Mr. Scollard?" Oridge interrupted to ask.

"Just a very wise friend." Courtney didn't mean to be curt, but she had neither the time nor the patience to deal with Oridge's anticipated skepticism of Mr. Scollard's gift. "Slayde," she continued, her mind racing. "As unnerved as we are to learn there's a criminal living at Pembourne, we cannot overlook the opportunity this affords us. Until now, we knew of only one accomplice to whoever orchestrated the blackmail scheme: Armon. And Armon is dead, leaving us with no one who can lead us to his employer. Well, if Morland is that employer, we now have another means through which to incriminate him." She nodded at her own half-formed notion. "I don't know how yet, but we must ferret out his other cohort—the one living at Pembourne—who can, in turn, lead us to Morland."

By dusk, Courtney, Slayde and Oridge were ensconced in the Pembourne carriage, beginning their return journey to Devonshire. After a brief reunion with her father's crew, bittersweet with the joy of survival and the remorse over those still missing or forever gone, Courtney was more eager than ever to return home to the ever-deepening mystery.

Home.

The very word brought her up short. Sometime between regaining consciousness after her near-drowning and now, Pembourne had become her home—thanks to Slayde, Aurora, and a houseful of loving servants.

A frisson of fear shivered up her spine. One of those loving servants was a thief and, quite possibly, a murderer.

"Courtney?" Slayde gazed at her from across the carriage. "Are you all right?"

"Fine," she reassured him. "Merely lost in thought."

"The sketch?"

A nod. "The sketch. We should put this travel time to good use by conjuring up a plan to unearth Armon's Pembourne contact."

"We'll be arriving at Pembourne the day after next," Oridge pronounced. "By midmorning on that day, if we make only brief stops. That gives us ample time to explore our best course of action. Before we begin, however, I think we'd best discuss the immediate, formidable challenge you should prepare yourselves for."

Slayde's brows rose. "Which is?"

"The way you're going to behave toward and around your staff." Oridge cleared his throat. "Sir, if our theory is correct and one of your servants was indeed Armon's accomplice, the last thing you want to do is alert the culprit to the fact that you're suspicious. You must treat everyone as you customarily do. Also, I must advise you not to converse openly with Miss Johnston or me about the situation, lest you be overheard, nor to mention our findings to anyone."

"What about Aurora?" Courtney put in immediately. She gripped the edge of her carriage seat, resolutely meeting and holding Slayde's gaze. "We've kept things from her far too long already. Slayde, she's your sister. She's also a grown—and trustworthy—woman. If you truly want to tear down the emotional barrier you've erected between you, you won't do it by lying to her. Please. I'm asking you to tell her the truth—*all of it,*" Courtney added, emphasizing the phrase as a clear indication that she included the revelation of the false diamond in her request . . . something even Oridge knew nothing about.

Slayde inhaled slowly, wrestling with his decision.

Oridge shifted uncomfortably in his seat. "Forgive me for intruding, sir, but I must speak up, given that keeping your family safe is my job. If Lady Aurora is as impulsive as you've described, the knowledge that there's a criminal among us could inspire her to do something rash to expose the culprit, thus endangering her life."

"Remaining unenlightened could endanger her life as well," Courtney countered, never diverting her gaze from Slayde's. "Aurora trusts the staff . . . and why shouldn't she? With you away so often, they're her only family and have been for years. Given how much of the mystery she's already privy to, it's more than likely she could inadvertently say the wrong thing to the wrong person. *Unless* she's instructed not to." A pause. "Slayde, please—do this for me."

Courtney could see the effect of her plea in the darkening of Slayde's eyes, the profound expression that crossed his face. His reply, when it came, was filled with husky tenderness. "Consider it done. With one modification. *I* won't tell Aurora the truth; *we* will. We'll take her to a private spot and tell her—together."

A riotous surge of emotion accompanied Slayde's use of the word *together,* intensifying at the realization that he loved her enough to base his decision on her feelings. "Thank you, my lord," Courtney managed to say in a quavering voice.

Slayde leaned forward, his knees brushing hers. "As it happens, we have a great deal of news to share with Aurora. Or have you forgotten?"

"Forgotten?" Courtney wondered if her heart would burst. Had she forgotten that she was soon going to become Slayde's wife? Forgotten the exquisite moments surrounding his proposal? Never in a million years. "No, my lord," she assured him with a secret smile. "I've forgotten . . . nothing."

Her veiled allusion to their magical night together, while lost to Oridge, rendered its full impact on Slayde. His jaw tightened, his penetrating stare delving deep inside her, unequivocally stating that, were they alone, he'd rekindle those memories here and now.

"Very well then," Oridge conceded, aware of the tension, misinterpreting its cause. "Share the details with Lady Aurora. But no one else. Is that acceptable?"

"Perfectly," Courtney agreed, tearing her gaze—and her thoughts—away from Slayde. "Difficult or not, we have no choice but to keep all this to the four of us, to behave as if we've learned nothing out of the ordinary."

"Agreed." Slayde, too, returned his full attention to their original topic—albeit reluctantly. "Getting back to the matter of resolution, there are over a hundred servants at Pembourne. How the hell do I determine which one is guilty?"

"You can start by compiling a complete list of your staff, then eliminating anyone who wasn't in your family's employ ten years past, at the time of your parents' deaths," Oridge suggested.

"The guards," Courtney put in. "You didn't hire them until after Aurora became your ward."

"True," Slayde conceded. "Moreover, I do keep written records concerning my staff, including the dates they've been at Pembourne, in my study."

"Excellent." Oridge nodded briskly. "Compiling that list and reviewing your records will be our first priority upon reaching Pembourne." He shifted, turning to face Courtney. "Miss Johnston, while we're on the subject of prudent actions . . ." A discreet cough. "Although I'm duly impressed with your quick mind, I must prevail upon you—given the dangers of the situation—not to rush off on any more reckless crusades like the one Lord Pembourne described to me this morning."

"You have Miss Johnston's word," Slayde answered for Courtney. "From now on, she stays at Pembourne, with me watching her every move. And, should I need to leave the estate, you will act as her substitute sentry."

Oridge's lips twitched slightly. "I see. Is that, too, acceptable, Miss Johnston?"

"Certainly, Mr. Oridge." Courtney's smile was angelic. "I have no intentions of causing Lord Pembourne— or you—any worry. I'll be a most obedient charge."

"Don't believe her for a moment, Oridge," Slayde advised, eyeing Courtney skeptically. "She's as inventive as she is beautiful."

"So I gathered from the details you relayed to me earlier. Speaking of which,"—Oridge reached into his portfolio and extracted a folded newspaper, his eyes twinkling—"I take it neither of you has had the chance to skim today's *Times*?"

Courtney nearly leaped from her seat. "Are the ransom notes in there?"

"The notes *and* your letter. Atop page two. A most visible location."

"Splendid!" Courtney was already reaching for the newspaper.

Slayde was a split second faster, relieving Oridge of the *Times* and opening it to the proper page. "I must admit you and Aurora did an astonishing job," he murmured as he read. "Even the phrasing of the letter sounds like language I would use."

"Why, thank you, my lord." Courtney's eyes sparkled. "Coming from you, I take that as the very highest of compliments."

"All in all, Miss Johnston's efforts look quite persuasive in print," Oridge assessed. "I suspect that, between the newspaper article and the ensuing gossip, people will soon be more than convinced that the black diamond and its alleged curse are no longer connected to the Huntleys."

"Precisely what I intended," Courtney said with great relish, reaching for the newspaper.

Slayde handed it to her, scowling as a new thought occurred to him. "I wonder how Morland will react to this public revelation."

"Not happily, I should say." Oridge rubbed his chin thoughtfully. "Unless he's innocent or, if he's guilty, unless he's already rid himself of the stone. After today, he'll be under public scrutiny, a prime suspect, given the history of your families. To try shipping or selling the stone at this time would be an enormous risk."

"And the diamond is useless to Morland if he can't profit from it," Courtney noted, triumphantly scanning her article.

"Profit from it or, if he wants only to rid himself of the curse, transport it to the royal family who paid for its recovery as soon as possible—something he'll be unable to do for weeks, perhaps months, until the uproar dies down."

"So Morland might very well be infuriated right about now." Courtney raised her head, a speculative gleam lighting her eyes. "How intriguing."

"Courtney, don't even think of approaching that man again," Slayde warned, eyes narrowed on her face.

"I won't." Idly, she refolded the *Times*. "On the other hand, maybe we'll get lucky. Maybe *he'll* approach *us*."

Chapter 15

A day and a half later, Slayde's carriage rolled through the gates at Pembourne, its occupants stiff and bleary-eyed, but no closer to devising a scheme for unearthing the culprit at Pembourne than they'd been two days past.

"We'll continue this discussion later, my lord," Oridge pronounced, glancing out the window as they rounded the drive, "after you've compiled that list of names and dates. We'll meet in your study, behind closed doors."

Slayde nodded. "Along with Miss Johnston and Lady Aurora," he added pointedly.

"Fine." Oridge gathered up his portfolio. "Again, I must remind you to make certain no one's about when you alert your sister to our findings. I can't stress that point enough; it's crucial to achieving our end *and* to remaining healthy in the process. Unfortunately, as things stand, we don't know whom we can trust."

"So we trust no one," Slayde decreed.

"Exactly."

Courtney sighed, shifting restlessly in her seat. She wished they'd already formulated their plan, something that would force the culprit to give himself away. Well, she intended to do so as soon as possible—if not with Slayde and Oridge, then with her favorite coconspirator: Aurora.

The carriage stopped, and a footman climbed down, opening the carriage door and assisting them out.

" 'Tis good to be home," Courtney murmured, assessing the manor fondly. There was that word again— *home*. An inner glow lit her heart.

"Yes. It is." Slayde stepped down beside her, the tension that had accompanied them from London temporarily held at bay. Smiling tenderly, he wrapped his arm about her waist. "Pembourne *is* your home, sweetheart," he added, as if reading her mind. "Now and always." He cast a dazed look about him. "Ironically, it's become mine as well."

Hearing the awed catch in his voice, Courtney reached up, caressing his jaw and reveling in the contentment she saw reflected on his face. "Welcome home, then," she whispered.

Slayde turned his lips into her palm. "Welcome home."

Euphoria bubbled inside Courtney like uncorked champagne. "When can we tell Aurora our news?"

"The instant we see her. We can shout it to the heavens, if you wish."

"I *do* wish," Courtney replied. "Perhaps then I'll believe it's really going to happen."

"Oh, it's going to happen," Slayde declared, his breath warm against her skin. "Just as soon as I can arrange it."

"Good morning, Lord Pembourne, Miss Johnston." Siebert opened the entranceway door and greeted them, evidently unsurprised by Courtney and Slayde's show of affection. "And good morning to you as well, Mr. Oridge," he said, noting the investigator as he walked up behind them.

"How prompt you are, Siebert." Courtney grinned. "You must have sensed our arrival."

"As a good butler, I sense a great many things." A pointedly arched brow, followed by a tolerant sigh. "However, in this case, it wasn't necessary. Lady Aurora has been dashing from window to window since yesterday, impatiently awaiting your return. I told her it could be another several days before you concluded your business in London, but there was no discouraging her. In any case, when she saw your carriage drive up, she bellowed the news of your arrival down the hallway. She should be along any—"

"Here I am." Aurora burst out the door. "I couldn't wait. Our surprise is too exciting. Courtney!" She hugged her friend. "I have something wonderful to tell you."

"What a coincidence." Courtney laughed, hugging Aurora in return. "I have something wonderful to tell you, too." A glance at Slayde. "We both do."

"Well, your news will have to wait. I've been exploding since yesterday, when this happened."

"Happened?" Slayde cocked a wary brow. "Aurora, you didn't try to leave Pembourne, did you?"

"No, Slayde." She rolled her eyes. "I've been here every minute. But, as of yesterday, I've had company."

"Company?" Slayde stiffened, as did Oridge. "Who?"

"Come see." Aurora tugged Courtney's hands, drawing her into the house, toward the sitting room.

Slayde cast a swift, pointed look at Siebert, who shook his head. "No, sir," he said quietly. "Nothing on the missives yet. Although I do believe the current surprise will lift Miss Johnston's spirits somewhat. Also, my lord, I thought you and Mr. Oridge would want to know that you had your own surprise visitor yesterday morning."

"Really? Who?"

"The Duke of Morland."

Courtney halted in her tracks, whirling about to listen.

"Morland?" Slayde repeated in amazement. "He came here?"

"Yes, sir."

"What did he want, Siebert?" Oridge asked.

"I'm not quite sure. He was seething with rage, spouting something about how Lord Pembourne had stolen from him again, wrested away his future. I couldn't make out all of it. The man was thoroughly foxed. But I did assure him I'd impart word of his visit."

"And so you have."

"Slayde, the duke was drunk," Aurora interrupted impatiently. "I listened to every word from the second floor landing, hoping he'd say something revealing. He didn't. His accusations were wild and incoherent, precisely as Siebert just told you. So let's discuss him later. Right now, I want to bring Courtney to our guest."

"Indeed, sir." Siebert surprised Slayde by concurring. "Lady Aurora is quite right. The duke's ramblings were vague, at best. And I do think you'd enjoy accompanying Miss Johnston to the sitting room. Mr. Oridge can remain with me at my post; I'd be happy to supply him with any pertinent details. You can join us in a few minutes. How would that be?"

With a puzzled expression, Slayde complied. "All right. I'll be back shortly."

He followed Aurora, who'd already dragged Courtney halfway down the hall.

"This guest actually came to see you," Aurora was explaining. "But he and I have become splendid friends in the interim."

"He?" Slayde demanded.

Aurora grinned at Slayde over her shoulder. "Yes—*he.*" She flung open the door to the sitting room. "Courtney, greet your guest."

A joyful gasp escaped Courtney's mouth. "Lexley!" She bounded across the room to the settee, hugging the stout man who had struggled weakly to his feet.

"Courtney." He clasped her to him, tears glistening in his eyes. "Thank God."

"Those were to be my words," she said, guiding him

back to his seat, carefully scrutinizing him as she lowered herself beside him. "Although somehow I knew Mr. Oridge wouldn't disappoint me."

"Oridge—as I hear it, he's the man I owe my life to."

"Yes. He's the investigator who sent those exceptional navigators I presume rescued you from Raven Island. Mr. Oridge works for Lord Pembourne, who hired him to find Armon's ship. Armon is—was—that horrible pirate who captured the *Isobel*, in case you didn't know his name. Which you probably did, given you spent more time topside than I did. Either way, he's dead now. He was killed by whoever paid him to steal the black diamond." Courtney paused to catch her breath. "Have I thoroughly confused you?"

A hint of a smile. "No. But not for want of trying. It's just lucky that Lady Aurora explained most of this to me while we waited for you and Lord Pembourne to return from London. The rest I knew from Booth."

"Booth?"

Lexley's smile widened. "He's the head of those exceptional navigators you just mentioned." Glancing toward the door, Lexley's gaze found and recognized Slayde. "M'lord," he said humbly, "I don't know how to express my gratitude. When Courtney fell from my shoulder and was swallowed up by the Channel, I begged you to save her. Somehow I knew you would. At the time, I had no idea that I, too, would benefit from your kindness and bravery. I thank you for my life. But, more importantly, I thank you for Courtney's."

"No thanks are necessary." Slayde walked over, perched on the arm of a chair. "Are you well?"

"I'm weak but unharmed." A chuckle. "Lady Aurora has taken excellent care of me. Why, I've even been promised a visit to the Windmouth Lighthouse to meet this extraordinary fellow Scollard."

"We could have gone today—Mr. Lexley is much stronger than he was yesterday," Aurora inserted. "But since I wasn't allowed to leave the mansion . . ."

Slayde shot her a look. "Tell me about the rescue," he urged Lexley. "And about the other crewmen who were abandoned with you. Did they all survive?"

"Each and every one of us," Lexley answered proudly. "Oh, we didn't eat much, and at night it got pretty cold. But our prayers kept us going. Prayers are the one thing that bloody pirate couldn't take from us. And look how well they worked. He's dead and we're home."

"Where are the others now?"

"By this time? With their families. Booth arranged everything. I told him I had no family, and he said he had instructions to bring me to Pembourne Manor."

"Oridge," Courtney murmured aloud. "He must have provided those instructions. What a kind gesture."

"Booth and his men were astounding," Lexley continued. "They navigated those waters as if the rocks and currents didn't exist. They got us off on longboats, all nine of us. They brought us food, water, and bandages— some of which they gave us right there in the longboats. The rest they administered aboard their fishing boat. Then they supplied us with enough ale to make us forget any aches and pains we might have. We slept most of the way to Cornwall. Three carriages were waiting there to take the men to their homes—no matter how far away they lived. One of those carriages brought me here." Lexley stared at a spot on the carpet. "I wish I'd had something to give Booth and his men, payment of some kind . . ."

"They'll be compensated," Slayde assured him. "I'll see to it at once."

Lexley looked up. "I'll repay you down to the last shilling. I don't care how long it takes."

"Your safety is payment enough."

Pride and gratitude warred on Lexley's face. "I'm not good at taking charity, m'lord. I work for my money."

"Fine. We'll discuss that when you're stronger."

"I'm almost myself. Which reminds me, I won't impose on your hospitality after today. First thing tomorrow, I'll be on my way. I just needed to see for myself that Courtney was all right. Although Lady Aurora did a fine job of assuring me she was."

"I'm sure you're eager to resume your life," Slayde responded smoothly. "But if it isn't too much trouble, I'd appreciate your postponing your departure, merely for a week or two. Courtney is still somewhat out of sorts, as you can imagine. You, of all people, know the full extent of what she endured—" Slayde shot Lexley a meaningful look, the name *Arthur Johnston* hanging between them as clearly as if it had been spoken. "I'm sure it would ease her distress to have a long-standing friend nearby. Surely you can understand what I'm saying?"

Bowing his head, Lexley nodded. "Yes, sir. I can well understand."

"Good. Then it's settled." Slayde turned to Aurora. "What bedchamber did you give Lexley?"

"I had Miss Payne make up the blue room."

"Splendid." Slayde stunned Aurora by giving her an approving wink before refocusing his attention on Lexley. "Is the room to your liking?"

The elderly sailor stared. "To my liking? I've never seen such elegant quarters in my life."

"Good. Then you won't mind keeping them for a while?"

Lexley swallowed. "No, m'lord. I won't mind."

Slayde rose. "I'll leave you and Courtney to catch up. I must speak with Siebert. Aurora?" He gestured for his sister to accompany him.

Aurora's face fell.

"Unless you object, m'lord," Lexley interceded, "I'd be honored if Lady Aurora would agree to stay. She's awaited this reunion nearly as eagerly as I have."

A corner of Slayde's mouth lifted. "Very well," he agreed, heading toward the door. "I'll return shortly, with Oridge. He'll want to meet and talk with you."

Courtney squeezed Lexley's arm. "I'll be right back." She scurried after Slayde, catching up to him in the hall. "Slayde?"

He waited, his expression tender. "Hmm?"

Without the slightest hesitation, Courtney rose on tiptoe, wrapped her arms about Slayde's neck, and tugged his mouth down to hers, kissing him soundly. "I just fell in love with you all over again," she whispered. With a radiant smile, she darted back into the sitting room.

Slayde stared after her, myriad emotions crossing his face.

Then, he resumed his walk to the entranceway, his pace and path the same as it had been countless times before.

Except this time he was whistling.

"He said nothing else?"

Pacing about the marble floor, Slayde digested everything Siebert had relayed about Morland's visit.

"No, sir. He just kept repeating himself, alternately demanding to see you and lambasting you for destroying his life, stealing from him yet again, and thus annihilating his future. He reeked of liquor, so deep in his cups he could scarcely stand upright."

"Obviously, he saw the letter and ransom notes printed in the *Times*," Oridge commented, carefully saying only that which was public knowledge.

"My thought exactly, sir," Siebert agreed. "The duke obviously believes Lord Pembourne's trading the diamond for Lady Aurora's life was akin to stealing it from the Bencrofts yet again."

Slayde halted, his gaze meeting Oridge's, each of them having the same thought.

Siebert's assessment *would* have made excellent sense, if Morland was not the person now in possession of the diamond.

But if Slayde's theory was correct and Morland was the criminal they sought, his fury could have been ignited only by the realization that the publication of the letter and ransom notes would thwart his attempts to restore the jewel and reap its profit.

Which made yesterday's diatribe totally baffling.

Oridge had prepared Slayde for Morland's rage. But the kind of rage they'd both expected had been the kind that incites murder, not childish tantrums. After all, he'd allegedly killed Armon and, just days ago, attempted to shoot Courtney down in cold blood.

That prompted another thought. If Morland was the person who'd followed them to Somerset, aware of the fact that they were en route to London, why had he driven to Pembourne yesterday, presumably to vent his rage at Slayde, knowing damned well Slayde wasn't there?

Was it all a ruse to divert suspicion from himself?

Was he clever enough to devise such a complex plan?

If he was sober, maybe.

But if he was as drunk as Siebert said? Never.

"You're sure Morland was foxed?" Slayde demanded. "He couldn't have been feigning it?"

Siebert's brows rose. "Not unless he's the finest actor in all of England. The stench of liquor came from his breath, not his person, which it would have, had he doused his clothing for effect. Moreover, his eyes were glazed, his speech slurred, and his balance severely impaired. No, sir, there's not the slightest doubt—the duke was totally, utterly soused."

"I see." Slayde frowned. Siebert wasn't prone to exaggeration. And if Bencroft was as deep in his cups as the butler implied, he'd be alert enough to devise nothing.

Unless, of course, Siebert was lying.

The very thought made Slayde's blood run cold. On its heels came a jolt of self-disgust and an explosion of denial. No. Absolutely not. He didn't care how emphatically Oridge had cautioned him. There were certain members of his staff whose loyalty he refused to question. Siebert was one. He'd been with the Huntleys since before Slayde was born, overseen Pembourne with unfailing pride, discipline, and principles, demonstrating nothing but honesty and dedication for nearly four decades.

If Siebert said Morland was drunk, then drunk he was. With a muttered oath, Slayde resumed pacing.

"Oh, and one other thing, sir," Siebert added, oblivious to Slayde's inner turmoil. "Mr. Rayburn was at Pembourne, as well. He followed the duke from Morland."

"Of course—Rayburn!" Slayde exclaimed. "I completely forgot. Did he stay hidden? Or was Morland aware of his presence?"

"His Grace was *aware* of nothing." Siebert sniffed. "That fact notwithstanding, he was restricted to the doorway, his back facing the grounds, and Mr. Rayburn, throughout his tirade. *I* spied Rayburn because he intended me to. He gestured to me from the shrubs, alerting me to his presence lest I need assistance. Needless to say, I didn't. Given the duke's wretched physical state, I was able to escort him to his carriage within minutes and without the aid of so much as a footman."

"I've got to ride to Morland." Slayde's frown deepened. "Not only to meet with Rayburn, but to hear firsthand what Bencroft has to say. However, I won't leave Courtney unguarded."

"Sir?" Siebert inclined his head quizzically. "Is Miss Johnston in danger?"

Feeling Oridge's warning look, Slayde answered, "Siebert, you of all people know my contempt for Lawrence Bencroft. I didn't trust the bastard while he was locked away in his fortress. Now, he's invading my home, evidently provoked by what he read in the *Times*, and drunk to boot. What if he returns and makes another scene? Or worse, what if he becomes violent? I don't know what he's capable of—and neither do you. I refuse to take that risk, either with Courtney's safety or Aurora's." A quick glance at Oridge. "If I leave Pembourne for several hours later today, would you stand vigil for me?"

"Of course, my lord. I'll use that time to speak with Lexley—since I'm certain Miss Johnston will be glued to his side."

"She will indeed. Incidentally, thank you for having him brought here. I can't tell you what seeing him meant to Courtney. Especially in light of losing her father." With those words, Slayde's gaze darted back to Siebert. "You're sure we received no responses to my missives?"

"None, sir," Siebert confirmed. "But it is early. You sent them out only a week ago."

"What missives?" Oridge inquired.

Slayde scowled. "I sent out letters to numerous clergymen along the coast of Devonshire. Just in the event that any of their parishioners recovered Arthur Johnston—or his body."

Oridge blinked. "Recovered? I thought you said the man was bound and weighted when he was thrown overboard."

"I did."

"Then how could he be anywhere but at the bottom of the Channel?"

"He couldn't." A pause. "Unless he wasn't bound and weighted."

"I don't understand."

"Nor do I—yet." Slayde raked a hand through his hair, glancing toward the sitting room. "But I'll advise you as soon as I do. In the interim, Siebert, keep me apprised. Oridge, we'll have our meeting in my study in an hour. I'll leave for Morland immediately thereafter. For now, I'm going to join Courtney."

Slayde stalked off, feeling Oridge's stunned stare boring into him. He realized the investigator had never seem him behave so irrationally. Hell, he never *had* behaved so irrationally.

But when it came to Courtney, rationality ceased to exist.

Before he left Pembourne today, he intended to get Lexley alone. And when he did, he'd get some answers.

"Slayde." Courtney looked up when he entered the sitting room, her beautiful face alight with a happiness that eclipsed his brooding humor, bathed it in sunshine. "We were just talking about you."

"Now *that* sounds ominous," he teased, helping himself to a brandy. "Lexley, would you care for a drink? I suspect I'll need one, if I'm being cruelly maligned."

"No, thank you, m'lord." The older man leaned forward, a bit more stiffly than he had a half-hour past. His color, too, had paled somewhat, indicating that the strain of the preceding weeks had taken more out of him than he was willing to admit. "I assure you, I've heard nothing but praise about you since you left the room. By Courtney's description, you're every bit a hero."

Slayde felt that odd constriction in his chest. "To the contrary," he disputed quietly, staring into his goblet. "If anyone is a savior, 'tis Courtney." Awkwardly, he cleared his throat, glancing up to see Lexley's moved, albeit tired, expression. "I've spoken with Mr. Oridge. He and I are in agreement that you should rest for a few hours. Then, the two of you will talk."

"Thank you, m'lord."

"Slayde." Courtney rose, crossing over to him, speaking softly and for his ears alone. "Before Lexley retires to his chambers, I'd appreciate if we could divulge our news . . ." She wet her lips. "That is, I do want Aurora to be the first to know, but with Papa gone, and Lexley having been as close to him as he was . . ." Her voice trailed off.

Placing his goblet on the sideboard, Slayde raised Courtney's chin to meet his gaze. "Would it make you happy?"

"Yes."

"That's all I needed to hear." Slayde shut the sitting room door, clasping Courtney's hand in his.

Instantly, Aurora's head came up. "Are we about to hear your wonderful news—the news I wouldn't listen to because I was too excited about Lexley's homecoming?"

Slayde nodded. "Yes, although given the magnitude of

your surprise, we forgive you for delaying our announcement."

"Announcement?" Now, Aurora jumped to her feet. "Is it what I think it is? What I hope it is? What I've prayed it is?"

Laughter rumbled from Slayde's chest. "I suspect it might be." He turned to Lexley. "I realize you're exhausted. But before you go up to rest, Courtney wanted you to be here, to join Aurora in being the first to know. And I quite agree." He stared at Courtney's small hand clasped in his, thanking the stars for teaching him that miracles did exist, for blessing him by bringing this extraordinary miracle into his life. "Courtney has agreed to bestow upon me the greatest gift I could ever ask for—her hand in marriage."

"I knew it!" Aurora shot across the room, flinging her arms about Courtney and giving her a fierce hug. "Oh, Courtney, I knew it from the moment we met. If anyone could unlock that bloody stubborn heart of Slayde's, it was you. I'm so happy for you—for both of you." She drew back, her eyes shining. "Think about it—we're going to be sisters, cohorts for life."

"God help us," Slayde muttered.

Sobering, Aurora turned to her brother, making a move to embrace him, then hesitating—uncomfortable, uncertain. "I needn't tell you how lucky you are," she said. "I'm so grateful you found Courtney before it was too late . . . not only for her, but for you. At last you can bid that lonely man good-bye."

"I agree." With a new and unknown instinct, Slayde squeezed Aurora's shoulder, bending to brush his lips across her brow. "Do you know, you're very insightful—for a child? Then again, you're not a child anymore, are you?"

An understanding glint flashed in Aurora's eyes. "No. I'm not."

"I'll try to remember that."

"I'll remind you if you forget."

"I'm sure you will." Slayde grinned, aware of Courtney's brilliant smile, feeling it wash through him and propel his own astounding metamorphosis yet another step.

"Marriage." Lexley had struggled to his feet and was now making his way toward them, beaming ear to ear. "How wonderful. I . . ." He caught Courtney's hands in his. "Your father would be so proud, so happy. More than anything, he wanted you to find the kind of love he shared with your mother. Well, you obviously have. Even an old man like me can see the exhilaration on your face."

"You're not old," Courtney refuted, her voice faltering. "Further, I expect you to regain every ounce of your strength. I'll need you to escort me down the aisle to embrace my future. Papa would have wanted it that way. So do I."

Lexley's eyes were unashamedly damp. "I'd be honored." He turned to Slayde. "You're a fine man. Take good care of her."

"You have my word."

"When?" Aurora demanded. "When is this wonderful day to occur?"

"I'm in the process of acquiring a special license," her brother answered. "As far as I'm concerned, the vows can be exchanged on the day it arrives. But that's up to Courtney. I want this wedding to be everything she's ever dreamed of." Slayde's lips twitched. "Which probably means she'll want to plan it with you. In writing. With a copy submitted to the *Times*."

Aurora's eyes widened. "He knows?" she asked Courtney.

"He knows. I told him."

"Oh, Lord."

"We have a great deal to discuss," Slayde assured her, exchanging glances with Courtney. "But first, I'm going to escort Lexley to his chambers."

"That won't be necessary, m'lord," the sailor murmured. "I can find my way."

"Even *I* get lost at Pembourne and it's my home," Slayde countered. "So let's have no arguments. I distinctly heard my betrothed order you to rest and regain your strength."

A weak smile. "I can't very well argue with that."

"No, you can't." Slayde opened the sitting-room door. "I'll return shortly," he advised Courtney, his knuckles brushing her cheek. "You and Aurora wait for me here."

She nodded her understanding. "We will."

Ten minutes later, Slayde stood by, watching Lexley settle himself on the bed. The poor man looked utterly exhausted, far too drained to converse. Unfortunately, the questions that had hammered at Slayde's brain this past week would no longer be silenced.

"Lexley," he began, making sure the door was securely shut, "I had another reason for seizing this opportunity to talk to you alone. I apologize for taxing your strength, but there is something I must know."

The elderly sailor blinked, propping himself on his pillows. "Of course, m'lord. What is it?"

Slayde clasped his hands behind his back, realizing he was grasping at straws and not giving a damn. "First, I want your word that this conversation will remain between us. Courtney has suffered far too much already. I will not allow her to be hurt."

"Of course," Lexley looked utterly bewildered. "I'd never hurt Courtney."

A nod. "Courtney's father gave her a watch, a timepiece with a moving scene of a ship and a lighthouse."

"Yes." A painful sigh. "Captain Johnston's wife gave that timepiece to him as a wedding gift. He wanted Courtney to have it after he . . . when he . . ."

"The watch stopped at the precise time Arthur Johnston went overboard. Since then, it has jumped ahead several times, inciting a great deal of anxiety, and questions, in Courtney's mind. Further, she's experienced repeated dreams in which her father is still alive, calling out to her, needing her. Her distress escalated to the point where I agreed to bring her to the spot where her father went down. It was horrible for her, reliving the entire occurrence a second time. I won't subject her to that kind of pain ever, ever again. Not without damned good cause. My question to you is, does that cause exist?"

"Dear God." Lexley's face had gone sheet-white, beads of perspiration erupting on his brow. "Courtney has actually dreamed . . ." A distraught pause. "I knew you'd traveled to where the *Isobel* was overtaken. Lady Aurora explained it all to me. But she said you'd found nothing. I asked her a dozen times. She said you'd searched—but to no avail. Is that not true?"

"Yes. It's true." Slayde's heart rate had begun to accelerate at the severity of Lexley's reaction. "The currents were powerful, the waters rough. 'Twould be very difficult for someone to survive."

"I know. But, dear Lord, how I prayed."

"Did you have reason to pray?" Slayde jumped on the first mate's statement, stalking across the room to grip the bedpost, all attempts at remaining calm having vanished. "I don't mean groundless reasons; I mean well-founded ones."

"At the time, I thought so," Lexley muttered brokenly. "Maybe it was just wishful thinking. But it was the only way I could try to save him. Heaven help me, it wasn't enough."

Slayde inhaled sharply, asking the crucial question that had gnawed at him for over a week. "Before Armon forced you to thrust Arthur off the *Isobel,* did you manage to loosen his gag? His bonds? Did you somehow find a way to increase your captain's chances of survival?"

Lexley stared. "How did you know?"

"God, then it's true." Hope and triumph converged, pounded through Slayde's blood. "I knew—or rather, suspected—because Courtney's memories include hearing her father scream as he went over. No gagged man can scream loud enough to be heard a deck below."

"I loosened the gag just before we reached the rail.

Armon was a dozen feet away. I turned my back on him while I maneuvered the captain to the side, positioned myself so Armon was unable to see what I was doing. I worked my blade from my pocket and slashed the bonds at Captain Johnston's wrists and the rope tying the weighted sack to his thigh. The end of that rope I shoved into his hand, where he clutched it low and against him so it would appear to Armon that it was still fastened to his leg. The bastard got only a brief view because, a split second later, I thrust Captain Johnston over the edge. I knew his chances were slim. He would have had to unbind his own ankles—I didn't dare risk taking the extra time to do so for fear of alerting Armon—and then battle that rough section of the Channel. But he was an incredibly strong swimmer and, with the currents in his favor, I prayed he could make it to shore. It appears my prayers were for naught."

"Did you say the currents were *with* him?" Slayde demanded. "I don't understand. Courtney and I sailed in those currents. They were powerful as hell, nearly dragging us out to sea."

"They're always fierce, almost impossible to navigate. But sometimes they change direction and surge inland. That was the case the day Captain Johnston went down."

"When we revisited the area, Courtney said she thought that the current on that awful day had been running in the opposite direction to what we saw—but then she assumed she was mistaken."

"Probably, she doesn't know the current can reverse. Courtney wasn't what you would call an avid sailor, m'lord. She rarely spent much time topside—only enough to know the route, not the more intricate challenges we encountered."

Slayde gripped the bedpost so tightly his knuckles turned white. "You're telling me those waters were moving in the opposite direction that day?"

Another nod.

"Then he could be alive." Slayde's eyes narrowed. "Courtney's father could very well be alive."

"No, m'lord." Lexley shook his head emphatically. "If I believed that, I'd be crawling my way along the Cornish coastline, searching. But I don't. Because if Captain Johnston was alive, he would have found his way to Courtney."

"Not if he was injured. Or ill. Or even unconscious. Hell, following such a furious bout with the seas, he could be any of those things."

"But if he'd been found, wouldn't his rescue have been reported?"

"Reported where? To whom? *If* Johnston was coherent, he would have realized the *Isobel* must have been destroyed. As for Courtney, the last he saw her, she was being held prisoner. He doubtless believed the worst. And that's assuming he was lucid. What if he wasn't? What if he was unable to identify himself? How would his rescuers know where to take him or whom to contact?"

"M'lord—" Lexley's hands balled into fists, refusing to allow hope for what he feared to be virtually impossible. "I want to believe this as much as you do. But if nothing's been reported, isn't it more likely the captain drowned?"

Slayde shook his head. "I don't think so. The currents were too strong for him to have sunk without the weight of that sack dragging him down. He must have been washed ashore. And if he were already dead when that happened, *I* would have received word. You see, I sent messages to every coastal clergyman I could think of. Had a drowned man been found washed ashore, one of those clergymen would have been notified, after which he would have notified me."

Promise flared in Lexley's eyes. "That makes sense." He sat up, his exhaustion forgotten. "Could this truly be possible? Do you honestly believe Captain Johnston is— might be—alive?"

A month ago, Slayde's reply would have been an unconditional no.

But now?

Solemnly, Slayde pondered Courtney's dreams, the periodic advances of her timepiece, the intensity of her faith, a faith that had been shattered by misleading currents too convincing to ignore.

Someone who looks but can't see . . . But now he sees . . .

Confidently, Slayde nodded. "Do I believe Johnston could be alive?" he repeated, the answer as clear as the vision he now possessed. "Yes. And I know just where to go to find out."

Chapter 16

Aurora gasped, all the color draining from her face as she examined the diagram Slayde had given her. "Someone at Pembourne is involved? My God." She sank into a chair. "Whoever penned this aided Armon not only with blackmail and theft, but with murder. They killed Mama and Papa."

"And they'll pay for it." Courtney lay a comforting hand on Aurora's shoulder. "Their crimes won't go unpunished."

"Nor will their intended crimes," Slayde added bitterly. Seeing Aurora's questioning look, he expounded, his face tight with remembered rage. "Whoever's orchestrating this scheme obviously believes Courtney to be a threat. When she and I left for London last week, we stopped in Somerset for the night. The moment Courtney alit from the carriage, a masked rider appeared out of nowhere and fired a shot at her. But for the grace of God . . ."

"No. Oh, Courtney." Aurora grasped her friend's hand, as if to assure herself that Courtney were unharmed. "Thank heavens he missed you."

"He didn't miss me for lack of skill," Courtney said softly. "Were it not for Slayde . . ." A shiver of remembered fear. "Your brother saved my life—again. He knocked me out of the way just in time."

"It had to be Morland." Aurora was on her feet again. "Your threats terrified him. He hadn't a clue they were contrived. He must have followed you here, then from Pembourne to Somerset—and tried to silence you."

"My theory exactly." For the third time in a quarter hour, Slayde glanced at the tightly locked sitting room door. "Let's keep our voices down. As Oridge reminded us, we haven't a clue who penned that sketch. Until we do, no one must be privy to our conversations."

"We have to unearth the traitor at Pembourne." Aurora's whisper was fierce, her expression murderous. "Then he can lead us to Morland."

"We spent the entire carriage ride home trying to do just that," Courtney said with a restless sweep of her palm. "We came up with nothing. That, of course, must change at once."

"Without question," Aurora concurred. "We'll think of a plan immediately."

Despite the gravity of the situation, a faint smile flickered across Slayde's face. "Not only are you both reckless and inventive, you're also impatient and strong-willed. I shudder to think what my life will be like with the two of you."

"Slayde," Aurora put in, unsmiling, "is there anything else you haven't told me?"

Slayde's amusement vanished, and he glanced at Courtney, who gave him an encouraging nod. "Only one thing more," he admitted quietly. "A truth I kept from you from the start—not because I didn't trust you, Aurora, but because I was desperate to protect you." A resigned sigh. "However, as Courtney finally managed to convince me, you're entitled to know."

"Know what?"

"The black diamond, the one I gave Armon—it was a fake. I paid a jeweler to craft it. I've never so much as seen the real black diamond. But I was terrified that your kidnappers would kill you if I didn't produce something. So I did."

Aurora sucked in her breath. "Why would you keep something of that magnitude from me?"

"Because you believe in that absurd, monstrous curse. I hoped my deception would afford you peace of mind. As it turns out, that peace of mind was shattered anyway."

"I see." Aurora shook her head, trying to absorb the ramifications of what Slayde had disclosed. "Right now, my feelings about the black diamond, its curse on the Huntleys—even my reaction to your deceiving me—are secondary. More important is the fact that given what you've just told me, Morland obviously still has the stone. If he'd tried to sell it or restore it to Russia, someone would have discovered it was a fake. Further, that explains why the letters we printed in the *Times* upset him so. We must have thwarted whatever plans he had."

"I agree wholeheartedly," Slayde replied. " 'Tis time to discern Lawrence Bencroft's plans *and* his state of mind. Hence, I intend to return his visit—today. I mean to find out exactly why he came to Pembourne, whether his intoxicated state was a one-time event or a reversion to his years as a drunken sot and what he's been up to. After that, I mean to seek out Rayburn and hear from his lips whether Morland left his estate the night Courtney was assailed."

"And then?" Aurora pressed.

"And then we'll see if we have enough incriminating facts to undo Morland on our own, or if we need the help of his Pembourne accomplice." Extracting his timepiece, Slayde glanced at the hour. "Speaking of which, we're due in my study in twenty minutes for a meeting with

Oridge. He'll want that list specifying all the servants who have been with us at least ten years."

"I'll help you compile it," Aurora declared at once.

"Good; then it will be ready when he is. After we mull over the possibilities, I'll leave for Morland. Incidentally, if you and Courtney become overeager during my absence and decide to take matters into your own hands—don't. Oridge has been instructed to adhere himself to you like a second skin until my return. I assume neither of you objects?"

Aurora arched a brow. "And if we did?"

"Then I'd remind you that while I'm just learning how to need and love, I've long since mastered the art of protecting those I care for." Slayde's jaw set. "Don't test me, Aurora. You won't win."

"Slayde," Courtney interceded, with a brief shake of her head at Aurora, "we won't leave Pembourne or do anything foolish. But that doesn't preclude our withdrawing behind closed doors, trying to conjure up a plan to unmask the traitor at Pembourne. Surely you wouldn't deny us that?"

A slow, indrawn breath. "No. I suppose I wouldn't. Nor would you listen to me if I did."

"That's true." Courtney's eyes sparkled. "On the other hand, Mr. Oridge's job will be infinitely easier if Aurora and I spend the afternoon together in one room. Just think: rather than dashing about the grounds, begging Cutterton for assistance, Oridge will only have to post himself outside one door and perform his sentry duty until your return. He can even alert us if, for any reason, our voices become discernible and need to be lowered." A beatific smile. "Now, doesn't that make sense?"

Slayde eyed her warily. "Unfortunately, yes—it does." A speculative pause. "I'm not sure why, but you always seem to bring me around to your way of thinking, even when I have no intentions of being swayed."

"Yes, I do, don't I?"

A scowl. "Aurora's defiance I can handle, and combat, but your . . . your . . ."

"Persuasiveness?" Courtney suggested. "Logic? Wisdom?" She crossed the room, laying her palm against Slayde's jaw. "Or perhaps it's just an ability that stems from loving someone the way I love you."

Slayde swallowed, emotion darkening his eyes. "Perhaps." He turned his lips into her palm. "In which case I'll learn to live with it."

The lighthouse was quiet when Slayde arrived two hours later. Awkwardly, he knocked, wondering if Scollard was even here during the afternoons and, if so, if he would welcome Slayde's visit.

"Ah, Lord Pembourne. You've arrived. Excellent."

Whipping about, Slayde stared at the elderly man who'd come up behind him.

"Forgive me. Did I startle you?" Mr. Scollard inclined his head. "You could have gone in and waited for me in the sitting room. I was just examining the area above the strip, away from where the tide waters strike the shore. An excellent location for a cottage." He reached past Slayde and opened the door. "Come in."

Slayde complied, feeling as off balance as if he'd been struck. "You were expecting me?"

"Of course." Scollard scratched his chin thoughtfully. "There was something I wanted to do . . . what was it?" An exasperated shrug. "No matter. It'll come to me. In the meantime, I'll make some tea. You haven't much time and we have a great deal to discuss. Incidentally, I'm relieved you left Oridge to oversee the ladies. He'll station himself right outside Rory's door and at the same time be able to review that list and keep an eye out for suspicious behavior. He'll even find a minute or two to chat with Lexley." The lighthouse keeper scowled. "It's Courtney I'm worried about, but for this one afternoon, she'll be safe, and after today, you won't be leaving her alone . . . ah!" he exclaimed, his eyes lighting up.

"That's what I wanted to do—offer my congratulations. You're a lucky man. Then again, Courtney is equally lucky. Two halves of what will soon be a far greater whole. I'm delighted. I can hardly wait to see what a beautiful bride she'll make." A curious glance. "I'll get that tea. You'll need at least two cups; your mouth's been hanging open so long it must be parched."

Slayde snapped it shut. "I . . . How do you know . . . Never mind." He dropped into a chair. "Please accept my apologies. This is all very new to me."

"No apologies are necessary," Mr. Scollard assured him. "Even Rory, who's been privy to my insights for years and who's far more open to the intangible than you, occasionally has difficulty accepting that which clearly is. As for this being very new to you, I know that only too well—and I'm as relieved by your transformation as I am proud. For a while there, I feared you might never find your way."

"Find my way?" Slayde asked with a faint smile. "Or see clearly enough to discern it?"

"Both. You'd wandered too far to realize you were lost, much less to distinguish your path home."

A harsh, indrawn breath. "How many times have we met?" Slayde managed. "Twice? Three times? And glimpsed each other perhaps a dozen times more? How is it you know me so well?" He shook his head in wonder. "Or is that one of those questions Courtney claims you won't answer?"

Mr. Scollard gave a profound sigh. *"Won't?* Perhaps *can't* is a better choice of words. No gift comes without its price. Mine is that I cannot envision at will, or block out what I'd rather not see." His probing stare met Slayde's. "I've prayed with all my heart to foresee your solution, yet I see only bits of it."

"I'll take those bits—gladly. Whatever you can offer me."

"So be it. The tea." Mr. Scollard vanished, only to return minutes later with a pot and two cups. "Rory says you don't much care for tea. So I've laced it with brandy. I considered doing that with Courtney, but she'd be either foxed or asleep after one cup. So I refrained."

Chuckling, Slayde accepted the proffered cup. "You're right."

Mr. Scollard seated himself across from Slayde, waiting only until his guest had downed several gulps of tea. "Ask," he urged simply. "I'll gift you with all I can."

Lowering his cup, Slayde got right to the point. "Is Courtney's father alive?"

"Ah, Courtney asked me much the same question. She asked if her father was gone. I told her he was gone from her eyes and ears but never from her mind and heart."

"That means only that he's elsewhere, not that he's dead."

A triumphant gleam lit Scollard's eyes. "Good for you. Courtney can't understand as such—not yet. And while it's true Lexley divulged his heroic acts to you, it was you who approached him."

"Why didn't you tell Courtney what Lexley had done?"

"I didn't know. Probably because Courtney wasn't ready to hear. I told her all that was in my power to grasp, explained that there are some ties that can be broken, others that cannot—and that it was up to her to discern the difference."

"Knowing Courtney, she must have assumed you were referring to spiritual ties."

A smile. "You know your betrothed well. In any case, I clarified the point as best I was able, reassuring her that if memories can't be silenced, spiritual bonds can't be broken, while physical bonds can. That *if,* however, was Courtney's dilemma. She couldn't recall what was never hers to know. Awareness of the Channel's currents was precluded by her perpetual seasickness. Therefore, her faith was splintered."

"Faith that was perpetuated by vivid dreams and a broken timepiece that moved at will."

"Ah, the timepiece. A remarkable treasure. A

thwarted ship; a lighthouse that beckons. Like an ailing man struggling to heal, and the quiet inlet that houses him. Yes, Courtney's mother gave her husband the perfect wedding gift. As you'll give to your wife." A faraway gleam. "Precisely what she's prayed for, in fact."

"What she's prayed for is her father," Slayde responded fervently. "For his safety. If I'm able to give her the perfect gift, then that gift would be her father. 'Tis all she's ever asked for. That and a puppy who needed her—" He broke off, Scollard's words striking home. "'Like an ailing man struggling to heal, and the quiet inlet that houses him.' Is that man Courtney's father?"

"A fortnight ago, that perception would have eluded you. 'Tis amazing how wisdom springs from faith. Like love and need, faith is an intangible entity, yet far stronger than that which the eye can behold. You've come a long way, my lord."

"You're telling me Arthur Johnston is alive."

With a flourish, Mr. Scollard finished his tea. "June birthdays are lovely, don't you think?" he inquired, setting down his cup. "Nearly as lovely as June weddings. The two together would be a bride's dream, wouldn't you say?"

"If that woman is Courtney, yes," Slayde agreed, his mind racing. "Where shall I look? Where can I find him?"

"You're so certain he's alive?"

"Yes. I'm certain."

The lighthouse keeper squeezed his eyes shut, then nodded. "You are indeed." A pause. "You've looked in the most crucial of places—and you've found what you sought. The rest is simple, for it involves only beginning with the information you've acquired and employing logic. And logic, my lord, is your forte." With a satisfied nod, Mr. Scollard opened his eyes. "I do believe Courtney's patience is paying off. Her confusion is, as I vowed, giving way to enlightenment. My insights alone could never have unclouded her vision. But the other I spoke to her of—he can accomplish what my gift cannot."

"He?" Slayde gripped his knees, leaned forward. "Am I the *he* of whom you speak?"

"As I told Courtney, listen with your heart. It won't fail you." Abruptly, Mr. Scollard went rigid, his mouth thinning into a grim line. "Danger," he muttered. "It stalks Courtney like a predator. After today, there will be no protection. 'Tis up to you, my lord. You alone can prevent the danger from seizing her."

"How?" Slayde demanded, his heart pounding in his chest. "What can I do to keep her safe?"

"You must be there to see. *Another* must search. You cannot place Courtney in any hands other than your own, not once you've made the brief visit fate now commands you to make."

Slayde didn't need to ask what the lighthouse keeper meant. Nor did he need to consider his reaction. "Fate doesn't take precedence over Courtney," he pronounced, coming to his feet. "If she's in danger, I'll abandon my plan to face Morland and head directly back to Pembourne."

"No." Scollard shook his head. "Go you must. So long as you're confronting the duke, the peril will be held at bay."

"In other words, Morland can't hurt her if he isn't there."

"Those are your words, not mine." Scollard rose as well. "But you have ghosts to put to rest. Do so. Then return to your home, your sister, and your future bride."

"I'll be back at Pembourne before dark." Slayde began pacing, hands clasped behind his back as he employed the logic of which Mr. Scollard spoke. "I'll speak with Oridge—his colleagues are all highly respected. He'll recommend someone qualified to find Courtney's father. That will allow me to remain at Pembourne while still recovering the gift I'm determined to give my wife-to-be."

"A sound plan."

Slayde's brow furrowed in concentration. "An inlet, you said? You picture nothing more?"

"A *quiet* inlet," Scollard amended. "Other than that, I sense only a will struggling to remain unbroken and a body struggling to heal."

"Just like Courtney when I first brought her to Pembourne," Slayde noted softly. "And she prevailed. So will her father. I'll see to it." His jaw set. "A quiet inlet—there aren't many of those along the coast from Devon to Cornwall. Yes, 'tis enough to go on."

"You're a fine man, Slayde."

The praise triggered a tightening in Slayde's chest. "Courtney proclaimed me the same. I never believed it—until Courtney came into my life." He stared at the floor. "She's a blessing. Her love for me is a miracle. I'll kill anyone who tries to harm her."

"I know you will."

Slayde swallowed, hard. "Starting tonight, I won't leave her alone for a minute. I'll carry a weapon, if need be."

"Your true weapon is already in your hands: your wits. The danger is within, the threat too subtle for a pistol to combat."

"Courtney told me your prophecy—that the danger lies at Pembourne." Slayde's fists clenched. "Who? Can you tell me who?"

"I perceive only undeserved trust and clawing fear. And outside—heartlessness and obsession haunting your doorstep."

"That's Morland," Slayde got out through clenched teeth.

"You're sure."

"Aren't you?"

"That matters not. What matters is your certainty. You must do with your mind what you did with your heart: clear it of the shadows that obstruct your sight. Once you've accomplished that, you'll see what is truly there, not what you choose to see. I think, at last, you're ready for that, Slayde."

"I don't understand."

"Soon you will."

"Damn it, I need to know!" Slayde exploded, slamming his fist to the mantel. "Tell me—is Morland behind all this? Did he try to kill Courtney? And the traitor at Pembourne—the one who drew that sketch, helped Armon kill my parents—who is it?"

A pained look crossed Mr. Scollard's face. "I wish to God I knew. If I did, so would you. But I only see that which is offered to me. Nothing more."

The torment in the lighthouse keeper's voice invoked a surge of guilt. "Forgive me, Mr. Scollard," Slayde said at once. "I had no right to attack you like that; nor to accuse you of keeping anything from me. I know how deeply you care for both Aurora and Courtney. 'Tis just that I feel so frustrated."

"I understand. There's a great deal at stake. Certainly enough to incite an emotional outburst."

Slayde gave a humorless laugh. "Funny, I was never given to those before."

"Which? Emotions or outbursts?"

The significance of the question struck home. "Neither," Slayde responded, meeting Mr. Scollard's gaze. "I felt nothing and expressed less. Evidently, both are outcomes of falling in love."

"Indeed they are. Savor those outcomes, Slayde. But balance them with your logic. Reserve the irrational for Courtney's loving hands; employ reason where no love exists. Now go. See the duke. Hear his words. Speak to Rayburn. Then return to Pembourne. Ruthlessness hovers at its portals. Resolution is in *your* hands—as is Courtney's life."

"Elinore, I really appreciate your visit," Aurora said, coming to her feet. "I'm sorry it has to be so short. I hope it wasn't me—I realize I'm not terribly good company today."

"Nonsense." Elinore rose from the yellow salon's curved settee, fingering her strand of pearls and studying Aurora's restless expression. "The reason I'm rushing off is because I'm expected at Lady Altec's in an hour." She rolled her eyes. "Doubtless, another boring gossip session. Still I did, in a moment of weakness, agree to go. So go I must." A pause. "But I'd be lying if I said I hadn't spent the week worrying, anxiously awaiting some word from you. 'Tis the real reason I stopped by today. Remember, when last I left, Courtney and Slayde were en route to London on a most unsettling mission."

"I know that, Elinore. And I should have contacted you; there was no excuse for my negligence. 'Tis just that when Lexley arrived . . ."

"Stop." Elinore pressed her finger to Aurora's lips. "No apology is necessary. Now that I've seen all that's occurred in my absence . . . goodness, you've scarcely had time to breathe! First, Mr. Lexley's arrival, then Courtney and Slayde's." An earnest sigh. "Thank heavens Mr. Lexley survived his ordeal. He seems such a fine man, and Courtney deserves something of her old life back again. 'Twas horrible for her to lose her father." Glancing toward the doorway, Elinore lowered her voice, brow furrowed in concern. "Although, despite her obvious relief, she does look a bit peaked. True, I only saw her for a moment before she went to unpack. But she seems pale, faraway. Is she all right?"

Mentally, Aurora bit her lip, honoring her promise to say nothing to anyone—not even their dearest family friend. "I think confronting the pirates who killed her father took a great deal out of Courtney. But given a little time, she'll be fine. Better than that, in fact." Aurora squeezed Elinore's arm, urging her toward the hallway as she desperately tried to curtail her own impatience. She knew precisely what Courtney's preoccupation stemmed from: her determination to find out who penned that sketch of Pembourne, a mystery they'd planned to spend the afternoon resolving.

Inadvertently, Aurora's gaze drifted upward. She only hoped Courtney hadn't succeeded in devising a scheme to unmask the culprit while she'd been down here entertaining Elinore.

"Aurora? Are you more troubled than you've let on?"

Aurora nearly jumped out of her skin at Elinore's astute assessment. Hell and damnation, why couldn't she be a better actress? "Absolutely not," she assured her friend. "Truly. Courtney is just contemplating . . . matters." Lord, that sounded about as believable as if she'd admitted Courtney were entertaining an army of men in her bedchamber. "I, too, am glad Mr. Lexley is here. He's a true balm for Courtney's pain."

"She said nothing more about what happened during the excursion to London?"

Elinore's particular choice of words elicited a tremendous idea, the perfect avenue for Aurora to take. There *was* a way she could be honest and yet reveal something that was not only innocuous but that would, with a modicum of luck, both convince Elinore and divert her.

"Wait." Aurora pulled Elinore aside just before they crossed the threshold into the hallway, lowering her voice to a whisper. "Courtney did share a secret with us—or rather she and Slayde did."

"A secret?" Elinore's brows rose.

"Yes. Thus far, they've told only Lexley and me, but I know they intend to share the news with you next. And, given your unnecessary worry, I'm going to divulge their announcement in order to ease your mind *and* to explain Courtney's faraway look." With an impish grin, she confided, "Courtney and Slayde are to be married."

Genuine pleasure erupted on Elinore's face. "Married?" she breathed. "How glorious! When?"

"Just as soon as Slayde obtains a license. Now don't say a word until the servants have all been told."

"My lips are sealed."

Aurora clutched her elbows. "You'll be at the wedding, won't you? I know how much Courtney wants that. She's come to care for you as much as I have."

"I wouldn't miss it for the world," Elinore vowed, eyes aglow with anticipation. "In fact, I think I'll contact my jeweler at once. I have a stunning new gown that would be perfect for the occasion and I must have just the right accessories fashioned."

"That sounds wise." Aurora grinned, thinking how typically Elinore it was to make provisions ensuring she'd be elegantly attired for a wedding whose date had yet to be announced. "Oh, Miss Payne?" Aurora nearly collided with the housekeeper as they rounded the doorway. "Would you please bring Mr. Oridge a tray? The poor man is going to starve to death if he doesn't eat."

The housekeeper startled, having been checking her list of inventory as she walked. "Of course, Lady Aurora. I'll see to it at once." Her gaze flickered to the viscountess. "Will you require anything further, Lady Stanwyk?"

Elinore shook her head. "No, Miss Payne, thank you. I'm about to take my leave."

"Very well, my lady." Miss Payne headed toward the kitchen.

"Is Mr. Oridge meeting with Slayde?" Elinore asked Aurora. "Is that why he's too busy to eat?"

"No. Actually, he's awaiting Slayde's return. My brother had an . . . errand to take care of."

Elinore assessed Aurora's expression. "What errand?" she asked, the worry back on her face.

A sigh. "He's at Morland, confronting the duke. That's one of the reasons I've been preoccupied. Lawrence Bencroft burst in here the other day. He was drunk and raving, demanding to see Slayde. My brother means to find out why."

"Oh, dear." Elinore frowned. "I was afraid of this. The duke evidently saw the article Slayde submitted to the *Times*. He must be livid."

"That's what we have to assume, based upon the timing of Morland's visit." Aurora had to swallow the urge to tell Elinore the whole truth: that it was she and Courtney who had submitted that article, not Slayde—*and* that the entire submission was a clever deception. But Mr. Oridge had stressed the fact that they weren't to discuss a single facet of the mystery with anyone. Thus, she held her tongue.

"The letter was a stroke of genius," Elinore was

declaring. "Now everyone will have no choice but to believe the diamond is gone. And the Huntleys will, at last, be free." Her eyes misted. "Perhaps now your parents can rest in peace."

"I hope so," Aurora managed to say, assuaged by an irrational surge of guilt. How could her parents rest in peace when the diamond remained hidden wherever her great-grandfather had secreted it?

"You're worried about Morland's reaction," Elinore put in softly. "Especially if Slayde's admission inhibits his ability to transport the diamond."

"Yes. I'm terrified he'll hurt Slayde," Aurora confessed.

"That won't happen, darling." Elinore turned as they reached the entranceway door, her smile restored—whether as a genuine display or merely as an act of reassurance, Aurora wasn't certain. "Slayde can handle Morland," the viscountess continued, slipping into the wrap Siebert held out for her. "Especially if the fool is drunk. Besides," she added with a conspiratorial wink, "your brother has more pressing matters on his mind. Right?"

"Right."

"Good." Elinore smoothed a stray hair back into place, gesturing toward the staircase. "Now scoot back to Courtney. And please—tell her I'm here for any assistance she requires. Any assistance at all."

"At last."

Sprawled in Aurora's armchair, Courtney greeted her friend, watching as she slipped back into the bedchamber. "We have only an hour and a half before Mr. Oridge reclaims this sketch."

"An hour and twenty minutes," Oridge corrected from where he stood guard in the hallway.

Courtney rolled her eyes. "In any case, I was hoping you and Elinore hadn't decided to make a day of it."

"Hardly." With a tolerant sigh, Aurora shut the door against Oridge's firmly planted back. "Much as I adore

Elinore, this is one time I couldn't wait for her to go. Did you conjure up something without me?"

A faint smile touched Courtney's lips. "Would you be devastated if I said yes?"

"Probably."

"Then rest easy. I've been staring out the window, worrying about Slayde. I've scarcely even glanced at the note and drawing, much less divined who penned them." She indicated the page they'd wrested away from Oridge following a ten-minute heated debate—the result of which was Oridge's grudging agreement to permit them two hours alone with the sketch, after which he intended to reclaim it.

"Well, we'd best start glancing," Aurora muttered. "Because the precise instant our time elapses, Mr. Oridge will be flinging open that door to snatch the sketch away. As you heard, he's already mumbling under his breath." She dropped onto the bed, her expression solemn. "I, too, am worried about Slayde. He's walking into the lion's den. Although Elinore seems to think he can manage Morland." A pause. "At least I think she believes that."

A pucker formed between Courtney's brows. "What is it? What else is upsetting you?"

"Nothing. Everything. To begin with, I'm not accustomed to lying. And I'm not very good at it."

"Nor am I," Courtney sympathized. "Did you say something to Elinore you wish you hadn't?"

"No. Other than the fact that I divulged your wedding plans. I'm sorry, Courtney. 'Twas the only way I could explain my odd impatience and your equally inexplicable distraction."

At the last, Courtney sighed. "I'm as poor an actress as you are."

"Do you mind that I blurted out your news?"

"Of course not. Elinore is like family. Slayde and I would have told her next anyway." Courtney leaned forward. "Aurora, what happened to unnerve you?"

Pain flashed across Aurora's face. " 'Twas listening to

Elinore extol the virtues of Slayde's penning his letter to the *Times*. Courtney, I can't explain it, but I feel as if I've betrayed Mama and Papa. Elinore kept saying how fortuitous all this is, that the Huntleys will finally be free of the curse and that my parents will, at last, rest in peace." Aurora's tormented gaze met Courtney's. "But they can't rest in peace, can they? Because the diamond hasn't left my family's possession. My great-grandfather remains the last known person to have handled the stone, stealing it for himself. 'He with a black heart who touches the jewel will reap eternal wealth, while becoming the carrion upon whom, for all eternity, others will feed,'" she recited aloud. "Oh, God, Courtney. The whole idea terrifies me. And now—I feel so horribly guilty for pretending we've set it all right, granted my parents some semblance of peace, when in fact, we have not."

Courtney rose and went to the bed, sitting down beside her friend and hugging her tightly. "Now you listen to me, Aurora Huntley," she commanded fiercely. "There is no curse. 'Tis as fabricated as every other dark tale or legend that spans generations, propagated by thieves whose best interests it serves to do so. Your parents were killed by greedy, monstrous criminals, not by some imaginary curse. That diamond is worth a fortune. Those who traverse the globe in search of it crave that fortune. None of them seems to be deterred by the black legacy attached to it, do they? And wouldn't they be, if they truly believed they'd become the carrion upon whom all others will feed eternally? I should think the answer to that—great wealth or not—would be yes."

Drawing back, Courtney caught Aurora's hands in hers. "Aurora," she continued, her voice quavering as she spoke, "when I needed the strength to resolve Papa's death, you gave it to me. You offered me friendship, support, and a tangible method to achieve my end. Let me do the same for you." She rose, crossing over to pick up the sketch. "If you want to grant your parents peace, *this* is the way to do it. Let's find and punish the scoundrels who killed them. That will avenge their deaths and ease your heart of its excruciating burden."

Aurora's haunted look vanished, supplanted by her characteristic—and welcome—determination. "You're right." Purposefully, she dashed the moisture from her eyes. "How did I ever survive before you came to Pembourne?" A hint of a smile. "More importantly, how did Slayde survive? Never mind. I know the answer to that: he didn't. The change in him these past weeks . . . I still can't believe he's my brother. He jokes, laughs—Lord, he even *winked* at me. And the way he looks at you—" She stopped, studying Courtney's face. "Is it wonderful?"

"More than wonderful," Courtney replied softly. "More than heaven. More than anything I've ever imagined." She arched a knowing brow. "You'll see for yourself when it happens to you."

"I?" Aurora laughed aloud. "Now *that's* an unlikely notion. First of all, Slayde never lets me out of the house to meet anyone. And second—well, I just can't imagine any man who'd be *interesting* enough to spend the rest of my life with. If the day ever comes that I'm allowed beyond Pembourne's walls, I want to go everywhere, see everything. I've had more than enough complacency to last a lifetime. And I highly doubt there exists a man who'd tolerate—no, welcome—such a restless bride."

"If you say so."

"I say so." With a definitive nod, Aurora reached for the sketch. "Let's get back to work before Oridge comes in to reclaim this."

For the next hour, they studied the drawing, trying to deduce who could have—would have—penned it.

"If only whoever drew this had signed the note, or at the very least, initialed it," Courtney finally muttered. "There's nothing in the wording that's distinctive enough to attribute to any one person."

"It has to be someone who can read and write proper English," Aurora noted. "Surely *that* must eliminate a portion of the staff."

"Yes, but do we know for a fact who can or cannot do that?" Courtney countered.

"Not without asking them."

"Or testing them." Courtney chewed her lip. "What if we were to invent a plausible reason for instructing each servant to pen his name, or some specific words, or . . ." She shot up like a bullet. "That's it!"

"What's it?" Aurora sat bolt upright.

"The last ransom note—not the one found in Armon's pocket, but the one Slayde received."

"The one that disreputable fellow Grimes copied."

"Exactly." Courtney's eyes sparkled. "Not only is Grimes a contact for stolen jewels, he's also a skilled forger. He studied the handwriting of that second note, then reproduced it. Other than confessing that— and the fact that he was Armon's contact—to Slayde, he's been of little use to us. But I think all that's about to change." Courtney rubbed her palms together. "As I recall, Mr. Grimes is amenable to business arrangements that consist of his being lavishly compensated while remaining wholly intact. We can offer him that. In fact, we can offer him more than enough to buy his cooperation."

"You want him to study the handwriting on this sketch?"

"Not only study it, but compare it to a host of others. We're going to assemble the staff and ask each and every one of them to pen a few words for us. We'll conjure up a suitable reason, then choose a fragment from the note, something innocuous enough for the culprit to have forgotten he'd written ten years past. That way no one will feign the inability to write so as not to participate. Once the task is done, we'll take all the samples to Grimes."

"Who will then match the culprit's hand with that on this sketch," Aurora jumped in, realization erupting like fireworks.

"Precisely." Courtney's small jaw set. "At which time, dear cohort, we'll have our traitor."

Chapter 17

"Thayer, tell the duke I'm here," Slayde commanded, looming in Morland's entranceway door like an avenging god. "And don't bother refusing me or telling me he's away. He's here. And I'm going nowhere until I've spoken with him."

The butler flinched at Slayde's formidable presence, the leashed fury in his tone. "To the contrary, Lord Pembourne," he countered, taking two backward steps, "His Grace has been expecting . . . rather, hoping—" Breaking off, Thayer whipped out a handkerchief, mopped at his brow. "I have instructions to advise him the moment you arrive. Please—wait here while I announce you." He turned, nearly sprinting down the hall.

Not three minutes passed before he reappeared. "The duke will see you at once. Follow me."

Thayer led Slayde down the same corridor he'd just traversed, pausing when he reached the open study door.

"Lord Pembourne," he trumpeted, his voice quavering a bit.

"Huntley—so you finally got my message." Unsteadily, Morland rose from behind his desk, bitterness contorting his features, hatred darkening his red-rimmed stare. "I planned to give you one more day before I descended again on Pembourne."

"To do what?" Slayde demanded. "Harass my staff? Tear apart the manor? Or something more ominous than either?"

From the doorway, Thayer gave a delicate cough. "If there will be nothing else, sir?"

Morland's gaze never left Slayde's. "No, Thayer, you're welcome to bolt. Shut the door behind you. Oh, and you're bound to hear shouts. Ignore them. The earl and I have a great deal of catching up to do."

"Yes, Your Grace. Thank you." The butler fled like a pursued rabbit.

"I could kill you, you filthy bastard," Morland spat the instant he and Slayde were alone.

"I don't doubt it," Slayde shot back. "You have a wealth of experience when it comes to murder." A pause, flashes of Courtney's near-fatality jolting through him. "And *attempted* murder."

Morland's eyes narrowed. "Attempted murder? Have you a new accusation to add to your demented list of crimes?"

"I have many. Are you sober enough to hear them?"

"I'm as sober as you are."

"As you were the day you burst into Pembourne?"

"No. That day I was drunk. Today I'm livid." Morland gripped the edge of the desk until his knuckles turned white. "Don't confuse the two. Now, where is it? Where is that blasted diamond?"

"You already know the answer to that, Morland." Slayde's voice was menacingly quiet. "So drop the façade and give me the answers I seek. I'm not leaving here without them. I'll drag them from your lips if I must, employing whatever methods are necessary to get them."

"*You* dare to threaten *me?*" Morland roared, picking up an empty goblet and hurling it against the fireplace, where it smashed into a hundred shards. "You, who handed my life over to that pirate along with the black diamond? You had no bloody right. I don't give a damn about your sister's life. That privateer was welcome to her—'twould be one less Huntley to contend with."

Slayde's control snapped. "You miserable . . ." He crossed the room in a heartbeat, his fist connecting with Morland's jaw.

"Go ahead," Morland taunted, panting as he regained his balance. "Thrash me. Beat me senseless. I'm condemned to an eternal hell anyway, thanks to the Huntleys. You're all animals, cursed thieves who have hoisted your curse onto us." He rubbed his jaw, words of enmity spilling forth of their own accord. "Four generations, my family has suffered, died, from your greed and hatred. Did you have the jewel all these years, you wretched scoundrel? Or did you uncover it just in time to relinquish it and damn the Bencrofts to immortal doom?"

Something penetrated Slayde's rage, gave him pause. Perhaps it was Morland's tone, his desperation. Perhaps it was instinct, the new awareness Slayde had only just acquired. In any case, he found himself waiting, deferring his next punch, listening to Morland's ramblings.

"What's wrong with you Huntleys?" he was demanding, raking both hands through his hair. "Don't you want to be rid of that curse? Do you enjoy being haunted by demons? Or is it just the sheer pleasure of tormenting the Bencrofts that stirs your black-hearted souls? You don't need the fortune that diamond would bring. Hell, you've got more money than you know what to do with."

"While you don't," Slayde said at once.

A harsh laugh. "You know damned well I'm in dire financial straits. The Bencrofts have lost countless fortunes thanks to your great-grandfather's piracy. We'll continue to lose countless more."

"So you view the diamond as payment for your suffering."

"Payment *and* salvation. Moreover, I was on the verge of finding the stone, restoring it to where it belonged so I could at last set things right. Oh, I could never obliterate the past, but I could grant my ancestors peace and myself a measure of security in my old age. I would have succeeded. I'd raised the money to begin my search. And then—this!" Morland snatched up a copy of the *Times* and flung it to the floor at Slayde's feet.

Slowly, Slayde's gaze traveled to the open newspaper, glancing from the article on page two to the vein pulsing furiously at Morland's temple to the unfeigned enmity—and trepidation—glistening in his eyes.

A deluge of stunned awareness struck, transforming Slayde's rage to shock, to doubt and, ultimately, to realization: Lawrence Bencroft was telling the truth.

Drawing in a slow breath, Slayde assimilated the snatches of information he'd just been given, fit all the pieces together.

"Morland," he somehow managed to reply, "are you suggesting that not only did you *not* pay Armon to steal the black diamond but that your sudden re-emergence in the business world was an attempt to finance a search for the stone?"

"Are *you* suggesting you didn't know that?"

"How would I?"

Morland's smile was grim. "Oh, come now, Pembourne. You told me yourself you'd delved into my business affairs. Quite thoroughly, I presume. What did you discover I'd been doing with my funds?"

"Transferring them. Amassing them. Spending an unusual amount of time meeting with your solicitor and banker discussing them." Slayde's eyes narrowed. "Let's put the results of my inquiries aside. If what you claim is true, why didn't you combat my accusations, or Courtney's for that matter, by revealing this convenient detail? She and I both, on separate occasions, appeared on your doorstep, accusing you of orchestrating the plan to pilfer the diamond. You said nothing to prove you weren't involved."

"I have nothing to prove, not to you or that crazed woman you sent here. And since my money was being invested in a search—the onset of which was a thorough investigation of your activities to ensure that you weren't, in reality, harboring the diamond at Pembourne—it hardly seemed prudent to disclose my intentions and alert you to that upcoming investigation. Moreover, since I knew I was innocent of all the allegations you and that insane Johnston girl were hurling at me, I never once doubted that, like your accusations, your claim to have relinquished the diamond was entirely fabricated. Until I read that contemptible submission of yours. Had I but known—" Morland leveled an icy stare at Slayde. "I'd have thrashed you before I let you hand over that diamond. But now it's too late. Some other greedy bastard has the stone, and it will take me months to track it down."

"You're not lying." Slayde said the words aloud, almost as if he needed to hear them to believe they were true. "Hell and damnation, you're actually telling the truth." Additional implications sank in. "Are you also going to deny taking a shot at Courtney last week? The night we were in Somerset?"

"What?" Morland countered. "Took a shot at . . . is that the attempted murder you were referring to?" Furiously, he shook his head. "The last I saw of that chit, she was tearing out of my home, presumably heading back to Pembourne. I never saw her again. I never knew you and she went to Somerset. And I damned well never tried to kill her." Morland's hands balled into fists. "Pembourne, not only are you a heartless thief, you're also a lunatic. For months after your parents died, you hammered me with accusations—that I was a murderer, that my father was a murderer. Now, ten years later, you've decided to rekindle the ashes of those accusations—inspired by some sick purpose that evades me. Moreover, you're also charging me with shooting a woman I met for but a few minutes and couldn't give a damn about one way or the other. Well, I have no intentions of allowing you to reopen old wounds or create new ones. Your claims were demented and unfounded then; they're demented and unfounded now. So are those of that sea captain's daughter. The two of you can threaten me with exposure 'til the end of time. Unless you've manufactured nonexistent evidence to incriminate me, I have nothing to fear. Not only didn't I try to kill *her,* but, for the hundredth time, I did *not* kill your parents." A lethal glare. "Don't misunderstand; I loathe the Huntleys. Murdering one of them would purge my soul and lighten my heart. But the particular one I'd have in mind would be your great-grandfather. I'd choke the location of the diamond out of him, then kill him without a shred of guilt. Unfortunately, he's already dead. And murdering the rest of you would serve no purpose other than to vent my rage and condemn me to Newgate. Frankly, you're just not worth it."

Slayde was reeling, too overcome by what he'd just learned to address Morland's venomous comments. Besides, they suddenly ceased to matter. Suddenly, everything ceased to matter.

Everything but Courtney.

With a gripping sensation, Slayde confronted the single most impending horror indicated by Morland's revelations: somewhere out there was the culprit who'd truly attempted to shoot Courtney. And that culprit was waiting, plotting.

Mr. Scollard's voice resounded through Slayde's head.

Ruthlessness hovers at your portals . . . heartlessness and obsession haunt your doorstep. . . . Danger stalks Courtney like a predator. After today, there will be no protection. You alone can prevent the danger from seizing her. . . . Resolution is in your hands—as is Courtney's life. Return to Pembourne . . . return to Pembourne. . . .

Everything inside Slayde went cold. God help him, he had to get to Courtney.

* * *

The phaeton couldn't reach Pembourne quickly enough. For the dozenth time, Slayde urged the horses to go faster, nearly jostling Rayburn from his seat in the process. "Sorry," Slayde muttered.

"Quite all right, sir." Rayburn resituated himself. "I understand. And if it's any consolation to you, you did the right thing by relieving me of my post. I can do you more good hunting down the real culprit than I can scrutinizing the duke's estate. It's quite obvious Morland isn't involved."

"You're sure he never left the manor?"

"Other than yesterday morning when he descended upon Pembourne, no—not from the instant I resumed my post six days past, having delivered Lady Aurora and Miss Johnston to Pembourne. In fact, not only has the duke gone nowhere, but no one has visited him—not his solicitor, not his banker, no one. The only person to arrive at Morland all week was the local delivery boy, who has long since checked out as legitimate."

"Couldn't Morland have left his estate during the time you rode to Pembourne—especially if he followed you, Courtney and Aurora to my home?"

"Of course. However, I was gone from my post for but a few hours. If the duke had pursued Miss Johnston from Pembourne to Somerset before returning to his estate, I'd definitely have witnessed his return, if not his departure. No, my lord, the Duke of Morland was not the person who took a shot at Miss Johnston."

"Then who the hell was?" Slayde growled, fingers tightening on the reins.

"Who indeed, sir."

Glancing about, Slayde realized Pembourne was nearly upon them. "Before we arrive, I have another pressing matter to discuss with you."

"Sir?"

"Until new evidence presents itself, there's little point in your blindly trying to hunt down the assailant. Moreover, I have an interim assignment I want you to pursue—a delicate, extraordinarily important assignment. It must be handled quickly, discreetly, and—with the help of God—successfully. I'd originally intended to get a recommendation from Oridge; I trust he'd supply me with the name of someone competent and reliable for the job. But needless to say, I'd much rather engage your services, as I'm already familiar with the high quality of your work."

"I'm honored and at your disposal, sir. What is this assignment?"

Slayde's mouth set in a grim line. "I need you to find someone for me. Someone who's been injured and is incapable—either mentally, physically, or both—of finding us. Or rather, of finding Courtney."

Rayburn blinked. "Who?"

"Her father."

"Captain Johnston? According to your notes, he was thrown overboard and drowned."

"He *was* thrown overboard. As for drowned, I have reason to believe that he survived, that the currents swept him onto the Cornish shore. The question is, where? My information says he's recovering in a quiet inlet. Thus, we have to locate and search every quiet inlet from here to the western tip of Cornwall. I'll pore over charts with you, make a list of all the inlets that fit that description. First thing tomorrow, you'll go off to explore each of them." A scowl. "I'd handle this myself, but I dare not leave Courtney—not until we've determined who tried to kill her. So I'm asking you to go in my stead, to work as thoroughly and painstakingly as I would have. To defy the odds and recover Arthur Johnston."

Rayburn gave a definitive nod. "I won't disappoint you, my lord."

"I know you won't." The phaeton passed through Pembourne's gates. "Oh, and Rayburn? Don't say a word of this to anyone. Especially Courtney. She's just coming to grips with the possibility of her father's death. And in the unlikely event that I'm wrong, that Johnston did perish in the Channel . . . I don't think she could withstand the pain a second time."

"I understand. This will remain strictly between us."

"Thank you. I'll tell Courtney and Aurora that you're spending the night, then pursuing other suspects. Which you are—eventually." The phaeton rounded the drive, and Slayde brought it to a stop. Leaping to the ground, he headed for the manor, adding, "We'll meet in my study later, to pore over those charts. Right now, I want to make sure Courtney's all right."

Slayde was already mounting the steps when Siebert opened the entranceway door. Assessing his master's grim expression, he announced, "Miss Johnston and Lady Aurora are quite well, my lord. In fact, they've been surprisingly quiet. I believe Mr. Oridge is becoming unnerved by their silence."

"I'm sure he is." Slayde visibly relaxed. "We had no unexpected guests?"

"No guests at all, my lord. Other than Lady Stanwyk. And even she stayed but a half-hour. Lady Aurora was too restless for a visit."

"Aurora—restless? Now *that* sounds like trouble." Slayde veered toward the stairs, calling over his shoulder, "Please have Miss Payne make up a room for Rayburn. He'll be staying the night."

"Of course, sir." A frown. "Actually, I've scarcely seen Miss Payne all day. That's odd." He shrugged. "Never mind, sir. I'll find her." So saying, he went off in search of the housekeeper.

Slayde reached the second-floor landing in record time, then stalked down the hall. *Rory's bedchamber,* Scollard had said. Very well, then that was where he'd go.

Oridge was jostling the door handle when Slayde appeared. The investigator glanced up, nearly sagging with relief when he saw his employer. "You're back, my lord."

Fear knotted Slayde's gut. "Why? What's wrong?"

"Nothing, sir," Oridge assured him. "'Tis only that Miss Johnston and Lady Aurora have barricaded themselves inside." An exasperated sigh. "They haven't attempted a window escape; I've listened intently for any indications of that, such as unusual rustles or squeaks, sudden lulls in their chatter. None of those has occurred—yet. However, the two of them must be plotting something, because they refuse to come out."

"Hell and damnation." Slayde pounded on the door. "Courtney. Aurora. Open this door before I break it down."

An instant later, a key turned and the door was flung wide. "Slayde," Courtney said, her heart in her eyes. "Thank God . . . you're all right."

"Thank God *I'm* all right?" He couldn't help it; he dragged her to him, enfolded her in his arms. "I've been half crazed with worry." He pressed his lips into her crown of red-gold hair. "Why are the two of you locked up like criminals?"

Courtney tilted back her head and smiled up at him. "We needed a few more minutes to finalize our plan. And Mr. Oridge refused to extend our agreed-upon allotment of time by even a quarter hour. So we took the necessary steps to protect our interests."

"What allotment of time? What plan?"

"First tell me Morland didn't hurt you."

"He didn't hurt me. I, however, punched him."

"Then he revealed something?"

"At that particular instant? Only that he believes Aurora's life is worth sacrificing in order to retain possession of the diamond."

Aurora rose, wide-eyed. "You struck Morland—for me?"

A hint of softness. "You *are* my sister, you know."

"I'm beginning to realize that," she replied with an equal measure of softness.

"Slayde," Courtney pressed. "Did you learn anything?"

"Too much and not enough." Slayde eased Courtney

inside the bedchamber, gesturing for Oridge to join them. "The four of us have a great deal to discuss." The moment the door shut behind them, Slayde turned to his investigator. "Did any of the servants behave oddly?"

"Not in the least. I've been posted outside Lady Aurora's bedchamber all afternoon, scanning the list and studying the staff. Other than a few maids and footmen who expressed sympathy that I'd been given the impossible task of thwarting Lady Aurora's escape efforts, no one's so much as spoken to me. They've performed their jobs in what I would call a customary fashion. Oh, I did have the opportunity to speak with Mr. Lexley. He's a most gracious fellow, but with no additional details to provide us."

"Then we're right back where we started, damn it." Slayde's arms tightened about Courtney. "I'm not letting you out of my sight," he informed her. "Not for a moment. So give up any notion of locking doors unless I'm behind them with you."

"Slayde, what is it?" Anxiously, Courtney studied Slayde's taut expression. "What's upset you so?"

A muscle worked in his jaw. "Morland's innocent," he stated flatly. "He's not the one who hired Armon. He doesn't have the diamond. And he didn't take a shot at you the other day."

Aurora emitted a shocked gasp.

"And your parents?" Courtney sounded more concerned than she did stunned. "Is he innocent of their murders as well?"

"According to him, yes. He vehemently denied any involvement in their killings. Of course, he's said that a dozen times before. We have yet to find proof of his innocence. There's every possibility that he's lying."

"But you don't think he is."

A weighted silence. Then: "No—I don't."

"What about Chilton? Do you still believe he committed the murders?"

Reason and emotion warred in Slayde's head, years of enmity screaming for acknowledgment.

Logic. Mr. Scollard's words sliced through his mental turmoil. *Reserve the irrational for Courtney's loving hands; employ reason where no love exists.*

"No," Slayde heard himself say. "I don't." He gave a dazed shake of his head. "How ironic. For ten years, I've been so certain, so utterly convinced Chilton was responsible. But today, listening to Morland, seeing him without allowing hatred to blind me . . . somehow my perspective altered."

"Did you speak to Rayburn, my lord?" Oridge interrupted.

"Yes, immediately following my confrontation with Morland. As a matter of fact, I brought Rayburn back with me. There's no point in his remaining there, scrutinizing Morland's every move. The duke is not the criminal we seek."

"I take it His Grace was at home the night Miss Johnston was attacked?"

"At home and alone. Morland hasn't left his estate all week. Nor has anyone visited him. So he neither fired that shot nor hired someone else to fire it. By the way, he was also fully sober during our altercation. Vicious and frightened, but sober. He disclosed things that made all the pieces fit: why he's stopped drinking, why he's rejoined the business community, why he's been conducting meetings with his banker and solicitor."

Quietly, Slayde elaborated, disclosing Morland's objectives, his plan to unearth the black diamond, his immediate goal to investigate the Huntleys.

"That explains his irrational reaction to our article in the *Times,*" Aurora concluded thoughtfully.

"Yes. It also leaves us with no name, no face—nothing but the realization that whoever orchestrated these crimes wants Courtney eliminated." Slayde swallowed. "If it isn't Morland, who is it? And how the hell do we find out before he tries to hurt her again?"

"Using the only other lead we have," Courtney pronounced, gripping the sleeves of Slayde's coat. "Our only hope of getting to the true culprit is to discern the identity of his other henchman—the one right here at Pembourne. Once we do, he'll panic and unknowingly lead us straight to whoever hired him."

"Which brings us to the remarkable plan Courtney's developed," Aurora piped up, her shock at Morland's innocence eclipsed by renewed excitement. "Thanks to her quick thinking, we'll have our traitor by tomorrow, and his employer soon after."

With a start, Slayde raised his brows at Oridge.

"This is the first I'm hearing of Miss Johnston's plan, sir," the investigator replied with a helpless shrug. "As I said, I've been in the hall all day—barred from the room." He glowered at Courtney and Aurora. "According to the agreement I made with these ladies—under extreme duress, I might add—they were to return the sketch to me twenty minutes ago. They refused to comply. I had no idea what they were using it for or what they were up to."

"We were finalizing our plan." Courtney frowned. "All but the reason we'll give the staff. Perhaps you gentlemen can assist us with that."

"What agreement?" Slayde demanded. "What plan? What reason?" He rolled his eyes. "And why am I surprised that I haven't an inkling what you're talking about?"

"I'll tell you." Courtney extricated herself from Slayde's embrace, crossing the room to fetch the drawing. "Look." She pointed to the note. "We've all been concentrating on the sketch, when we should have been concentrating on the message written above it." Her eyes glowed with purpose. "The idea came to me when I considered the letter Aurora and I submitted to the *Times* and how long it took Aurora to copy your hand. Everyone's writing is distinctive, especially when examined by an expert. Well, we know the perfect expert, don't we?"

"Grimes," Slayde muttered. "But what is it we're asking of him? To copy the note?"

"No, to compare it. We're going to assemble the entire

staff—which we intend to do anyway, to announce our wedding plans. Once the jovial atmosphere has been established, we'll present our dilemma—which must be something that would require each of the servants to pen a phrase. An innocuous phrase, using words contained in the message on this sketch—so innocuous that no one will feel threatened; therefore, all those who know how to write will comply. Once they have, we'll collect all the samples and bring them to Grimes."

"And he'll match the writing on the sketch to that on one of the samples," Slayde concluded. With a gleam of triumph, he turned his head to meet Oridge's astonished gaze. "I believe you should offer Miss Johnston an apology. It appears she made extraordinary use of her time with the sketch."

"I believe I should offer Miss Johnston a job," Oridge returned dryly. "Her plan is ingenious."

"Thank you, gentlemen." Courtney grinned. "But the plan is useless without a plausible excuse to give the staff. Why on earth would we ask them to do this?"

"Because we suspect one of them has been aiding me in my escapes from Pembourne," Aurora announced.

Three heads whipped about to face her.

"'Tis the perfect dilemma!" she continued. "Every servant at Pembourne knows how incensed Slayde becomes when I manage to escape, successfully eluding detection. Well, what if I've been managing more frequent and successful escapes of late? What if the guards were ordered to investigate—and they did, only to find an unassuming note propped alongside the back entrance, maybe concealed by a portion of the shrubs that frame the door. A note that read 'Use this door for coming and going.' Delivering the note to Slayde, they would all conclude that I'd been receiving help in my attempts to flee—help from someone inside Pembourne. Slayde, of course, would be irate, determined to find out who my coconspirator was. Thus, the need for writing samples—to compare with the original note, which no one will actually see. 'Tis ideal, because we needn't fabricate an elaborate and unbelievable lie. Every staff member will know *what* we are doing—but not the truth behind *why* we're doing it. Why, even Courtney would be required to participate. After all, she is the likeliest candidate for my accomplice. And if Slayde would go so far as to question the honor of his betrothed, not even the culprit will guess our true purpose. He'll participate—*and* play right into our hands. Because if you look closely, you'll see that every one of the words in my fictitious note is contained in the message on this sketch. So we'll be providing Grimes with all he needs to do his job."

"Aurora, how brilliant!" Courtney grabbed her friend's hands and led her into a victorious jig. "Not only brilliant, but flawless. Isn't it, Slayde?"

Slayde stared from Aurora to Courtney to the sketch. Then, he turned to his investigator, a grin of disbelief curving his lips. "Oridge—you're fired."

Chapter 18

"I'm glad you reconsidered and kept Oridge on," Courtney teased as Slayde escorted her to her bedchamber.

"Only because I can't be in two places at one time," Slayde joked back. "Else he'd be gone." Sobering, he added, "I intend to stand guard over you all night and have him do the same for Aurora. I'm not taking any chances with either of you."

He opened the bedchamber door—and collided with Miss Payne.

"Oh, pardon me, my lord," she said, turning three shades of red. "I didn't hear you coming. But 'tis Matilda's night off. So after I turned down Miss Johnston's bed, I awaited to see if she needed anything."

"Thank you, Miss Payne," Courtney replied. "That's very kind of you. But there's nothing I require." She hid her smile as Slayde strolled into the bedchamber, causing the housekeeper to blanche.

"I'll see to Miss Johnston," Slayde informed Miss

Payne, unbothered by her reaction to his scandalous behavior. "Despite Matilda's absence, she'll want for nothing."

The housekeeper looked as if she might faint, and Courtney felt a wave of sympathy. "I'm sorry if we've shocked you," she leaned forward to murmur. "Despite appearances, 'tis only a minor indiscretion. Lord Pembourne and I are to be married within a fortnight."

Miss Payne swallowed. "Married?"

"Yes, but don't breathe a word. We've told only Lady Aurora, Lexley, and the Viscountess Stanwyk. We'll be announcing it to the entire staff tomorrow. So, please, keep our secret. And, again, forgive Lord Pembourne's less than proper behavior—and mine."

"Yes. Of course. Congratulations. I understand. Good night." Miss Payne backed off, then hastened down the hall.

"Slayde, you're impossible," Courtney said, shutting the door and biting back laughter. "The poor woman nearly collapsed, she was so mortified."

"I really couldn't care less. I've never lived my life for others. I don't intend to start now." He paused, glancing at Courtney. "Unless it upsets you."

"I've never made a secret of how little protocol means to me," Courtney answered. An impish grin curved her lips. "Although I had wondered if you, like Mr. Oridge, planned on spending the night in the hallway."

Slayde's gaze intensified, his eyes darkening to a deep, smoky gray. "I'd planned on spending the night in your arms," he said in a husky voice that sent shivers down her spine. "Unless you turn me away."

In answer, Courtney turned the key in the lock, crossing over to stand before him. "Never," she breathed. Reaching up, she untied his cravat. "I'll never turn you away." She unbuttoned his waistcoat and shirt, parting the material and pressing her lips to his exposed, hair-roughened skin. "I love you too much."

Slayde growled deep in his throat, swinging Courtney into his arms and carrying her to the bed. He dispensed with her gown and chemise in several sharp, urgent motions, lowering her to the waiting sheets and stepping away only long enough to tear off his own clothes, his restless gaze raking every bare inch of her as he did.

Unashamedly, Courtney drank in his magnificent nudity, reaching her arms out to him and whispering, "Slayde—hurry."

It was all he needed.

With a wracking shudder, he covered her nakedness with his, tangling his fingers in her hair and angling her mouth to receive his kiss.

"Yes," she said against his lips, her fingers caressing the powerful muscles of his shoulders and back, stroking down to his buttocks, which went taut at her touch.

"God, you drive me crazy," he muttered, devouring her mouth with hot, hungry kisses, melding her tongue with his.

"I can tell." Experimentally, she arched, feeling the answering pulse of his body, his rigid length throbbing against her belly in its desperate need to be one with her.

"Do that again and I'll be inside you in a heartbeat," he rasped, lowering his head to her breast. Slowly, deliberately, he drew her nipple into his mouth, licking maddening circles about the aching tip until Courtney thought she'd die. Abruptly, he gave her what she craved, his lips enveloping the peak, tugging powerfully—once, twice, then in a hard, steady rhythm, punctuating each motion with a lash of his tongue.

"Oh . . . God." Courtney bit her lip against the scream threatening to erupt. Lightening shot from her breasts to her loins, her womb clenching as liquid heat pooled between her thighs.

Wildly aroused by her response, Slayde shifted to her other breast, inflicting the same torture, gently holding her hips to prevent their undulating motion. "Not yet," he answered her unspoken plea. "Not yet." He reached down, slipped his fingers between her thighs—and was nearly undone by the satiny wetness that greeted his touch. "Perfect," he said thickly, his fingers gliding inside, his thumb finding and stroking the tiny bud that begged for his touch. "So . . . utterly . . . perfect."

Courtney sobbed his name, arching against his hand, begging him to stop, each roll of her hips wilder, more abandoned.

"You're so beautiful." Feeling her inner muscles quiver against his fingertips, Slayde quickened his motions, shuddering as he battled back his own release, which clawed at his loins despite the fact that he had yet to enter her. "So close," he rasped. "You're so close. Let me feel you."

"No . . . Slayde, no." Courtney shook her head, her hair a glorious tangle on the pillows. "I . . . no." Blindly, she reached between them, her fingers finding and surrounding his turgid shaft, caressing skin too achingly sensitized by nerves too raw to breaking.

"God . . . Courtney." Slayde went utterly still, gritting his teeth against the feral shout exploding in his chest, flames igniting in his loins. Of its own accord, his body moved against her palm, seeking a more erotic contact, desperate to know the effects of her touch.

Taking full advantage of the moment, Courtney squirmed away, wriggling down the bed until she could worship him with her mouth, love him in the same magnificent way he had her.

She'd scarcely begun when Slayde dragged her back up.

"Stop!" he commanded, lifting her hips and plunging deep, deep inside her. "Courtney . . ."

He poured into her even as he roared her name, throwing back his head and succumbing to the shout he'd fought to suppress. Unendurable pleasure screamed along his nerve endings as Courtney convulsed around him, cried out his name, hard spasms of completion overtaking her, clasping at his length and intensifying his climax beyond bearing. He gripped her thighs, opening them wider, lifting her into him to give her every iota of sensation, every drop of his essence.

Courtney cried out again, clutching Slayde with arms

and legs and inner muscles that contracted around him in what had to be the most exquisite of tortures.

They collapsed in a joined heap, dragging air into their lungs, shuddering with the lingering tremors of their release.

Minutes drifted by, melded into a blissful stretch of timelessness, a bone-deep contentment—of their bodies, yes, but more profoundly, of their souls.

An eternity later, Slayde raised his head, kissed Courtney's closed eyelids, her flushed cheeks. "I love you." Tenderly, he framed her face between his palms, brushing her lips with all the soft kisses he'd intended, but which their urgency had earlier precluded.

Courtney's arms came up to encircle his neck. "Am I still alive?" she murmured.

A chuckle. "If not, then neither am I. In which case, I don't give a damn. So long as I'm with you, I don't care where I am."

"Either way, it's heaven." Courtney's lashes lifted and she smiled. "Utter, eternal heaven." She kissed the damp column of Slayde's throat. "I love you, Lord Pembourne."

Fierce emotion darkened his gaze. "And I adore you, soon-to-be Lady Pembourne."

That caused a pucker to form between Courtney's brows. "Lady Pembourne—I hadn't considered that. In marrying an earl, I become a countess."

Slayde rolled them to one side, wrapping his arms securely about his future bride. "Is that approval or disapproval I detect?"

"Would it matter?"

"No. You're marrying me anyway."

She laughed. "Tell me, then: are countesses permitted such abandoned behavior in the bedroom?"

"Absolutely. 'Tis a requirement of the peerage."

"I see." Courtney's shoulders were shaking. "And are countesses permitted to ravish their poor, unsuspecting earl husbands repeatedly?"

"Without so much as a moment's recovery time."

"Ah. And are countesses—"

"Yes." Slayde covered her mouth with his, kissing her until her breath was coming in quick, heated pants. "Most definitely—yes."

"Very well, then," Courtney managed to say, quivering as Slayde hardened inside her. "I suppose I'll adapt."

"Slayde?" Courtney whispered, securely nestled in the warm circle of his arms.

"Hmm?"

"Earlier, when you spoke about your confrontation with Morland, the sudden change in your perspective— what caused it?"

Slayde gathered her closer, gazing across the dimly-lit room. "Several things: you, the new depth of understanding your love has brought me . . ." A smile. "And a very unusual cup of tea."

Courtney twisted about, raising up so she could make out Slayde's expression. "You went to see Mr. Scollard."

"I did indeed."

"Oh, Slayde." She flung her arms about his neck. "I'm so glad."

"So am I, actually. He's astounding, your Mr. Scollard. 'Tis as if he can see inside you. Oh, speaking of seeing," Slayde teased, caressing Courtney's cheek, "I evidently both see and hear quite well now. Whatever deficiency I had is gone. According to Mr. Scollard, I've found my way." All teasing vanished, supplanted by an emotion too vast to contain. "Thank God that way led to you."

Courtney's eyes misted. " 'Tis the same for us as it was for Mama and Papa—you, the ship, and I, the lighthouse. Neither is complete without the other." She brushed her lips to Slayde's, her prayer as reverent as his. "Thank God we *both* found our course."

Her choice of analogies reminded Slayde of the fierce commitment he'd sworn to fulfill. "I'm going to make everything right, Courtney," he vowed fervently. "You'll see."

Puzzled, she searched his face, somehow sensing he referred to more than just the mystery they had yet to resolve. "I know you will." A speculative pause. "Tell me about your visit with Mr. Scollard."

Damn, but her insight was staggering.

Warning bells sounded, and Slayde cautioned himself to tread carefully, to refrain from any mention of Arthur Johnston and the possibility that he was alive. "I stopped by on my way to confront Morland. Mr. Scollard was expecting me."

"Naturally," Courtney murmured.

"He congratulated me on our forthcoming marriage *and* on my amazing transformation. Then he made me tea."

Courtney grinned. "Given your preference for rational explanation, you must have been utterly astounded."

"At first, yes. But once I stopped grappling with what I couldn't understand and just accepted it, I began enjoying our chat. He commended me on leaving Oridge to oversee you and Aurora, and urged me to go on to Morland, to face my ghosts." Slayde's expression darkened. "He did caution me that after today, I was not to leave you alone, that you would be in danger. When he said those words, I nearly gave up the idea of riding to Newton Abbot and dashed back to Pembourne. But Scollard insisted that, for this one day, you'd be fine without my protection. Now that I consider it, he already knew Morland was innocent. He also knew that I had to recognize it for myself. His exact words when he sent me off were 'So long as you're confronting the duke, the peril will be held at bay.' Naturally, I assumed he meant the peril and Morland were one and the same; that if Morland was at home, engaged in a confrontation with me, he couldn't be at Pembourne hurting you. But when I verbalized that thought, Scollard replied, 'Those are your words, not mine.' If that wasn't an allusion to the fact that my suspicions were misdirected, I don't know what was."

"Yet you didn't realize it then."

"No," Slayde admitted. "I suppose, as Scollard said, I had to clear my mind of the shadows that obstructed my sight in order to see what was truly there, not what I chose to see."

"He's a wonderful man, isn't he?"

"Yes. He's also worried sick about you." Slayde sifted his fingers through Courtney's hair. "So am I. Every reference he made led back to the fact that the danger lies at Pembourne. And not only as far as the traitor we're harboring—although Scollard did sense that bastard's clawing fear—but as far as our main quarry as well. Scollard kept using phrases such as 'outside—heartlessness and obsession haunting your doorstep' and 'ruthlessness hovers at its portals.' Again, given that I believed Morland was the culprit, I assumed those references were to his drunken visit to Pembourne, his intentions to return. But now, with Morland eliminated as a suspect, we have to view Mr. Scollard's insights in a new light."

Courtney paled. "You believe that whoever's at the helm of these horrible crimes is close by?"

Slayde studied Courtney's frightened face, torn between his innate compulsion to protect her, which urged him to lie in order to assuage her fears, and his love for her, which commanded that he speak the truth. In the end, there was no choice. "Yes. I do." His thumbs stroked her cheekbones. "But I also believe that scoundrel's downfall is imminent, thanks to the plan you and Aurora conjured up." A sudden memory flashed through Slayde's mind, spawning a glimmer of comprehension. "What's more, Mr. Scollard believes the same."

"He told you that?"

"Indirectly. What he said was that wits, not pistols, would be my true weapon." A discerning grin. "What he failed to mention was that the wits involved would be yours."

* * *

Over a hundred servants crowded Pembourne's ballroom, the only room large enough to hold so vast a number of people. Most of them shifted nervously, murmuring among themselves about the possible reasons for Lord Pembourne's request that they gather here after breakfast.

Undetected, Slayde surveyed the room from the hallway. "Do you understand what I expect of you?" he muttered to Cutterton.

"Of course, sir," Cutterton said quietly. "Mathers and I will support your story. We'll concur that we found the note yesterday, and advised you to take instantaneous action. As for our immediate responsibility, we'll distribute the writing materials and collect the handwriting samples—after we've publicly advised Miss Johnston that her participation in this task is mandatory."

"Excellent." Slayde shot Cutterton a grateful look. "I know you haven't a clue why I'm doing this. I hope I'll be able to fill you in soon. In the interim, I appreciate your cooperation."

"That's my job, sir." Cutterton's gaze flickered to the left and he gave a terse nod. "Mathers is here with the paper and writing implements."

"Good. Then let's proceed." Slayde turned to Courtney, who was standing beside him, her eyes bright with anticipation. "Come, love," he said softly, extending his hand. "We have an announcement to make."

"Yes, my lord." She placed her hand in his. "Indeed we do."

A hush fell over the group as their master entered, Miss Johnston by his side.

Courtney looked from one face to the other, pained by the apprehension she saw reflected there. Many of these people had cared for her, nursed her back to health, and, in the process, become like family to her—especially Siebert and Matilda, who stood near the front, their worried gazes softening with affection as they met hers. For their sakes—for *all* their sakes—she prayed this nightmare would soon end.

As Slayde cleared his throat to speak, Courtney's eyes met Aurora's, and she smiled at the vivid excitement revealed in the turquoise depths. Not an ounce of fear, she noted. Not her Aurora. Only joy at Slayde's and her impending marriage, and exhilaration at what Aurora was convinced was the greatest and soon-to-be most successful scheme of all time.

"First, let me thank you all for taking time away from your duties," Slayde began. His brows drew together as he sought just the right words to convey his announcement. "Many of you have been with my family for years, yet doubtless view me not as a resident of Pembourne, but as an infrequent and short-term visitor. 'Tis no secret why. I've spent little of my life within these walls—especially since my parents were killed a decade ago, after which Pembourne became only a hollow chasm of pain and anguish. Thus, it's been anything but a home—not for me or, I suspect, for many of you." A meaningful glance at Aurora. "Certainly not for my sister, who spends half her life trying to flee from it."

A few of the servants coughed uneasily.

"Last month, a young woman came into our lives who, in a very short time, has managed to accomplish what I could not: she's made Pembourne feel like a home and its occupants like a family." His fingers tightened around Courtney's. "We all owe Miss Johnston an incredible debt—most especially, I.

"In the true spirit of the family she's helped to create, I've summoned you all here this morning to share some wonderful news. Pembourne's transformation, and mine, are destined to endure, thanks to the extraordinary gift Miss Johnston has agreed to bestow upon me— that being her hand in marriage." A murmur went up from the crowd, and Slayde turned to Courtney, his expression tender. "I'm proud to announce that Miss Courtney Johnston will soon become Mrs. Slayde Huntley, the Countess of Pembourne . . . my wife."

Unanimous, enthusiastic applause erupted.

Courtney blinked, staring from one beaming face to

the other, tears stinging her eyes at the unexpectedly fervent response. She'd anticipated polite approval, in some cases pleasure, but exuberance such as this? It was humbling.

"Thank you," she managed, her voice lost in the din.

Aurora rushed forward, embracing both her brother and future sister-in-law, her own eyes damp.

"Why are you crying?" Courtney laughed through her tears. "You already knew."

"So did you," Aurora retorted. "Yet you're crying."

"Please wait," Slayde called out loudly, holding up his palm. "Unfortunately, there is another, more sobering matter I need to address before any celebrating takes place."

The clapping quieted, then ceased, apprehension once again swelling to fill the room.

"As I just mentioned, Lady Aurora is notorious for her attempts to escape Pembourne."

"Oh, but Slayde," Aurora inserted on cue, "all that will change now that Courtney's—"

"Nevertheless," he interrupted, "it's come to my attention that, over the past few days, someone at Pembourne has been assisting her in her attempts to outwit the guards." Slayde clasped his hands behind his back, his bold silver-gray stare sweeping the room. "This is not mere speculation. I have proof of my claim. What I now ask is for the guilty party to step forward and admit what he or she has done. If that party complies, he or she will be firmly dealt with, but not dismissed. Otherwise . . ." Slayde left the rest of his sentence hanging. Jaw set, he waited.

Seconds ticked by.

"No one is willing to claim responsibility for this?" he pressed.

Silence.

"Very well, then there is but one other way to achieve my end." Half turning, Slayde gestured for Mathers to enter. "Mr. Mathers will be handing each one of you a blank sheet of paper. Once that's been done, I will read to you the contents of a note left for Aurora by her accomplice at the rear door of the manor. You will pen the sentence precisely as I read it. When each of you has completed that task, you will hand your paper to Cutterton, who will place a number on your page and make a corresponding entry on a list that I alone will keep. After all the pages are collected, I will retire to my study, where I will compare each of your hands with that on the note. When I find a match, I'll have what I need. Are there any questions?"

One stableboy raised his hand nervously. "Pardon me, m'lord, but I can't write."

"Those of you who can't write are excused. Please check with Mr. Cutterton at the door and he will make note of that fact for the list." A muscle flexed in Slayde's jaw. "I strongly suggest the guilty party does not feign the inability to write as a means of evading his task. I have files on every person I hire. I intend to verify who can and cannot read and write." A weighty pause. "In the interim, Mathers, you can begin."

Twenty minutes later, there were half the number of people in the room as there had been initially, and each of the remaining occupants held a sheet of paper and a quill.

Cutterton left the doorway and approached Courtney, signaling to Mathers to join them. "Forgive me, Miss Johnston," he said, "but I must ask you to participate as well."

Courtney's jaw dropped. "I?"

"Yes." Cutterton turned to Slayde and explained. "I apologize for embarrassing your betrothed, sir. But I must be thorough. And Miss Johnston is Lady Aurora's closest friend, constant companion, and most willing cohort. I'd be remiss if I didn't ask her to take part in this exercise."

"Really, Cutterton . . ." Slayde began.

"It's all right." Courtney waved away Slayde's protest,

her chin held high. "If Mr. Cutterton feels it necessary, I'm more than willing to participate." She extended her hand to Mathers.

"You're sure?" Slayde asked her quietly.

"Perfectly sure." She accepted the paper and quill. "As you yourself just said, Pembourne has become my home and its occupants my family. There should be no doubts or deception between us."

"Very well. Then we're ready to begin."

"Slayde," Aurora protested, "how could you ask Courtney . . ."

"You are excused," Slayde pronounced. "Please retire to your chambers at once."

Aurora stared at him in a show of disbelief. Her mouth opened and closed once, twice. Then she gathered up her skirts and fled.

"As I was saying," Slayde continued, "we can now begin. Each of you pen the following phrase: 'Use this door for coming and going.'"

Dutifully, the servants complied.

Slayde waited until they were all staring at him once more. "You're all free to return to your duties," he said. "Hand your papers to Cutterton as you leave the room. Oh, and one other thing. If the person responsible should experience a change of heart and decide to confess, I'll be in my study. If not, I'll eventually be sending for you." Pointedly, Slayde surveyed the room. "Thank you all. Once this incident is behind us, we can begin the more joyful task of planning a wedding."

The servants came forward, turning in their papers, some nervous, others matter-of-fact. Siebert bowed and congratulated Courtney and Slayde, his pleasure warm and genuine. Miss Payne offered her congratulations as well, although, Courtney noticed with amusement, she couldn't quite meet their gazes after what she perceived as last night's indiscretion. Matilda harbored no such reservations. She stepped over, squeezing Courtney's hands and beaming ear to ear. "I'm so thrilled for you," she murmured. "I wish you all the happiness you and Lord Pembourne deserve."

"Thank you," Courtney whispered, her throat tight with emotion. "Matilda—" She knew she shouldn't be doing this, not before everyone was exonerated, but she just couldn't help herself. Matilda was innocent. No one could convince her otherwise. "When all this is over, when Slayde and I are married . . ." Courtney swallowed. "Would you do me the honor of staying on, not just at Pembourne, but with me? As I understand it, a countess requires a lady's maid. And, while I know I'll be terribly difficult to train, given all the years of fending for myself, I can think of no one better equipped with the necessary love and patience to tackle the job. Nor anyone I'd rather have beside me. Would you consider it?"

Tears gathered in Matilda's eyes. "'Twould be an honor, Miss Courtney."

"Pardon me, ma'am," Cutterton interjected, stepping over to address Matilda. "Your paper?"

Matilda dabbed at her eyes. "Of course, sir. Here." She presented it, giving Courtney's arm another squeeze before hastening off.

"Don't bellow at me, Cutterton," Courtney muttered, seeing his disapproving frown. "Else I truly will help Aurora by telling her about the half-dozen escape routes I've discerned from my bedroom window—routes even she has yet to find and try." Courtney inclined her head at Cutterton, smiling at the stunned expression on his face. "I think you and I are going to get on famously, don't you?"

"I think you and Aurora are going to have to conduct classes for my investigative and security staff." Slayde's dry retort came from just behind her.

Courtney whirled about to face him, noting that the room was now empty. "Is it time?"

"Yes." A scowl. "I still don't like the idea of your accompanying me to such a seedy section of Dartmouth."

"Slayde—don't." She lay her hand on his forearm. "We've come too far for this. I need to be there. Besides, Oridge's message said everything is under control. He's keeping our friend company until we arrive."

A terse nod. "All right. Let's go." He turned to Cutterton. "You'll post yourself outside my study?"

"Yes, sir. So far as everyone will know, you're closeted within."

"Good. Given the circumstances, I don't anticipate any visitors."

"Understood. Now let me ensure that your path is clear and that you and Miss Johnston can reach the phaeton we concealed around back without being detected. Oh," Cutterton added, "you asked me to advise you when Mr. Rayburn had taken his leave. He did so about an hour ago."

"Thank you." Slayde pondered the charts he'd given Rayburn at dawn, praying that one of the six inlets he'd mapped out would lead them to Courtney's father.

"Slayde?" Courtney touched his hand. "Don't look so troubled. I know Mr. Rayburn is investigating other avenues, perhaps even dangerous ones. But I have the utmost faith in him, whatever the challenge."

"So do I, sweetheart." Slayde pressed his lips to her forehead, reiterating his silent prayer. "So do I."

Grimes leaned back in his chair, rubbing a dirty hand across the stubble on his chin. "I've been lookin' at these for an hour," he complained. "And none of 'em has matched up." He picked up the original note, now neatly folded so only the message—not the date or sketch— was revealed. "What's on the other side of this, anyway?"

"A drawing of my house," Slayde answered smoothly, perched on the edge of the desk. "Which I don't intend to let you see. If I did, I might suddenly find my home divested of all its worldly goods." He gave Grimes's shoulder a shove. "Now get back to work. We're paying you a bloody fortune for what amounts to nothing more than a few hours of risk-free work."

"Sure, but it must be pretty important for you to send your henchman on ahead." He jerked his thumb in Oridge's direction.

Oridge sighed. "Shall I convince him to shut up and resume working, sir?" he inquired, arching a brow at Slayde.

"Now, now, just calm down," Grimes answered nervously, bending forward again. "I'll do your job."

Courtney bit back her impatience, pacing restlessly about the cramped quarters.

"Tell her to stand still," Grimes muttered. "I can't concentrate with her walkin' around."

"Learn," Slayde shot back. "And if you address the lady with anything short of respect, I'll break your jaw."

With a sullen look, Grimes resumed his chore.

Another twenty minutes passed.

Grimes was down to the final five or six pages, and Courtney was about to scream in frustration, when the fence sat back in his chair, flourishing a page for Slayde to see. "Here's your man."

"You're certain?" Slayde asked, seizing the paper.

"Hell, yes. 'cuse me," he added quickly to Courtney, recalling Slayde's threat. "Look at the curve of the *s*'s and the half-crossed *t*. Also, there are slight breaks between the first and second letters of each word, and every letter is tightly curved. This is the one. You want it copied?"

"That won't be necessary." Slayde tossed a wad of bills on the desk. "There's our agreed-upon thousand pounds plus an extra hundred. That more than concludes our business." He gathered up all the papers, crossed over, and yanked open the door, guiding Courtney out and to the phaeton.

The instant Oridge had joined them, Courtney turned to Slayde. "You brought the list, didn't you?"

"Right here." He reached into his coat pocket and extracted it, simultaneously glancing at the number atop the page Grimes had designated. "Eight," Slayde murmured, unfolding the list. "Now let's see who the hell number eight is."

Courtney peered over his shoulder, her gaze darting to the appropriate line. "Slayde," she gasped, gripping his arm. "It's Miss Payne."

Chapter 19

"Remember, no one knows we've been away," Slayde reminded Courtney, slowing the phaeton down as they neared the rear gates of Pembourne. "To their knowledge, I'm still in my study. We have that fact going for us. Oridge, you divert Miss Payne. I don't care how. Tell her you need additional pillows. Tell her you found an insect in your bed. Just keep her occupied. Courtney and I will search her room, just in case there's anything in there to identify her employer."

"As good as done, sir."

"After that, I'll reassemble the staff and tell them the real reason for our writing exercise: that I've recently acquired evidence proving the fact that someone inside Pembourne aided in the robbery that resulted in my parents' murders, that the evidence in question is a note written in the culprit's hand. I'll further elaborate that, after careful scrutiny, I've been able to narrow the writing samples down to only three possible suspects. I'll explain that, given the magnitude of the crime, I would never accuse anyone without being totally certain of that person's guilt. Therefore, I'll be riding to London immediately to seek out a proper handwriting expert. Having made that declaration, I'll go so far as to climb into my carriage and ride off. That should give Miss Payne ample opportunity to rush off to either warn or seek refuge with her employer."

Courtney inclined her head, an admiring smile curving her lips. "Aurora and I must be rubbing off on you, my lord. Why, that plan is almost as ingenious as ours."

"Coming from you, I'll consider that the highest of compliments. Perhaps Mr. Scollard did mean to imply that my wits would be called upon as well." A shadow crossed Slayde's face. "Miss Payne has been with my family for decades. 'Tis hard to believe she's capable of the kind of crimes we're addressing."

"Theft and murder are quite different from one another, Slayde," Courtney reminded him. "All we know for sure is that Miss Payne was involved in the robbery. There's no indication that she meant for your parents to die, much less that she helped kill them."

"But they did die," Slayde said grimly. "And she didn't exactly come forward and identify Armon as their killer, nor admit her own part in the theft that lead to their murders. Worse, she's stayed on at Pembourne as a trusted employee, when she should be rotting in Newgate."

"I've not found Miss Payne to be particularly warm or endearing," Courtney replied. "However, I don't think she's ruthless, either. My guess is that whoever she's working for ensured her silence—perhaps with Armon's help. They probably threatened her position, her health, even her life if she said a word, or refused to help them in future endeavors."

"Such as seizing your father's ship in order to extort the black diamond."

A pained nod. "And afterward, when I came to

Pembourne, she was doubtless instructed to keep an eye on me, see if I told you anything damning about Armon, anything that would implicate them. It would certainly explain why she spent so much time hovering about during my recovery. I never understood her concern, given that nurturing is hardly her way."

"It also explains why she was in your room last night. Most likely, she was searching for something that would tell her how much information you'd gained during our excursion to London."

"That makes sense. No one would think to question a housekeeper's presence in someone's sleeping quarters—" Courtney broke off. "That explains Aurora's note!"

"Which note?"

"The one she left you when she went to London. Remember? She found it lodged behind her headboard and assumed it had dropped there on its own. Well, it hadn't. It was removed, then replaced on the day Aurora returned. Miss Payne must have known of Aurora's intentions to travel to London and used it to her employer's advantage. With the absence of Aurora's written explanation, you had no reason to doubt the legitimacy of the ransom notes and the 'fact' that Aurora had indeed been kidnapped. Thus, the ruse was successful, with Miss Payne knowing all the while that Aurora was quite safe, frolicking about London with Elinore."

"That conniving . . ." Slayde drew a slow, inward breath. "Forgive me, Courtney, but I can't be as charitable as you."

"I'm not charitable. Nor do I expect you to be. Because of Miss Payne's involvement, my father is gone. As are your parents." Courtney clasped her hands together to still their trembling. "But Miss Payne did not act alone. Nor did she act solely with Armon, who's already paid with his life. She acted upon the orders of another. And it's that person we want to expose, that cold-hearted animal we want to see punished. We can't let our enmity cloud our reason."

Slayde's fingers closed over hers. "Are *you* preaching logic and level-headedness to *me,* Miss Johnston?" he teased gently.

His loving quip found its mark, and Courtney managed a faint smile. "It appears I am, Lord Pembourne."

"Astounding." He brought her palm to his lips. "It seems we've encountered yet another miracle together."

Slayde checked the hallway of the servants' quarters for the third time before beckoning Courtney forward. "Now," he hissed.

They slipped into Miss Payne's room, shutting the door quietly behind them.

"The desk?" Slayde questioned.

"No," she countered. "The wardrobe drawers. You go through those on the left, and I those on the right."

Courtney crossed over, dropping to her knees and pulling open the first drawer.

"Why the wardrobe?" Slayde asked, squatting down beside her. "I'd assume any written material would be in her desk."

"Not if it's of a personal nature." Courtney scanned the contents, then carefully rearranged them before sliding the drawer shut, tugging open the one beneath it. "Women have a tendency to hide private things in private spots—spots no one would be apt to invade. Which is precisely why we're invading them." She shook her head, shutting the bottom drawer. "There's nothing here."

"Nor here," Slayde concurred, completing his task. He surveyed the sparse furnishings. "Is the bureau personal enough?"

Courtney grinned. "Yes. I'll search it. Why don't you look through the nightstand."

A wary glance at the closed bedchamber door. "Ten minutes more. Then we leave."

"But Slayde—"

"You're the one who told me to employ reason. Well, I'm employing it. If Miss Payne should discover us, our entire plan to get to her employer will be dashed. Therefore, if we find evidence, splendid. If not, we'll rely upon her to lead us where we need to go. Either way, we're leaving this bedchamber in ten minutes."

A reluctant nod. "Very well." Courtney scooted over to the bureau, gauging the drawer that would hold underclothes. She yanked that one open, lifting a pile of prim nightgowns out of the way and groping behind them.

Her fingers brushed something smooth and flat.

"Slayde," she said in an urgent whisper. He stalked over just in time to see her remove what was clearly a journal of sorts. "The entries look to be sporadic," Courtney noted, skimming the pages. "But they begin in 1796 and span the entirety of Miss Payne's employment here at Pembourne. Look—" Smoothing the page for closer perusal, Courtney indicated the date at the top: 5 January, 1807. "'Tis her first entry of the year your parents were killed."

"Two months prior to their deaths," Slayde concurred grimly.

Courtney held up the journal and together they read:

I'm growing old. My skin is coarse from scrubbing and my shoulders are stooped from carrying. I came here a young girl, with grand dreams and a romantic heart. Now, I look in the glass and see a bitter spinster with no future and a housekeeper's wages. The countess is ten years my senior, yet her skin is smooth, her eyes bright. 'Tis easy to see why. She's bathed in jewels, showered with attention. While I'm alone, without so much as a decent sum put aside for the future. If there's one thing life's taught me, it's that there's no justice.

Courtney frowned. "Clearly, Miss Payne was a very unhappy woman."

"Clearly, she still is," Slayde muttered. "The question is, what did she do about that unhappiness?"

The muffled sound of approaching footsteps reached their ears, and Slayde's head came up like a wolf scenting danger.

Courtney held her breath, waiting, as the brisk strides grew closer, reached Miss Payne's bedchamber . . . and passed it.

She sagged with relief. "I knew Mr. Oridge wouldn't disappoint us."

"Even Oridge can keep Miss Payne only so long before she becomes suspicious," Slayde worried aloud, casting another furtive glance at the closed door. "We can't take that chance. Nor, obviously, can we take the journal with us and risk Miss Payne's discovering it missing. So, let's accelerate this process, skip ahead to dates closer to when the murders took place. Maybe she'll name names."

Nodding, Courtney sifted through a few short, inconsequential-looking pages, until she came to the page dated 18 March, 1807, which was covered, top to bottom, with writing.

"Let's try this," she murmured.

She hasn't a clue how humiliating it was for me to ask for that increase in wages. And she refused me. She said I was already earning nearly as much as Siebert. Well, that's as it should be. I work harder than that aged fool. And to further humiliate me by offering me a loan? I don't *need* the money; I've *earned* it. Far more than she's earned her wardrobe of exquisite gowns or that treasure chest of jewels the earl keeps locked away in the library. Well, I know just who to turn to, just the person to convince Lady Pembourne of my worth. The Viscountess Stanwyk. I'll approach her. She thinks highly of me; heaven knows she's always saying how invaluable I am, what an asset I am to Pembourne. And the countess respects her opinions. Yes, that's what I'll do. I'll talk to Lady Stanwyk. She'll understand. She'll help me.

And then just beneath that, dated 20 March, 1807:

She's agreed to see me tomorrow. We managed to chat for only a few minutes before Lady Pembourne returned to the salon, but the viscountess said she had the ideal solution to my dilemma. And she smiled so reassuringly when she said it. Perhaps she intends to offer me a position at Stanwyk. More money, a brighter future. I can hardly wait.

"This tells us nothing," Slayde proclaimed, "Other than the fact that Miss Payne is brazen as well as deceitful. 'Tis inconceivable that she'd consider overstepping her bounds by approaching one of Mother's peers for assistance—her closest friend, no less."

" 'Tis equally odd that Elinore would agree to see her. Given the circumstances, I should think she'd have gone straight to your mother with word of her housekeeper's faithlessness."

"She probably did."

"Then why wasn't Miss Payne dismissed?" Courtney frowned, skimming ahead only to find page after blank page, devoid of any writing at all. "Now I'm truly at sea. If Miss Payne was so enthralled by her upcoming meeting with Elinore, why didn't she pen the results of the meeting?"

"Maybe there were none. Maybe she came to her senses and never went to Stanwyk. Or maybe Elinore thought better of her kindness and threw Miss Payne out the moment she arrived." Slayde grasped Courtney's arm, tugged her to her feet. "Put the journal back where you found it. It tells us nothing but Miss Payne's motivation, which I could have guessed anyway. Theft is usually motivated by greed. Let's go."

Courtney shook her head, hanging back. "Slayde, there's too much here that screams discord. Elinore is the essence of protocol. She'd never agree to a meeting with your mother's housekeeper. Yet, she obviously did just that—Miss Payne might be cold and greedy, but she's not delusional. And why do her entries stop here? Don't you find it a tad coincidental that they break off precisely a week before she becomes immersed in a plot to steal your mother's jewels? Something had to precipitate her involvement—or rather someone—the same someone who instructed her to draw that sketch and send it to Armon. Whoever that was, Miss Payne would have had to meet with him between the twentieth and the twenty-seventh. Yet, there's no reference in this journal to any such meeting, or any meeting at all, other than the baffling one agreed to by—" Courtney broke off, all the color draining from her face. "God . . . no."

"No," Slayde echoed with a firm shake of his head. "You're letting your imagination run amok, Courtney. 'Tis impossible."

"Is it?" she asked in a small, shaken voice. "You're probably right. I'm probably so overwrought that I'm no longer able to see clearly, so eager to resolve things that I'd stoop to doubting someone Aurora adores—someone I've come to consider a friend. If that's the case, I'll detest myself when all this is behind us. But, Slayde, we must explore every possibility." Courtney inhaled sharply. "Suppose Miss Payne did have that meeting with Elinore? Suppose Elinore had a damned good reason not to mention it to your mother? Suppose she offered Miss Payne money, position, Lord knows what else, in exchange for something much more valuable?"

Slayde stared. "The diamond? You think Elinore was after the black diamond?"

"I think whoever orchestrated this scheme was after the black diamond. So, assuming Elinore was guilty, yes, I think she saw a way to acquire that stone." An agonizing pause. "Not once, but twice. Ten years ago, she was your mother's dearest friend. For all we know, that was a calculated effort on Elinore's part, designed to help her learn of the diamond's whereabouts. When Miss Payne approached her, it provided the perfect opportunity to go after the stone without endangering herself."

That sparked a thought, and Courtney glanced down at the journal, pointing to the March eighteenth entry. "Look. Miss Payne makes mention of your mother's strongbox of jewels *and* its location, so she obviously knew of both. If she revealed that to Elinore, Elinore doubtless assumed the strongbox housed the black diamond and decided to go after it. I don't know where she found and hired Armon, but he was perfect for the role she had in mind. She didn't count on your parents interrupting his robbery. And then, after all that, the stone wasn't even there. So she resumed her original plan, only now, with your mother dead, she ingratiated herself with Aurora. How hard do you think that was, given Aurora's need for affection? And all the while Elinore would feel so utterly safe, knowing you were convinced that Lawrence and Chilton Bencroft were guilty."

A muscle was working in Slayde's jaw. "Chilton's mind snapped a month before my parents' murders. That's when he and Lawrence burst into my home, shouting their accusations. Of course I thought they were guilty." On the heels of his admission, Slayde was assailed by Mr. Scollard's words of advice, resounding as clearly as if he were speaking them now. *Do with your mind what you did with your heart: clear it of the shadows that obstruct your sight. Once you've accomplished that, you'll see what is truly there, not what you choose to see.*

Drawing a sharp breath, Slayde met Courtney's gaze. "The fact is, I was wrong. The Bencrofts weren't guilty. But I was too blinded by emotion to be objective. I don't intend to make that mistake again. So let's follow this theory through."

Shakily, Courtney nodded.

"What about the second attempt to steal the diamond," Slayde pursued, "the one that brought you to me?"

"Again, assuming Elinore is guilty, 'twas another perfect opportunity for her to achieve her goal," Courtney replied. "Aurora was restless, desperate to see the world. You were in India, scheduled to return at what was the height of the London Season. All Elinore had to do was arrange things with her henchmen: Armon would send the ransom notes and make the exchange, Miss Payne would ensure that you hadn't a clue where Aurora was by seizing the note she left you. Then, Elinore could get her hands on the diamond and no one would be the wiser."

"But Armon got greedy," Slayde continued, looking utterly ill. "He undermined Elinore, made the exchange a day early, and fled with the stone." A pensive pause. "That, however, raises another question. Can you honestly equate the charming woman who takes tea at our home with a ruthless killer? Because whoever hired Armon also shot him down in cold blood. That's no longer accidental death, Courtney. That's premeditated murder."

"I realize that. But, if Elinore is behind this, her entire personality is a façade, and we don't really know her at all. She's feigned friendships, dismissed her own responsibility for your parents' murders, even pretended to mourn them—and to care for their children. She's manipulated, plotted, stolen, and, indirectly, killed. Could that kind of person commit premeditated murder? I would say yes."

"She could have taken that shot at you," Slayde reasoned aloud. "She'd have had ample time to follow us to Somerset, just as she'd have had ample time, upon returning from London and discovering Armon's subversion, to ride to Dartmouth and kill him. But she had a motive for doing away with Armon. Why would she want to kill you? What would suddenly render you a threat?"

Memory exploded like firewords. "Dear God," Courtney breathed. "*I* gave her reason to feel threatened. Just before you and I left for London, I told her I intended to scour Armon's ship until I found evidence of his employer's identity. Slayde, no one but Elinore and Aurora were with me when I said that."

"Hell. Bloody, bloody hell." Slayde ran both hands through his hair. "No wonder Mr. Scollard kept talking about danger being at Pembourne's portals, on its doorstep."

"That's right. He said that to you yesterday." Courtney gripped Slayde's arm. "Yesterday afternoon—at about the same time Elinore was visiting with Aurora. Lord, it all makes sense. Horrible, unbearable sense."

"Courtney—" Slayde's expression was haunted. "If you're right, if all this speculation turns out to be true, I've blinded myself to a reality that could have endangered Aurora's life."

"Don't think that way. Aurora is fine. She will remain fine." Courtney turned, punctuating her claim by shoving the journal back in its spot beneath the nightgowns and shutting the drawer. "Let's not react until we determine if all this speculation is fact. We have no proof, no confession. We don't even know what Elinore intends to do with the diamond, if she has it. Obviously, she hasn't tried to sell it, or she'd be aware that it's fake. Which she definitely is *not* aware of; only yesterday she told Aurora how delighted she was with your decision to reveal the truth in the *Times,* so that your parents could at last rest in peace." Courtney felt bile rush to her throat.

Eyes ablaze, Slayde seized Courtney's arm. "Let's go. 'Tis time for answers."

Pembourne was silent as a tomb.

Long after Slayde exited the ballroom, having reconvened the entire staff and shared the real purpose for their earlier writing exercise—right down to describing the document that had provoked it—the servants huddled together, whispering in horror. The fact that one of them was a conspirator to murder was unfathomable.

Miss Payne shrugged into her coat and passed by Siebert, trembling so badly she could scarcely speak. "Siebert, I need some air."

"I understand, madam." He himself was sheet-white. Exiting the manor, she collected the phaeton, disappearing down the drive and through the gates in a cloud of dust.

"That's our cue," Slayde muttered to Courtney and Oridge, from where their carriage was concealed by the roadside. "Let's go."

Elinore strolled about the garden, admiring her new emerald brooch and contemplating—with a surge of anticipation—the matching earrings that would soon be arriving. It was such a lovely treat to actually wear some of her prized possessions, she mused. So many of her treasures were far too precious to risk removing from their special case, much less don. Treasures such as the countess's magnificent collection—especially, at long last, the majestic black diamond. She didn't dare wear that, or any of her dear, departed friend's gems lest someone recognize them and try to wrest them away. Nonetheless, 'twas well worth the sacrifice. She could still gaze at them each day, watch them sparkle on their velvet bed as they were captured by sunlight or shimmering in moonlight. How perfect they were—unflawed, unrivaled, and—in contrast to all else—immortal.

And they were hers.

A speeding phaeton shattered Elinore's reflections, and she started, watching it race up the drive and come to a halt before her.

Her eyes smoldered as she saw who the driver was.

"Are you insane?" she hissed as Miss Payne leapt to the ground. "What are you doing here?"

"They know," Miss Payne panted. "Lord Pembourne and the girl. They know."

Elinore tensed. "Just what is it they know?"

"They found the sketch. I don't know where, or how. All I know is they have it, they realize someone at Pembourne helped with the burglary, and they're about to learn who that someone is."

"And how are they doing that?"

"Lord Pembourne had all the servants write some words—giving us a fabricated reason as to why. Now, he's on his way to London, seeking a handwriting expert. He's going to match our hands with that on the sketch. Once he does, my identity wil be known."

"I see." Frowning, Elinore stroked her brooch, its cool emerald surface a comforting balm. "How terribly unfortunate."

"Unfortunate? Our entire lives are unraveling, and you consider that to be unfortunate?"

Elinore's hand stilled. *"Our* lives?"

"Forgive me—*my* life," Miss Payne hastily corrected herself. "Lady Stanwyk, you must understand. I can't go back there. They'll send me to Newgate. Please—you must give me that job you promised when I first approached you ten years past. I understand why, after Armon killed the earl and countess, I couldn't leave Pembourne without arousing suspicion. But none of that matters any longer. If I go back, 'tis as good as a death sentence." A choked sound. "Armon is no longer alive to be persuaded to vouch for my innocence. Lord Pembourne will assume I aided in the murders. I can't take that risk."

"No, indeed you can't." Elinore's jaw set. "Nor can I."

"Then you'll offer me a position?"

"What good would a job do, you fool? Stanwyk isn't a sanctuary from Newgate. Bow Street would simply come here, rather than Pembourne, to collect you. Not only you," she added, her fingers tightening about her brooch, "but me, as well."

"What shall we do?"

"I'm afraid that to remain in England is no longer an option. The only solution is to leave the country—now." A delicate frown. "Armon is dead," she mused aloud. "That leaves only you and Grimes. And Grimes is so unreliable. I did a thorough job of convincing him to keep quiet about the fact that I was forced to eliminate Armon, but he is so easily intimidated. Lord only knows what he'll tell Lord Pembourne under pressure."

"In that case, do we dare leave him behind?" Miss Payne asked.

"No. No one can be left behind." Elinore's eyes narrowed thoughtfully. "No one at all." With that, she gave a firm nod. "Here's what I want you to do. Ride to Dartmouth and alert Grimes to the situation. Both of you wait for me there. I'll pack my things and make arrangements for safe passage to the continent. Then I'll join you. By sunset, you'll be gone."

"Will Grimes cooperate—leave England on such short notice?"

A reassuring smile. "Grimes will present no problem."

Grimes was pacing beside Miss Payne, wiping sweat from his brow, when Elinore arrived. The viscountess climbed gracefully down from her phaeton, pausing only to remove a solitary bag before gliding toward her waiting companions.

"Listen, your ladyship," Grimes began, "I don't know what the hell's goin' on here. I know you keep me in business. Hell, you buy ninety percent of the jewels I get my hands on—with or without Armon alive to supply them. But the only pirates and smugglers I know are here in England. I don't have a clue who to connect with on the continent."

"Why are you bothering to tell me all this?" Elinore inquired. She glanced down to ensure that her bag was beside her, safe, Grimes's claim reminding her that it would be some time before she secured another fence— certainly one as accomplished and easily manipulated as he. Well, 'twas a small and temporary setback. She had an extensive collection to content herself with in the interim. Why, the black diamond alone could occupy her for weeks, simply admiring its facets, marveling at its incomparable beauty.

Grimes was regarding her oddly. "What do you mean, why am I tellin' you this? Miss Payne says we're leavin' the country."

"Is that what Miss Payne said?" Elinore raised inquisitive brows. "She was mistaken." Swiftly, she extracted a pistol from beneath her mantle. *"I'm* leaving the country. *You're* simply leaving."

A shot rang out, striking the barrel of Elinore's pistol. With a cry of surprise, she dropped it.

Oridge stepped out of the trees, his own gun aimed carefully at Elinore. "I think you've killed enough people, Lady Stanwyk."

"More than enough," Slayde concurred, striding around to confront Elinore. "If you were a man, I'd beat you senseless," he ground out from between clenched teeth.

"I harbor no such reservations." Courtney stalked out from her concealed position, marching directly up to Elinore, who watched Courtney's approach without so much as batting a lash.

"You're a monster," Courtney bit out. "A murderous, cold-hearted monster. Well, this is for Slayde's parents. For Papa. *And* for the pain that learning of your guilt will cause Aurora." Courtney drew back her hand and slapped Elinore across the face with all her might. "I hope you and your jewels rot in prison."

"Rot?" Elinore scarcely flinched, looking more amused than pained. "That's where you're mistaken, Courtney dear—you, Slayde, Aurora, and all the other ignorant fools you just mentioned. 'Tis people who rot. Jewels, on the other hand endure." An odd light flickered in Elinore's eyes. "They endure forever."

Epilogue

"Courtney, wake up!"

One eye opened and regarded the semidark room. "Aurora, what time is it?"

"Half after five," Aurora declared cheerfully. "Far too late to sleep on one's birthday." She yanked off the bedcovers, tugged at Courtney's arms. "Come."

"Come? Where?" Both eyes were open now, the final wisps of sleep gradually eclipsed by amusement. "Not even the birds are awake yet."

"Oh, yes they are." Undaunted, Aurora hugged her friend. "Happy birthday," she said. "Oh, Courtney, by next week at this time, you'll be my sister."

"I know." Courtney returned her friend's embrace, then eased back to study her expression, for the first time in days seeing the old Aurora. "Are you all right?"

With a prolonged sigh, Aurora nodded, her jubilant mood temporarily held at bay. "Yes. I'm sorry I've been so morose all week."

"You needn't apologize. You were in shock. 'Tis just that it hurt me so to see you in pain. And I felt helpless to appease it."

"As you and I both know, there are some things we each must face on our own. In my case, it was more than the shock of Elinore's guilt I was coming to terms with. It was the realization of my own stupidity. How could I not have known? How could I have trusted, befriended a deranged woman who killed just to gain possession of an unlimited supply of jewels, who murdered my parents, shattered my childhood—and Slayde's?"

"It wasn't your fault," Courtney defended at once. "Elinore is insane, Aurora. She's also very clever. She fooled everyone—right down to Miss Payne, who worked for her and knew the evil that existed beneath that elegant veneer. Think about it. Miss Payne actually believed Elinore meant to bring Grimes and her to the continent rather than leaving their bodies as food for the gulls. And why? Because—despite all she is, all she's done—Elinore appears to be so bloody composed, in total control of herself and the situation, a lady to the core." Courtney shook her head in amazement. "Aurora, you should have seen her. She never showed remorse, never flinched or looked away, not even when I slapped her. Nor did she look the slightest bit perturbed when Mr. Oridge announced they were going to Bow Street. All she did was open her bag, ensure that all her gems were accounted for, before smoothing her hair, readjusting her brooch, and announcing she was ready to go. If you'd seen the regal way she walked off . . . as if Oridge were leading her to a ballroom rather than to a jail cell." Courtney drew a harsh breath. "A woman like that could deceive anyone."

"I realize that now." Aurora squeezed Courtney's hands. "And I promise you, I'm fine. 'Tis time to bid the past good-bye. There's a grand and glorious future awaiting us." So saying, she shook off the momentary melancholy, leaping to her feet and glancing at the clock on the mantel. "Speaking of the future, I'm to deliver you, dressed and ready, to the lighthouse, by eight o'clock. That's when your birthday celebration commences."

"At eight A.M.?" Courtney began to laugh. "Does poor Mr. Scollard realize he'll be expected to eat cake just after dawn?"

"Oh, I think so." A mysterious smile. "I think Mr. Scollard is well prepared. Now, I'll go fetch Matilda. She wanted to select a special gown for you in honor of the occasion."

Watching Aurora dash off, Courtney smiled, feeling more blessed than she'd ever dreamed possible. Even the past week's painful events—Elinore's arrest, the announcement to the staff of Miss Payne's betrayal, and Aurora's understandable distress—couldn't obliterate the joy of knowing she was about to become Slayde's wife.

Although, between the emotional aftermath of Elinore's guilt, Slayde's unexpected business trip to Cornwall, and a wondrous array of wedding plans, they'd scarcely seen each other all week—other than during the darkest hours of night when Slayde would come to her, make love to her until neither of them could breathe, whisper over and over how much he loved her.

For Aurora's sake, he always left before dawn.

But soon, that discretion would no longer be necessary.

Because, in five short days, Courtney would be Mrs. Slayde Huntley.

At that joyous thought, Courtney climbed out of bed, thinking that this was indeed the most wonderful of birthdays—far different than what she'd anticipated one short month ago when her life had seemed over, her heart empty.

Pausing, she slid open her nightstand drawer, lifting out her father's timepiece. "Papa," she whispered, snapping open the case. "I only wish you could share—" She broke off, her breath expelling all at once.

The watch was moving.

As she stared, the lighthouse beam shed its light across the waters, and the ship sailed forth, seeking its path. The scene unfolded like a shimmering ballet, not once, not twice, but repeatedly, making no move to slow down or stop.

Courtney stared, transfixed, wondering if this was heaven's way of smiling down on her, blessing her future with Slayde as the time drew near for their lives to merge, to become one..

Emotion constricted her throat as she watched the scene unfold again. The beam. The ship. The journey. Each time, the sequence was the same.

And each time, the ship found its way home.

"Are you sure Mr. Scollard is expecting us?" Courtney asked anxiously as they approached the lighthouse door. "It seems utterly still."

"Let's go in and see." Aurora turned the handle, guiding Courtney inside.

They'd scarcely crossed the threshold when a small flash of gold tore across the sitting room.

Yipping excitedly, it crashed into Courtney's legs and collapsed in a tangle of squirming fur and impatient limbs.

"What on earth . . . ?" Courtney stooped, picking up the wriggling pup, who immediately began lavishing her cheek with enthusiastic licks. Courtney was laughing so hard she could scarcely speak. "When did Mr. Scollard get a dog?"

"He didn't," Aurora replied. "This little lad is a visitor. He won't be staying."

"He's precious," Courtney said, inspecting the pup, who, momentarily nestled in the crook of her arm, then broke free, leaping to the ground and racing after his tail. "He's a babe, scarcely a few months old." She glanced at Aurora. "How did he get here?"

"He's ten weeks," Aurora supplied. "As for his background, his mother belongs to a family in the village.

Unfortunately, their cottage isn't large enough to accommodate a litter of pups. They managed to find homes for all of them—except this fellow. Evidently, he was too spirited for his own good. His wild racing about discouraged those families who came to look at him. 'Tis a pity. When he came to the lighthouse, he was quite homeless."

"Homeless?" Courtney stared at the dog, who, unaware he was being discussed, continued to rush in circles in avid pursuit of his tail. "Oh, Aurora, he can't be homeless. He's too young to survive on his own. And he's not too spirited—Lord knows, if people were condemned for that trait, you and I would have been put away long ago."

"True." Aurora nodded, her expression oddly solemn. "In any case, I said he *was* homeless. He no longer is. In fact, I think he's quite eager to go to his new home—and his new mistress." With that, she squatted, capturing the pup in midspin and placing him in Courtney's arms. "A puppy, you said. More specifically, one who needed you." Aurora's turquoise eyes glistened with tears. "Well, he does. And so do I. Happy birthday, Courtney."

Courtney's gaze widened. "He's for me?"

"For you. From me." A watery smile. "I don't know if *you'll* always thank me for this gift, but I know for sure the pup will."

"Oh, Aurora." Courtney stroked the tiny golden head, melting beneath velvet brown eyes filled with equal measures of warmth and mischief. "I don't know what to say."

"Tell me what you plan to name him."

With another burst of energy, the pup leapt from Courtney's arms and tore off, this time upsetting papers off a small end table before dashing partway up the stairs, then back down.

Both women began to laugh. "How about Tyrant?" Courtney suggested, gathering up the pages that had fallen. "I think the name's fitting, don't you?" She glanced at the papers she held, her brows arching in surprise. "I didn't realize Mr. Scollard was building himself a cottage."

"He isn't."

"But look: these are sketches, not far from the water's edge, it appears. He's obviously planning to build this cottage."

"He is."

"But you just said—"

"I meant he wasn't building it for himself."

"Then who is he building it for?"

"I'll let Mr. Scollard tell you. . . . Oh, here he is. Good morning, Mr. Scollard."

"Good morning, ladies." With a warm smile, the lighthouse keeper approached them from the kitchen, placing a tray of tea and cakes upon the table. "Happy birthday, Courtney. Ah, I see you've found your gift."

Courtney blinked. "Oh—you mean Tyrant." She glanced over to where the pup was now contentedly chewing on a biscuit that had definitely not been there before. Then, again, in Mr. Scollard's lighthouse, one expected magic.

"No, I didn't mean your new friend—although he is a charming devil. I meant the drawings."

"I don't understand."

Mr. Scollard pointed. "The cottage. Do you like it?"

"It looks lovely. But why would . . . ?"

"A place to call home when on land. 'Tis most important, wouldn't you agree?"

Courtney felt a slash of pain as she remembered having used those words to describe what she'd wanted for herself and her father. "Of course I agree. And I don't mean to appear ungrateful. I'm just puzzled."

"Why?"

"Because I'll be residing at Pembourne with Slayde and Aurora."

"Of course you will," Mr. Scollard said patiently. "I don't expect you to live in the cottage, only to accept it as a gift."

"But then, who . . . ?"

"Happy birthday, Courtney."

It was Slayde's voice, deep and resonant, that reached her ears, and Courtney looked past Mr. Scollard to see her future husband emerge from the bedchamber, guiding a weak but beaming man into the room.

All the color drained from Courtney's face. "Papa?" she choked out.

Arthur Johnston took the remaining steps on his own, holding out his arms to his daughter. "Courtney—" His voice broke. "Happy birthday."

"Oh, God—Papa." She rushed to him, hugged him fiercely, tears of joy coursing down her cheeks, drenching his shirt. "You're alive. Dear God, you're alive. Not just alive, but here. With me."

Amid her emotional litany, she heard her father's murmured assent, felt the trembling of his hand as he stroked her hair. Desperately, she focused on that reassuring motion, the gentle pressure of his palm tangible evidence that she wasn't dreaming, that this impossibly wonderful illusion was in fact reality.

It was the slight falter in his touch that brought her head up.

"Papa, you're weak. You need to rest." Capturing his hand, Courtney guided him into a chair, then knelt at his feet, afraid to look away, afraid that, if she did, he'd vanish. "You look so thin, so tired . . ."

Arthur Johnston leaned forward, patted his daughter's cheek. "I'll mend," he said quietly. "Just seeing you is enough to ensure that. Now stop worrying."

"I'd given up," she whispered. "I'd stopped praying for this miracle. But it's occurred nonetheless. The watch . . . it wasn't wrong . . . and today—it wasn't just Slayde and me that made it start anew. 'Twas you . . . the fact that you're here . . . alive . . ." Knowing words could never convey all she longed to explain, she tugged the timepiece from her pocket, opened the case. "It stopped the day you went overboard," she got out, her voice quavering. "Several times, it moved, only to stop

again. And then this morning, it resumed—for good."
She studied her father's beloved face, watching tears
glide down his cheeks as he absorbed her words, reached
out to touch the precious gift his wife had given him all
those years ago. "Here, Papa—" Courtney snapped the
timepiece shut and pressed it into his palm. "The watch
is back where it belongs—with you."

Reflexively, her father's fingers closed around the
engraved case. "Yet another miracle." He bent to kiss
Courtney's forehead. "Not only have you been restored
to me, but now your mother has as well."

Still dazed, Courtney struggled to think straight, to ask
all she needed to know. "How did you survive? How did
you find me?"

A muscle worked in her father's jaw. "I owe my life to
Lexley," he said fervently. "It was his loyalty and
courage that gave me a fighting chance. He severed as
many of my bonds as he dared before casting me to sea.
The remaining bonds, I managed on my own. The
currents were with me; they dragged me into a peaceful
inlet, where I crawled on shore and collapsed for Lord
knows how long. Eventually, a fisherman found me,
brought me home. He and his family took me in, gave
me food and as much care as they were able. I don't
remember much; I faded in and out of consciousness."
Again, Courtney's father leaned forward, smoothing her
hair off her face, pain lancing his weathered features. "I
kept seeing flashes of you, crying, weak and bandaged,
needing me. And your mother, begging me to help you.
Twice, I crawled from the house—I suppose I was
delirious with fever—to look for you. Each time, I
collapsed. I'd all but given up when Mr. Rayburn located
me."

"Mr. Rayburn?" Courtney gasped.

Her response elicited that cherished twinkle she loved
so much and had thought gone forever. "Um-hum. You
asked how I found you. Well, my future son-in-law hired
one hell of a fine investigator. Rayburn unearthed me
within two days of searching. The news he gave me—

that you were alive, cared for—was the best medicine on earth. The next day when Slayde came to fetch me, I was more than ready for the carriage ride from Cornwall to Devonshire. He brought me to Mr. Scollard's lighthouse. That's when we decided on this birthday surprise." A grin in Aurora's direction. "I never thought Lady Aurora would keep it to herself."

Courtney's head whipped about. "You knew?" she demanded of Aurora.

A beatific smile. "I knew. In fact, yesterday when you were being fitted for your wedding dress, I managed to sneak Mr. Lexley down here for a little reunion with your father. The three of us and Mr. Scollard had a grand time. And with each cup of Mr. Scollard's tea, your father grew stronger."

"Speaking of which, what's in that brew, anyway?" Courtney's father asked Scollard. "I feel more fit by the minute."

"Well, of course," was the matter-of-fact reply. "You need to regain your strength. How else would you be able to walk Courtney down the aisle?"

"You notice he didn't answer your question, Mr. Johnston," Aurora commented. "'Tis his way. It means he likes you."

"He must. He's building that cottage for me."

"For you?" Courtney's breath suspended in her throat.

"Well, certainly for me. You're not going to need it. You'll have a huge estate to keep you busy. But I need a place to stay when I'm on shore."

"You can stay at Pembourne with us."

Her father shook his head. "Not for the amount of time I have in mind. I'll need a place of my own. Besides, I promised you a birthday gift as well, remember? Even if Lady Aurora did steal away half of it." He grinned at Tyrant, who was lapping up stray droplets of tea and becoming more energetic by the minute.

"Papa, you promised me only a week," Courtney reminded him. "I'd never ask for more than that."

"Well, I would," he replied gruffly. "I want many, many weeks—months—in the years to come."

"But—the sea is your life."

"Only a portion of my life. I want time for the other portion as well—on land, with you." A hard swallow. "I wouldn't miss seeing my grandchildren grow up for all the oceans in the world."

"Excellent," Mr. Scollard inserted. "Because the cottage will be fully built by the time Courtney and Slayde return from their wedding trip."

"I don't doubt it," Courtney's father replied with solemn gratitude. "You're an astounding man. From what I understand, you helped Slayde figure out where I was, and for that I'm eternally in your debt."

"Don't be. 'Twas Slayde's belief, not my vision, that brought you here."

"I agree." Arthur's gaze returned to his daughter. "Courtney, I'd all but given up, too. Were it not for the remarkable man you're to marry—who made sure I was found and brought back to you—I'm not sure I would have endured much longer."

For the first time, Courtney allowed herself to look at Slayde, having known from the onset that once she did, every shred of her composure would vanish. "Thank you," she said in an aching whisper. She felt her father squeeze her hands, then release them, a silent conveyance of his approval and understanding.

Courtney rose, walking toward her future husband, gazing up at him with her heart in her eyes. "I love you," she choked, her voice breaking as she reached him, her shoulders shaking with sobs. "I don't know how to thank you."

Slayde enfolded her against him, hugging her fiercely to his heart. "You just did."

Courtney closed her eyes, savoring the absolute rightness of Slayde's embrace, the exquisite balm of being surrounded by those she loved, beckoned by a future that held naught but happiness. *No other moment can ever be this perfect*, she thought fervently. This overwhelming sense of joy was an incomparable, once-in-a-lifetime experience.

She was wrong.

Five days later, on her father's arm, Courtney knew an even greater joy as, clad in exquisite yards of white and silver, she walked down the aisle of a small Devonshire chapel and, before God and man, became Mrs. Slayde Huntley.

The chapel was filled to capacity, the wedding attended by the entire Pembourne staff—including Rayburn, Oridge, Cutterton, and a swarm of guards, all of whom were relaxed for the first time in ages, secure in the knowledge that, just this once, neither Courtney nor Aurora had any intention of bolting. At the head of the chapel were Lexley and Mr. Scollard, beaming from ear to ear and, of course, Aurora, her face aglow, her smile wrapping itself around Courtney as it declared them sisters.

Courtney's heart swelled as she reached Slayde's side, saw the pride and love reflected on his handsome face. He held out his hand to her, then paused, giving Arthur Johnston a reassuring look that told Courtney's father all he needed to know—that his child would be loved and protected for the rest of her life. With an answering smile, her father squeezed Courtney's arm and turned her over to the man she loved.

They exchanged vows, Slayde's voice strong and sure, her own equally certain, their gazes locked as Slayde slid the gold band onto the fourth finger of her left hand.

"Two halves, now a far greater whole," he murmured, brushing her lips with his.

"Far greater." Tears shimmered on Courtney's lashes. "Greater than all life's obstacles combined." She swallowed. "I love you, Slayde."

Slayde's eyes darkened and, defying protocol yet again, he framed Courtney's face between his palms, lowered his mouth to hers for a deep, binding kiss. "God, I love you, Mrs. Huntley."

As if on cue, the entire chapel rang with applause.

Chuckling, Slayde raised his head, capturing Courtney's hand in his. "Come, love," he said, "I believe our future awaits."

With that, he guided his bride into the throng of well-wishers.

And the Huntley name lived on.

Author's Note

Guess what? This time we don't have to say good-bye!

Courtney and Slayde will be returning from their wedding trip, starting their marriage . . . only to have Aurora turn their entire world upside down, taking her future in her own hands—and by doing so, destroying the fragile tendrils of peace and kindling an unexpected and unthinkable passion.

The Black Diamond reaches from the sequestered gates of Pembourne to the forbidden grounds of Morland Manor—*and* its newly ascended and equally reluctant duke. Julian Bencroft, transient adventurer and mercenary extraordinaire, intends only to tie up the loose ends of his father's estate before sailing back to his dangerous existence far from English soil . . . until Aurora Huntley catapults into his life, upsetting it and altering it forever.

Bound by a twist of fate, Aurora and Julian begin a search amid the dark caves of Cornwall, seeking the only thing that can end their families' curse: the black diamond. What they find in the process is something neither of them expects. . . .

Enjoy the following preview of *The Black Diamond* Pocket Books has provided. And trust me—with Julian, Aurora has more than met her match!

As always, I look forward to hearing from you. Write to me at:

P.O. Box 5104
Parsippany, NJ 07054-6104

Include a legal-size self-addressed, stamped envelope if you'd like a copy of my latest newsletter.

Love,
Andrea

POCKET STAR BOOKS
PROUDLY PRESENTS

THE BLACK DIAMOND

Andrea Kane

**Coming soon
from
Pocket Books**

**The following is a preview of
The Black Diamond. . . .**

Devonshire, England
January 1818

"I will not marry him!"

Lady Aurora Huntley nearly toppled the study chair, leaping to her feet as if she'd been singed. With a look of utter incredulity, she stared across the desk at her brother, her chest tight with unspeakable fury. "My God, Slayde, have you lost your mind?"

"No." The Earl of Pembourne unfolded from his chair, his silver-gray eyes narrowed in warning. "I assure you, Aurora, I am quite sane. You, on the other hand, are bordering on irrational. Now, sit down."

"Irrational?" Aurora ignored the command, tilting back her head to gaze up at her tall, formidable brother. "You've just announced to me, as casually as one would announce the time of day, that in a matter of weeks you'll be marrying me off to an affable but uninspiring man who is no more than a chance acquaintance and for whom I feel nothing, and you find my anger irrational?"

"The Viscount Guillford is a fine man," Slayde argued, hands clasped behind his back as if prepared to do battle. "He's honest and principled. I've done business with him for years and know that firsthand. He's also financially secure, well respected, even-tempered, and generous, not to mention nice-looking and charming, as is evidenced by the number of women reputedly vying for his affections—and his name."

"I'm not most women."

A muscle flexed in Slayde's jaw. "I'm only too well aware of that. Nonetheless, the viscount is everything I just described and more. He's also—for some very fortunate and equally baffling reason—thoroughly smitten with you, even after a mere four or five meetings. In fact, according to him, he fell under your spell on his first visit to Pembourne. That was the time I was unavoidably detained for our business meeting and, to quote Guillford, you entertained him with your delightful company until I arrived."

"Entertained him? We chatted about White's and the finer points of whist. He made a gracious attempt to teach me to play. You were a quarter hour late. The moment you walked into the sitting room, I excused myself and left. That was the extent of the 'entertainment' I provided."

"Well, you must have made quite an impression. The viscount found you refreshing and lovely. Further, he's one of a select and rapidly diminishing few who remain unperturbed by the Huntley curse and by the scandal surrounding our age-old feud with the Bencrofts. When you consider the events of the past fortnight, that last factor could be the most significant of all Guillford's attributes. So, contrary to your protests, you are indeed going to marry him."

"But Slayde—"

"No." Adamantly, Slayde sliced the air with his palm, silencing Aurora's oncoming plea. "My decision is final. The arrangements are under way. The subject is closed."

Aurora sucked in her breath, taken aback by the unyielding fervor of Slayde's decree. It had been months—last spring, to be exact—since she'd seen that rigid, uncompromising expression on his face, felt that impenetrable wall of reserve loom up between them.

She'd thought the old Slayde gone forever— along with his obsessive hatred for the Bencrofts. That Slayde had vanished last May when he'd met and subsequently married Courtney Johnston, who, with her spiritedness and unwavering love, had stolen Slayde's heart, helping him make peace with the past and granting him hope for the future.

Until now, when all the wonders Courtney had effected were in danger of being shattered—and by the very man Slayde had so loathed: Lawrence Bencroft, the Duke of Morland.

Fury swelled inside Aurora as she contemplated the hell Morland had resurrected with his bloody investigation, his false accusations. Damn him for stirring up doubts that had, at long last, begun to subside. Damn him for casting aspersion on the Huntleys, then dying before he could be disproved.

Most of all, damn that bloody black diamond. Damn it *and* its heinous curse. For four generations, it had haunted her family. Would they never escape its lethal grasp?

With a hard swallow, Aurora struggled to compose herself. "Slayde," she tried, reminding herself, yet again, that her brother's irrationality was founded in fear, not domination or cruelty. "I realize that the *ton*'s focus has returned to the diamond with a vengeance since Morland's accusations, and now, his death. But—"

"The *ton?*" An implacable look flashed in Slayde's eyes. "Cease this nonsensical attempt to placate me, Aurora. You know bloody well I don't give a damn about the fashionable world or their gossip. What I *do* give a damn about are the three attempted break-ins, half-dozen extortion letters, and equally as many threats that have besieged

Pembourne over the past ten days. Evidently, Morland's sudden demise, on the heels of his commencing an investigation that—according to his *very* public announcement—would prove I was harboring the black diamond, has once again convinced numerous privateers and scoundrels, prompting them to act. Clearly, they intend to ransack my home and threaten and browbeat me into producing the stone—a stone I've never seen and haven't the slightest clue where to find."

"But how can anyone invade Pembourne? You have guards posted everywhere."

Slayde scowled. "That offers reassurances, not guarantees. Aurora, I'm your guardian. I'm also your brother. That means not only that I'm responsible for your safety, but that I'm committed to ensuring it. I won't see you harmed or vulnerable to attack."

"I'll take my chances."

"Well, I won't." Slayde's tone was as uncompromising as his words. "I intend to see you safely wed, severed from the Huntley name for good."

Wincing, Aurora tried another tactic. "How does Courtney feel about your insistence that I marry the viscount?"

One dark brow rose. "I think you know the answer to that."

"She fought your decision."

"Like a tigress."

Despite her careening emotions, Aurora smiled. "Thank God."

"Don't bother. 'Tis a waste of time. You won't win this battle, not even with Courtney's help."

A knowing look. "Why not? She's not only my closest friend, she's your wife—*and* your greatest weakness. I have yet to see you refuse her anything."

"Well, there's a first time for everything." Slayde inhaled sharply. "In any case, Courtney is not the issue here. You are."

"I beg to differ with you. Courtney *is* the issue here. As is your unborn child. How are you going to protect *them* from the curse?"

Pain flashed in Slayde's eyes. "With my life. I have no other means. I can't protect them, as I can you, by severing their ties to me. 'Tis too late for that. Courtney and I are bound in the most fundamental way possible—my babe is growing inside her. I cannot offer her freedom, a new life, even if I chose to. But with you, I can." Slowly, he walked around his desk to face his sister. "There's no point in arguing, Aurora. I've already accepted Guillford's offer. You'll be married in a month." He paused, studying Aurora's clenched fists from beneath hooded lids. "I realize you're furious at me right now. I hope someday you'll understand. But whether or not you do, you're marrying Guillford. So I suggest you accustom yourself to the idea." Slayde's expression softened. "He adores you. He told me himself that he wants to give you the world. As for you, I know you enjoy his company. I've seen you smile, even laugh, in his presence."

"I behave similarly in the presence of Courtney's pup, Tyrant."

Another scowl. "You'll learn to love him."

Vehemently, Aurora shook her head. "No, Slayde, I won't." She turned and marched out of the study.

"I spent all last night pleading your case." Courtney Huntley, the very lovely, very pregnant Countess of Pembourne, sighed, shadows of fatigue etched beneath her sea-green eyes. "He's adamant that this union take place."

"The whole idea is ludicrous." Aurora paced the length of her friend's bedchamber, her red-gold hair whipping about her shoulders. "Slayde, of all people, should realize that marriage must be founded in love, not reason. After all, that's why you two wed. My brother is so in love with you he can scarcely see straight. How can he want less for me?"

"He doesn't want less for you," Courtney defended Slayde at once. "I promise you, Aurora, if there were someone special in your life, someone you cared for, Slayde would refuse Lord Guillford's offer in a heartbeat."

"But since there isn't, I'm being forced to wed the most acceptable substitute?"

Courtney sighed. "I can't argue that Slayde's plan is a dreadful mistake. All I can do is explain that his worry for your welfare is eclipsing his reason. I've never seen him so distraught, not even when we first met. Since Morland died and speculation over the black diamond's whereabouts have escalated into a host of threats, it's as if he's reliving years past. He's no more rational about me than he is about you. I'm not even permitted to stroll the gardens alone. Either he or one of the guards is perpetually glued to my side."

"Well, perhaps you're willing to accept it. I'm not."

A flicker of humor. "Willing? No. *Resigned* is a better choice of words." Tenderly, Courtney smoothed her palm over her swollen abdomen. "I'm a bit more unwieldy than I was a few months past—or hadn't you noticed? I suspect I wouldn't prove much of an adversary to the guards if I tried to outrun them."

Aurora didn't return her smile. "I can't marry Lord Guillford, Courtney," she whispered, coming to a halt. "I just can't."

Their gazes met.

"I'll talk to Slayde again," Courtney vowed. "Tonight. I'll think of something—Lord knows what—but I'll fight this betrothal with every emotional weapon I possess."

With a worried nod, Aurora looked away, contemplating her options. Customarily, Courtney's assurances would have been more than enough. But not this time. Slayde had been too vehement, too single-minded, and there was too much at stake.

She'd have to ensure his cooperation on her own.

The manor was dark when Aurora slipped out the back door and through the trees. She'd mentally mapped out her route five times since the last of Pembourne's lamps had been doused, grateful she had a new escape route the guards had yet to discern.

That was because she'd only just discovered it.

She'd come upon the tiny path last week, by pure chance, while romping about with Tyrant. He'd raced off, thereby leading her to the small clearing. Curious, she'd explored it, discovering, with some surprise, that the path wound its way to the southern tip of the estate. She'd stored that knowledge away by sheer force of habit, never expecting to use either the information or the route. Her escape attempts had come to an end last spring, along with Courtney's arrival.

But today's decree called for drastic measures.

And, come hell or high water, she intended to take them.

Inching through the fine layer of snow that clung to the grass, Aurora made her way to the narrow section of trees behind the conservatory, then slipped through them, careful not to disturb the branches or make a sound. However, given the current circumstances, she was sure none of the guards were concentrating on her whereabouts. First, because they were keeping vigil for intruders. And second, she thought with a grin, because her restlessness had so thoroughly vanished they'd become lax about keeping an eye on her. Well, all the better.

As she cleared the branches, Aurora's grin widened. The rear gates of Pembourne loomed just ahead. Beyond that, she knew, lay the dirt road which led to the village.

She gathered up her skirts and sprinted forward.

The first part of her plan was complete.

Dawlish Tavern, as the pub's chipped sign identified it, was dark and smoky. Aurora's eyes watered the instant she entered, and she paused in the doorway, impatiently rubbing them as she tried to see.

Perfect, she thought a moment later. The occupants were definitely what her past governesses would refer to as riffraff, clusters of ill-kempt men gathered about wooden tables, laughing loudly as they tossed off tankards of ale and flung playing cards to the table.

The ideal spot to be ruined.

Look for
The Black Diamond
Wherever Paperback Books Are Sold

Let
Andrea
Kane
romance you tonight!

Dream Castle 73585-3/$5.50

My Heart's Desire 73584-5/$5.50

Masque of Betrayal 75532-3/$4.99

Echoes In the Mist 75533-1/$5.50

Samantha 86507-2/$5.50

The Last Duke 86508-0/$5.99

Emerald Garden 86509-9/$5.99

Wishes In the Wind 53483-1/$5.99

Legacy of the Diamond 53485-8/$5.99

Available from Pocket Books